MIRIAM

La Colombe Blanche

Wendy Waters

\#

APS BOOKS

YORKSHIRE

APS Books,
The Stables, Field Lane
Aberford, West Yorkshire,
LS25 3AE

APS Books is a subsidiary of the APS Publications imprint

www.andrewsparke.com

This one's for Charlie, my grandson, and Liza, the sister I always longed for.

GLOSSARY OF TERMS

Bowe bell – *the bells of Saint Mary le Bowe Church that rang the hour.*

Budget – *bag.*

Burning ague – *typhus or typhoid fever.*

Caroche – *a luxurious or stately coach or carriage.*

Cheaps – *markets.*

Chine – *meat cut across the backbone.*

Coffyns – *pie cases.*

Cuckquean – *a woman betrayed by her husband.*

Cup-shotten – *drunk.*

Dell – *a pregnant runaway woman.*

Demander of glimmer – *a beautiful woman who approaches men in alehouses and lures them out of town where her upright man robs him.*

Doxy – *a runaway woman dependent on a man for protection on the roads.*

Flux – *dysentery*

Frater – *steals from women in the markets.*

Galleon – *large sailing boat of Spanish design, used for cargo and war.*

Goodinycakes – *an unleavened cake made of cornmeal and water or milk.*

Hennins – *conical Medieval ladies' hats with veils.*

Jeremiads – *a long, mournful complaint about society.*

Ketches – *two-masted sailboats.*

Kickie-wicky – *wife.*

Kinchin-cos – *runaway boys.*

Kirtle – *gown.*

Manchets – *loaves made of fine white flour.*

Mazer – *cup.*

Marchpane – Marzipan.
Nightrail – nightgown.
Palfreys – horses.
Palliard – beggar in a patched coat.
Paps – breasts.
Pinnaces – light sailing ship, often used as a tender for a galleon.
Pottage – pot of stew made from available ingredients.
Pox – smallpox.
Sallats – Salads.
Shifting – changing into night clothes.
Skiffs – small, flatbottomed river boats.
Squillerie – a room off a kitchen where coal is kept.
Staithes – wharves on the river.
Suckets – sugar plums and dried fruit in thick syrup flavoured with ginger and other spices.
Swive – fornicate.
Trenchers – plates usually made of wood.
Upright man – a man who carries a staff and roams the highways and rules the other rogues in the area.
Vellum – writing material made from calfskin.
Wait – musician, entertainer.
Wherries – the ferries that carried Londoners across the River Thames.

PROLOGUE

The handsome prince who woke me eases closer for a kiss
A tingling troubling pressure, rude awakening on my lips
The breaking dawn puts out the fires and guilty is the prayer
Of love-stained mouths that whisper, cant
There was no lover here.

So light is her footfall, the miles beneath her feet leave no mark upon her flesh. No sweat beads her brow, no blisters pock her heels, nor does the earth record her passage. She does not tire or thirst. No heart protests in her breast, no hunger claws at her belly, no sleep delays the distance she must put between London and sanctuary.

The child is dead. No flutter of foot betrays life in her womb.

She is utterly alone and in that hollow silence the recent horror chambers: the leering crowd marking her passage to the pyre, the raucous cries of "burn the witch" as coarse ropes bound her to the stake, the silence trembling with lust when the executioner lit the pyre, the screeches and groans of orgiastic pleasure as flames enveloped her.

'Find an abandoned Abbey. Wait there till I come for thee,' said the man who gave her his cloak when the fire that spared her flesh consumed her modesty. 'I promise you vengeance.'

'Swear.'

'I swear. Now go. Follow the old Roman road Watling out of London and then turn south and find the sea. Follow the sea until you find an Abbey.'

'I would comfort my mother first.'

'No time. Go now before they find you and make a freak of you.'

1

PART ONE

I

London, 1588

Miriam Tilby shed her first moon-blood the year Captain Drake defeated the Spanish Armada and the Welsh printed their own bible. Her mother Eirinn cared not a jot for the Spanish or the Welsh but feared her daughter's step into womanhood foreshadowed an ending.

'The river's song is so loud today. Can you hear it, Mam?'

'No sweetling. Only you hear music in everything.' Eirinn Tilby looked across the wide, brown Thames towards Southbank, her gaze distracted, her fingers twisting the fabric of her gown into agitated pleats. 'Try not to hum sweetling.'

'I'll try Mam but the song is so lovely. The river sings of the sea.'

Late autumn and circlets of leaves swirled along the river protesting the seabound tide. The sun wept its failing light into dusk as the day's meagre warmth resolved into chill. Wavelets shivered the furled sails of rivercraft fretting to tether on staithes along the banks and slapped against the hull of Drake's famous galleon, the Golden Hind, now permanently moored at Deptford.

'Do you think the world ends in a great fall of water?'

'Only God knows.' Eirinn gathered up the remains of their Sunday picnic. 'Come now, we must be home before dark, I've supper to cook.'

'Oh please, Mam, a few more minutes. I want to know how this song ends.'

Eirinn gave her daughter a long sad look. 'A few more minutes.'

Miriam closed her eyes and swayed to the music only she could hear. Moments later she sighed. 'That was lovely.'

Eirinn stood up, lifted the basket onto one hip. 'Try not to hum around Thomas. He would make trouble of it if he could. He already thinks you're a witch.'

'Thomas thinks every woman is a witch.'

'You're not a woman, you're a girl.'

'I've shed moonblood.'

Eirinn shivered. 'I wish you could remain a girl; the world is …'

'Full of music.'

'Full of men who prey upon beautiful young women. They will beckon and you will follow as I followed your father. Come now.'

Miriam brushed the slivers of grass from her gown and trailed her mother up the bank. 'Was my father handsome?'

Eirinn's dark eyes flashed. 'Handsome as the Devil.'

'Let me carry it.' Miriam took the basket from her mother. 'Did you love him?'

'More than life itself, fool that I was. Your father made a wanton of me and a base-born of you when he left us.' Eirinn stopped walking, looked up at the purpling sky. 'Love is a terrible urge but no man will marry a base-born woman even if there is love.' She resumed walking at a brisk pace. 'I'm sorry for the life I've cursed you with, sweetling.'

'We live in the finest part of London, we've food and ale, wine on Sundays, we sleep in warm beds and want for nothing. What a life to be cursed with. Do you believe in Hell?'

'So many questions! Heaven wouldn't make much sense without Hell now would it and I do believe in Heaven.' After a moment she added, 'Hell is where your father belongs.'

An Unexpected Visitor

Their footsteps echoed on the cobbled lanes that threaded the city. As they passed the Mermaid Tavern a wait's melodious voice softened the drunken exchanges that ebbed and swelled like the river's tide.

Miriam paused, listening. 'His voice is so true.'

'I'm sure it is but we have to be home before the light fails completely.'

Onwards to Saint Paul's Cathedral, its long shadow gloaming the empty marketplace. Here they trod carefully, avoiding the fetid puddles of waste cast from upper floor windows, holding their noses to avoid taking in the noxious fumes that delivered flux, pox and burning ague upon the breath. Once safely home, Eirinn rang the bell for Jonas, the ostler, to unlock the gatehouse door.

'Be careful,' Eirinn said as they waited for Jonas. 'You are passing fair. Men will want you but –'

Miriam silenced her mother with a kiss. 'I will never fall in love.'

**

Sunday nights were fish nights for the servants at Radclyffe House, indeed for servants all over England, even though the law decreed that fish nights were Wednesdays, Fridays and Saturdays, servants ate their Masters' leftovers, and that often occasioned breaking the law created by the Queen to protect the fishing industry. Eirinn Tilby did her best to limit their fare on fish nights to veal, game and poultry, which was allowed, but in the warmer months when meat was hard to keep, it was either break the law or starve.

'Thomas help set the table for supper.' Eirinn glanced over her shoulder as she stirred the pottage. 'Don't sit there ogling the maids.'

Thomas drained his mazer and dragged himself to his feet. 'Mistress Tilby, I've been up since first Bowe bell tending the Master and his palfreys.'

'It's your free day, Thomas, you've not been tending anyone but your friends in the tavern. Jonas tends the palfreys. Fetch the linen and call Jonas in for supper.'

'Maybe I'll marry,' said Thomas. 'Get myself a servant and comforter in one fair sweetling. What say you Rosamunde? Will you share my bed?' He slid over to Rosamunde, fondled her breast.

'I'd rather share my bed with lice,' said Rosamunde, slapping his hand away.

'If it pleases you to scratch. What say *you*, Abigail? I've a yearning for a kickie-wickie with white paps and rosebud nipples.' Sliding his hand under Abigail's basquine.

Abigail's pale cheeks scorched red. 'Thomas stop touching my – my –'

Eirinn clanged the ladle against the pot. 'Thomas, keep your hands to yourself. Your flesh-mongering will see you swinging at Tyburn before you're twenty.'

Thomas released Abigail and headed to the dry larder. On his way past Miriam who was filling the flagons with wine for Sunday supper, he stopped. 'Are you hearing music again?'

Miriam ignored him.

'I asked you a question,' said Thomas.

'And I gave you an order,' said Eirinn. 'Are you simple-minded that you cannot remember a command?'

8

'No, Mistress Tilby.' He leaned over Miriam, tweaked her curls savagely and hissed. 'You'd curdle milk, you red-haired witch.'

Eirinn swept across the kitchen and smacked Thomas across the face with the back of the ladle.

Thomas' yelp of pain caused everyone, even Master Simon Trenery, the valet and head man, to stop what they were doing and look up.

Mistress Tilby raised the ladle above her head, ready to strike again. 'Apologise to my daughter.'

'You'd best do it, lad, unless you want another clip,' said Master Trenery.

'I meant no harm, Mistress Tilby.'

'Apologise to my daughter.'

'I'm sorry, Miriam.' Thomas rubbed his cheek where a pink welt was blossoming.

Eirinn lowered the ladle. 'Now fetch the linen and tell Jonas to come in for supper. See that he shuts the courtyard door after him. He will leave it open and it's deathly chill in here. The fire's as cold as Puritan faith. Stoke it, Abigail.'

'Yes, Mistress Tilby.' Abigail glared at Thomas. 'You delight in mischief.'

Thomas gave Miriam a withering look, his eyes glittering hatred. After shouting Mistress Tilby's orders at Jonas, he collected twelve napkins from the dry larder and slapped them down at each place.

'Rosamunde fetch the mazers and trenchers,' said Eirinn, stirring the pottage bubbling on the hob. 'Abigail, the platters of fish when you've finished stoking the fire. Thomas help Abigail and keep your hands to yourself. When there's hairs on your chin and you're earning 2 shillings and 4 pence a week you can turn your mind to marriage, not before.' She paused. 'And if you ever insult my daughter again it won't be the back of my ladle you'll be feeling but the stocks.'

Master Trenery frowned. 'The stocks, Mistress Tilby? It would mean the assizes for you and a strong case against the lad.'

'I know what it would mean. A day in the stocks might cool that hot head of his.'

Master Trenery said no more but returned to his book of Italian Madrigals, his fingers presently tapping out the rhythm of a new song. 'You must sing this tonight, Miriam. I yearn to hear it sung with an angel's voice, and Thomas, you'll accompany us on the cittern. I'll play the lute as always.'

'Your voice is a gift from God, Miriam. That's why you hear Heaven's music and those deaf to it are jealous,' said Abigail, glaring at Thomas.

Eirinn bestowed upon Abigail a smile that lit the gloaming room like sunlight. 'Abigail, leave off stoking and light a candle for the table, we need more light than this sullen fire is throwing.' Turning back to the pottage, her smile faded. God could not protect her daughter from the kind of malevolence that sent innocents to the gallows. A young woman had been hung for witchcraft only the week before, accused of bewitching her neighbour's husband. Even Queen Anne Boleyn's execution had sprung from a web of lies. And hadn't the virgin Queen burned Mary Cleere for calling her base-born? Words had the power to kill and it was not the first time Thomas had called her daughter a witch but as long as he kept his mischief in the kitchen Miriam was safe from him but sooner or later trouble would find her. Her beauty was a beacon, a blessing in the highborn, a curse in the low and

Miriam was the lowest of the low, a base-born, no man's child.

Eirinn glanced at her daughter, head bent over her task, red-gold curls framing a face that might have won the heart of a knight or a lord had she been conceived in a different womb. Her beauty was the kind playwrights frame in tragedies. It would draw ruin to her, a man like her father would emerge from the world beyond the gatehouse and bait her with words of love just as she herself had been baited. Too late her daughter would taste the poison of prejudice and indifference.

Jonas erupted into the kitchen, a blast of cold air in his wake.

'Jonas! The door!' Eirinn snapped.

'Beg pardon, Mistress Tilby.' Jonas plodded back and closed the door.

Eirinn rubbed her back and sighed. 'I am easily vexed this evening.'

Miriam put the flagons of wine on the table and took the ladle from her mother. 'Sit down. I'll finish the pottage.'

'Thank you sweetling.'

'Everyone sit down for supper now,' said Master Trenery. 'It's been a long week.'

When all the servants had washed their hands and taken their places at the table Master Trenery pressed his palms together and gave thanks.

'Amen,' they all declared with varied sincerity before plunging their knives into the remains of Saturday night's fish dinner.

'Valentyne and Fyndern,' said Master Trenery. 'Remember the Marchioness in your prayers before bed for it was only her mercy that saved you from starvation.'

11

The two kinchin-cos, recently rescued from the streets by the Marchioness, stared at him but did not answer. In the firelight their pinched cheeks looked ashen, their eyes hollow and dark as empty wells. In their birdlike hands, clawed and blistered from hard winters and scavenging, they gripped their manchets as if someone might steal their bread. Judging by their narrow-eyed silence, Miriam feared remembrance of the Marchioness was unlikely. Indeed, it was unlikely prayers were remembered.

As the platters emptied and the trenchers groaned, conversations rose in bubbles of gossip and laughter.

'Drake found monsters in the New World.'

'They say the Queen will die of a broken heart now Lord Dudley is dead.'

'The Master comes home later and later. The ostler says he visits a lady in Bishopsgate.'

Jonas looked up, a dribble of sauce running down his chin. 'I never –'

'John Dee is back from France and they say he talks to angels with Edward Kelley.'

'People have been burned for less but then Master Dee has the Queen's special favour.'

'How do you know it's a woman he meets, Jonas?' asked Thomas, knife raised perpendicular to the table upon which his elbow rested. 'He could be playing cards at the Mermaid Tavern.'

'It must be a woman,' said Rosamunde. 'The Mistress is always in tears and their fights are fierce enough to wake the children. I sing to them to soften their parents' squabbling.'

'You sing?' asked Master Trenery, glancing at her with sharp interest.

'Not as beautifully as Miriam but I can make melody enough to settle the children.'

'I heard you singing last night,' said Miriam. 'Your voice is lovely.'

Rosamunde smiled at her. 'And you with the voice of an angel.'

'Maybe he meets a Catholic priest who takes him to midnight Mass in some popish nobleman's attic.' Thomas pierced a slice of eel and transported it to his mouth without a moment's pause upon his trencher.

'That sort of talk could send the Master to the Tower,' warned Master Trenery.

'And me handsomely rewarded,' said Thomas with a sly wink at Rosamunde. 'Then I could marry Rosamunde and set up a fine little house for us to make babies in.'

'I wouldn't have a scurvy knave who hangs his betters for a swive,' declared Rosamunde, returning to her conversation with Abigail.

Thomas stabbed another slice of eel furiously. 'Maybe I wouldn't have a demander of glimmer for a wife neither.'

'Enough,' said Master Trenery. 'Rosamunde, have you heard from your mother?'

'Not since I moved to London, Master Trenery.'

'Have you written to her?'

'I've not had time to buy ink.'

'I can furnish you with some iron gall ink and a sheet of vellum if you wish.'

'You would spare vellum and ink for Rosamunde?' Thomas smirked. 'You must be sweet on her, Master Trenery.'

'Every lewd comment brings you closer to the stocks, Thomas,' said Master Trenery. 'A mother and daughter should maintain communication. It's a holy bond and Rosamunde is a long way from her mother.'

Dark-eyed, raven-haired Rosamunde had arrived in London after the winter solstice when the roads had hardened from mud to clay and were passable again. She came with a reference that was barely glanced at, for the household had just lost a gentlewoman to the sweating sickness. Rosamunde could read and write as well as help in the kitchen and Eirinn seized upon the opportunity to have her daughter taught a skill that might earn her a few extra coins in due course. Rosamunde proved an excellent teacher and soon Miriam was consuming ideas with a hunger that made Eirinn nervous and Master Trenery proud.

'I can write your letter for you, Rosamunde, if you tell me what to say.'

'Thank you, Miriam. You're so clever. It took me fifteen years to learn to read and write. You learned in one.'

'I had a good teacher.'

'She cast a spell,' muttered Thomas.

Eirinn raised her knife and pointed it at Thomas. 'I warned you.'

'It *is* a woman,' said Jonas, derailing another argument. 'He do meet her Friday nights when the young Mistress and 'er Ladyship are at cards with their friends.'

'He might be going to the tavern,' said Abigail.

''Tis a woman,' Jonas insisted. 'He bade me hide a gift for her in the stables so Lady Elizabeth wouldn't find it.'

'What kind of gift?' asked Thomas, instantly distracted. 'Jewellery?'

'It were small enough to hide under the hay, but I won't say no more. I've said too much already.'

14

The table fell briefly silent before the company split into huddled conspiracies, pairs and trios leaning in for exclusive exchanges. Rosamunde and Abigail spoke softly, heads pressed together. Master Trenery and the two footmen discussed the possibility of civil war now that the Queen had withdrawn into grief over the death of Robert Dudley.

'If she does not name a successor England is vulnerable to the Spanish,' said Master Trenery. 'She's not a young woman anymore and without a son –'

'Or a daughter,' said Eirinn.

'An heir,' said Master Trenery. 'The Spanish will strike.'

'Could we beat the Spanish again, Master Trenery?' asked Jonas nervously.

'If the tides are favourable and Drake is at the helm.'

'I'd rather slice my throat than be raped by a Spaniard,' murmured Rosamunde.

'Let's not frighten ourselves,' said Eirinn. 'The Queen will rally soon enough. One cannot grieve over a man forever.'

Miriam pulled the latest jeremiad out of her apron pocket. 'Rosamunde, I've finished reading this. Would you like it?'

'What is it?' asked Master Trenery.

'A book of spells!' Thomas snorted. 'They say you need three witches to make a spell stick. That's Miriam, Rosamunde and Abigail, between them they could turn us all into toads.'

'It's a literary work lamenting the state of society, Master Trenery,' said Miriam.

There was a momentary hush at the table.

'Sweetling, we are servants,' said Eirinn. 'We don't need an education beyond reading recipes and writing letters.'

'The Queen is well-educated, Mam,' said Miriam. 'Surely the woman who is the highest in the land sets an example for all women?'

'Women should know their place,' said Thomas. 'God made men stronger and wiser. Satan could never deceive a man.'

'Thomas in this modern age men and women are more equal than ever before but the Queen does rely on her advisers, Miriam, and they're all men,' said Master Trenery.

'Unbalanced empires topple according to this.' Miriam tapped the jeremiad. 'Do you have time to read this Master Trenery? We could have a lively discussion about it.'

'I would like to read it,' said Rosamunde, rallying, 'but with my duties in the kitchen and tending the children – Lady Elizabeth is poorly with the new child on the way and the little ones are forever in need of shifting. Sad little sweetlings, they cry for their mother but between the arguments with the Master and the sickness that plagues her she has no interest in them. I give them all the love I can but I'm not their mother.'

'Where do you buy your books, Miriam?' asked Abigail.

'The booksellers near Saint Paul's and Paternoster Row. I could teach you to read if you like and then we can discuss the state of the world.'

'When do we have time for lessons?' said Abigail, shrugging.

Miriam stabbed her knife into a lamprey. 'Rosamunde taught me on Sundays after Church.'

'I am not as sharp-minded as you. It would take years of Sundays to teach me.'

'We have years,' said Miriam. 'Everyone should know how to read and write. I can teach anyone else who wants to learn, even you, Thomas.'

'Maybe I don't want to learn,' snarled Thomas. 'A woman should accept a man just as he is, isn't that so Master Trenery?'

'No,' said Master Trenery. 'Men and women alike should be judged by their merits.'

'The bible says women are men's servants,' muttered Thomas.

'How do you know when you can't read?' Abigail laughed.

Fyndern and Valentyne, following this conversation, shifted their attention from one speaker to the next as they wolfed down their supper. When they thought no-one was watching they stuffed more manchets into their jerkins, the habit of a lifetime learned in taverns where men were too cup-shotten to notice a pair of grimy hands relieving them of their bread and purses. The boys would eat their bread later that night when the household writhed in dreams of lust, piracy and betrayal, of soured milk and wheyey butter and bodies bruised purple with fairy pinches.

But before bed and dreams: music.

***

After the remains of supper had been handed out to the paupers at the gatehouse and the kitchen had been cleaned ready for Monday service Master Trenery pulled his chair close to the fire. 'Fetch my lute, Abigail, and Thomas, your cittern. Miriam here is the music. Thomas listen closely and play when you are ready.'

Miriam studied the twined notes and words that would presently resolve into song. Thomas returned with his cittern and sat by Master Trenery, a picture of amiability that belied the earlier devilment and teasing. Presently Master Trenery plucked the lute, shimmering a melody glamoured with visions of a land they would never see, Italy. After five bars Miriam began to sing, her pure voice conjuring images of streets made of water and gondolas festooned with flags the colour of ripe berries. The river-streets, the boats, the tale of a love won and lost, the counter melodies of lute and finally cittern wove an exotic chimera. No-one moved or murmured until the last notes flew sky born as lanterns on a moonless night and then a sharp intake of breath shattered the enchantment.

'Who is this fairy, Master Trenery?'

The entire assembly rose and bowed to the Marchioness who stood in the doorway.

'This is Mistress Miriam Tilby, your Ladyship,' said Master Trenery.

The Marchioness looked from Miriam to Eirinn. 'She favours you, Mistress Tilby, a beauty to be sure, and that halo of red curls is much like mine when I was young. Master Trenery, teach Mistress Miriam how to serve my family in the main hall. We must be sure she knows how to behave amongst her betters when I have need of that beautiful voice.'

And that was the first time in fifteen years Miriam had ever seen one of the family.

Later that evening, after shifting into her nightrail and cap, Miriam picked her teeth and rubbed them with a cloth soaked in rock alum, a tedious routine, but her mother stressed the need to keep their teeth healthy or it was a visit to a barber-surgeon who would remove a decaying tooth with a pelican. Eirinn said the black teeth of the Queen were nothing to romanticise or copy with a rubbing of coal as so many gentlewomen did for it signified decay from too many sugary cates.

Miriam was already snuggled under the sheets when Eirinn finished picking her own teeth and came to their shared bed.

'Sweetling, please be careful what you say. Thomas is a troubled lad and will make mischief if he can.'

'He is all talk, Mam.'

'Still, be careful. Curb your tongue around him.'

'It seems the only place a woman is free is in her dreams.'

'What do you dream about?'

'Oh, a handsome man who charms ladies out of their baubles in exchange for a kiss. Abigail and Rosamunde have the same dream.'

'How is it that you all have the same dream?'

'Blame Master Trenery for his tales of highwaymen who wear their Spanish leather boots thigh-high. Don't worry, Mam, these dreams that fever our nights, cool at dawn when the Bowe bells summon us from our beds. I will live and die a servant in Radclyffe House and so will Abigail. Rosamunde will marry one day if only to have a child of her own for she does adore children. I just hope she doesn't marry Thomas.'

II

The only man I loved betrayed my body to the pyre
Of all the judges who condemned me his cruel silence lit the fire
But the flames did not release me, seared my soul into my flesh
I did not burn, I did not die, my seal and fate enmeshed.

Why the flames spared her, why the man helped her, why she yet lives she does not know. Nor what kind she has become – angel, imp, demon. Perhaps she is the first of her kind, for no wait has ever sung of one such as she – the living dead, spared by the flames. She craves not food nor water nor sleep. Breathing, the habit of one and twenty years, is the only remaining pulse of life. Heart, hunger and thirst are stilled but her senses have heightened. She hears the snapping of a twig hours before footfall reveals the deer, notes the flash of fur or feather through knitted canopy miles ahead and fragrance is so strong she becomes ripe berry, sown field, or laden bough. The perfume of apple blossom dances in her breast but ignites no hunger.

She knows not how long this flesh will last or for what purpose. All she knows is she must find an abandoned Abbey away from the world of men.

'How will you find me?' she asked her rescuer as she drew his cloak around her.

'I find all my witches one way or another.'

'I am no witch!'

'You were just burned for one. These God-fearing people are evil. The fallen angel himself would never stoop as low as these good Christian judges. You must stay hidden until I rule the earth.' He handed her a bundle. 'Clothes. Put them on when you are far from London. It is not safe to linger. When you reach the sea head west until you find Lands' End. Make haste now. The moon will light your way.'

A Restless Night.

Miriam lay in the dark listening to the night sounds: her mother's spirant breathing, the squeaking and scratching of the clawed and furred hunters and their prey, the hissed curse of a cup-shotten knave slipping on the frost-bitten cobbles, the sudden swishing descent of a barn owl followed by the screech of its prey – a mouse, or a rat, perhaps a kitten – and sometime in the pre-dawn hours an argument between the Master and Lady Elizabeth followed by the faint mewling of their children and the soothing strains of Rosamunde's singing, the melody followed by tense silence. Finally, a few hours before dawn, she drifted back to sleep, her dreams shifting to a handsome dark-eyed man who covered her mouth in an urgent press of lust and need.

The Bowe bells tolled the dawn hour, shattering the restless night into fragmented images of claws and coal-black eyes and a kiss that burned yet upon her lips. Her mother stirred and reached for her chamber pot. A tinkling relief prompted Miriam to slip out of bed and squat shivering over her own pot, the morning air snapping with frost.

'You did not sleep well, sweetling?' Eirinn's voice an anchor in the shapeless dark.

'Did I wake you? Sorry.'

Miriam felt for the linen rubbing cloth on her bedside table, slipped back into their warm bed and began rubbing her body clean, raising the bright red flush of cleansing blood that would carry away the noxious humours that festered flux and burning ague.

'What do you think the Marchioness means to do with me?'

'She will have you sing for her rich and powerful friends.'

Miriam heard the swish as her mother threw on her smock, felt the renewed pressure as she sat back down to pull on her socks and hose. Miriam dressed quickly, her smock, hose and kirtle night-cold and bitter with lye from yesterday's washing. Presently her mother was behind her, lacing up her basquine. Turning, she performed the same service for her.

'She'll want you dressed in cambric – a new gown, new kirtle, a fine bodice. All white. New slippers.'

'How can we pay for cambric?'

'She'll give us coin. Abigail will make new clothes for you.'

Eirinn said nothing more as they combed and rubbed their hair and washed their faces in a basin of icy water that chased away the last vestiges of sleep.

'I can't protect you once you leave the kitchen. Your beauty will draw the kind of attention a base-born girl cannot refuse.'

'The kind of attention my father gave you?'

'I went to his bed willingly. Be careful whose eyes you meet and whose smile you return. Come now, Abigail will have set kindling for the fire. The kitchen will be warmer.'

Miriam pulled on her buskins and collected yesterday's soiled smock, kirtle and hose and followed her mother along the dark hallway and into the kitchen where a chorus of "Good morrow Mistress" and "Good morrow Master" was exchanged before the footmen and the gentlewoman departed for their various upstairs duties before breakfast. Abigail had already lit the hearth fire and

22

was now feeding the oven fire ready for the day's baking, the gathering warmth dispelling the chill. The two kinchin-cos were up, yawning and about their first task, collecting and emptying the chamber pots in the cesspit. That done, they washed their hands without being reminded and huddled shivering by the fire awaiting Mistress Tilby's orders.

'Fetch two chickens,' said Eirinn, cutting into a sack of flour. 'See that you break their necks with one clean snap. Don't make them suffer.'

The boys nodded and made their way back out into the cold, dark courtyard. Presently terrified squawking followed by a heavy silence indicated the job had been done.

'I hate it,' murmured Abigail, feeding another handful of twigs into the oven fire.

'Everything preys upon everything else,' said Eirinn, pouring a quarter of a bushel of fine white flour into a wooden trough. 'It's nature's way.'

'Is it God's?' murmured Abigail.

'His ways are stranger still,' said Eirinn. 'He'd let us starve.'

The boys returned with the dead chickens, settled on stools by the fire and began plucking, the feathers raining into a bucket, fresh stuffing for mattresses and pillows, the longest and best kept apart for Master Trenery to sharpen and fashion into quills.

Miriam chopped the ingredients for the alowes pies at one end of the table while her mother kneaded the dough at the other. No-one spoke as the rhythms of plucking, kneading, chopping, and the snapping of twigs filled the room. Shattering the comparative silence, Thomas stumbled in with armfuls of the family's soiled garments.

'More washing than usual,' he said, piling the family's clothes next to their own mound of hose, smocks, bodices,

23

jerkins and aprons. 'Look at the Master's boots!' He dumped a pair of mud-splattered gamaches, the ribbons frayed and soiled, next to the pile. 'He took more than one tumble last night.'

'Thomas –' Eirinn raised a flour-frosted hand.

'Yes, Mistress Tilby.' Thomas slunk closer to the fire to wait for his next order.

A ring of the gatehouse bell meant the water-bearer had arrived with the day's water: a three-gallon container of fresh water drawn from the fountain in Cheapside.

'Here's the water. Thomas. Valentyne.' Eirinn fished in her apron pocket for a penny which she gave to Valentyne. 'Pay the water-bearer and rouse Jonas to help Thomas carry it to the kitchen door. He'll be sleeping in the barn with the palfreys. He rarely finds his own bed when he waits up for the Master. On your way back collect a basketful of eggs.'

The boy grabbed a basket and scurried off. Moments later Jonas and Thomas plopped the day's supply of water outside the kitchen door and Miriam and Abigail began filling the cauldron suspended over the fire for the day's washing.

Eirinn nodded at Fyndern. 'Leave off plucking and fetch the Castille soap for Mistress Abigail.'

When the water came to a boil Thomas and Jonas lifted the cauldron down and placed it next to the piles of soiled clothes.

'Thomas, add a bucket of cold water to the cauldron to spare Abigail's hands,' said Eirinn.

Presently, Abigail plunged the family's cambric shirts, smocks, petticoats, ruffs, hose, and socks into the tub. 'What does the Marchioness mean to do with Mistress Miriam?'

24

Eirinn looked up sharply. 'You've work to do. I won't have idle chatter in the kitchen.'

Abigail bent her head over the tub and said no more as she rubbed the family's cambric clothes with the hard white cakes of Castille soap that would preserve their whiteness.

'I'm sorry, Abigail,' said Eirinn. 'She'll have her sing for her fine friends.'

Abigail looked up again. 'Isn't that an honour, Mistress Tilby?'

'No, it's not an honour. The gentry do not see us as human beings. Miriam will be a moment's distraction, nothing more…I hope.'

Rosamunde tumbled in. 'Good morrow, Mistress Tilby, Abigail, Miriam, lads, Thomas.' Yawning and holding her basquine with both hands, she stood by the fire shivering while Abigail tightened her laces. 'I wonder what the Marchioness intends to do with your angel voice, Miriam?'

Eirinn tapped the table with her ladle. 'Rosamunde, the manchets, if you please.'

'Yes ma'am.' Rosamunde took over kneading the dough.

'As I told Abigail, she'll have Miriam sing for her fine friends,' said Eirinn. 'Now let that be an end to it.'

Rosamunde fell silent and then moments later, 'Miriam might sing for the Queen!'

'The Queen!' cried Abigail.

'The Queen,' Eirinn murmured, gaze unfocused, worry momentarily suspended. 'My daughter singing for the Queen.'

'Miracles do happen,' said Abigail.

'Not to servants,' said Eirinn, snapping out of her reverie. But a few moments later she murmured. 'My daughter singing for the Queen.'

**

The kitchen fell into a chorus of industry: the scrubbing of the washing, the plucking of the chickens, the chopping and slicing of ingredients for the pies and the sucking sound of Rosamunde kneading wove their way into a song and presently Miriam began to hum.

'Don't hum, sweetling,' Eirinn whispered as she prepared the coffyns for the pies. 'Rosamunde, the dough's ready. Leave it to rise and hang the clothes out in the courtyard. Valentyne, light the way for Mistress Rosamunde.'

The morning was still dark, their only light, the stuttering fire. Valentyne lit another candle, half-gutted from last night's supper and lit the way for Rosamunde. There was a sudden draft of chill air as the kitchen door swung open guttering the candle and sending the fire into spasms of palsied flames.

'See to the door, Fyndern.'

The boy dropped his half-plucked chicken on the floor, slunk after his brother and closed the door, settling the fire and steadying the candle.

Miriam touched her mother's hand gently. 'I will never sing for the Queen. She has the finest waits in England at Court.'

'You heard her Ladyship. She means to use your voice as a weapon. Who else would she need to impress? She is second only to the Queen in rank.' Eirinn sighed. 'It would be a rare honour but you're safer in the kitchen. I wish she had never heard you sing.'

Abigail looked up from the tub. 'But she did Mistress Tilby and Miriam's beautiful voice should be shared with the world.'

'The world?' Eirinn slapped her palm on the table. 'Everywhere outside this kitchen, even the Cheaps, is dangerous for a –'

'Base-born girl.' Miriam finished the sentence. 'All these hopes and fears over a song. Life will continue unchanged, you'll see. I will never sing for the Queen and the Marchioness may already have forgotten about me. The alowes fillings are ready.' Miriam handed her mother the bowl of chopped mutton seasoned with parsley, thyme and saueri and tossed through with plump raisins and dates rolled in mace and salt.

'Check the oven, sweetling,' said Eirinn.

The oven fire had burned down to a bed of hot coals with flickering blue tongues of flame and the dome threw off a heat radiant enough to raise the pink in Miriam's cheeks. She raked the coals out of the oven and mopped the remaining ash clear. Eirinn put the manchets on a long-handled shovel and placed them in the oven before sealing it with a wooden door that had been soaked in a bucket of water overnight.

Meanwhile Abigail had finished washing their own clothes with the cheaper black soap made from beast's tallow and lye. The water had turned the dull frothy grey of a receding tide.

'Our clothes are ready, Mistress Tilby.'

'Rosamunde, hang out the clothes. Valentyne light her way.'

'The chickens are ready for gutting, Mistress Tilby,' said Fyndern.

'Good lad, put them on the table and wash your hands. I'll have something else for you to do presently.'

Eirinn sliced the birds from gullet to tail and collected the glutinous coils of steaming intestines in a dish to be used for stock. After rinsing the hollowed cavities, she set them aside

27

and began preparing the family's breakfast: ale and an omelette for the Master, a pint of wine with a piece of salt fish and a dish of sprat for the Marchioness and frumenty for Lady Elizabeth who only took a small dish of spices boiled in milk while her morning sickness persisted.

By the time Rosamunde had hung out the washing the manchets were ready. Miriam unsealed the oven door, removed them quickly and as swiftly replaced them with the alowes pies. Master Trenery stopped in briefly to let Eirinn know the table in the main hall was set and ready for the family and the footmen were on their way to collect the breakfast trays.

Tendrils of sunlight crept through the shuttered windows, gilding a dusting of flour on Eirinn's wrists and gold leafing Abigail's flaxen hair as she emptied the washing tub one bucketful at a time on the vegetable garden in the courtyard. The strengthening morning light elucidated the mellow stone walls and glistered the furred and feathered carcases hanging from blackened hooks beneath a glittering of ladles, knives, pots and pans.

The two young footmen appeared suddenly, the morning sun making haloes of their pale brown curls. For a moment they stood there blinking and yawning before collecting the breakfast trays of manchets, ale and wine, and disappearing into the shadowy hallway. Crossing their path, Master Trenery and Thomas arrived ready for the next portion of the family's breakfast: the Marchioness' fish, the Master's omelette, and Lady Elizabeth's frumentary.

As she worked, Miriam pictured the family stirring in their feather beds, yawning, pushing back the curtains that kept the night chills out, deciding whether to rise and dress for breakfast or sleep in. Many mornings Master

Trenery and Thomas returned to the kitchen with the entire breakfast untouched. But Eirinn always prepared it and Master Trenery, the footmen, and Thomas always delivered it, the routine order of their lives uninterrupted by choice, fancy, or fatigue.

The family's breakfast delivered; Eirinn told the servants to clear the table for their own breakfast: a casual affair taken piecemeal between chores.

'Wash your hands, lads. Must I keep reminding you?' said Eirinn. 'You're not on the streets now.'

The two kinchin-cos duly washed their hands, and without thanking the Lord, slung themselves down at the table and gobbled up two manchets. Within minutes the lads were joined by Abigail, Rosamunde, Eirinn and Miriam. They passed the tankard of ale around and ate their fill of fruit and fresh-baked bread. By the time Thomas, Master Trenery and the footmen returned with the trays, trenchers and soiled mazers, the women and the kinchin-cos had finished eating.

Master Trenery put the uneaten omelette down on the table. 'Another late night.'

Eirinn nodded. 'Divide it up. It won't keep.'

Midday Dinner

'Valentyne, fetch two cream pots from the dairy, a tub of butter from the buttery and a wheel of cheese from the cheese chamber, Fyndern pluck these six pigeons.' Eirinn removed them from hooks above the bench and tossed them onto the table. 'Add their feathers to the chickens', Rosamunde fetch pepper, saffron, cloves, mace, vergis and salt from the malt chamber, Abigail bring me the dish of soaked damsons from the larder and heat up water in the chafers. Miriam fine chop more thyme, sauery, margeron and parsley.'

Eirinn chopped up the chickens that had been soaking in the bucket of water and rolled the pieces in fine white flour before glazing them with a paste of beaten egg yolks rubbed into a dish of butter flavoured with saffron. Miriam prepared six coffyns before peeling the swollen damsons and cutting the stones out. The ingredients ready, Eirinn placed the glazed chicken pieces in the coffyns and arranged the damsons around them. A final sprinkle of currants and the pies were ready for their lids.

Eirinn nodded at the oven. 'The pies are ready.'

Miriam removed the alowes pies, now golden brown, set them on the board to cool and replaced them with the chicken and damson pies. For the next three hours the kitchen buzzed with activity, everyone too busy with their tasks to speculate about the Marchioness's plans for Miriam. Chafers boiling over the fire saw a procession of ingredients: the six plucked and drawn pigeons, a rump of beef for shoes, beef bones for broth, damsons in claret. A broth for pottage simmered in the cauldron over the main fire and capons seasoned with thyme stewed on the hob.

Eirinn sliced the wheels of cheese for tarts and handed them to Abigail to soak in a dish of sweetened milk while Miriam beat a pot of cream together with the yolks of ten eggs and a dish of sugar-sweetened butter for the French-style cheesecakes. Rosamunde prepared coffyns for the pigeon pies and Fyndern and Valentyne scampered back and forth to the larder for fresh ladles, chafers and skimmers, to the buttery for more cream pots and to the courtyard for fresh water and more eggs as needed.

By midday, the table groaned with a feast of four alowes pies, five French cheesecakes, five cheese tarts, four chicken and damson pies, six baked pigeons, seven beef shoes, a dish of cates and four damson tarts. The family's midday dinner.

At midday, Master Trenery, the two footmen and Thomas relayed the feast upstairs and the servants sat down to their own midday dinner. Afterwards work began again with the preparation of the family's supper and by mid-afternoon the clothes were brought in and arranged on racks to dry completely before being folded and delivered to the various rooms. After the family's supper the kitchen was cleaned and made ready for service the next day. Around midnight the servants tumbled into their beds to snatch a few hours' sleep before the Bowe bells summoned them at dawn when the cycle would repeat, each day an identical link on a chain that was severed the day they died. No servant expected alteration or surprise but change hovered over Eirinn and Miriam like a circling hawk and all because the Marchioness happened to hear a song.

The Marchioness

By 1588 there were no more dukes in England for the Queen had executed the last one, Thomas Howard, the Duke of Norfolk for treason in 1572. Keeping the nobility deliberately weak, the Queen created no new viscounts or Marquesses and very few barons and earls.

But there remained one Marchioness: Elin Ulfsdotter Snakenborg, Marchioness of Northampton, known in Court circles as Helena the Red for her magnificent red hair. When she arrived at Dover on the 8th of September 1565, Helena so enthralled the elderly Sir William Parr, 1st Marquess of Northampton and brother of the late Queen consort Catherine Parr, that he offered her marriage. The Swedish beauty accepted him, confident that his attentions would be short-lived for he was an elderly fifty-two and she a maid of sixteen.

Helena became a wife in May 1567 and by October she was a widow: a very rich widow. Upon her husband's death, she inherited a house in Guildford Surrey along with the magnificent Stanstead Hall in Essex, plus a substantial dower and the gift of the manor of Hemingford Grey granted her by the Queen.

Her husband's body was scarcely cold when she married again.

Thomas Gorges of Longford, Wiltshire, was a handsome young gentleman, second cousin of the late Anne Boleyn but this did not spare the young couple the Queen's wrath when she learned that the last remaining Marchioness had married a mere gentleman.

Helena was exiled from Court and Thomas incarcerated in the Tower of London. It was only the interception of a friend, Lord Chamberlain Thomas Radclyffe, 3rd Earl of Sussex, that softened the Queen's heart. Helena was forgiven and Thomas released but to shore up advantage they named their firstborn child Elizabeth and their newly acquired matrimonial home in Cheapside, Radclyffe House, out of gratitude to their friend.

Helena was happily-married and deeply in love when in 1573 a pregnant, unwed girl knocked on the gatehouse door of Radclyffe House begging for food and work. Simon Trenery, the newly-appointed valet, gave the young woman a hot meal and spoke to the Marchioness about a position for her in the kitchen as a scullery maid.

The Marchioness took Eirinn Tilby and her unborn child into service: risking her own neck, for despite her power as the one remaining Marchioness, taking in a pregnant doxy was a hanging offence, and Swedish or no, she was living under English law which forbad the sheltering of a vagrant. Perhaps it was because they were the same age and their fortunes so different that Eirinn's plight elicited sympathy in Helena or perhaps it was because the Swedish outsider had the compassion lacking in so many others of noble birth, including the Queen.

Eirinn learned the workings of the kitchen under the tutelage of the cook, Master George, and when he died of ague a year after she arrived, she took his position while Master Trenery looked for his replacement but the meals Eirinn prepared were so excellent the Marchioness gave her the post and with it a room of her own, an honour almost unheard of for a base-born servant in England.

Miriam was just a babe in arms when the Marchioness was widowed for the second time. Thomas Gorges was snuffed out by a brutal flux in 1574. The young Marchioness grieved prodigiously and withdrew from society. Unable to bear the vibrance of her children: five healthy little half-Swedes, two sets of twins in addition to Elizabeth, she packed them off to Stanstead Hall where the young Gorges exhausted a succession of wet-nurses and gentlewomen. Helena wore widow's weeds for the next twelve years and Radclyffe House, once lively with masques and banquets and the laughter of children, grew silent and wintery.

Then in 1586 summer returned. The Marchioness discarded her black weeds, and sent for her eldest daughter, Elizabeth, now a fecund and fetching fourteen-year-old. The still-young and beautiful Marchioness acquired a dazzling new wardrobe in gem-coloured velvets and lace and distributed her weeds amongst the servants, but since the sumptuary laws forbad the wearing of clothes above your station, these superior garments were packed away in chests scented with lavender to preserve them until they might legally be worn or sold to the theatre where sumptuary laws did not apply, at least for the duration of the play.

Now, magnificently garbed, Helena Gorges renewed her connections at Court for the sole purpose of securing a suitable husband for Elizabeth.

Within a month she had found him.

Rathe Courteney was the son of a wealthy wool merchant from Halifax. His father, Sir Geoffraie Courteney, who could boast a lineage dating back to Henry Ist, had made a fortune out of sheep after the Queen made it compulsory for everyone, except the few remaining nobles, to wear a wool cap to church on Sunday. Sir Geoffraie enclosed his Halifax estate, invested in twenty thousand sheep, and transformed the east range of his crumbling old castle into a factory for processing wool. Glass windows provided light and long working days for the spinners and weavers. The exemplary fine cloth he produced was sold at home in England and abroad in the Netherlands. It was a lucrative business created through pragmatism and the ability to produce raw wool and process it into textiles on site. Sir Geoffraie's enterprise saved the decaying Courteney fortune and secured a spectacular marriage for his son with the one remaining Marchioness' daughter.

Sir Geoffraie Courteney and the Marchioness of Northampton brokered the union of their eldest children over a bottle of Malmsey, the sweetest, richest and most persuasive Portuguese Madeira, usually only weaponised for romantic trysts.

Rathe Courteney did not meet his bride until the day before the arranged marriage. The introduction was made over midday dinner at Radclyffe House in the company of his father and his prospective mother-in-law. Initially relieved to meet an exquisite young woman, fragile as a piece of porcelain, Rathe became increasingly frustrated with her inability to make conversation beyond a demure assent. While their parents planned the union of their houses and fortunes, Rathe struggled to find common ground with Lady Elizabeth. Finally, having exhausted every topic from oceanic exploration to the presence of fairies, he narrowed his questions down to fashion (her taste thereof), the weather (her preferred season) and flowers (her favourite). Her responses were monosyllabic and to the point: farthingale, spring, roses, each answer punctuated by a sip of Malmsey which turned her alabaster cheeks an alarming shade of scarlet.

Rathe pretended interest while his mind wandered to his recent investment in two galleons, which, if they survived storms, pirates and reefs, promised a fortune independent of his father's. As a wedding present his father had given him £3,000 "to play with as he saw fit" and he saw fit to risk a speculative investment: half-shares in two sleek galleons made to the specifications of ex-pirate, John Hawkins. Hawkins' galleons with their lower superstructures, were much more manoeuvrable and seaworthy than previous ships like the carrack and could serve as both cargo-carrying vessels and warships should the Queen command it.

If Elizabeth and Rathe were pawns in their parents' game, they accepted their roles for the advantage their union would bring to their families. Geoffraie Courteney believed in old titles and the Marchioness believed in new money.

After the nuptials, the new Master left ancient Halifax and moved to modern London where a young man of means could afford multiple distractions. He brought no servants, not even a valet, and for all the impact he made he might have been a ghost for no servant apart from Master Trenery and Thomas ever saw him. Jonas only saw him fleetingly when he collected his horse on Friday evenings and returned it in the early hours of Saturday morning after an evening spent in his mistress's bed.

III

The sounds of life tease at my heart
The ringing laughter, conversation, joy, and song
The echoes chamber in my soul and cant a curse
I don't belong.

'Follow the coast west to Lands' End, Arthur's County.' He frowned. 'You doubt Arthur?'

'He's a myth.'

'He's no myth. He was Welsh, that was his problem. The English Kings wrote him out of history, but he was a great warrior and a fair peacetime leader, unlike these Tudors. He resides in Anwen now – the Underworld of delights and eternal youth. You may yet preside over such a world here among the living.'

'The same living who burned me?'

'I promised you vengeance and you shall have it once my plan takes root. But hasten now to Cornwall where they hate the Queen. You'll be safe there.'

'I have no coin for a journey.'

'You will not need coin for you will not hunger or thirst and I will find you. Soon.'

'My mother?'

'Send for her later perhaps. Not now. If they catch you, they'll make a freak of you.'

And so, she left London and all she had known – her mother, her home, the man she had recklessly loved – trusting a stranger would help her understand what she had become and in time, help her effect vengeance.

***

A week after she heard Miriam sing, the Marchioness gave Master Trenery two gold sovereigns for Mistress Tilby – more money than she had ever seen in her life – and instructions to buy three ells of cambric for her daughter's new clothes and a pair of fine white slippers. Her old brown buskins grimed with kitchen grease would not do in the upstairs dining room.

'Miriam is to be ready for service by the end of the month,' Master Trenery told Eirinn. 'I am to teach her how to serve the family.' He pressed the coins into her palm. 'It's a great honour given her –'

'An honour? I know what this world does to base-born women.'

'The Marchioness has been good to you and she will be kind to Miriam for your sake.'

Eirinn glanced at the winking coins, snapped out their glitter with a fist. 'What's to become of my girl, Simon?'

'More than we hoped for, Eirinn.'

The autumn sun cast long curling shadows of bean and gourd vines across the turned red earth of the kitchen garden and sent elongated echoes of the gatehouse roof snaking across the cobbled courtyard. In this fractured light beads of dew quivered on clods ripe for new planting.

'You're late,' said Eirinn, cuffing the kinchin-cos when they tumbled into the kitchen.

'Mam, please don't cuff them. They've no caring mother, no father to see that they are fed and shod.'

Eirinn softened. 'I'm sorry, lads. I'm much troubled at present. Now mind Mistress Miriam in the Cheaps. Master Jonas is busy with the palfreys today so I'm relying on you to protect my daughter.'

'With our lives,' said little Valentyne earnestly.

'No need for sacrifice.' Miriam laughed. 'If you can carry your loaded panniers without dropping them, I'll be satisfied.'

The boys were scarce nine years old, strong enough to fetch and carry but hardly much protection. They were still having trouble rising at first bell after their rootless life on the streets. Many mornings the lads were red-eyed for lack of sleep, no doubt after a night fretted with dreams of parents long gone to God or absorbed into the shiftless poverty of the London boroughs.

Eirinn handed her daughter the coin purse for the produce and eight pence, her own wage, for her books.

Miriam tucked the coins into her pocket. 'I'll be eighteen in three years and then I'll earn my own coin for my books.'

'And it will be a fraction of what useless Thomas will earn.' She sighed. 'Why should male servants earn two shillings four pence a week while hardworking women get eight pence? I suppose God never trusted our sex again after Eve gave Adam the apple. Ah well, it always falls to women to feed men and the good Lord punishes us for it one way and another.'

'The Queen doesn't treat women any better than God does.'

Eirinn shuddered. 'Keep these thoughts to yourself, sweetling.'

'She could change our lot for the better. She has the power. She could make sure we got an equal wage if not an education.'

'Hush now, don't criticise the Queen. Mary Cleere was burned at the stake for saying the Queen was base-born. It were a loose tongue sent Mistress Cleere to the pyre.'

'And it was the Queen gave the order to light it.'

Eirinn shivered. 'Come along now, the best produce is gone by mid-morning. Watch out for fraters and palliards in the Cheaps. You won't have Jonas to scare them off.'

Miriam turned to the boys. 'Frater and palliards – your old friends. Can I trust you?'

'You can trust us, Mistress. We 'ad no friends save each other,' said Fyndern.

Eirinn pressed the two gold sovereigns into Miriam's palm. 'For your new clothes.'

Miriam stared at the coins glinting in her palm, frowned. 'So much money for clothes when people are starving. Is it right?'

'Nothing is right in this world but we are better off than most.'

Eirinn walked them to the gate and roused Jonas to unlock it. 'See that you're home by dinner time.'

'Rosemary and bays!' cried a girl on the street with a laden basket.

'Hie girl!' cried Eirinn. 'I need both.'

They left Eirinn haggling over a pannier of rosemary and bays and made their way towards West Cheap, the larger of the two markets, which began at the Great Conduit on Old Jewry Street and ended at the smaller conduit near the gates of Saint Paul's Cathedral where the most exotic fruits and vegetables were sold – carrots and tubers from the New World, cabbages and ropes of onions from Flanders – and of course where the booksellers had their stalls.

Cheapside, both a street and a market, was the beating heart of London. It was here that most of the important celebrations took place and all the market buildings had viewing platforms for jousting tournaments and foot parades. The narrow tributary side streets off the arterial main road had names that indicated their trade: Honey Lane, Milk Street, Wood Street, although every housewife knew that the fishmongers traded on Friday Street.

'That's the Church that rings the bells you ignore most mornings,' said Miriam, pointing up at the great stone spire of St. Mary-le-Bowe Church.

'We try to wake,' said Fyndern.

'But it's hard for you after having no cause to rouse yourselves for so many years. When did your parents die?'

Valentyne subtly shook his head at his younger brother.

Miriam caught the exchange. 'Well, never mind the past. You're safe now. You have pallets to sleep on and food in your bellies.'

Perhaps they had reason to keep their parents' whereabouts secret. If they were still living the Marchioness would be obliged to give them back to their parents. Passing the Cheapside Cross they entered the busiest part of the markets near St. Peter's Church. The morning rang with a chorus of sound: the rumbling of coaches and drays on busy Watling Road, the clanging, banging and rasping of lathe and hammer as new houses rose on nearby streets where windmills once turned, criers delivering news, street vendors announcing their produce, a woman in an apron calling, "Who will buy my fine sausages?" another with a basket on her head chanting, "Hot pudding pies, hot!" another singing "Come buy my glasses, glasses, fine glasses!" the disparate sounds resolving in a song of life, roiling yet arrowed as London's arterial river.

Miriam hummed along and the boys smiled at each other.

'Sorry, lads. I always hear music. Sometimes I make up words.'

'We know. We hear'd Master Thomas teasing you,' said Fyndern.

41

'We like your singing, Mistress Miriam. It's lovely like birds,' said Valentyne.

Even though it was early, the market was already crowded with housewives and servants haggling over produce. Waits and makepieces entertained for coin and wags looking to steal a kiss or a cob shuffled through the crowd. The autumn sun, warm and sharp, lit a morning alive with the sounds of industry and it seemed all England was bent on improvement now that the Catholic Queen Mary was dead and the Spanish threat eradicated.

Miriam read that in the sea-furbelowed counties now protected by the might of their invincible navy, brand-new houses rose moatless and shining with glass and light-filled manors replaced the glowering old stone castles. Modern London also glittered with glass-tiered mansions. It was a new and exciting world and who knew what opportunities the future held? Perhaps one day servants would enjoy the same freedoms their masters took for granted.

Miriam glanced at the boys trotting along behind her. 'You lads have never seen the markets like this have you? As customers rather than thieves.'

'We only stole to eat, Mistress Miriam,' said little Fyndern.

The Bowe Bells had peeled six times when they passed a shop fragrant with fresh-glazed cates and pies, the sun heightening the heady blend of sugar and minced fruit. The boys slowed to a dawdle, sniffed.

'Come along now. Mam can bake finer than these and there will be a treat for you later.' They looked up at her, eyes narrowed and distrusting as wild things. 'I promise.'

Shouldering their panniers, they tore themselves away from the tantalising scent. Miriam only had a few calls to make – Bread Street for some fresh-made cobs to supplement their manchets, Fish Street for the day's catch, Milk Street for the warm frothy nectar her mother used to bake her cates, lemons and cherries if they were fresh, the booksellers, and lastly, a visit to the Royal Exchange for the cambric for her new clothes and a pair of white slippers.

The road had been recently gravelled with sand which made the walking easy and pleasant. Miriam stepped lightly, delighting in the cheer of life, the sight and sound of haggling and bartering, the sudden trill of laughter over a shared joke, the criers announcing the latest news abroad and in Court, the merchants crying their wares and the sudden fountain fall of notes from a lute. The sun gold-leafed a cloudless day throbbing with youthful promise. A gaggle of farmers ushered their livestock – cows, sheep, pigs, chickens in cages – through the crowd to sell to slaughtermen and butchers. Miriam stopped a farmer and bought a brace of coneys for 10 pence, dropping the rabbits into Valentyne's pannier.

Fyndern stared at the dead rabbits as if they might spring up and hop away.

'They ain't goin' nowhere but home, Fyn!' Valentyne laughed.

'Home?' he asked.

'Radclyffe House is your home now,' said Miriam. 'Mam wants five pints of fresh cream, a dozen lemons and a pound of cherries. Do you know how much those things cost?'

They shook their heads.

'One lemon is 3 pence, so a dozen will cost three shillings, the cream will cost one shilling and threepence and a pound of cherries costs 10 pence. It pays to know the right price so you don't get robbed. You say nothing, just listen while I haggle and stay close to me, 'tis easy to get lost in a crowd.' She paused. 'If that's what you're planning.'

43

They looked up at her, dark eyes wide and wary.

After haggling, Miriam placed the lemons, cream and cherries into Fyndern's pannier. 'Too heavy?'

The boy shook his head.

'Tell me if the load gets too heavy and we'll take it home. We can always come back out for more before dinner. Now about running away –'

'We won't run nowhere Mistress Miriam,' said Fyndern. 'Like you said Radclyffe House is our home now.'

'Yes, it is, but you have to get up before dawn and work for Mam and you don't like that.'

'We're not used to it, is all,' said Valentyne.

'Still, if you've a mind to escape me here – it may seem a grand adventure to return to your life of ignoring the Bowe bells but come evening when your bellies are roaring and you've no safe place to lay your heads, you'll be prey to those that prowl the streets looking for lads about your age. Do you know what they do with young lads?'

They shook their heads.

'They chain them up and remove them to the sea.'

'Who does?' asked Valentyne.

'Pirates. Soulless fellows who want gold and anything they can steal. Little hands like yours are prized for picking foreign pockets but if you're caught in a foreign market, you'll swing like any English lad at Tyburn. Pirates will spirit you away in the night and by sun-up you'll look out on naught but blue, swaying and pitching in your chains.'

'How do you know all this?' asked Fyndern with narrow-eyed suspicion.

'Master Trenery said it at supper before you came. He overheard the Master who owns two galleons complaining about the practice of stealing lads and forcing them into a life of piracy.'

'Would they make us row like the wherrymen?' asked Valentyne.

'They'd make you row all day and in a storm they'd make small lads like you climb a mast as high as yon belltower to untie the sails.' She turned away, smothered a smile, certain the little ones thought better of any silly escape plan they may have hatched in the night, this being their first day abroad since the Marchioness took them in. 'And don't think you'd share the treasure neither.'

Fyndern tugged on her sleeve. 'Mistress Miriam, I heard them ships do fall off the ends of the earth.'

'Who told you such?'

'Our Ma afore she died o' the Black Death.' This last comment received a sharp nudge in the ribs from Valentyne.

Miriam stopped walking. 'Your parents died of the Black Death?'

Fyndern nodded, his eyes brimming with tears. 'Ma did. We never knew our Da.'

'Don't tell 'er we was base-born,' snapped Valentyne. 'She'll tell 'er Ma and then we'll be turned out and back to stealing.'

'She won't turn you out. I'm base-born, too.'

'You're never,' said Fyndern, blinking up at her.

'But you're so beautiful,' said Valentyne. 'How could you be base-born?'

'Many are, even some of the great and powerful.'

'Who was Mary Cleere?' asked Valentyne.

'A woman who should have held her tongue. You will hear things in the kitchen that should never be repeated, things that could get us burned just like Mistress Cleere.'

'You said the Queen herself did light the pyre,' Fyndern whispered.

'I was foolish to say it so close to sharp little ears.' Miriam lowered her voice. 'Mind me now, you must be very careful who you speak to. A careless word could send an innocent to the Tower. Come now, we have much to do before dinner.'

The lads fell quiet and trotted along behind Miriam as they made their way deeper into the market. 'About the earth – your mother was wrong. It's round not flat. Sir Francis Drake proved it by sailing all the way round. It was announced here in the market. He found a new world on the other side of the earth. I know it's hard to believe but the earth is round like a ball.'

'But how do we not fall off?' asked Valentyne.

'God keeps us stuck on if we're good and say our prayers.'

The children once again fell silent until Valentyne spoke. 'But how do the sea and the animals and the carts – everythin' 'cept the trees as have roots in the ground stay stuck when they cannot pray and know nothin' of God?'

It was a good question, one that had vexed her, too. She ventured the only answer that seemed both reasonable and safe. ''Tis God's will.' She lowered her voice. 'And magic.'

'Magic,' they whispered, clearly finding this more likely.

'Does Mistress Tilby know your mother died of the plague?'

'No, our talk only goes one way,' said Valentyne. 'She talks and we listen and do 'er bidding.'

'Come now, let's finish our errands and not worry about things we cannot fix or understand.'

Their mother had died of the plague. Miriam wondered if her mother had burned their clothes, for plague lingered in cloth. Even lye would not kill the humours that carry plague. Health, so delicate and fleeting, depended on balancing the four humours – yellow bile, black bile, phlegm and blood. All had to be balanced for life to thrive but only prayer could stop illness caused by divine intervention – the punishment for sin.

Putrid smells made people sick. Even a bad alignment of stars could cause an imbalance in the humours as could a fairy's pinch in the night. These things could be managed with care but the greater elements that governed life – fire, earth, air, water – were beyond their control and had their own power to sicken. Too much fire and a body grew choleric. Too much time outdoors in the dry and cold and your bile turned black. Even a splash of cold water could build up the phlegm that drowned the lungs and stopped the breath but most dangerous of all was the hot, wet air that brought the Black Death and a noxious smell, even a faint one lingering on the clothes of the dead had the power to …

'They burn women with red hair like hers.' A voice blistering, shattering and near.

Miriam swung around, met the glacial gaze of a stout woman with washerwoman's arms and a snivelling child dangling from one bunched fist. 'And them green cat-eyes of hers are casting spells on my child. She's bewitching my son!'

'She never –' Valentyne took a step towards the woman, fists bunched.

Miriam pulled him back. 'Valentyne, be still.'

A red-faced fellow, half the woman's size, popped out from behind her. 'Hush now, Constance, times have changed since our dear Queen was crowned. It was her father hung witches.'

47

'And her sister burned 'em.'

'My dear, 'tis a lovely day. Come Dorcas, let's buy a poppet for you.' He seized the child by his free hand and tugged but his mother held firm.

'Witches have hair the colour of fire and eyes like a cat's … like hers.' She glared at Miriam. 'It's unnatural that hair and them eyes.'

'The Queen has that colour hair, my dear.' Once again, the man tried to free the child from her grip. 'Come Dorcas.'

'But not them eyes the colour o' leaf.'

'My dear, it will not do to criticise a lass whose hair favours the Queen's.'

Now the woman tore her judging eyes away from Miriam and skewered her companion with a hateful glare. 'Maybe she's bewitched you, too, Samuel.'

Just then a minstrel began to sing in a voice true and clear. Miriam knew the song, had sung it often. The Foy Porter, written by long dead French composer Guillaume de Machaut. She had never heard a finer interpreter, so moving was his rendition, so pure his voice, it quietened the haggling crowd, the carping harridan, the vendors' repetitive cries until it seemed the very air rang with the beseeching melody of a lover whose lady compared to that rarest of all gems, a sapphire. Using this momentary lapse of attention Miriam spirited the boys away to the Royal Exchange to purchase three ells of cambric and a pair of white slippers for her new situation.

After their errands they returned home with laden panniers and eight pence change.

'No books today, sweetling?' said Eirinn as she unloaded the panniers.

'We ran out of time,' Miriam lied.

'We 'ad to leave, Mistress Tilby, there were trouble in the Cheaps,' said little Fyndern.

Eirinn almost dropped the pots of cream. 'What happened? Miriam? Valentyne?'

'A lady did call Mistress Miriam a witch for her red hair and green eyes. She did say she put a curse on her son,' said Fyndern. 'Valentyne was going to jark her with his fist.'

Eirinn patted Valentyne on the head. 'Good lad. Go to the larder and fetch a dish of cates off the lowest shelf. I baked them specially for you.'

'I told you she would,' said Miriam. 'You were brave lads today. Thank you.'

When the boys left the kitchen Eirinn whispered, 'What happened?'

'Nothing that a song couldn't cure.'

'You sang in the Cheaps?'

'Not me, a minstrel with a voice so true it silenced trade. We left quickly and went to the Royal Exchange. There was no trouble.'

Eirinn sank down onto a stool. 'This time.'

The boys returned with the dish of cates.

'Wash your hands. I'm tired of reminding you!' said Eirinn, and smiling, added, 'You're good lads.'

While the children devoured the cates Miriam took her mother aside and spoke low so they could not hear. 'Their mother died of plague. Their clothes need burning. Maybe even their bedding.'

Eirinn shook her head. 'They were on the streets longer than six weeks. If there was danger, we would have sickened by now.' Her face shadowed. 'This business of calling you a witch is what I've been afraid of. Your beauty is a danger to you now. I will send Abigail for supplies from now on. She's fair but not uncommonly so.' She touched the fine white cambric. 'Everything is changing.'

That evening Miriam's lessons began. After supper Master Trenery had her practice delivering laden trays and refilling glasses without spilling a single drop of wine.

'Now,' he said, 'unlike our meals, there is no glass at the family's places. They will raise their fingers thus.' He held his index finger aloft. 'When we see this signal one of us will fill a glass with their preferred drink and deliver it. When their glass is empty, we collect it and rinse it in a wooden basin and replace it on the buffet, ready for service. The wood protects the precious glass. Delicate Venetian glass is more highly prized than a gold or silver cup and the Marchioness has ten. We must handle them with great care. Here try now. I will be the Master and you will bring me wine.'

Over the next week Master Trenery taught Miriam how to set and clear the table and light the tall tallow candles. Abigail made her a white cambric kirtle, gown and bodice, and for her final lesson Master Trenery explained she must stand silently in the shadows watching for a raised finger or a nod indicating the clearing of a voider or the delivering of a drink. She must never speak unless spoken to and she must not stare at the family or appear to be listening to their conversation, even though she would be privy to every word – their darkest secrets and their privately-held views.

'They are trusting us with their lives,' said Master Trenery. 'A faithless servant looking to enrich herself could send her betters to the Star Chamber and report a Master's heretic view or a Mistress's hatred of the Queen. The family will be careless in front of us.' He paused. 'They forget we are there you see.'

The Family

'They're tearing down ancient piles and filling in moats now that Drake has quashed the Armada. So much history lost.' The Marchioness stabbed a slice of conger eel. 'I prefer fish nights. Meat sits heavily on my stomach these days.' Popping the eel into her mouth.

'Who are?'

The Marchioness stared at her son-in-law across the candlelit table. 'Who are what, Rathe?'

'Tearing down ancient piles?' He raised his index finger and Master Trenery poured a glass of his preferred drink, Capri wine, into a delicate Venetian glass on the buffet, delivered it, and stepped back into the shadows to wait, silent and unmoving as a statue.

'The new rich, the sailors and merchants, the folk who made their fortunes –'

'Honestly,' said the Master, completing her sentence and taking a long draft of wine. 'This is splendid. I must import another barrel.'

'I prefer Malmsey,' said the Marchioness. 'You call piracy and commerce honest?'

'It's more honest than inherited wealth.'

'Count yourself fortunate you have both,' said the Marchioness, her breasts bulging above a stomacher of purple velvet threaded with gold.

'I know how fortunate I am.' The Master's coal-black eyes slid over to Miriam, his gaze lingering a moment before returning to his mother-in-law. 'Will you renovate, Helena?'

'Perhaps. Will your father?'

'He's already renovated the east range for wool processing but he won't touch the rest. That drafty old castle was a gift to the first Geoffraie Courtenay from Henry 1st. It's full of musty old tapestries and hideous family portraits and no doubt the odd skeleton but Papa likes to remind himself that the Courtenays were once important.'

'And will be again when I persuade the Queen to give you a knighthood.'

'The Queen isn't making any new knights, Helena.'

'She will.' The Marchioness smiled. 'I have just the weapon for her persuasion.'

The Master shrugged. 'I don't care for titles.'

'Maybe not but your son might.'

'What did Geoffraie Courtenay do for King Henry?' It was the first time Lady Elizabeth had spoken since the family sat down to supper.

'He paid off the King's gambling debts,' said her husband, his gaze once again drifting to Miriam.

**

It was Miriam's first evening in service, the first time she had seen the family apart from the fleeting visit by the Marchioness a month earlier. The Master was as handsome as the highwayman in her dreams, coal-black eyes and hair dark as a magpie's wing. He was dressed in black, the most fashionable and expensive of velvets and his cordwain gamaches were also black. In contrast, his wife, Lady Elizabeth, was pale and delicate as one of their Venetian glasses. Her hair was the colour of spun-gold and worn high much like a porcelain doll Miriam had once seen in the Cheaps. The candlelight illuminated threads of lilac veins on breasts all but revealed above her pink silk bodice. She ate little, spoke less and drank constantly, her eyes sliding across to the Master again and again but he either did not notice or did not care for he ignored her.

'Your father's right to maintain the castle. It's our son's inheritance,' murmured Lady Elizabeth. 'Good breeding.'

52

'Yes, I've a mind to renovate,' said the Marchioness, cutting her daughter off mid-sentence. 'My estates in Surrey and Essex are surrounded by houses made almost entirely of glass. Imagine the light within, and those Italianate gardens that are all the fashion: mazes, fountains, curves and contours. I could sit at my window and admire my garden all day.'

'What about all that lost history, Helena?' Master Rathe laughed.

'Are you planning a move to the country, Mama?' asked Lady Elizabeth.

'If I refurbish Stanstead Hall I may.' She raised her little finger and Master Trenery poured her wine, stepped forward, delivered it and removed the soiled glass in one smooth movement. The Venetian glasses caught and threw back the candlelight in rainbows. Miriam had seen them of course when she and Abigail washed them after the family's meals but to see them candlelit and raised to lips that sipped casually as if wine and ale flowed as freely as the fountain in Cheapside was miraculous. Their own mazers were wooden and they gulped their ale down fast as they were only allowed two flagons between them. The family had three flagons of Malmsey and two leatherjacks of Capris wine. Unlike their plain wooden trenchers, the family's trenchers were made of silver and their knives had glass handles with etchings of flowers on the bronze clasps. In the centre of the table a silver candelabra held three tallow candles that cast a golden glaze over the room.

'I do not trust the Spanish,' said Master Rathe, raising his finger again. 'We may have need of our moats yet.'

Master Trenery filled a fresh glass, delivered it and handed the cleared glass to Thomas to wash. Lady Elizabeth raised her finger. This time Thomas filled the delicate glass and without so much as a beat between filling and turning he delivered the wine to Lady Elizabeth before slipping back into the shadows. This was a very different Thomas from the teasing lad in the kitchen. This Thomas was quiet and orderly, all devilment dissipated. Miriam pressed back into the shadows next to him and Master Trenery, watching and waiting for her cue to serve or clear. As the evening wore on her attention drifted back and forth between the astounding room and the attractive family and even though her feet and back ached after working all day and her stomach grumbled, she reminded herself that it was a great honour to serve her betters, to be trusted with their fine trenchers and glasses, to overhear their private conversation.

'The peace agreement will hold them off,' said the Marchioness, settling the matter of the warlike Spanish. 'No army or pirate would dare trespass now thanks to Drake.'

'Drake is a pirate himself, Helena, and this peace is as fragile as the paper it was written on, as easily burned as forged.' Once again, the Master's gaze shifted to Miriam.

'Burned? Forged? You are being disagreeable. Too many late nights, Rathe?' The Marchioness glanced at Miriam. 'Perhaps we can find something that will keep you home.'

Lady Elizabeth stabbed the conger eel on her trencher, then dropped it and emptied her glass in one long swallow, tapping the glass impatiently for a refill. Master Trenery poured a fresh glass of wine and was about to deliver it.

'No, Master Trenery!' said the Marchioness. 'Lady Elizabeth has had enough to drink. Eat something, Eliza, if not for you then for the baby.'

'Why?' snapped Lady Elizabeth. 'You've already got your precious grandson. What does it matter if this one dies and me with it?'

'Elizabeth –' The Marchioness sighed.

'I feel ill Mama.'

'A little more food and a little less wine would ease your choler.'

Lady Elizabeth ate a morsel of food and then looked longingly at her husband.

It seemed to Miriam that sorrow stalked the rich as intently as it tortured the poor. Indeed, in this matter alone fate dealt an even hand. Still, Miriam reasoned she would rather sit at this table and lie abed past the summoning Bowe bells and wear silk and velvet next to her skin rather than lockram and kersey. For a life of ease, she would put up with an errant husband and an indifferent mother.

'If you're so certain the Spanish can't be trusted to honour the peace treaty, Rathe, then explain the new building ravening the countryside. Clearly some people have confidence in the Queen's ability to negotiate a treaty.'

'I have every confidence in the Queen, Helena. I just don't have much in the Spanish.'

'Mama, may I be excused?'

'Stay where you are, Elizabeth, and attempt to contribute to this conversation.'

Trying to ignore the turbulent currents, Miriam studied the room. The walls were hung with tapestries depicting ancient wars, knights on horseback, swords raised above their heads, maidens waving favours from towers. In the far corner a leather and chainmail suit of armour stood to attention on a frame, a sword buckled to its bulging leather cuirass. She wondered which ancestor had worn it and which sovereign he had fought and died for, shuddering at the

55

horror men had to endure for ungrateful sovereigns. Master Trenery said there was a highwayman who had fought bravely for the Queen, a loyal soldier who had command of his own squadron. He believed she would reward him when the war was over, but the virgin Queen cared little for the men who served her. Even as she revelled in the victory, she forgot about the men who had secured it. There was no reward for them, no castle – those were given out like confyts to her favourites like Robert Dudley. So, this ex-soldier, a second son with no hope of inheritance, turned to highway robbery, stealing from the rich and distributing his spoils amongst the local poor. Master Trenery said he single-handedly staved off starvation in his county one winter. And still the Queen hung him.

**

'Rathe, how goes it with your galleons? Any profit?'

'I've a mind to import sugar this year.'

The Marchioness shook her head. 'Slaves are where fortunes are made.'

'I won't be part of that evil trade.'

'You'll miss out on a fortune.'

'I'd rather keep my soul, Helena.'

'And *my* title,' said Elizabeth. 'Oh, I forgot, titles don't interest you.'

The Master ignored the jibe, raised his knife, and used it as a pointer. 'Hawkins stole kings and princes along with commoners. Kings and princes chained up and sold as slaves to Portuguese plantation owners in the New World.'

'Savages,' said the Marchioness.

'Human beings,' said the Master.

A livid flush crept up Lady Elizabeth's neck, inflaming her cheeks. 'Ungodly savages.'

Master Rathe laughed. 'You and the Queen are of the same mind, my dear, for she profits handsomely from the capture and sale of ungodly savages.'

It seemed to Miriam that the Queen profited handsomely by turning a blind eye to the suffering of others. Selling foreigners for a profit was one crime but what of her own poor wretches? Why would she who possessed the greatest fortune in the land fail to feed her own poor? She had asked Master Trenery this question once and he just shook his head and said hers was the greater view and she knew what was best for her people. But Miriam could not see how starvation was best for anyone. And didn't Master Trenery feed the poor their leftover food each day? He said it warmed his soul to feed the less fortunate. Did the Queen who wanted for nothing lack a soul?

'Ungodly savages can expect no mercy until they accept our Christian faith,' said Lady Elizabeth. 'Kings or no.'

Miriam wondered where God stood on this issue. His was surely the greater view and yet his indifference to human suffering – the pox that suffocated a person to death within a week, the babies who died shrivelled by starvation, the endless wars, the enslavement of kings – argued for a lack of compassion and in Miriam's mind these sins lay at God's door and his failure to right them was enough to make even a saint question heaven. Why were God and the Queen so careless? She had no answers and who was she to seek them? A base-born servant.

'Mama please, I need to lie down.'

'Elizabeth, I said no.'

Miriam felt a stab of pity for the young woman who was a reluctant mother, neglected daughter and cuckqueaned wife. Perhaps no amount of luxury made such misery bearable.

The Bowe bells chimed the midnight hour. Miriam looked at the almost untouched feast her mother had spent all afternoon preparing. She and Thomas and Master Trenery had not eaten since midday. Feeling faint with hunger, the room and its contents began to fold into an altered light – the tapestries, the armour, the family, the red velvet curtains frothing on the polished stone floor – seemed to meld and she imagined herself a bystander at a fairy feast: the silver trenchers, mazers, spoons, salt vessel and pepper box, the bowls of sauces, the voiders for gristle and waste, all winking silver in the candlelight.

'But Mama –'

'No!'

The fairy feast shattered and once again the pangs of hunger clawed.

The Marchioness smiled at her son-in-law. 'I have a little treat for you after supper. You might even enjoy it too, Elizabeth.'

The Master yawned. 'Are we playing cards?'

'It's not Friday, is it?' Lady Elizabeth glared at her husband; her face set in a mask of swallowed fury. 'Friday when you pretend you're going to the Mermaid Tavern.'

Miriam steadied herself against the wall. Why wouldn't the Marchioness let her daughter leave and end this interminable supper that no-one appeared to be enjoying?

'I *do* go to the Mermaid Tavern.' The Master's sharp retort echoed. 'It's where the playwrights meet and exchange ideas. I learn more from them than I do in church.'

'Blasphemy!' cried Lady Elizabeth.

The Master sighed. 'What's your surprise, Helena?'

The Marchioness motioned to Thomas to clear her voider. He swooped on the overflowing bowl and disappeared into the gloaming hallway. 'Master Trenery fetch your lute.'

Master Simon gave Miriam a swift look before quitting the room and leaving her alone with the family. The two footmen had vacated after delivering the trays and would only appear again when it was time to clear after the family had gone to bed.

Once Master Trenery was out of earshot the Marchioness nodded at Miriam. 'What do you think, Rathe? Fair enough to keep you home on Friday nights?'

'Mama!'

'Hush Elizabeth and Rathe don't even bother protesting, I know it's not a cultural liaison that lures you away from your family every Friday. If you must stray, I'd rather you did so under your own roof. The cocks and crows that raven the streets of London after dark are death to a peacock like you. I need you alive and knighted and I want my daughter free of the French disease.'

Lady Elizabeth pushed back her chair. 'I've had quite enough of this.'

'Stay where you are! I'm saving your marriage and your health.'

'A servant.' Lady Elizabeth spat the word.

'She is clean and fair enough to amuse your husband for a while and she has the voice of an –'

Lady Elizabeth slammed her fists on the table. 'Am I not fair enough for you, Rathe?'

'Angel!' finished the Marchioness. 'And if she has issue, we can be rid of her.'

Miriam leaned against the wall for ballast, her head hammering. Her mother was right. Having quit the kitchen she was now in the kind of danger that would see her turned out. Where would she go? The savage streets of London would not welcome a base-born doxy and how long before her red hair made her a witch? An apothecary might risk his neck for eight pence in exchange for a draft of poison. Poison ...

'Wait until you hear her voice,' said the Marchioness. 'I have never heard finer in Court.'

The Master was watching her, candlelight flickering over his face as he reached for the pomander attached to a silken cord at his waist. Looping the cord around his index finger he teased the ball into a casual hypnotic swing releasing the scent of cloves, nutmeg and cumin. A twitch of a smile and he released Miriam too and turned to his wife.

'Elizabeth my dear, I may be persuaded to stay home and join you and Helena at cards on Friday nights. Are we playing gleek, primero, prima-vista, maw, cent, or saint?'

'Gleek,' muttered Lady Elizabeth.

'Delightful,' he said with the hint of a smile. 'Delightful, Helena.'

'You'd best reacquaint yourself with the rules of the game,' said the Marchioness, raising her finger for more wine.

Miriam poured the wine into a precious glass, took a deep breath and stepped forward to deliver it, candlelight teasing auburn lights in her hair as it fell forward over her shoulders. Out of the corner of her eye she caught Lady Elizabeth's furious, worried glance, felt the Master's dark eyes upon her, ravening, assessing, deciding.

'The game has always favoured the rich, Helena, but if it's cards you're referring to I'll let Elizabeth win.' He leaned back in his chair, watching Miriam.

'If I am not sufficiently interesting –' began Lady Elizabeth.

'You were too long in the country, Eliza,' said the Marchioness. 'You know nothing of real life and how to manage it. Ah, here's your surprise.'

Master Trenery had returned with his lute.

'Play that enchanting song I heard the other night, Master Trenery and Miriam, sing for us, my dear.'

Master Trenery plucked the strings and Miriam stepped forward into that strange and altered light. The Master watched her, a smile teasing at the corners of his mouth. Lady Elizabeth raised her chin, a look of hatred spreading across her porcelain face. The Marchioness watched them both with quiet confidence.

And then she sang.

**

Lady Elizabeth swung around in her chair, pink mouth agape, blue eyes widened and round as coins. The Master tipped his head back and closed his eyes, allowing the song to wash over him, as water might if you were brave enough to risk immersion.

The Marchioness watched her daughter and son-in-law the way a cat watches an unsuspecting mouse, but whether she meant to catch them or lull them into trust Miriam knew not. Master Trenery had said the Marchioness was a shrewd woman, clever enough to survive a jealous Queen's wrath over her second marriage whilst maintaining her singular status as the sole surviving Marchioness in England. Such people finesse in the shadows and keep their heads, Master Trenery said.

61

If the music spun a singular enchantment over unsuspecting prey Miriam could not tell but for her it was momentary salvation, a space uniquely hers. If the Marchioness still intended her as swive for her son-in-law, she prayed her voice might persuade her of the wasted application. She and her voice could surely be put to better use seducing the great and the powerful into giving Master Rathe a knighthood.

When the last notes rang out, the Marchioness signalled to Master Trenery. 'Thank you. Tell the footmen they may clear now.'

Master Trenery caught Miriam's eye and smiled before removing himself and his lute.

'Well, Rathe, did you like your surprise?'

'Very much. How do you intend to make use of this luminous little gift?'

'I was thinking a midsummer banquet at Stanstead Hall after the renovations. Yes, I am resolved to renovate, Rathe. I will create a fairyland theme for the Queen –'

'You'll invite the Queen, Mama?' Lady Elizabeth's mood brightened considerably.

'I've a mind to. This fairy's singing could earn your husband a knighthood. I remember my days at Court. Music and beauty made the Queen very generous.'

'Music has the power of alteration,' said the Master.

The Marchioness raised her finger for more wine. 'So, you subscribe to Christopher Marlowe's view?'

Miriam delivered the glass, the candlelight making firefly lights in her magnificent hair and the Master, gazing at her, did not answer the question.

'Rathe!'

He turned his head slowly. 'Yes Helena?'

'I asked you if you subscribe to Marlowe's view about the Music of the Spheres.'

'I have great sympathy for Marlowe's views but it wouldn't do to express them outside this room.'

'Did you hear them at the Mermaid Tavern?' asked Lady Elizabeth, her mood shifting.

'Marlowe tends to drink in Deptford when he's not summoning the Devil in the woods at Cambridge.' He laughed.

'Depraved heretic.' Lady Elizabeth pressed a napkin to her lips.

'His Devil can't be any worse than their Protestant God. Only last month those good Christians disembowelled a Catholic priest for sport.'

'Careful Rathe,' warned the Marchioness.

Master Rathe shrugged. 'Who's listening?'

So, Miriam was nothing more substantial than air now the song was over, but music fell like arrows upon the rich and the poor alike and where they lodged, they had the power of alteration. Poison and magic work slowly, leavening the most socially uneven terrain and she hoped her song may yet take effect.

'Marlowe is a dangerous heretic,' said Lady Elizabeth. 'The Devil whispers in his ear.'

'He would love that,' said the Master. 'But by all accounts, his beseeching has gone unanswered.'

Lady Elizabeth tossed her napkin down on the table. 'Marlowe's views are pagan.'

'His views are borrowed from Pliny the Younger,' said the Marchioness. 'Read, my dear and widen that narrow little mind of yours.'

'I only read the Bible. You are risking the flames of Hell, Mama, reading the Devil's bait.'

The Marchioness caught the Master's eye and they exchanged a look of barely veiled contempt for the young Mistress. 'Rathe, have you read Pliny the Younger on the subject?'

The Master raised his finger for more wine and Miriam stepped forward to deliver it. 'The Elder. It was Pliny the Elder not the Younger.'

'A pair of Godless Greeks.' Lady Elizabeth sniffed.

'Romans,' said the Master with a sigh. 'Pliny wrote about the Music of the Spheres: a beautiful, ordered mechanism, both mathematical and musical, a way to measure the distances between celestial bodies mirrored in the spaces between notes. An exquisite concept and one that impresses Marlowe.'

'Marlowe who claims God does not exist,' Lady Elizabeth, sniffed. 'Can you not see the devilment in this?'

'I see only the power of music to elevate, soothe and harmonise our otherwise dislocated world.' The Master leaned back in his chair. 'Neither Pliny nor Marlowe believe in God.'

'But they do believe in the Devil,' said Lady Elizabeth. 'Is one possible without the other?'

'I believe in music,' said the Master. 'The *musica universalis*, the Music of the Spheres.' And he went on to explain how there were spheres made of glass that circled each other. It was their movement that caused the music. Miriam forgot her hunger and fear, her lucid mind absorbing a concept enchanting, beautiful, harmonious, and musical.

'Have you heard this music, Rathe?' asked the Marchioness.

'Sometimes when the night is still, I believe I hear it.'

'The Pastor has never made such a claim,' said Lady Elizabeth.

'Perhaps he is a little deaf, my dear.'

The footmen and Master Trenery returned and waited to clear the table.

'May I be excused now?' said Lady Elizabeth.

'You may, Elizabeth,' said the Marchioness.

Lady Elizabeth rose and swept past Miriam, the scent of her pomander a sudden overwhelming sweetness that lingered in her wake.

'There's a fortune to be made in slaves, Rathe,' said the Marchioness, pushing back her chair. 'Think on it.'

The Master leapt up and offered the Marchioness his arm as they departed the room. When they were gone, Master Trenery gave a swift nod and Thomas, the footmen and Miriam cleared the table. In the kitchen after eating their own supper in exhausted silence the men rose.

'God save and prosper you, Master Trenery,' said the footmen. 'And you, Master Thomas.' As usual they ignored the base-born serving girl.

'God save and prosper you, Mistress Miriam,' said Master Trenery when the young men had departed. 'You sang beautifully tonight.'

'Thank you, Master Trenery. God save and prosper you, sir.'

Alone, Miriam washed all the mazers, trenchers, spoons and trays and as she did, she imagined a celestial chorus singing a song of life, its greater view so far above the troubled earth as to be blind to human suffering and that settled the matter of God's indifference – his head was full of music.

That Night

Eirinn was still awake when Miriam crept into the room. 'How was your first night of service?'

'Well enough.' Miriam did not want to trouble her mother with the Marchioness' proposal. Not yet. 'Mam, have you ever heard music from the stars?'

'Sweetling only you hear music in everything.'

'I haven't heard this music.' Miriam shifted, picked her teeth, and slipped into bed.

'This music plays in the heavens. The Master called it the Music of the Spheres. Everything in the sky is made up of spheres one within the other and these spheres are clear as glass. The last sphere is the firmament that holds all the stars. The spheres inside it hold the sun, the moon and the planets and at the centre of all in its very own sphere is the earth and as these spheres spin they make music, such music as brings grace to all who hear it.'

'I've never heard that in church.'

'Pliny the Elder wrote about it and Christopher Marlowe believes it and they both say God doesn't exist at all. Just this music.'

'I warrant they don't say that too loudly.'

'Pliny the Elder is long gone but Christopher Marlowe wrote it in one of his plays. The Master believes him, but Lady Elizabeth says it's heretic talk.'

'It is.'

'They're cruel to her. They pretend she's not even there, invisible like a servant.'

'I am sorry to hear it and she carrying his child. But don't you go repeating what they said. We are God's finest creation, made in his image and privileged to reign over all his creatures. Even the sun and moon spin around the

66

earth and it would serve us to remember and honour such distinction.' She paused. 'Did they say anythin' about your singing? I saw Master Trenery collect his lute.'

'They said I might sing at a banquet in midsummer after Stanstead Hall is renovated with glass windows and an Italian garden.'

Eirinn was silent for a long minute. 'I will need marzipan.'

'What for?'

'Confits. Banquets needs confits.' Eirinn was quiet for so long Miriam thought she slept until: 'Did the Master look kindly upon you?'

Miriam caught her breath. 'Very kindly.'

'Keep a steady course around the Master. The Mistress may be poorly with a new bairn on the way but her eyes are sharp and Master Trenery says she vexes easily.'

'Mam, there is something else. Her Ladyship means to invite the Queen. She said if I sing for her she might give the Master a knighthood, she being much moved by beauty and music.'

'So you will sing for the Queen.' She sighed. 'Abigail and Rosamunde will be pleased.'

Miriam felt for her mother's hand, squeezed. 'Don't worry, rich folk forget you are there once the song is over. The Queen being the richest person in the land probably won't even listen to me.'

Eirinn shuddered. 'My daughter will sing for the Queen. It's a great honour sweetling.'

Miriam pulled the blanket up to her chin and fell straightaway into dreams of stars spinning around a circlet like jewels in a crown, their dance orchestrating music such as she had never heard in her life. Fairy music. Other.

Sunday

Eirinn hurried her daughter out of the church, avoiding the woman standing at the door dressed in a white shift and confessing her whoredom to parishioners as they entered and left.

'She'll be lucky if she isn't carted,' said Eirinn. 'Lying with her neighbour's husband.'

'Why isn't he confessing his sin?'

'You heard the sermon, she tempted him.'

The sermon had been all about Eve tempting innocent Adam with fruit, an act of disobedience that got them both evicted from God's Garden, and as a special punishment for Eve's sin, women were cursed with the pangs of childbirth and a secondary position in society for they could no longer be trusted after a woman abused God's gifts. Still, Miriam reasoned, Adam didn't need to bite the apple.

'Adam could have said *no*.'

Eirinn laughed. 'Men can't say *no*.'

'What's wrong with them?'

'Sweetling, that sharp little brain of yours would test the patience of a saint. Some things we just have to accept. Shall we feed the swans while we have our picnic?'

Eirinn had prepared a fine feast for their Sunday picnic but after seeing the woman in the white shift with her white wand of shame, her haunted eyes and trembling mouth, Miriam felt sick. If the Marchioness made her swive for the Master it would be her standing at the church door confessing her sin.

'Did you hear me, sweetling? Shall we feed the swans?'

'Yes, of course, they depend on the likes of us for food. Mam, if a servant was to get pregnant to her Master would

68

she have to stand at the church door in a white shift, being spat on and called a whore? Is that what happened to you?'

Eirinn sucked in a breath. ''Tis a lovely day, sweetling. Let's try to forget the lady at the church door.'

They walked towards the river, the sun treacling every surface, warming and echoing the benevolence of a heaven where God was so raptured by angelic music he was blind to human suffering.

'Mam, is there an herb that would bring on an unwanted child?'

Eirinn stopped walking, lowered her voice. 'Who needs it? Abigail? Rosamunde?'

'No, but if they did?'

She looked around, checked no-one was in earshot. 'There is a remedy but 'tis a hanging offence to use it.'

'What is it?'

'A blending of equal parts laurel, madder, pepper, sage, and crushed savin juniper seeds. It will bring about a thorough purging. We have most of those ingredients in the dry larder except savin juniper seeds.'

'Could they be bought in the market?'

'No. They are hard to come by, but I know a woman, she'd be an old lady by now if she still lives.'

'You've been to her?'

She looked down. 'Once after you were born but I have sinned no more since then.'

'It was not your sin to carry alone if sin it be. Was it Master Trenery?'

'No. He's a good man, a God-fearing saint.'

'Then who?'

'He is long gone and no, I never confessed my sin. You put my thoughts in a muddle when you speak of sin as if it were his burden to carry as well as mine.'

'Where is this woman to be found if we need her?'

'Close. But we don't need her, do we?'

'No, but 'tis good to know there is something can be done.'

''Tis a hanging offence.'

'Not for the man.'

'A woman's lot was never equal after Eve sinned.'

Miriam took a breath. 'Let's go to the theatre after our picnic. Have you enough coin?'

'I have enough coin for the wherry and the theatre now that you no longer buy your books.'

'I have no time to read.'

Eirinn linked her arm through her daughter's as they walked to the riverbank. 'What play would you like to see?'

'Anything by Christopher Marlowe.'

***

The Thames glittered like broken glass, sunglow refracting rainbows on every crest and eddy. Eirinn spread a cloth on the verge and laid out their feast – leftover meats, tarts, cates, and glazed fruits from the family's supper. A minstrel was playing for a group of merrymakers nearby, his voice lilting over the melody of a popular pastoral by William Byrd *Where fancy fond for pleasure pleads*. The mournful tune, the fine quavering voice, light as a girl's, the tale of shame and desire was lost on the noisy revellers but found its mark with Miriam and filled the lonely arch of sky above the serpentine river.

But shame will not have reason yeeld, though griefe doe sweare it shall be so: as though it were a perfect shield, to blush and feare to tell my woe: where silence force will at the last, to wish for wit when hope is past.

70

'To wish for wit when hope is past,' she murmured. 'Ah, that we may laugh at injustice and loss.'

'Sweetling, what has happened? Has Thomas –?'

'No, 'tis nothing. Look! Here come the swans for their dinner.'

Two swans, a beautiful white cob and his pen lurched up the bank followed by a freckling of grey cygnets. Now that the minstrel had finished his song the sounds of life returned amplified, laughter bright and feckless as the tide, the swans honking to be fed, the susurration of the river, and the merrymakers giving each other the week's news.

'Why don't they fly?' Miriam tossed a piece of bread to the swans. 'Why would any creature gifted with wings not fly?'

'Not all 'as have wings will fly.' Eirinn lowered her voice. 'The Scottish Queen Mary should have flown back to France instead of trusting our Queen for mercy. 'Tis a troubling time when one sovereign despatches another. 'Tis felt on the streets. We simple folk feel the ground shifting beneath our feet.'

'Maybe our Queen learned from the father who murdered her mother. Is that why she does not marry? Because she is afraid her husband would send her to the block?'

''Tis not for the likes of us to question, sweetling.'

'No, the great must never be questioned.'

Eirinn glanced at her daughter sidelong. 'Something ails you.'

'I am tired is all. Look at how the cob shares the bread with his little ones. He's a good father. We can learn much from nature.'

Eirinn tossed more bread to the swans. 'Food brings all sorts together. Before the Lord cast Adam and Eve out of the garden they had a feast every day – the sweetest fruits and wines fit for a queen and all for the taking. Sometimes the wisest course is not to question.'

The sun poured liquid gold over the bank that slid into the river rushing to the sea where pirates and sailors charting that blue expanse believed themselves more powerful than God and unbridled by law. The sky melted violet-blue into the spaces between chimney pots and spires and it seemed everything fused together like one of Eirinn's sauces when all the ingredients resolved into ambrosia. A daubing of cambric clouds drifting across the sun momentarily cast indigo shadows as if to say perfection is a mask, a lure.

'If God created all this beauty, why does he let humanity sin unchecked?'

'Your mind is too sharp for your own good. Let's just enjoy the day.'

Miriam took a cate from the basket, bit into the luscious sweetness. 'Do you think they had cates in Eden?'

'I'm sure the Lord did bake the most divine cates and tarts for his guests. If Eve had not been greedy, all folk, rich and poor, high and low, could feast every day and never pay a penny for the pleasure.'

**

After their picnic, Eirinn and Miriam paid a penny for a wherry ride across the Thames and joined the crowds on the South Bank moving through Paris Garden on their way to the playhouses. All manner of folk were headed in the same direction – workingmen, gentlemen, wives accompanied by their husbands and servants, tourists from Holland and France. Outside every theatre was a queue, a throng of almost two thousand people chatting, laughing, and speculating about the plays and the players.

'The crier says there are two Marlowe plays today,' said Eirinn.

'Let's go to Tamburlaine at the Rose Theatre.'

'We'll sit upstairs. I have sixpence.'

'We could stand in the yard for a penny.'

'No, my back aches. We'll sit.'

**

They took their seats in the upstairs gallery and watched the theatre fill. Fine ladies in ornate headdresses fanned themselves and chatted while the gentlemen with their pipes and feathered hats scanned the crowd for rivals, friends, or conquests. Suddenly Miriam caught her breath in a sharp, hissed inhalation.

'What is it?' asked Eirinn.

'The Master.' She nodded at the box opposite where the Master sat with a woman dressed in a ruby-coloured kirtle and stomacher, her dark curls escaping a heavily beaded gable hood in the style of the late Queen Anne. Her breasts were heaved up so high they almost touched her chin.

'That must be the woman he meets on Friday nights,' Miriam whispered.

'Sweetling, we did not see him.'

'Let's pray he does not see us.'

But just as the trumpets sounded for the play to begin the Master caught sight of Miriam and their eyes locked, the hold remaining fast until the first player took the stage. Throughout the opening scene Miriam was intensely aware of his gaze shifting away from the stage and across to her but as Marlowe's genius imposed itself in language, ideas, and revelation, she forgot all else, caught in the playwright's singular web, his retelling of the fate of a 14th century Mongol conqueror whose brutal rise to power was equally matched by his inglorious fall. The story unfolded in a rhythmic way, the words rising and falling like music, hypnotic and spell-binding and it transported Miriam to a place where magic seemed not only possible but more real than her life of service and the Master who might compromise her with the Marchioness's blessing.

Marlowe's genius levelled the crowd and drew new divisions – kindred and connate, disparate and incongruent. Some heard the message hidden in the rhythm of his words, the exposé of the human condition and no doubt many were in lockstep with his march into a modern world distanced from the Dark and Middle Ages. Marlowe's ideas had a currency that superseded lineage and gold but could they change the world fast enough to spare her the Master's lust? Would it give her rights?

Miriam remembered the Master saying that Marlowe had summoned the Devil when he was an undergraduate. She wondered if he had forged some kind of deal – his soul in exchange for a genius that would elucidate the transformation of a social order that went all the way back to Eden where a tyrannical Lord evicted a curious Eve, a transformation that would unseat a queen so sensitive to criticism she kept the executioner's blade sharpened and the pyres stacked. That Christopher Marlowe was brave enough to deny God and a regime that ruled through superstition and fear showed a spirit both doomed and divine. But had he done so at the expense of his soul in allegiance to a darker Lord?

'Are you still hungry, sweetling?' asked Eirinn as the woman selling apples, nuts and beer shouldered her way through the crowd.

'Save your coin for the wherry ride back.'

Eirinn waved the woman on. 'This Marlowe is brave to write as he does but he must be careful. There is always a price to pay when you criticise those in power.'

Miriam dared not look across the yard where the Master and his lady-friend sat but she felt his gaze upon her just as keenly as she had felt it when she served him and the thought of where it might lead filled her with dread for what voice had she in the matter? Indeed, in any part of her life. For now, the words of Marlowe gave her a temporary voice – his.

'Tamburlaine will fail,' said Miriam at interval. 'Marlowe has planted the seeds of his fall in Act One. A mirror of life? Will God and the Queen also fail through their vanity?'

'Hush, only speak thus when we are alone.'

Miriam lowered her voice. 'The Master said Marlowe once summoned the Devil but can he trust the dark lord? Would it not be wiser for a man of genius to trust only himself?'

Eirinn shuddered. 'And to think we came to this play after Church.'

Miriam laughed. 'An unbalanced empire will topple, Mam.'

***

Throughout the play Marlowe's ideas found traction where the ground was well-prepared by hardship and inequality. Change was in the air, Miriam felt it and revelled in the hope of it but as always occurs with the onset of alteration the shackles of bondage tighten as the beneficiaries of an old system constrict their grip. But nothing, not even superstition, can hold back a tsunami of social change when the time is ripe. The new writers' poetic and philosophical meditations were blooming in harmony with madrigals and airs and a silvery mesh of scientific and geographic discoveries that rounded the flat earth and released the heavens from the wrath of an implacable God. These visionaries held a mirror up to mankind and revealed them in all their frailty and majesty: not as unsalvageable sinners trapped in the miasmic fantasy of a trespass in Eden but as people with souls worth saving.

After the play, Miriam and Eirinn retraced their footsteps and paid their fee to the wherryman. As he rowed them across a river now urgent for the sea, they were silent, lost in contemplation of fresh ideas and the knowledge that the Master knew they had seen him with his mistress. Eirinn shuddered to think what action he might take, if any. But hopefully he knew he could count on their silence for a life on the streets with an empty belly guarantees discretion.

Walking home along the cobbled streets, Miriam eased closer to her mother. 'There was more truth spoken at the playhouse than there was from the pulpit earlier this day.'

'Miriam –'

'Don't worry, I'll never marry so no husband need find offence in my irreverence.'

Supper

'The earth is round like a ball and spinning through space dark as night and empty of air.' Master Rathe took a long draught of wine. 'Night is nothing at all.'

'Where is Heaven then?' Lady Elizabeth was yet again pushing what little food she could manage around her trencher.

'Eat something Elizabeth,' said the Marchioness with an irritated tap on the side of her glass.

Master Trenery motioned for Miriam to refill.

Miriam filled a fresh glass on the board, stepped forward into the halo of candlelight and delivered the Marchioness' wine before removing her soiled glass as she had been taught. The Master watched her, his fingers toying with his knife, his dark eyes narrowed. Miriam dared not meet those eyes for fear her look would betray his indiscretion at the theatre.

'This heretic idea of emptiness is Marlowe's no doubt. How *was* the play?' asked the Marchioness.

'Dull.' The Master yawned. 'Some 14th century conqueror falls victim to vanity. Never lead an army. That's what highwaymen are for.'

Lady Elizabeth eased back in her chair, the baby, now a protuberance, forbad her sitting closer to the table. 'I hardly think a common thief adequate for the task of leading an army.'

'A man with nothing to lose has uncommon courage, my dear. Tamburlaine was a vainglorious fool to harbour dreams of conquest. I can think of better ways to spend a vast inherited fortune.' He paused. 'Of course, Marlowe's meaning may be lost on the privileged. It would be interesting to hear the thoughts of those in the yard.' He glanced at Miriam.

The Marchioness, following his look, half smiled. 'Why should we concern ourselves with the thoughts of those who do not share our finer sensibilities?'

'Because they outnumber us, Helena.'

'Did someone toss it then?' asked Lady Elizabeth suddenly.

'Toss what, my dear?' Master Rathe yawned again.

'The earth. If it spins through a dark night someone must have begun its course.' She rubbed her bulging stomach, arched her back to relieve the pressure under her ribs. 'There is naught in the deacon's sermon about God tossing the earth upon its course so what is Master Marlowe suggesting? The Devil pitched it?'

'No-one pitched it, my dear. The sun grips it and the earth spins to get away from his grip but like many a flawed union they depend upon each other for life.'

'As we depend on God,' said Lady Elizabeth.

The Master raised his glass to her. 'Not all entwining is governed by fear. Some forces are hidden from us.'

'If they are hidden then it is not for us to pry.' She shifted uncomfortably. 'It was curiosity that saw Eve evicted from Eden.'

Miriam tried to picture the earth as a ball spinning through space supported by nothing but divine pitch. If there was no up, no down, no place to fall then where was Heaven as Lady Elizabeth had asked? Where Hell? And what would happen to humanity if the sun lost its grip and the earth flew off into that endless nothingness that lay beyond the firmament? Would everything die? Her head ached imagining the emptiness of that black night devoid of the spheres and their circling paths and their music. Where was safety if there was no restraint? Where was harmony and the song of songs? Where was meaning? Was God truly so prankish he would risk a flawed aim?

'Marlowe is an atheist,' said the Master. 'The question of obedience to God does not shackle him.'

'Must you speak of that profane man at the dinner table?' said Lady Elizabeth.

'The Devil or Marlowe?' asked the Master with a grin.

The Marchioness took a breath so deep it threatened to split her bodice. 'This war between you must be settled if we are to benefit from our combined fortunes. It is tiresome, Elizabeth.'

'You blame me alone while my husband whores?'

'Rathe you might consider staying home,' said the Marchioness with a heavy sigh.

'Not all of us are fortunate enough to find contentment in marriage,' said the Master. 'But for the sake of our fortunes I will try to stay home more often.'

'And avoid plays,' said Lady Elizabeth.

The Marchioness sipped her wine. 'I was at cards with one of the Queen's Ladies-in-Waiting and the word is that Dee and that sorcerer, Edward Kelley, are trying to speak to angels through their seances. I don't know who tempts the flames more, Marlowe or Dee.'

'Dee will never burn while he has the Queen's favour,' said the Master, raising a finger for a refill. 'And Kelley is an alchemist not a sorcerer.'

'They should all be burned for sorcery. Queen Mary would have seen to it,' said Lady Elizabeth.

'An ugly practise,' said the Marchioness. 'The rancid smoke clung on for days quite ruining our carriage rides in the park and making me cough horribly. I am relieved our virgin Queen is more tolerant. You would do well to learn tolerance, Eliza. Allegiances change so rapidly.'

For want of occupation Miriam looked around the room, her attention caught on the portrait of Lady Elizabeth. In the painting she looked happy, if distracted. Alongside her portrait were others, ancestors dressed in armour, ladies in Medieval hennins with flowing veils, their long-dead eyes watching the present diners with languid ennui.

'Slaves,' said her Ladyship, snapping Miriam out of her reverie, 'the New World is clamouring for slaves.'

'I remain firm, Helena. I won't be part of that sub-human practice.'

'Hawkins and Drake grow rich on the trading of slaves.'

'Drake has gone mad, Mama,' said Lady Elizabeth. 'Drunk on sun and sea and the power that comes of being your own man for too long without the constraint of Church or Crown.' She paused. 'But let's not discuss freedom from service in front of the servants.'

'They would need the Golden Hinde and a lifetime of seafaring experience to acquire such freedom,' said the Marchioness. 'Drake may have gone mad but he has also grown rich.'

'Hardly any wonder when his pirate cousin encourages him to steal,' said the Master.

'You were happy enough to invest in galleons designed by Hawkins when you looked to make an independent fortune,' said the Marchioness.

The Master sipped his wine. 'I may be a hypocrite, Helena, but I am no pirate. It is a great pity that pair of rogues weren't hung in the Americas. I agree with my wife for once. The Queen should not have rewarded Drake with a knighthood. He and his cousin are little better than highwaymen and she hangs *them*.'

'Drake is clever enough to juggle his piracy with service,' said the Marchioness.

The Mistress sniffed. 'Why do we speak of that horrid little man?'

'If it's any comfort, my dear, King Philip has put a high price on Drake's head.'

'The Spanish may be thanked for ridding the world of a snake if they catch him,' said Lady Elizabeth.

'Be sure, his charmed life will end on the gallows or as sustenance for sharks,' said the Master. 'No man can maintain such uncanny luck.'

In a moment of agreement husband and wife smiled at one another and the smile worked on Elizabeth like a charm. She ate every morsel on her trencher, earning another smile, this time from her mother.

'I admire your principles, Rathe, and your father's. However, wool is not as profitable as it once was,' said the Marchioness. 'Slaves are where the profit is. Think on it.'

'Sugar,' said the Master, tapping the table with his knife for emphasis. 'There's a fortune to be made.'

'Sugar from the New World?' asked the Marchioness.

'Yes,' said the Master, tapping his glass for a refill.

At a nod from Master Trenery, Miriam poured a fresh glass of wine and delivered it. When she placed the glass at the Master's hand, she could smell the pomander he wore at his waist, the heavy scent mingling with the faint smell of sweat, musk and the Castille soup Abigail used to wash his cambric shirts. She felt his eyes upon her and it took all her willpower not to meet those eyes.

'Thank you, Mistress Miriam,' he said gently.

At the sound of her name Miriam met his gaze and saw there fire and longing. With a nod and a trembling smile she collected his soiled glass and retreated into the shadows where Thomas and Master Trenery stood silent as statues.

Lady Elizabeth stabbed her knife into the table. 'You know her name?'

'I told you her name when she sang,' said the Marchioness.

'Why should I recall the name of a servant?' Lady Elizabeth cast a glistering, contemptuous glance at Miriam before giving her husband a beseeching look he neither acknowledged nor returned.

'Be kind Eliza, she cannot help being base-born and her pretty voice will be useful at the banquet I am planning.' The Marchioness leaned her elbows upon the table. 'Rathe, John Wynter has five ships. He captains one himself and sets sail again next month. We could invest in his cargo.'

'What is his cargo, Helena?'

The Marchioness looked away. 'I did not enquire.'

'Investing in unknown cargo is a fool's gamble and a gentleman sailor like Wynter is no match for a Barbary pirate.'

'And yet you speak of importing sugar from the New World,' said the Marchioness.

'I said I'll think on it. There is much risk and I am making a handsome profit sailing between England and France delivering wool and returning laden with barrels of wine and bales of silk. It is a steady fortune and a sure one but if I can find an experienced sea Captain, I'll send him to the New World for an even handsomer profit in sugar.'

The Marchioness huffed. 'Why not deliver slaves and return with sugar? Double your fortune.'

'Some fortunes come at the cost of a soul.' The Master looked at his wife, pale and wan in the candlelight, shivering despite the warmth of the fire. 'Are you feeling quite well, my dear?'

'Wait till I am cold in my grave before this serving wench warms your bed.' Lady Elizabeth eased herself around to face Miriam, her eyes darkened to slate, the colour of a gathering storm and Miriam felt the hatred in those eyes as a jag to the heart.

'Eliza calm yourself,' said the Marchioness. 'This ecstasy of the mind is bad for you and the baby.'

'This ecstasy was curried by you, Mama.' She pushed her chair back and rose unsteadily. 'You put thoughts of bedding this wench into his head and as for you,' she levelled a look of dismay at her husband, 'do you think I do not see how you gaze at her every mealtime?' And lastly, to Miriam. 'Wait till I'm dead, wench.' With that she hurled her trencher dripping with sauce at Miriam and dashed from the room.

Thomas knelt and collected the dish as Miriam wiped up the sauce on the floor.

'Mistress Miriam what delightful cates has your mother prepared for us this evening?' asked the Marchioness as if nothing unusual had happened.

At this cue Master Trenery and Thomas cleared the meats and soiled silverware and left Miriam to lay out the platters of cakes, pastries, jelly, custard, sugar bread, gingerbread, pudding, and her mother's marvellous Shrewsbury cake.

The Marchioness ran her tongue over her lips, stabbed a Shrewsbury cake with her knife, took one bite and sighed. 'Heavenly! What is your mother's secret? Come now, tell us.'

'If it please your Ladyship, Mam uses butter, flour, eggs,' she paused, 'and sugar.'

'Sugar!' cried the Master. 'Our next investment.' He skewered a fruit pie and took a bite, eyes half-closing with pleasure.

The Marchioness took another bite. 'And there is something else. Come now, my dear, what is it? Betray your mother's secret.'

Miriam bowed her head. Her mother's recipes were their guarantee of a roof over their heads.

'Come now,' the Marchioness prompted. 'We know how to keep secrets in this house.'

The Master smiled at Miriam. 'And we are very grateful.'

'Lemon zest.'

'What is lemon zest?' the Master asked, leaning back in his chair so that the light pooled on his face and lit the hand that now tapped the side of his glass.

''Tis the peel of a lemon.' She poured a fresh glass and as she delivered it, the Master slid his hand to rest beside the glass, his fingers brushing hers in a warm, deliberate contact coupled with a look that sent a fire through her. His eyes and the touch of flesh on flesh, said so much without words and his desire for her was easily read.

'Everyone should go to the theatre,' he said, tracking Miriam. 'More enlightening than church. If you will not go to the theatre, Helena, you must read, expand your understanding of our swiftly-altering modern world.'

The Bowe bells tolled midnight. 'What would you have me read? Your pagan Marlowe or your mad Ben Jonson?'

'Marlowe, even if his ideas are disturbing.'

'And his plays dull.' The Marchioness laughed.

'Not everyone finds them dull.' He glanced at Miriam. 'Some could barely tear their eyes away from the stage.'

The Marchioness leaned her chin upon her hand. 'Be careful whom you sanction, Rathe. While you were safely tucked away in Halifax the London sky was black with the smoke of burning Protestants & Catholics. Marlowe courts the Devil and that is unwise. A word, an incautious glance, a play could lead him to the flames.'

'You earlier denounced the burnings as inconvenient and unlikely.'

'That was for my daughter's sake. Be careful whose company you keep in the Mermaid Tavern.' She stood unsteadily. 'Better yet, stay home. I bid you good evening and may God keep you.'

The Master stood as his mother-in-law left the room and without a word followed in her wake, ghosting into the gloaming hallway that led to the rooms where the family dreamed, loved and wept.

IV

The only man I loved betrayed my body to the pyre
Of all the judges who condemned me his cruel silence lit the fire
But the flames did not release me, seared my soul into my flesh
I did not burn
Could not die
I lived on
Lingered on
Linger on

And so, she left London and all she had known, her mother, her home, the man she had recklessly loved, trusting a stranger would help her understand what she had become. By first light she was miles from London and had gained the open fields dotted with husbandmen's cottages scant and rude, clinging together for safety beside the pale clay road rutted with the passage of coaches. The incidental sounds of night hunters – owls, foxes, badgers, stoat – had accompanied her throughout the long night and in between the death cries and squeals of their prey, silence. She wondered if she had lost her soul as punishment for the nights she had allowed his embrace. The child's soul had flown but hers was seared into her flesh as if God could not bear her presence, sullied maid, doxy, unworthy of the saints who had charred in the flames and departed.

If indeed God had abandoned her to some strange fate as yet undefined then she was like one of those sailors adrift on a windless sea echoing the starry firmament, freed of the rule of land but lost none-the-less.

No laws constrained her now. She was Other, bound to no-one. Free. Lost.

Radclyffe House – 1588

'What's this then?' Abigail held Miriam's apron up. 'Sauce?'

Miriam added peas to the pottage bubbling on the hearth. 'Lady Elizabeth threw her trencher at me.'

'She sickens with this new babe,' said Rosamunde, kneading the dough for the manchets. 'Her moods turn like the tide. She yells at the children and weeps over the Master. Pay her no mind, Miriam, she treats us all ill.'

Thomas, sprawled at the table, refilled his mazer. 'Miriam casts a spell o'er the Master and Lady Elizabeth sees.'

Master Trenery clicked his tongue. 'I see the same as you, Thomas, and 'tis not as you paint it. The Master has a wandering eye and it has strayed to Miriam. She bears no fault in it at all. Your loose tongue will see you hanged if you do not curb it.'

Thomas glowered into his ale. 'I am just reporting what I see.'

Eirinn frowned as she poured verjuice onto the meats from last night's supper; the sour pressing of green grapes and crab-apples to lengthen their healthful life for another day or two. 'We must all hold our tongues these days. The very pillars our lives have been built on these long centuries are like to crumble under the scrutiny of sharper minds than ours. Clever men say the earth spins through a long dark night and is only held in place by the mercy of our sun. But who saves us by night when the sun is gone?'

Miriam smiled. 'Remember I said the earth is a spinning ball? She turns her face away from the sun at night so other parts of her grow green and lifeful.'

Thomas almost dropped his mazer and Rosamunde ceased kneading the dough.

'Which book did you read this in?' asked Rosamunde. 'Not the Bible surely?'

'And you say she's not a witch,' Thomas muttered.

''Twas the Master said as much last night at supper,' said Miriam.

''Tis true. I heard it too,' said Master Trenery. 'Where was your mind, Thomas?'

Thomas made a small sound in the back of his throat. 'I heard naught that was blasphemous. All I heard and saw was Miriam casting her green eyes o'er the Master and him sinking under her spell until the Lady cried out for her to stop her thoughts of bedding her husband.' He sniffed. 'And then the Lady tossed sauce on her gown.' Eirinn reached for the longest knife, raised it. 'I am sorry Miriam,' he said quickly. 'Perhaps I mistook what I saw and heard.'

Eirinn returned the knife to the table. 'See that you keep a still tongue in your head or you will spend a day in the stocks.'

Thomas glowered into his ale. 'Yes, Mistress Tilby.'

'You heard nothing about the slaves her Ladyship wants to sell in the New World?' asked Master Trenery.

Thomas clutched his mazer with both hands. 'I heard the Master say it were an evil trade he'd have naught to do with.'

'Slaves?' asked Eirinn and Abigail at once.

'From Africa,' said Master Trenery, 'to be sold in the New World.'

'And what are they to do there?' asked Rosamunde.

'All the work their masters will not do for themselves,' said Master Trenery.

'No different from us then,' murmured Rosamunde.

'But far from home,' said Master Trenery.

No-one said anything for a long moment, each contemplating the plight of innocent folk corralled into ships and taken far from their homes to work for people whose language and customs were foreign.

''Tis a dangerous time to be alive,' said Eirinn. 'These sailors have opened up a strange world that may have been better left alone just as I wish the Marchioness had never heard my daughter sing.'

'The Master has a wandering eye. His gaze will shift soon enough.'

'Thank you, Master Trenery,' said Eirinn, a soft edge to her voice.

Master Trenery nodded. 'I wonder how much evil has been unleashed with New Worlds being settled on the other side of the earth. There will be a want of slaves to work the soil, cook the meals, tend the children and clean the houses and not all will trust foreigners. They'll be sending us next.'

'Us?' asked Abigail, voice trembling.

'Folk like us,' he said.

'Would you have to be on a ship to get there?' asked Valentyne.

'You would, lad,' said Master Trenery.

'They make lads my age climb the masts in storms,' added Fyndern. 'Mistress Miriam did tell us so in the markets.'

'I should like to be a sailor,' said Thomas. 'In the tavern I heard stories from sailors who survived pirates and storms and reached islands where women who wear naught but flowers offer love in exchange for trinkets.'

'If the ladies were so generous why did these sailors come home?' asked Rosamunde with a wink at Abigail. 'These are cup-shotten fancies, Thomas.'

'Many a man was tempted to stay and live a life of exotic ease but it would cost them their souls for these are not God-fearing people.'

"Twould involve a mutiny too. Still and all, they might have stayed if they'd seen Marlowe's new play,' said Eirinn, lidding the pies. 'He says God does not exist. 'Twould be a pity to live our whole lives in fear of a reckoning that never comes.'

'When Fyn and I were on the streets we heard tales of scaled monsters that could consume a ship in a single mouthful,' said Valentyne.

'And who told such tales?' asked Abigail, ringing out the clothes.

'Sailors,' said Valentyne.

'Sailors who survived the belly of such a monster?' Abigail laughed. 'Help me with these clothes, Val.'

'Val, is it?' asked Eirinn, exchanging a glance with Master Trenery.

Valentyne left the chicken he was plucking and took the other side of the basket. 'They may not have actually seen a monster, only heard tales of them in foreign ports.'

'From other sailors who survived the swallowing no doubt.' Abigail laughed as they headed into the courtyard.

'Val.' Eirinn shook her head. 'As I said, 'tis a shifting world we live in. The sea has brought new horrors along with strange and marvellous wonders.'

London 1589 – The Mermaid Tavern

Midnight and the atmosphere in the Mermaid Tavern was rowdy, the sack persuading playwrights and patrons alike of a literary genius that must be translated to velum and secured in ink as soon as their headaches wore off the next day. The air was thick with pipe smoke and cries of "more sack" intersected stories as improbable as the creature the tavern was named for.

He stood a moment in the open doorway reflecting on his plan, an audacious plan even for him, the progenitor of so much deception masquerading as intervention. Hopefully, his mark was there. The gentleman who would partner him if all went well had summoned him once long ago in the woods so it should not come as so startling a revelation that he appeared. Good manners aside, necessity bade him answer the invocation.

A week ago, he had been in France burying his treasure. He had just levelled the last shovel-full of soil when a knife thrust into his back relieved him of the perfectly good body he had acquired in the Jardins des Tuileries during a romantic interlude with a married lady. Furious and inconvenienced, his soul had flown to England where hangings were such a frequent occurrence, he had only to wait a brief while for a suitable host. When the handsome young highwayman mounted the gallows incurring a vexatious wailing from the young women in the crowd he knew he had found his next vehicle. Luckily, the neck had not broken in the long-drawn-out suffocation that ultimately evicted the errant soul. Being a small country village the corpse was not left dangling for two days as was the practice in London but hastily buried to alleviate the feminine fury that would result in a lack of affection for the remaining menfolk.

He had taken possession of the naked corpse the moment it was tossed into a criminal's shallow grave. Slipping into the body he began the painful process of reanimating it, flooding the congealing blood with warmth, shocking the arrested heart into a stuttering rhythm before clawing his way free of a choking layer of soil.

That evening, as he lay on top of the grave, suckling air, he reflected on the events that led to his murder: a mangle of religious wars, an assassinated King, Henry III, and an angry Third Estate eager for revolution. It was these events that had led him to secrete his tangible wealth – a priceless collection of ancient coins and jewellery – beneath the shrouds of lepers, and it was there in the graveyard that he had been murdered for a modest coin purse that wouldn't even buy one of the coins presently glistering in the swaddling around the decomposing corpse.

When it was safe to go home he would do so armed with a Will written in his own hand leaving all his worldly goods to his English cousin but until then he would use his considerable charm to fill his belly and line his pockets. Having settled upon that much of a plan he stole some clothes off a careless line and set off for London on foot. Enroute, he charmed his way into a comely woman's bed, and after eating her husband's dinner he left wearing the cuckold's best gamaches, breeches and jerkin.

It was on his way to London that he conjured the audacious plan that led him to the Mermaid Tavern seeking the man who would secure his sovereignty on earth. News had reached France that an enterprising fellow called James Burbage had thrown together a pile of planks and a platform upon which men strutted and pronounced words that skewered the hearts and minds of rustics and nobles alike. The London playwrights were making a name for themselves, some of them even transcending the greatest French equivalents: Theodore Beza, Étienne Jodelle, Robert Garnier and Alexandre Hardy.

As he walked, he came up with an ingenious fraud – if the brilliant young playwright who had once summoned him could be persuaded to forfeit both his soul and his work he could secure a future that would transcend his expulsion from Heaven and grant him dominion over earth. He could not offer fame and fortune in exchange for his soul, the usual deal, for the man in question was already famous and well enough off, but if he had read his mark correctly, he would leave the Mermaid Tavern this night in possession of unparalleled works of literary genius for the young man's troubles were legion and only just beginning. Soon he would need rescuing and in return for his genius he would offer him sanctuary in his Chateau where he would inspire plays that would inveigle the audience with a philosophy so twining they would lose faith in God and follow him. Where he would lead, he had yet to determine. But first, the deal.

The night was still, the full moon blistering the cobbles and lighting his way. Saint Paul's Cathedral loomed, silvered and spectral, and he shuddered as its shadow fell across his path. The Mermaid Tavern in contrast cast a welcoming flare across Bread Street, dispelling the Cathedral's gloomy holiness. He took a deep breath, his body thrilling to the influx of chill air. He pushed open the tavern door and stood a moment, peering around the room.

The gentleman who stood in the doorway of the Mermaid Tavern, the watering-hole of writers, artists, intellectuals and philosophers that Friday evening in late 1589 bore an uncanny resemblance to a young highwayman who had recently been hung in Bedford but no-one in the tavern would have had occasion to meet him and be relieved of their coin at gunpoint. The clientele of the Mermaid Tavern rarely ventured further than Bishopsgate.

The interior glowed in autumn colours, bronze and gold, the fire flickering across the stone walls, gilding the tables, the cluttering of mazers, and the sea of flushed faces. He scanned the room, peering through clouds of pipe-smoke at the patrons toasting their triumphs, drowning their failures, and nourishing their dreams with cheap ale. Listening keenly, distilling conversations down to embellishments, he sought that voice that had registered as a summons a few brief years ago. If he was out tonight, he would be here, engaged in debate with fellow playwrights or drinking alone at a corner table pondering his future. He hoped, the latter.

As the tableaux gained definition he saw his quarry. Christopher "Kit" Marlowe sat alone at a table near the fire, nursing his mazer, his lips moving over one side of an unreciprocated conversation or perhaps he was dismembering a speech from one of his plays. The stranger shouldered his way through the crowd, stood a moment before taking the seat opposite his quarry.

'Good evening, Kit. I believe you've been expecting me.'

The young man with a shock of golden-brown hair and eyes the colour of Gascon claret tossed a couple of angels on the table and stood up to leave. 'I've never seen you before in my life.'

'Sit down please, Kit,' said the stranger, fingering the coins. 'Angels. How fitting. You called me and I came. A little late to be sure. What can I tempt you with?'

'You are neither young enough nor pretty enough to interest me.'

The stranger lowered his voice. 'Then why did you call me?'

Marlowe sat back down and drew his hands through his mane of golden-brown curls. 'Are you claiming to be –?' he stopped speaking, shook his head.

'I am. Now shall we get down to business? I want fame and fortune and,' he paused, 'I will need your work to achieve it.'

'Well, there's a reversal. The Devil asking me for fame and fortune. What do I get in exchange? Your tarnished soul?'

He lifted the leather jack of sack. 'May I? My funds are a little scant at present.'

Marlowe shrugged. 'Help yourself.'

He refilled Marlowe's mazer and drank from it. 'I've walked miles and this new body is still healing.' He lowered the lace at his throat, revealing a ring of purpling flesh. 'Hung.'

Marlowe let his breath out slowly. 'Why didn't you answer me when I first called you? I was a student then. I'm famous now. I have no need of you, and you have offered me nothing in exchange for my work.'

His mind raced, he needed Marlowe, but Marlowe did not need him … yet. The man was a virtuoso and required no Faustian deal to attain genius but his attitude, his preferences, his philosophy would send him to the flames one day. However, he could not wait for *one day*.

'You've made it plain enough that you do not believe in –' He almost choked on the word.

'God?' Marlowe laughed. 'Superstitious nonsense.'

'But your words may yet trip you up and if, *when*, they do, you will need my help.'

'That's kind.' Marlowe stood a little unsteadily. 'I wish you good evening and would add may God keep your soul, but I fear he is the last person you'd entrust it to.'

'Wait.' He played his last card. 'If they send you to the flames, I will save you and in exchange for your life all your future work is forfeit to me. Agreed?'

Marlowe paled, swayed. 'If my loudly proclaimed atheism is my undoing I will sell you my work in exchange for my life.'

'Your hand on it, sir.'

And so, Marlowe shook hands with the Devil.

'One more thing,' said the Devil, 'could you see your way clear to lending me –?'

Marlowe tossed a bag of coins on the table. 'Your nemesis would turn water into wine.'

Radclyffe House – 1590

Despite the hunger in his eyes, the Master had neither touched nor spoken to Miriam since that evening two years earlier when he heard her sing. Lulled into hope, she abandoned her plans to acquire a poison that would send her soul either to Heaven or Hell, depending on God's will. The Master also gave up his mistress in Bishopsgate, remaining home on Friday nights to play cards with his mother-in-law, his wife, and their friends. On these nights, Thomas, Master Trenery and Miriam were in attendance until dawn, ready to refresh a drink or supply a confit. Lady Elizabeth had been safely delivered of a baby boy who mewled and fretted along with his two neglected siblings in the nursery, deepening the dark rings beneath Rosamunde's eyes and filling her soft heart with maternal tenderness.

Miriam's life settled into a routine of working in the kitchen by day, serving the family at night, feeding the swans on Sundays after church and sometimes going to the theatre. This cycle was unrelieved by variation or incident. The banquet at Stanstead Hall planned for the midsummer of 1589 had been postponed due to a long, wet season that made quagmires of the roads, bogging coaches, and rendering travellers easy prey for highwaymen and rufflers.

Apart from the Friday night card games, the Marchioness occasionally had company for tables or the charged games of dice where money changed hands. On these nights Miriam, Master Trenery and Thomas fell into bed at dawn after the guests had taken their leave, lighter or richer of purse, cup-shotten and tumbling into waiting carriages just as the sun inflamed an aubergine sky. On Friday nights and after these long gaming evenings Eirinn let her daughter sleep through the dawn Bowe bells for there was a goodly chance the family would not appear until mid-afternoon and the servants could have a sit-down breakfast with the chance to gossip and speculate about a wider world they would never intersect.

Now that her reading had all but ceased due to her workload Miriam learned about the outside world by listening to the family's mealtime conversations which were laced with ideas few would dare commit to velum.

According to Master Rathe life beyond London was exotic and dangerous in equal measure and to access it one needed a sturdy ship, a quadrant, an astrolabe, an experienced Captain and clement weather, and the timing of such a journey depended on the tidal rush of the arterial Thames, the conduit that ferried the intrepid, the desperate and the curious out into a world beyond the reach of English laws and English society. There was a fortune to be made, he said, but it was risky for many a ship had sunk with a speculator's investment drowned along with the sailors and a Captain who had not heeded the height of the Pole Star above the horizon.

The Master told stories of El Dorado, a fabled city made entirely of gold, and a fountain that restored youth. A century earlier in 1493 the nineteen-year-old Ponce de León joined Christopher Columbus on his 2nd voyage to the New World and upon arrival he struck off alone to explore. He discovered waters that restored youth simply by bathing in them or drinking from them. He called these waters the Fountain of Youth.

'And Raleigh still seeks it along with El Dorado,' said Rathe. 'Imagine finding it.'

'Do you believe such fables?' asked the Marchioness.

'There is a map, rough to be sure, but Raleigh swears by it. More recently one of the sailors in Pedro de Silva's 1570 expedition was captured by the Caribs and taken to a city made of gold next to a great lake. He said the locals threw gold into the lake to buy favour with their gods.'

'A golden city and captors who released him? A likely tale to explain a year spent with a mistress.' Lady Elizabeth scoffed. 'Are you planning on sailing away, Rathe?'

'I am too comfortable on land.' He glanced at Miriam. 'But I'd like to see this map. If we could find the Fountain of Youth imagine the fortune we would make! Better than sugar, much better than slaves.'

'A fine use of your ships,' said Lady Elizabeth, tapping the side of her glass. 'If God wanted us to be immortal he would have numbered us amongst the angels.'

'There are wonders beyond our narrow shores, my dear,' said the Master, and he went on to describe tables of latitude drawn by Portuguese navigators of such genius they could reduce the vast ocean to a scroll of velum stored in elm tubes.

'They're called plats and this Portuguese genius has made pioneering experts of Drake, Hawkins and Cavendish. 'Tis glory and wealth for Captains, misery for the men who sail with them. The poor wretches do all the hard labour and sleep on deck or crammed together in a hold no bigger than this room.'

'Why do they choose such a life?' asked Lady Elizabeth.

'They have no choice, Eliza. Tens of thousands of boys and young men have no prospects beyond starvation or the gallows. They sail with the likes of Frobisher, Drake and Raleigh in the hope of a small share of their fortune. For this they risk drowning if their ships are smashed to pieces by waves that tower as high as Saint Paul's Cathedral. Sailors are never taught to swim. They must go down with the ship.'

Lady Elizabeth shuddered. 'And yet you invested in two such ships and against such odds.'

'I have the luxury of risk, my dear, unlike so many others.' Again, he glanced at Miriam. 'But for those of us with wealth and opportunity why not risk a little of our inherited fortunes for profit? A man willing to take a risk can make a fortune greater than any investment on land. When Drake captured the annual Spanish convoy of gold bullion in 1572, he gave 1.5million pesos to our Queen and received a knighthood for his theft.'

'You may yet receive a knighthood without risking anything,' said the Marchioness. 'If our little songbird enchants the Queen.'

The Master raised his glass to his mother-in-law. 'A knighthood for a song. How noble. How monstrous. Still, I don't have to risk a tide or kill a dragon for it.'

'Or steal gold from the Spanish. Did Drake keep any of the fortune for himself?' asked the Marchioness.

'He kept half like the pirate he is. He rewarded his crew with a tiny portion of the theft, a pittance compared with his bounty and the Queen's but enough to transform their years of pitching, heaving and misery into a comfortable retirement upon dry land. And now our Queen thinks to expand her empire, marauding the world of so-called savages and stealing their land and their wealth. If El Dorado can be found the Queen will strip it of every ounce of gold. 'Tis our nature, I'm afraid, to feel superior to those whose land we trespass upon.'

'You would not leave El Dorado without a chest of gold,' said Lady Elizabeth.

'You're right, my dear, I have been raised to believe in my entitlement. A pity our Queen gave Humphrey Gilbert the right to steal lands not already in the hands of Christian monarchs. I would have liked the ships and the opportunity. But in 1578 I was still a boy.'

'He achieved nothing but a desolate piece of ice-bound waste,' said the Marchioness. 'Newfoundland proffers us little and he suffered a premature death on the return voyage.'

'But what an adventure,' said the Master.

'Adventure is fine when someone else is paying for it. Safer to trade with established merchants like The Muscovy Company and the Cathay Company and the Barbary Company. If you refuse to sell slaves best avoid the New World, there is nothing but death and misery there. Still, I would love a draft of that water from the Fountain of Youth and a nugget of Eldorado gold.'

'You're both heretics,' said Lady Elizabeth. 'Lusting after fountains of youth and golden cities as if God had cheated you of decent lives.'

'Shall we plan our banquet for next midsummer?' asked the Marchioness, ignoring her daughter. 'We need to get that knighthood for you Rathe without Spanish gold or maritime adventure.'

Standing in the shadows, waiting for a cue to serve or clear Miriam learned the ways of the privileged and puzzled over why the music supposedly orchestrating creation made no beneficent mark upon humanity, for if these heavenly spheres spun so comfortably one within the other why couldn't men occupying different spheres not find harmony? It seemed to Miriam that fortune dealt a remarkably uneven hand and Heaven's favours altered on the toss of a dice, much as fortunes ebbed and flowed on gaming nights.

Queen Mary burned Protestants. Queen Elizabeth burned Catholics. The Marchioness thought these clerics brave but vainglorious to burn for an idea fleeting as air, an idea even God didn't stoop to counter or confirm. The conversations between the Marchioness and her son-in-law revealed a world filled with wonder, danger and vanity and Miriam was glad to retire to her safe little bed and dream of small things like the sweetness of cates, daryoles, warm custard and the kiss of an imaginary lover.

'Something must be done about the poor,' said the Marchioness one evening. 'It is not safe to visit one's estates without the threat of violence and I am determined to have this banquet.'

'Perhaps stricter punishments,' suggested Lady Elizabeth.

'Even hanging doesn't deter these rogues.'

'Helena imagine having to feed your family when harvests fail and there is no work to be had,' said the Master. 'Their lot is intolerable and when the bounty acquired through piracy is counted as private wealth –'

'Do not think I lack sympathy, Rathe. I have saved several unfortunate souls, given them work at a time when taking in doxies and kinchin-cos was a hanging offence.

But for the safety of all concerned something must be done.'

'What would you suggest, Mama?'

'This vast bounty from piracy should be distributed as stipends to the destitute. It will cost our nation nothing for it was never ours to depend upon.'

The Marchioness' views, many of which showed tolerance for the poor, were bravely stated given that those views could still see her hung should a greedy servant succumb to the temptation of a reward. Many a wealthy man or woman rotted in the Tower on the word of a servant, the rights to their estate and fortune dissolved into the voracious maw of the Crown.

***

'Be careful not to return the Master's glances,' said Eirinn one Sunday as they picnicked on the riverbank. 'Men are drawn to a woman's ripeness as bees to a spring bower but come autumn their interest fades. Such swift alterations of affection could see you out on the street. Your own father turned me out when I was heavy with you and but for the generosity of the Marchioness we would have starved.' Eirinn tossed another piece of bread to the cob. 'We must never forget her Ladyship's kindness and Master Trenery petitioned her on our behalf. He is a saint.' Eirinn smiled and it seemed to Miriam there was something soft in that smile.

'Why did Master Trenery never marry?'

''Tis not too late.' The smile faded. 'We owe her Ladyship a great debt. Do not meet the Master's eyes.'

But she had. Often. How could she not when his gazes were so frequent? And there were nights when he replaced the highwayman in her dreams, his lips pressed against hers as he murmured words of love. But those dreams faded at dawn only to be reignited at supper when his eyes found hers like a ship finds harbour in a storm-tossed sea. But she dared not linger too long in that visual embrace. If she was turned out life would be cruel for the virgin Queen ruled the land with a harsh, unforgiving hand and the gallows at Tyburn permanently groaned with naked paupers whose bodies swung for two long days as a warning to would-be thieves. But when hunger claws and your children wither what soul would not risk the noose?

The Queen had never known hunger and Miriam wondered at her lack of mercy. Surely a woman who lived in a palace and surveyed her kingdom from a glass barge canopied with cloth of gold could find it in her heart to feed the poor in her care. Surely, she could share a table that groaned with pottage, sallat, herring, ling, eel, pike, lampreys, figs, apples, raisins, pears, venison, veal, peacock, tarts and sweetmeats with the beggars at her gate as Master Trenery did? And yet, as the Queen and her Court gorged on feasts washed down with the finest ale and sack, accompanied by the music of the best waits in London, the starving poor foraged for weevilly bread and soured ale right outside her gate.

'The rich are different from us,' said Eirinn. 'They do not have the same prickling of conscience.'

'And yet they pray so fervently on Sundays.'

'The Queen is God's anointed vessel. We must not question her ways. Certainly not in earshot of Thomas.'

**

While the Queen was above judgement but still apparently in need of God's mercy, she showed little of this quality to the poor who riddled her domain like judgement. Miriam decided it was a strange kind of arrangement between God and the Queen that she was given charge over the most vulnerable when she had no conscience.

But confusing as it was Miriam plodded through her routine days grateful for the small mercy shown her mother by the Marchioness and she determined to think more fondly of the woman who had offered her up as swive for her son-in-law. There was only one pathway in life for the lowly-born – servitude and mindful silence around their betters.

The Mermaid Tavern – 1593

By 1593 Marlowe had composed the 2nd part of *Tamburlaine, The Jew of Malta, Doctor Faustus, Edward 11,* and *The Massacre at Paris* and should have been the premier playwright in London but ...

William Shakespeare was born in 1564, the same year as Marlowe. The pair were a mere two months apart. Marlowe was the son of a Canterbury shoemaker, Shakespeare the son of a glovemaker from Stratford-upon-Avon and even though Marlowe had the advantage of a university education, the uneducated glovemaker's son was enchanting Londoners with plays exhibiting a vast and luminous knowledge of the world and its occupants. But how, when he had never travelled or acquired an education?

**

Marlowe ordered another flagon of sack. Halfway into a much-needed state of forgetfulness it occurred to him that Shakespeare may have met the Devil and signed away his soul in exchange for genius, but then he remembered the Devil who had approached him in 1589 was wanting plays and Will Shakespeare would sooner part with his soul than his plays, so hungry was he for social leverage. So, if it wasn't a Faustian deal what was the key to Shakespeare's success?

Uncanny luck, supernatural talent or the intervention of a genius who wished to remain anonymous?

Marlowe shivered and moved closer to the fire. His own success should have secured his social status and filled that place in his soul where purpose resides but lately he had been feeling distinctly uneasy and friends had warned him to curb his vitriolic atheism, at least in public. The world was changing, they warned, but too slowly to catch up with the free-thinking Kit Marlowe. The Queen was elderly, ill. Her moods were unpredictable and recently she had started executing witches. Alice Samuel and her family, the Witches of Warboys, who had been tolerated for years now lay in their graves, hung on charges of witchcraft and this hypocrisy on the Queen's part sat ill with the people when her own seer, John Dee, practiced sorcery, seances and fortune-telling at her behest. The aging Queen's tolerance of alternate thinking had shrunk to a very narrow field, even turning on one of her favourites, Sir Walter Raleigh, whom she accused of presiding over a school of Atheism. Kit doubted the buccaneer explorer had the imagination for such an enterprise but perhaps he was making new friends now he was landlocked.

Kit took a long draft of sack, his thoughts curdling. How had a glovemaker's son scribbled so many brilliant plays in an elegant verse form similar to his own when he had no learning? The crown that had rested so easily upon Kit's head was now askew and threatening to tumble altogether as the "Bard" captured the public imagination and filled the theatres.

Shakespeare was even eclipsing Sir Philip Sidney and Edmund Spenser. Performances of his plays were taking place each afternoon, not just in the theatres in Southbank but in the yards of galleried inns on the less cultured side of the Thames. The Boar's Head Inn in Whitechapel High Street, the Bell Inn and the Cross Keys Inn in Graceland Street, the Belle Savage Inn in Ludgate Hill and the Bill Inn in Bishopsgate Street regularly aired plays by Shakespeare and those mercenary innkeepers were creating a monopoly for his rival. Even the smaller companies of six or seven players taking multiple roles playing in provincial inns and privately in houses of gentlemen were favouring Shakespeare over the more complex and dangerous works of Marlowe.

Kit took another long draft of sack, his head ached, his palms itched. Was it an innate, untutored understanding of humanity that gave Will's work such lustre or was it simply that he made people laugh? True, his jokes were crude and his jesters ill-bred ruffians but the people couldn't get enough of them. Even the actors loved him. Will Kempe triumphed as Falstaff and the great Richard Burbage demanded the lead in *Titus Andronicus*, Edward Alleyn roared his way through *The Taming of the Shrew* as Petruchio and the crowds roared for more.

Kit dropped his head into his hands and groaned.

'Kit Marlowe, what a state I find you in.'

Marlowe lifted his aching head, peered at the stranger blearily. 'Who the devil are you?'

'Who the devil indeed. I am wearing the same body and I have come here to tell you that yours is forfeit unless I help you.'

'Are you threatening me?'

'Not me, Kit. Your dear friend, Thomas Kyd, betrays you even now, albeit under torture. You will be arrested tomorrow on charges of treason and heresy.'

'I have been careless.' A beading of sweat broke out on his smooth pale forehead.

'I can help you…for a fee. Your life in exchange for –'

'My work. I remember.'

'And safe passage to France and shelter.'

'I am an atheist and yet I believe in you.' He gave a hollow laugh. 'Ironic, isn't it?'

'I came. He did not.' The Devil lifted the flagon of sack, poured a measure into Kit's mazer, and drank.

'Still drinking my sack.'

He raised the mazer. 'Your health. Well, that's what we're here to decide. I enjoyed your *Doctor Faustus* by the way, gave me some splendid ideas, refined my technique.'

'Who are you really? A Lord? A French nobleman?' He leaned forward, whispered. 'The one who writes Shakespeare's plays?'

'Alas, I can barely scratch my own name to reframe my Will let alone write works like yours and Shakespeare's. I'm just a simple fallen angel, albeit an ambitious one. If I could sell my soul for any price it would be music for no teacher in this vast firmament has been able to unlock melody in me, no instrument sings at my touch, no symphonies rise winged in my soul. I am mute in this most exquisite expression and the pain is like,' he paused, 'hell. But enough of my agony, I am here to help you. Be glad I did not frighten you to death in the woods all those many midnights past. Be grateful I ignored your earnest pleas. I have only one use for young men and that is when I need a new body. Oh yes, I would have frightened you to death and taken refuge in your beautiful young body. Let us both be glad your pleas fell on deaf ears for you are of far more use to me alive than dead.'

'So, I am to hide away in France and you will pass my new work off as your own? How will I live? How will I eat? More importantly how will I drink?'

'I am about to inherit a Chateau in Provence with a well-stocked cellar and discreet servants. You will live and write there. All your most pressing needs will be met, however, I am rich enough for generosity – for every new work I will pay you sufficient coin to impress the locals. But try to keep a low profile. There are strange new currents afoot in France. The chasm between privilege and poverty widens and the French are not so meek as the English.'

'Is that why you left France?'

'Let's just say I was evicted rather hastily. I was murdered.'

'Is it safe to return?'

'Safe enough. My Chateau is a long way from Paris and I won't be visiting any graveyards in the foreseeable future.'

He drank the sack, refilled.

'Yes, your *Doctor Faustus* is splendid and your *Jew of Malta* with that delightful ghost of Machiavelli declaring, "I count religion but a childish toy and hold there is no sin but ignorance." Music to my ears and the best of you is yet to come when I tell you what to write. Consider me your Muse and patron.'

'And you'll put your name to my work.'

'That was the plan initially but I need the cloak of anonymity a little longer. Religion must loosen its grip before I declare myself but now we must make haste. Your death is near.'

Kit Marlowe looked around the Mermaid Tavern, at the mellow stone walls, the tables strewn with half-empty tankards, mazers and over-turned jugs. 'This has been my sanctuary. Will I ever see it again? Is it possible for a ghost to return unmarked?'

'No. I will save your genius but you must disappear. Even now your friend betrays you and tomorrow you will be escorted to the Tower unless I spirit you away tonight. Unless we feign your death.'

'Whose name will you put to my work?'

'A young man whose pen almost rivals your own. The alteration in style will be so slight as to go unremarked. He will write prodigiously but the words, the ideas, the philosophy will be mine, the genius of expression, yours, the fame, his.'

'Shakespeare.' Kit Marlowe squeezed his eyes shut, moaned. 'He stole my blank verse, stole my crown and now he steals my work and what price does he pay?'

'He sold his soul long ago but not to me – to posterity.'

'He may not agree to take my … *your* plays and pass them off as his own.'

'He will once he buys shares in the Globe. He will need a steady supply of new work now that he has run out of Kings. His popularity dries his pen. He will accept my offer.'

'How do you know he'll buy shares in the Globe?'

'I heard a rumour. Fear not, Kit, the Bard will immortalise your words and my message. Now I have my boat ready and waiting with a crew paid for their discretion. I will buy the taverner's silence and furnish the Queen's guards with the story of your death. I have even secured a grave for you and a fresh corpse.'

Kit shivered. 'So, the world will think I died this night, while my genius lives on in my rival's name. A Faustian deal indeed. I could not have penned something as diabolical as this.'

'You will.'

The Devil tossed a bag clinking with sovereigns onto the bar.

'What's this for?' asked the taverner.

'Kit Marlowe's payment.'

The taverner opened the bag, gaped. 'But this is far more than he owes.'

'Kit Marlowe was stabbed to death in a brawl tonight, his body removed by persons unknown and disposed of in an unmarked grave in St Nicholas churchyard in Deptford.'

The taverner laughed as he counted the coins. 'Escaping a shrew?'

Marlowe winced. 'Shakespeare taunts me even now.'

**

Marlowe and the Devil hurried out into the night and when they were safely afloat on the English Chanel Kit asked: 'Last time we met you were borrowing coin from me now you have a caravel, a crew, and a Chateau. How?'

The Devil laughed. 'Let's just say I came into an unexpected inheritance.'

'You forged a Will.'

'Is it forgery to inherit your own property? I have lived and died a thousand times and retained my fortune.'

Marlowe scanned the sky, noting the arrangement of stars, the razzle of worlds. 'If Shakespeare agrees to this deception, what do you hope to achieve?'

The Devil also gazed at the stars. 'The complete disintegration of life as we know it – the Church will crumble, the State will fall, the Monarchy will lose its grip, chaos will shatter the sanity of nobleman and rustic alike and when they tremble at each knock on the door, when they distrust their neighbours, their sovereign and their God, I will rise up like a new dawn and take control.'

Marlowe took a deep, satisfied breath. 'Shakespeare won't even know he is the font of such monumental havoc.' He tipped his head back, drank in the night blinking myriad stars. 'Oh, how I would love to see the world you create.'

'You never will, Kit.'

Stanstead Hall – Essex 1593

Three soggy summers and slow progress on the renovations of Stanstead Hall delayed the planned banquet until midsummer 1593 when all the stars aligned: the sun shone for weeks, allowing the completion of the renovations and the Queen accepted the invitation.

Four hired coaches and the family's carriage turned off the Great Road and rumbled along a trunk road overgrown in places with wild bramble. Repeatedly the coachmen were forced to stop and hack away the twists of impeding branches.

'I see no-one has passed this way recently,' said Eirinn. 'I wonder at the state of the larders if the markets are not easily accessible.'

'There must be another way in,' said Rosamunde who was nursing a tousle-haired boy of seven who sucked noisily on the corner of her mantle. 'How else will the Queen get here?'

'That child should not be suckling at his age,' said Eirinn.

'If it brings him comfort,' said Rosamunde, pushing the boy's damp hair back from his forehead. 'He gets little enough love.'

'At least he is sleeping now,' said Abigail, upon whose lap the younger child, a girl, slept peacefully after fretting for many wretched hours. The baby boy had died of sweating sickness a year after his arrival. Only Rosamunde mourned his passing.

'If there is a better road why do we not take it?' asked Eirinn, rubbing her aching hip.

110

'Perhaps it is riddled with highwaymen,' said Rosamunde, stroking the boy's forehead.

'I'm hungry,' said Abigail, yawning and rubbing her eyes.

'We're all hungry,' said Eirinn. 'And somehow I must conjure supper out of an empty larder.'

Miriam shared a coach with Rosamunde, Abigail, Eirinn and the children who had scarcely ceased snivelling for two long days and one sleepless night in a noisy, crowded Inn. Rosamunde did her best to soothe them until exhaustion overtook her and then Miriam sang to them, a lullaby that settled them for the span of the song. Around midday the little ones fell into an exhausted sleep, giving everyone a few hours' peace.

Finally, mercifully, they arrived, the coach wheels crunching over a gravel drive, the horses' hooves beating a counter rhythm that slowed and came to rest beneath a looming pile of red brick, banks of windows showered late-afternoon sunlight upon the company as they alighted, stretching, after their long confinement. Everyone including Lady Elizabeth gaped at the shining edifice that braced the rise of the hill.

The façade was divided into three parts conjoined by a limestone balustrade on the uppermost level suggesting a recessed balcony from which one might enjoy an uninterrupted view of the park, landscaped artfully to merge the wild with the tamed. The garden immediately in front of the house was a formal arrangement of knots comprised of rosemary, thyme, hyssop and kitchen herbs. Contouring the garden were paths coloured with red brick dust, doubtless left over from the renovations.

'Is that the kitchen garden?' asked Rosamunde.

'I would be afraid to forage there for fear of poisoning everyone,' said Eirinn, studying the intricate weave of clipped shrubs and hedges. Trees that might have towered over them in years to come were dwarfed and fashioned into animals, their branches clipped into absurd little paws and stumpy hind legs.

'Look at those statues!' Miriam pointed at a folly adorned with life-size marble statues of naked men carrying scrolls and discuses. 'One might mistake them for living men in the moonlight.'

'Only if you're cup-shotten!' Rosamunde laughed, waking the young master who ran to his mother who boxed his ears and sent him whimpering back to Rosamunde.

'The light within the house must be like daylight,' said Eirinn, turning her attention to the banks of windows.

'We won't need candles during the daylight hours like we do at Radclyffe House,' said Valentyne, materialising at Abigail's side after alighting from the coach he had shared with his brother and the two footmen. 'Can I help you with the child?'

Abigail smiled up at him, no longer a boy but a handsome lad on the brink of manhood. 'Thank you, Val. She's only just fallen asleep.' She handed him the little girl still sleeping fitfully in her arms.

Fyndern joined them. He was taller than his older brother and slender as a sapling but already showing promise of the handsome man he would become. 'Can I help you with anything, Mistress Abigail?'

Abigail looked from one handsome lad to the other. 'You two spoil me. Is there no servant to show us the way to the kitchen?'

***

'What do you think of my renovations, Rathe?' The Marchioness asked her son-in-law as they alighted from their carriages.

'Handsome to be sure. Where are your children, Helena? One might have expected them to greet you.'

'I am a stranger to them and they to me. I expect we'll be introduced at supper.' She laughed. 'Come along now, Rathe, inspect your inheritance. Eliza will be your guide if she remembers her way around. I'm going to rest before supper.'

The family entered via a portico to the right-hand side of the triple-fronted edifice, leaving the servants of Radclyffe House and the four London coachmen standing uncertain and lost on the driveway.

Presently a young male servant rushed around the side of the Hall, stopped in front of them and scraped off his woollen cap, releasing an eruption of gold curls. 'Follow,' was all he said before skittering away like a rabbit. The servants followed piecemeal and entered a kitchen far superior to the one at Radclyffe House. The Stanstead Hall servants stood in a line awaiting instruction and with the clear expectation that the cook from Radclyffe House would take charge.

'Good evening,' said Eirinn after a moment. 'I'm Mistress Tilby, the cook. Please don't introduce yourselves. It's been a long two days. Your names will lodge better in a refreshed head. If someone could see to the horses and refresh the drivers.'

At this, two young men scampered outside, and a serving girl offered the coachmen a leatherjack of ale, four mazers and a trencher of cheats to be taken "outside under yon oak, the weather being fair".

Eirinn looked around at a kitchen replete with two large, brick ovens already lit, a huge, scrubbed worktable, spits, pots, posnets, chafing-dishes, graters, mortars and pestles, boilers, knives, cleavers, dripping-pans, pot-racks, gridirons, frying pans, sieves, kneading troughs. Everything and more that she would need to create a banquet fit for the Queen. Checking the pantry, she found fresh-baked bread and clean linen, a well-stocked buttery, barrels of wine, and meat seethed in verjuice ready for the family's supper.

'This is very well-stocked, Mistress Tilby,' said Abigail, gaping at the dazzling array of pots and chafers. 'The road to market must be clearer than the one we just took.'

'You have everything you need then Mistress Tilby?' asked Master Trenery.

'If it please you, ma'am –' a young woman with florid cheeks stepped forward and gave a little curtsey.

'You may call me Mistress Tilby and there is no need to curtsey. I'm just a cook.'

'If it please you Mistress Tilby, the Masters and Mistresses say we must obey you and help with the banquet and not bother you with questions.'

'The Masters and Mistresses?' asked Abigail.

'The Marchioness' children,' said the girl. 'They live here. None be married yet.'

'How many am I preparing supper for?' asked Eirinn.

The same girl answered and Eirinn noticed now that the servants were very young, many of them scarcely out of childhood. 'There be four living here and with your party that brings the family to seven. The Lady Elizabeth's children will eat in the nursery and remain out of sight. They be Master George's instructions.'

'Master George?' Eirinn cast an inquiring glance at Master Trenery.

'The Marchioness' oldest son,' said Master Trenery.

'Oh yes, I remember the lad now. Headstrong even as a toddler.' She looked back at the girl. 'Rosamunde is settling the children into the nursery now. I will prepare their supper and send one of you up with it.' She flicked the edge of the table irritably. 'Are the children permitted to play outside or are they to be jailed in the nursery?'

The girl glanced around at the others who shook their heads. 'Master George do not want to see or hear his sister's children, Mistress Tilby.'

Eirinn took a deep breath. 'So the little ones are not to see sunlight or run on the grass because Master George fears they might live long enough to steal his inheritance, is that it?'

Master Trenery stepped forward. 'We will make sure the children do not intrude upon the family. I am Master Trenery, the valet at Radclyffe House. Any questions you have bring them to me and do not disturb Mistress Tilby.'

'Which one of you is the cook?' asked Eirinn.

'We all cook, Mistress Tilby, but none so well as a London cook. We will take orders from you.'

Eirinn gave the kitchen another sweeping glance. 'Very well. I will have my daughter, Mistress Miriam, write out a list of everything I will need for the banquet and,' she paused, 'can any of you read?'

The girl who had spoken for them all, nodded. 'I can read, ma'am.'

'I trust the road to market is better than the one we arrived on?' asked Master Trenery.

The girl nodded. 'The road into Stansted Mountfitchet is well-kept and busy, especially on Market days when all bring their livestock to town. It leads on from where you set down.'

**

Eirinn took command of the kitchen and prepared the first supper for the Marchioness' grown children. Master George's instructions were that only his servants were permitted to serve in the grand dining room, so it was an early night for the Radclyffe Hall servants after two long days' travelling. They sat down to a hasty supper after the family had been served and as swiftly washed, scoured, and set to dry all their utensils.

'Now, if you'd be good enough to show us to our pallets –' Master Trenery began.

'Master Trenery, you sleep on featherbeds,' said the same young fellow who had shown them to the kitchen. ''Tis the Marchioness' orders since you'll prepare the banquet for the Queen.'

Master Trenery smiled. 'We won't know ourselves for luxury. I'll bid you all good evening.' He collected a lighted candle. 'If you will lead the way, young Master.'

See how the moon lights up my smile
Ignites my hair like summer fire
And splashes silver in the corners of my eyes
My eyes are green
A summer field bewitched with dew
And emeralds too, and in my heart a woman's innocent desire.

She walked through nights febrile with a chorus germane to the landscape, loneliness a constant companion. She spoke aloud to this shadow presence when the small, dark hours closed in and missing her mother became a physical ache.

By day, the land grew lively with industry: yeomen farmers pulled ploughs across the dark earth, the young flirted while the old watched hollow-eyed from their places by the door, their children long-gone. From a safe distance she witnessed the misery wrought by greed – the young withered old, the old scarce more than bones. Vagrants with the strength of mind and body to speak told her engrossers had hoarded food and pushed prices up so high poor men could not feed their families. Famine forced them into a life of vagrancy. Could she spare a coin? She saw what she could not see when she served a rich spoilt family who thought only of their next fortune.

From behind hedgerows she watched the wealthy pass by in their caroches, velvet curtains drawn protecting them from the sight of beggars whose hollow eyes shadowed pain.

She walked and wondered where God was in all this.

Free to observe the troubled world from the distance of immortality she hated what she saw and that hatred fed a growing yearning for a general reckoning and personal vengeance.

Banquet – Stanstead Hall 1593

Five days before the banquet the servants were clustered in silent hives of occupation. The creation of a banquet with such an illustrious guest of honour required a cook with a firm sense of command and a keen imagination for the Queen was enamoured of Fairyland and Eirinn must create the illusion of magic. The mainstay of any banquet was the cornucopia of marchpanes and Eirinn used these little follies to create the denizens of Otherworld. She had sent the lads to the local Cheaps the week before for a dozen hessian bags of almonds.

The almonds had been crushed into a sticky paste sweetened with honey and sugar – the marchpane base – and separated into tubs. One tub was dyed blue with azurite, another green with the juice of spinach, another pink with rose petals steeped in boiled water, another yellow with saffron and egg yolk, and the last whitened with milk curds to be gold-leafed.

The servants watched carefully as Eirinn sculpted the marzipan into mushrooms, mice, bees, leaves, flowers, butterflies, fairies, elves, and tiny birds, and then she left them to sculpt while she moulded the white marchpane into petals to be gold-leafed. Valentyne and Fyndern proved especially gifted at sculpting the pink marzipan into tiny roses which Eirinn arranged in fairy-sized bouquets.

Once the marchpane follies were ready they were stored in the dry larder, high up on shelves away from hungry mice. Being sweetened with honey and sugar they would keep for days without spoiling. Over the following days various meats were boiled until they were soft enough to be minced, then they too were preserved with sugar and spices ready for confits, sweetmeats and pies.

On the night, the banquet would begin with a variety of sallats: green, boiled and specialties made with sliced boiled eggs and cuts of salted meats. These would be followed by the savoury meat dishes: shields of brawn with mustard, chines of roasted beef, a baked peacock dressed in its own feathers, wings, fanned tail, neck and head all carefully reconstructed, a whole turkey roasted and presented with feathers, wings and head, a haunch of roasted venison, olive pies, a whole roasted pig presented with head and trotters, twenty roasted capons, and lastly, bowls of coloured custards. This would be followed by an assortment of cates, pies, tarts, confits, sweetmeats, and more follies.

The banquet was to be set up in the ballroom, a vast pillared expanse that ran the length of the Hall, sunlight pouring in through floor-to-ceiling windows lit the room by day and when night fell hundreds of candles would cast an aureate glow. For days, the servants of Stanstead Hall had been winding ropes of fabric flowers around the pillars and through hooks affixed to the walls so that the room appeared to be an extension of the garden. Banquet tables garlanded with green velvet cords laced with pale pink silk roses and fabric leaves were pushed up against the walls leaving the floor clear for dancing. On the day of the banquet Eirinn would lay these tables with a feast served on silver and gold platters.

The day before the feast the Marchioness visited the kitchen.

'Mistress Tilby, I'd like to speak to your daughter.'

Eirinn looked up from the pot of oranges and lemons she was steeping for marmalade. 'Fetch Mistress Miriam, please Fyndern. She is storing platters in the dry larder.'

Fyndern disappeared into the warren of rooms off the kitchen and returned moments later with Miriam.

'My dear,' said the Marchioness, 'follow me.'

119

Miriam followed the Marchioness out into the brilliantly lit main house and up a winding flight of stairs into a small dark room where a maid hovered. The girl, for she was scarce past girlhood, did not speak, nor did she make eye contact, her sights cast down demurely.

'This is Avice, she will help you dress for the banquet. Show her the gown, Avice.'

The girl opened a wardrobe revealing a magnificent white gown fitted with gossamer wings and hanging next to it was a white mask twined with silver roses.

'You will wear this costume when you sing for the Queen. I have hired minstrels from London so there'll be no need to keep Master Trenery from service. On the night, you will not help your mother. You will come to this room, dress in this costume, and wait until I send for you. A servant will fetch you and lead you to the banquet room where you will sing the song that so enchanted my son-in-law,' she paused, 'and me. Do not make eye contact with the Queen but do face in her direction when you sing and afterwards do not speak to any of my guests but return to this room and wait. I may need you to sing again. I will send for you if so. Otherwise stay here until the guests have departed and rest. On the morrow you will resume your usual duties.'

Having established the rules, the Marchioness turned to leave but turned back as if she had remembered something. 'Save your voice, Avice is mute so expect no conversation from her. You may go back to the kitchen now and help your mother but remember, save your voice.'

The Day of the Banquet

At sun-up Eirinn laid out the first part of the banquet: a cornucopia of marzipan follies bedded in nests of fabric flowers and leaves. Around them she arranged silver bowls of suckets and dishes of candied fruits with little pots of marmalade for the goodinycakes and tarts.

At midday four minstrels from London arrived, ravenous, thirsty, and anxious to tune their instruments after two days travel. Eirinn fed them in the kitchen and tolerated their flirting with the maids but cautioned them not to slow down the preparations.

At sundown, the torches along the driveway were lit along with hundreds of candles in the Hall and soon the guests started arriving, spilling out of coaches, caroches and carriages in a frothing of jewel-coloured costumes and fabulous masks. The waits serenaded the panoply of pirates, jesters, counts, courtesans, princes, princesses and fairyland creatures – elves, sprites, fairies, goblins – all chittering in anticipation of the fairy Queen herself, Queen Bess.

While they waited for the Queen, the guests plucked at sweetmeats, preserved fruit and the marvellous marzipan confections. Male servants dressed as elves moved among them with trays of Giacomo Verzelini glasses filled with a variety of wines, ale, and the Queen's favourite, metheglin, a drink distilled from honey and herbs, while the female servants dressed as milkmaids offered nosegays to be pressed into belts and bodices.

The setting sun irradiated a horizon corrugated with an interlacing of ancient oak and elm and as the last vermillion rays flamed the sky the finest caroche in the land drew to a halt outside Stanstead Hall. The waits stopped playing and the guests sank to their knees as the Queen alighted from her carriage, splendid in royal purple and gold thread, her hands gripping the shoulders of two liveried young courtiers. The Marchioness, Master Rathe, Lady Elizabeth, and her siblings descended the stairs and knelt on the gravel before the fragile, elderly woman who had reigned over them all their lives.

Shaking off her young attendants the Queen cast her rheumy eyes over the hushed assembly, her gaze coming to rest on the kneeling minstrels. 'Rise and play on.'

At this, the entire party rose and the minstrels struck up a melody lately arrived from Italy, a jaunty piece that set toes tapping and couples seeking out partners for a lively dance. The Queen paused at the bottom of the stairs and watched the dancers turning and twirling, some of the younger ones leaping and adding impressive acrobatic flourishes.

'In my youth I could leap higher than a roe deer,' she said, crazing the thick white paste on her cheeks with a sad smile. 'I should have danced more but I was too worried. Spain. Catholics. Pox. However, I survived them all. I could have danced more.' Her fan, an ornate fluttering of white ostrich feathers shivered over the carmine gash of her mouth, hiding the blackened teeth. 'Show me to my seat, Helena, and bring me a glass of metheglin and a bowl of suckets.'

The Marchioness offered her arm but the proud old lady refused it only to grasp it on the first step when her balance faltered. Once the Queen was installed in a chair resembling a small throne the festivities gained a heady gaiety, laughter and conversation rippling over the music. The servants kept the feast replete in a seamless delivery of tray after tray of food, moving like will-o-wisps through the leaping, twirling, giddy assembly of masked phantasms. Drinks were invisibly replenished and tables maintained a groaning opulence on this faultless midsummer night. Myriad brilliantine stars blazed and a full-bellied moon silvered the garden statuary into a lifelike haunting. The evening flew by in a haze of rainbow-coloured silks and velvets as guests parried, removed, and reassembled in the familiar patterns of the Galliard, the Almain, the Paval, that formal procession of only slightly touching fingers and finally, the seductive Volt where partners openly embraced.

At midnight the Queen's head was beginning to droop and Helena leaned close and whispered into the wizened ear, 'Your Majesty, I have something very special for you.'

The pale head, spent as a faded flower, lifted. 'What is it, my dear?'

'A fairy.'

As arranged Miriam materialised beside the minstrels and began to sing, her pure voice settling the heady revellers and drawing every eye. A whisper passed around the room that a fairy had blown into their midst. The Queen blinked several times, her red-rimmed eyes settling at last on the vision in white standing or floating, she wasn't sure which, perhaps hovering, near the open door. Moonlight shining through her gossamer wings added a mystical lustre to the song and glamoured the winged apparition.

Even though she had been instructed not to, Miriam looked directly at the Queen and met there the loneliest gaze she had ever encountered, lonelier even than the eyes of the starving waifs foraging for scraps in the Cheaps. A current of understanding passed between them, vibrant as a musical cord or the fine mesh of umbilical plasma said to tether soul to flesh whilst there is breath. If Miriam was the embodiment of all the elderly Monarch's longing, the Queen was a sad reminder of what it means to be base-born and socially erased, even for the highest in the land. The outliers found communion in this altered light, this song and this moment and there shivered between them a momentary bond.

The last note rang out and as instructed Miriam retreated. In vain the Queen searched the moonlit cavity, raising a vein-threaded hand as if to touch the denizen of Fairyland so recently materialised. 'Did I imagine her?'

Helena smiled. 'Perhaps we all did.'

'My heart is full,' said the Queen. 'My dear, I would like my bed now. I would like to dream.'

Helena subtly nodded, cueing Rathe. 'My son-in-law will escort you to your room, Your Majesty.'

As the old lady rose, the entire company knelt.

'To have seen a fairy just once before –' The ancient eyes squeezed shut. 'Heaven or Hell.'

'Heaven surely,' said Helena, glancing up at her sovereign.

'I think I would prefer Hell.' The Queen laughed, a throaty, earthy guffaw that ended in a fit of coughing. When she regained her breath she sighed. 'I expect I'll know soon enough. Now where is this lad of yours?' Rathe was at the Queen's side in an instant offering his arm. 'A handsome man taking me to bed,' said the Queen. 'Now the fantasy is complete.'

Rathe led the Monarch through the kneeling crowd which presently rose and resumed dancing. After delivering the Queen to her ministering ladies-in-waiting Rathe paused in the corridor but instead of returning to the banquet where his wife was giddying herself with an array of dancing partners headed to the servants' quarters.

The Master

He wore black velvet breeches, doublet and cape, a frothing of white lace at his throat winked with a single ruby-coloured Indian gem, his black leather gamaches were up to his thighs and behind a mask of black silk, his coal-black eyes glittered, amused. His black leather hat bore a further twinkling of Indian gems in the buckle and sprouted three ostrich feathers dyed black.

'You may retire now Avice,' he told the mute servant. 'I will take Mistress Miriam back to the banquet to sing once again for the Queen.'

Avice departed the room in a rush, eager to quit her strange charge.

Miriam reached for her mask but he shook his head and closed the door. 'The Queen's abed. You have no further need of mask or wings.'

Miriam stood quite still as the Master slipped behind her and eased the harness from her shoulders. Dropping the wings onto the floor in a mesh of pale gossamer and silver thread, he removed his mask and tossed it on top of her wings. She could hear him breathing light and fast as if he had exerted himself.

'Did you enjoy Marlowe's play?' he murmured, his breath on her neck.

She shivered, nodded.

'My mistress didn't but then she hasn't your fine instincts.' He turned her around to face him, his fingertips exploring the naked skin of her neck and shoulders, tracing the undulations of bone and muscle. 'You are different from other women, Miriam. Certainly more beautiful.'

She met the coal-black eyes, saw them widen, his breath drawn in rapid, shallow drafts that shuddered the feathers arching from the hat he presently tore off and tossed.

'You are not quite of this world. The Queen thinks you are a fairy. I think you are –'

But he did not finish the sentence, his mouth pressed against hers with a feverish force that raised in her an equal fire. He wrestled her out of the diaphanous gown, unbound the loosely stayed bodice and tore off the cambric smock revealing her naked and pale and lit by the fecund moon that had so recently augmented an illusion created to gain a knighthood for him. Now he tore off his own garments careless of popping buttons and unhinging buckles.

The moon, their witness, lit a coupling almost violent in its consummation. No words as they heaved, tossed, twined, and tasted, testing the limits of pleasure until they lay spent in each other's arms silently retracing the patterns of joy with their fingertips. When dawn broke translucent and too soon he helped her into her work clothes and she helped him into his velvet. She had not spoken a word but now as he kissed her she murmured his name against his lips.

'Tonight after your mother has gone to sleep come back to this room. I will make sure no one trespasses upon us. Wait here for me until I am free to come to you. The Queen –' he shuddered. 'The Queen remains our guest for three weeks and I am to play lover to the old lady until she knights me and satisfies my mother-in-law.' He kissed her again. 'But every word of love I whisper into that wizened ear belongs to you.'

Three weeks of love

And there followed three weeks of feasts and tournaments replete with sword fighting, wrestling, jousting and card games where vast amounts of money was won and lost by people who scarcely noticed the difference. Midweek there was another masque but with fewer guests, most having returned to London.

Miriam moved through the crowded room delivering trays of confits and removing discarded glasses, invisible to all but Master Rathe whose eyes found her while his wife and mother-in-law were busy flattering the Queen. Once Miriam was close enough to the lonely old Monarch to observe her desolate inward gaze but the Queen, so used to guarding her flagging soul, did not recognise Miriam or sense the momentary bond that had silvered between them when she sang. Miriam was once again part of the shadowy legion that made the lives of the privileged flow so effortlessly, once again part of the illusion that life was equitable and God even-handed. But whilst she was unseen by day, by night she was near worshipped in a lather of lust that left them both hungering for more.

Too soon the real world imposed its timing and its sanctions. The Queen departed with the promise of a knighthood for Rathe and Court invitations for the Marchioness's remaining unmarried children. The servants were instructed to pack trunks for the journey back to London. Miriam waited that last night for Rathe but when he did not appear she crept back downstairs to her sleeping mother, doubts ravelling. Had he changed his mind about her or would their liaison continue in London sanctioned and orchestrated as it had been by the Marchioness? Of course he would soon be made a knight. Perhaps then he would be too socially elevated to till a base-born maid.

Or had he lain with a fairy?

London – 1593

After Stanstead Hall Miriam suspected but two months of missed courses confirmed she was carrying the Master's child. For weeks she clung to her secret uncertain whether she should ask her mother for that special brew that emptied the womb or risk bringing a base-born child into the heartless world. She knew the Marchioness was unlikely to show her the same compassion she had shown her mother, not when the father was her knighted son-in-law. She would be turned out of Radclyffe House, forced to beg on the careless streets of London. Of course a purging might solve the problem but the idea of snuffing out an innocent life tortured her.

Night after night she pressed her hands to the minute swell of her belly, hoping, praying for a bleed that would set them both free. Night after restless night she was tormented with dreams of the man who had whispered words of love as they lay twined on sheets of linen, the man now disappeared behind a mask of cold-eyed indifference. No longer did his gaze track her when she served the family at supper, nor did he find a bed for them to share. Life at Radclyffe House returned to the same patterns of service as if the three weeks of love had never happened and indeed but for the child growing in her womb Miriam would have wondered if those magical nights in his arms had been part of some imagined world fleeting as the illusion of Fairyland, his moans of pleasure the constructs of a dream.

She pressed a trembling hand to the embryonic life that would soon show itself. 'It would be better if we both died, sweetling. A fast and thorough poison would free us.'

After much deliberation she decided to end her life before the baby showed but her course dramatically altered when Lady Elizabeth collapsed one night at supper, gasping for breath, ripping at her gown, claiming it burned her. The Marchioness sent for a doctor but the

128

doughty old man fled the house. She sent for an apothecary but he likewise fled.

'Sweating sickness,' he cried, backing out the door.

When Lady Elizabeth's gentlewoman declined to tend her, the Marchioness turned her out and ordered Miriam to move into her daughter's chamber, there to wash, feed and shift her daughter until she either recovered or passed from this world.

And so Miriam moved into Lady Elizabeth's room where she slept on a palette, snatching a few hours rest between wiping the curdling sweat from her Ladyship's brow and attempting to feed her. In the days and nights that followed no-one else dared enter the room, not even her own mother. Eirinn left trays of food and drink outside the door and collected the soiled sheets and nightrails each morning. The Marchioness ordered them burned lest the contagion spread. Miriam's life became a twilit world of managing the pain of a dying woman and snatching a few precious hours' sleep for herself. She scarce had time to worry about her own future or her child's.

One night she was roused from a fitful sleep by a strange rasping sound unlike Lady Elizabeth's usual laboured breathing. She wiped the burning forehead with a clean linen cloth dipped in water and for a moment Lady Elizabeth gained clarity.

'His child. I know.' Her voice hoarse, her cracked lips parted revealing a swollen tongue and black teeth, her breath putrid and reeking of death. 'You bewitched him.'

'Lady Elizabeth, you must eat something.'

The lips peeled back into a cadaverous grin. 'You'll both burn for my death.'

'Please try to eat something.'

The eyes, so full of hatred, grew dark and one last rasping breath stilled her agued body and set her spirit free. Miriam stood for a long moment staring at the sightless eyes, the stiffening corpse. She had seen dead bodies in the streets but never so close and the absence of life was both terrifying and fascinating, one minute a living, breathing and accusing woman, the next an inert, silent lump of wax. Finally she crept to the door and opened it to report the death to the Marchioness but it was the Master who stood there.

'Lady Elizabeth is dead, my Lord.'

Rathe pushed past Miriam and went to his wife's bedside, studying the dead face for a silent beat before issuing a single order.

'Dress her in her pink gown.' The first words he had spoken to her since their return.

'I am carrying your child.'

Now he looked at her, panicked. 'You are quite sure?'

She swallowed, nodded.

He took a few sharp breaths and then lifted the bowl of broth next to his wife's bed. 'What's this?'

'Chicken broth.'

'See that her nightrail and bedding are burned.' He left the room without another word.

She removed the soiled nightrail and bedding, dressed the poor emaciated body in the pink gown that would cover her bones in the family's crypt.

'I'm sorry,' she murmured to the corpse. 'I meant you no harm.'

She had scarcely completed the task of dressing the corpse before Master Rathe burst into the room with two bailiffs.

'That's her,' he said, pointing at Miriam. 'That's the witch who poisoned my wife.'

Miriam gaped at him, disbelief choking a protest, and what happened next seemed part of a nightmare from which she must surely wake. Her lover leaned against the wall, watching as the two bailiffs grabbed her roughly and shoved her out into the corridor where she almost collided with the Marchioness.

'Lady Helena –' Miriam began.

'What are these men doing in my house?' The Marchioness eyed the bailiffs coldly.

'Elizabeth's dead,' said Rathe flatly.

This news elicited no emotion from her mother.

'But what are you doing with her?' She nodded at Miriam. 'Tidying up.'

Bridewell Prison and Trial

The charge was petty treason. The punishment burning at the stake. The Master accused her of poisoning the Mistress and bewitching him. Her trial would take place in the highest court in the land, the Star Chamber and while she waited she would be held in Bridewell Prison, once Bridewell Palace, the residence of King Henry VIII in the early part of his reign, now an orphanage and correction centre for wayward women. The wretches who entered through the kitchens and gatehouse rarely ever saw the light of day again for most died in their dark cells.

Day and night the cries of the hungry and frightened echoed unheeded for who remembered the effluence of a social order that blamed the less fortunate for their miserable lots? Miriam lay on her pallet, hands resting on her womb, on the child that kicked and squirmed, eager for life. If she

131

was sent to the stake the babe would be boiled alive when she was engulfed in flames. She stifled her sobs, determined not to give the gloating bailiffs the satisfaction of her misery.

Every afternoon, after the family's midday dinner her mother brought her food, a supplement for the meagre rations pushed through her bars each day. They would sit on her pallet knotted together, Eirinn weeping openly, Miriam silent and stunned by the twist of fate that had sent her there awaiting a trial that would almost certainly end in her death, for what was her word against the testament of a knight?

The trial was set for the next quarter, a fortnight away, in the dreaded Star Chamber, the court that dealt with the most serious breaches in the land. The accused may not be allowed to say anything in their own defence and would be tried on written depositions brought by witnesses. After consideration, the judges meted out any punishment they wished, including torture and execution, and no-one escaped their verdict for they were appointed by the Queen.

Miriam wondered what the lonely old sovereign would think if she knew her fairy was about to face the flames, authorised by her own henchmen, the royal judges.

No song could save her now.

***

Eirinn arrived with the usual basket of food and a bribe of cates for the guards who left them alone to say their goodbyes. The younger guards felt the imminent death of such a beautiful creature was a shame, but a witch is a witch and beneath her mesmerising exterior she must have hidden a black heart like all witches and didn't the scriptures say the Devil himself had a beautiful face?

Eirinn opened the basket and removed a leatherjack of wine along with two manchets and some cold chicken. 'There's a clean gown in there for you as well, sweetling. Change now and give me your soiled gown. Abigail will wash it.'

Miriam shifted quickly, folded her soiled gown and placed it in the now-empty basket. Eirinn trembled. 'I keep thinking the Master or the Marchioness will help.'

'They won't.'

'But why?' Eirinn shook her head from side to side in agony. 'You sang for the Queen. Your voice gave the Master his knighthood. You tended Lady Elizabeth when her own gentlewoman was too afraid to. Everyone knows she died of the sweating sickness. Why would he accuse you of poisoning her? Why?'

'I will quit this world without fear of the next. My only fear is the pain and –'

'I will poison him and the Marchioness,' Eirinn spat the words. 'I don't care what they do to me.'

'Don't. They're not worth your soul. I'll see you in Heaven where we will listen to the Music of the Spheres.'

'Then I will poison myself and join you. But why would he do this to you?'

Miriam pressed her hands to her belly, looked down. 'Because of this.'

Eirinn followed her daughter's gaze, gasped. 'His child? But when? Where?'

'Stanstead Hall after I sang for the Queen.'

'He forced himself upon you.'

Miriam shook her head. 'No, I was willing just as you were. I'm so sorry. You warned me.'

As if a candle had been lit dispelling the dark, Eirin understood. 'The child is an impediment. Ladies of high standing frown on such couplings.'

'But Lady Elizabeth is dead.'

Eirinn squeezed her daughter's hands. 'Sweetling, he plans to marry again, a Countess.'

'While his child boils to death in the flames!' Her voice caught in a strangled sob.

'No, it won't.' Eirin rose with sudden resolution. 'And you won't burn. I know what I must do.'

Miriam rose also. 'Do nothing. I won't have your death on my conscience.'

'You won't, sweetling. Trust me, you won't feel any pain and neither will the child.'

***

The day before the trial Eirinn arrived but not alone. She had Master Trenery and surprisingly, Thomas, with her. The guards took their bribe of cates and left them alone as usual. Once the guards were out of earshot, Thomas fell at her feet weeping.

'Forgive me! I never really thought you were a witch and when he lusted after you I was jealous. I wanted you for myself. Forgive me.'

Miriam pulled the weeping lad to his feet. 'Thomas, I hold no malice in my heart for you. Marry Rosamunde.'

'She won't have me any more than you would have.'

'She might if you treat her kindly.'

Thomas bunched his fists and shuddered. 'Valentyne and Fyndern are ready to kill the Master. So are Abigail and Rosamunde.' He clenched his jaw. 'So am I.'

'But you won't.'

'No, we won't,' said Master Trenery. 'We have something for you.' He pulled a small vial out of his pocket and pressed it into her hand. 'It will work quickly.'

'It won't hurt. You'll go to sleep forever.' Thomas sniffed. 'The babe too.'

'You knew?'

'I told them. Take it with food and you won't –' Eirinn stifled a sob.

'And you'll keep it down,' said Master Trenery gently.

The sound of footsteps marching in syncopation halted the conversation. Miriam hid the vial in her bodice just as two grey-faced bailiffs unlocked the bars and bid her accompany them to the Star Chamber.

'But the trial's not until tomorrow!' cried Thomas.

'It's been brought forward. It's this afternoon.'

Eirinn leapt up. 'No! No! It's tomorrow.'

The guards leered at her. 'She'll burn tomorrow.'

Master Trenery placed a steadying hand on Eirinn's arm. 'Come now, be calm, we have said all we need to.'

Eirinn pulled her daughter into a fierce embrace, whispered, 'I'll see you in Heaven.'

Miriam gave them all such a look of love it shamed the guards into momentary silence.

'If you'll come with us now, Mistress.'

Master Trenery held Mistress Tilby tightly and Thomas stood quite still, his jaws clenched, his fists balled but he remained silent as Miriam left with the guards, head held high, her soul half-flown from a life that had been little else but service and a song.

***

It was over in a blur of black-garbed indifference. Master Rathe read his accusations aloud, the sentence passed as the words "petty treason" "witch" and "murderer" rang out. She would be burned at sunset on the morrow and may God have mercy on her soul. Master Rathe quit the court without a backward glance and as quickly as she had been shuffled before these hardened judges she was back in her cell.

It was a feeble moon that ghosted her, a feeble resolve that steadied her as she uncapped the vial and raised it to her lips. Remembering what Master Trenery had said about keeping the poison down she forced herself to eat one of the manchets, the dry bread catching in her throat, jagging, teasing in this last hour of her life.

She caressed her belly in gentle soothing strokes. 'I'm so sorry, sweetling. You must come with me. Heaven may be kinder.'

'It isn't.'

She almost dropped the precious poison. He was dressed in black, hauntingly like the highwayman Master Rathe had pretended to be the night of the banquet and for one startling moment she thought he had come to gloat but the man who presently stepped forward into the spectral light was a stranger, darkly handsome, his eyes a piercing glitter of polished ebony that held hers in a hypnotic stare.

'You won't need that.' He passed his hand through the bars, palm up. 'The flames will not touch you.'

'My baby –'

'Ah.' He raised his hands and brought them down in a sharp sweep. 'Free.'

The movement in her belly ceased.

'Give me the vial, please. Trust me, you will not die tomorrow.'

'Am I to be released?'

'After a fashion. You won't be returning to your former life. I will protect you from the flames.'

'How?'

He smiled. 'Let's call it magic.'

'Who are you?'

'Someone stronger than anyone or anything you have ever known. The vial, please.'

As if a snake compelled a mouse she moved to the bars and gave the handsome stranger the vial that would spare her the flames.

He took it, closeted it in his vest. 'I can make better use of this. Now sleep.'

She drifted back to the pallet and fell into a deep, dreamless sleep, not waking until almost sunset the next day when she was dragged from her bed, removed from Bridewell and taken in a tumbrel to West Smith Field where a pyre was stacked with rushes and logs. A crowd shotten with hatred had gathered and when they saw her they chanted "Burn the witch" and "Enjoy Hell". In vain and with rising terror she looked around for her deliverer, but he was nowhere to be seen in the glut of faces twisted with lust and hate.

Feeling betrayed she submitted to her fate, the coarse ropes that fixed her to the stake, the leering crowd, her only relief the knowledge that the child was dead and would be spared the agony of being boiled alive. She did not pray for who could trust a God who allowed such savagery. When the pyre was lit, accompanied by a wave of putrid breath bellowing glee, she resolved to take great gulps of smoke and suffocate but as the first tendrils curled their misting miasma around her, she saw him. His arms were raised, his hands articulating patterns in the air, strange, angled shapes, as if he orchestrated music and a great calm engulfed her and

137

stilled her fear. The ravaging crowd grew impatient for her agony, some shrugging and departing, disappointed, others looking around for a tavern.

Meanwhile her deliverer continued his strange weaving enchantment as the flames towered into a brilliant, living wall of scarlet and gold, his incantation holding her suspended within the encincturing fire that sizzled off the restraining ropes and burned her gown to ash, leaving her naked. Through the blazing luminescence she imagined she saw his eyes, mesmeric, glittering through the flames that caressed her flesh like a cooling zephyr.

The night fell hard and fast, a brittle moon silvered the city, driving the disappointed and bored remaining crowd to taverns or beds and when the last embers spat and snarled, the square was empty. He stepped out of the shadows, gave her his cloak to cover her nakedness and helped her down onto the dew-damp street. He handed her a linen budget.

'Clothes for your journey. Find an abandoned Abbey. Wait there until I come for you.'

'How will you find me?'

'I find all my witches one way or another.'

'I am no witch!'

He laughed. 'You were just burned for one! Be glad I found you in time. These God-fearing people are evil. The fallen angel himself would never stoop as low as these good Christian judges. You must stay hidden.'

'For how long?'

'Until I rule the earth.'

'Who are you?'

'Your saviour.'

'How did you know I was to die?'

'I make it my business to know who is to hang and who is to burn and this time I intervened.'

'Why?'

'All in good time. Take Watling Road out of London and walk south. When you reach the sea head west until you find Lands' End. The moon will light your way.'

Miriam looked at the silver arrow of cobblestones, the old Roman Watling Road, that would lead her away from the only life she had ever known, away from her mother, broken with grief over her death and planning her own.

'I would ease my mother's pain first.'

'No, you must leave now. They must not cage you and make a freak of you.'

'I have no coin for the journey.'

'You won't need coin. You won't hunger or thirst.'

'I may need to rest.'

'You won't tire.'

'What am I?'

'Immortal. I have seared your soul into your flesh.'

'I cannot die?'

He shook his head.

'No matter what they do to me?'

Again, he shook his head.

'Then I will have vengeance.'

'You will have it when I rule the earth.'

She grasped his hand, dug her nails into his palm. 'Swear.'

'I swear. You may kill as many as you need to for there will be no punishment. You will never die, never see Heaven, never be judged. Now go. When you find an abandoned Abbey stay hidden. I will find you, my dear.'

'Miriam. My name is Miriam.'

PART TWO

I

So light is her footfall, the miles beneath her feet leave no mark upon her flesh, no sweat beads her brow, no blisters pock her heels, nor does the earth record her passage. She does not tire or thirst. No heart protests in her breast, no hunger claws at her belly, no sleep delays the distance she must put between London and sanctuary. The child is dead. No flutter of foot betrays life in her womb. She is utterly alone.

She walked over fields starred with wildflowers, avoiding the roads and villages, the haunts of men. Sometimes she followed the riverbanks where birdsong and the susurrus of flowing water calmed the longing for her mother and purged the horror of her incineration but when the wind rippled the grass into a song that sounded like rain she remembered the warmth of the kitchen on long wintery evenings when her "family" gathered around the fire, feasting on cates her mother had baked for them as Master Trenery strummed his lute.

These thoughts stewed into an aching for vengeance. She imagined creeping up the stairs into Master Rathe's bedroom and plunging a kitchen knife into his evil heart. But that was too kind. She wanted him to linger in his agony. Something slower and crueller: a poison that twisted his bowel into knots, stopping the flow of excrement until his body exploded, and then she would seek out the men in black gowns in the Star Court, the cold-hearted elite who sent innocents to the gallows or the pyre, and evict their putrid souls by appearing in their bedrooms and frightening them to death, and lastly, she would haunt the snaggle-toothed ghouls who cheered for her death.

But these delicious plans would have to wait. First she must find an abandoned Abbey and wait there for the saviour who would help her take her revenge. She walked on through the days and nights without pause. By day, when the world awoke, distant clangs, grumbling cartwheels warned her to keep her distance from humanity. By night, the hooting of owls and the scurrying of their prey in the hedgerows twinning her path made an eerie adjunct to her footfall.

A few days' and nights' walk from London she observed a noticeable increase in vagrants, sad bundles of rags sleeping in hollows by the riverbanks or drifting blindly by her half-dead. Those possessed of the strength of body and mind to speak told her about the loss of commons through enclosure, the practice of the rich who wanted to hunt in their Elysium fields, denying the common man pasture for his one milker or coneys to feed his family. With little available land for trapping or grazing, starvation was rife. After her life in service and her "death" she bracketed the rich into a single entity: contemptable leeches who bled the poor and created enclosure, the cause of all vagrancy.

On through rain, sun and storm she walked, immune to discomfort, becoming a part of the elemental pulse of nature. When lightning forked, illuminating the night, it irradiated a different creed from the sermons she had heard in church, conjured a god far removed from the patriarchal despot who credited believers with righteousness and non-believers with sin. Nature with her ruthless appetite for life, fed, bled and bred, contemptuous of ennui.

One day out of curiosity she approached a village, dared a glimpse through leafy apertures, observed that the cobbled high road was littered with beggars, mostly women and children. The itinerant poor she had seen on the byways and by the riverbanks were mostly men. Recalling the hubbub and pulse of London she winced at the threadbare Cheap, the ubiquitous jail, the sole Inn, the clutch of hovels bracing a single resplendent house made of pisé cross-stitched with ebony timber and she wondered why, so far from London, the locals lacked the imagination to create a fairer social order. Sunlight glinting off the lone spire of the church shafted a graveyard promising Heaven, a convenient lie when Hell burnt as fiercely in rural England as it did in London. Despite its distance from the capital she thought the plague must have reached this bucolic hamlet for there were children in every recess, huddled like kittens in a basket. Even here the poor died in plain sight just as they did in London, lying in the dirt and mire until the dead cart delivered them to a lime powdering in an unmarked grave.

The plague had made orphans of many children in London, including Valentyne and Fyndern, the two little changelings who would have dangled at Tyburn had it not been for the intervention of the Marchioness: an act of convenience rather than mercy, for it meant the acquisition of two sturdy little workhorses. The memory of those two lads, now handsome young men, filled her with a grief she could not express so dangerously close to humanity where her sobs might draw attention. She crept away. There were miles to go before she could weep safely.

**

Days melded into weeks, and quitting the riverbank she changed course and headed south towards the sea, reaching the coast one moonless night, her senses assailed by an admix of salt and moisture that did not resolve into dew. She paused her journey, entranced by the hypnotic rhythm of the waves, intensely aware of the quixotic presence of the sea, and thus occupied, she remained fixed all night, listening to the siren song. At dawn, she discovered she stood on a clifftop, only a few feet from the edge, pale slivers of wind-whipped grass and glazed rocks surrounding her.

Her first sight of the sea, an upended sky, deeply blue and seemingly infinite, woke in her the promise of eternal thrall. She felt a deep respect for the sailors who dared that wide expanse until she remembered it was only greed that fortified them. Suddenly the sun quit the horizon in a burst of flame, glistering pathways across the blue, signposting a tranquil inlet. A scattering of ketches tethered to a jut of rock lay on the sand, and then in a spectacular aureole, dawn fired a hulking stone edifice on the opposite cliff.

It looked like an Abbey.

Pimpled on the green furbelow adjacent to the cove a small town was stirring awake, and before the fishermen arrived to pursue the day's catch, she hurried down to the cove and onto a plateau honeycombed with tidal pools, there to search for a path to the Abbey. On the seaward side, half hidden in a mesh of greenery, she found steps carved into the cliff-face, and taking them, climbed up to the eerie perched on the edge of the bluff.

It was indeed an Abbey. Abandoned. Inside, she found evidence of the slaughter that had cleared it. Traces of blood rusted the flagstone floor and stained the walls. A bible lay where it had been tossed. She picked it up, saw that it was written in Welsh. The men who had carried out King Henry's vicious orders were thorough for nothing remained of the once thriving community, not even bones.'Where was your God?' she asked their ghosts.

She placed the holy relic of their abandoned religion on a hall table floured with dust and set about exploring, wandering from room to room, ghostlike. Upstairs she found a warren of cells with straw pallets and cracked chamber pots but no other evidence of past or present occupation other than a few terns' nests lively with chicks.

'I don't mind sharing with you,' she told the seabirds. 'I would like the company while I wait for my deliverer.'

She drifted back downstairs to the kitchen where the familiar fixtures – oven, table, pots, ladles – reignited her grief. Sinking to the floor, she wept for her mother and her extended family: Master Trenery, Abigail, Rosamunde, the kinchin cos, Jonas, even Thomas. A guttural animal cry rent the dank space, and she rocked back and forth in an orgy of release, but no tears flowed for there remained no lifeful juices. At length she found respite in the silent space within where a heartbeat once measured her days. She touched her cheeks, dry and waxy as an unlit candle, cold as winter, and wondered anew what she had become. Staring out the window, the vast reach of silent blue chimed with the silence within, extinguishing all thoughts as the sun set, plunging the sea into grumbling grey.

As evening fell, she stirred and retraced her footsteps, conjuring the spirits of the nuns who had once filled the Abbey with prayer. She hoped they had been brave enough not to scream when they were butchered, depriving the soulless savages of their fun just as she had done at her incineration. Finally, she wafted into a room on the uppermost level, a vast, yawning chamber that echoed her footfall. It may have been a prayer room or a dining room or both for there was a long refectory table in the middle littered with more bibles, a few sheets of music, presumably hymns, a dozen or so trenchers and some wooden mazers. Chairs lay overturned, scattered as if they had been violently tossed. Against the far wall a rough-hewn sideboard carried a dozen sealed leatherjacks and a single silver goblet. She wondered how the murderers missed that when they ransacked the place. Cringing in a dark corner, a lute, also untouched. Why the murderers left the lute, the goblet and the wine was a puzzle unless they had not discovered this room. Perhaps the overturned chairs signatured the nuns' attempts to flee to their cells before their butchers found them.

She righted one of the chairs, remarked its corrugated planes as if the hands that wielded the axe and gouge had been unaccustomed to joinery. Had the nuns made their own furniture? Placing the chair in front of a shutterless window, empty as a vacant eye socket, she had an uninterrupted view of sea and sky. She sat there watching the stars claim their places in the firmament, gaining brilliance as the night's cloak welded sky to sea. Far below, the village moved from work to play, casting a feeble light as candles were lit, and presently the strains of a familiar song drifted up. For want of company she sang along, her voice winging out into the velvet night, the song accompanying the transverse of stars and sickle moon across the sky. When the moon was almost overhead a star fell, protesting the extinguishing of its light in a streak of silver fire and she wondered again about the veracity of separate spheres, for how could a star, even a dying one, pass so readily through an impregnable wall of glass?

But perhaps after all there were greater mysteries governed by stranger forces than the bible allowed and in her lonely state she needed heaven's music for company so she forgave the trespass of a fallen star. All night she listened for the Music of the Spheres but apart from the lash of waves against the cliff, the eerie caw of a homebound gull and the intermittent sounds of revelry from the village below, she heard nothing. In the small hours when sea and sky were still an undifferentiated mass the sea grew suddenly calm. Nothing moved. Nothing breathed. When she stilled her own habitual inhalation, it seemed the world ceased to exist. Cloaked in pristine silence she intensified her vigil, every sense tuned to the registration of something, *anything*, that would inform her fate and refine the vengeance she now lived for.

Sometime in the long dark night she imagined she heard her mother's voice calling her from beyond the veil and she sank into despair cavernous and bleak. She would never see her mother again for she was eternally chained to the earth now that she was immortal.

Provence – 1594

'What have you got for me?'

The young man laughed, shivering the auburn curls that hung halfway down his back. 'You find our arrangement amusing?' He lifted a jug on the sideboard, filled a Venetian glass with a measure of ruby-coloured liquid. 'I see you've left some burgundy for me.'

The laughter eased to a ripple and the young man rose, collected a wad of velum etched with dusky ink and dropped it on the board. 'There.'

'Your hair is unfashionably long.'

'I am dead. Who cares?' He nodded at the manuscript. 'The scavenger should be thrilled to be credited with this play. It's my best work.' He refilled his glass, sauntered over to the window and looked down at the garden. 'It's a lovely prison. Thank you.'

'You are free to leave once you've honoured our contract.' He took his glass and the manuscript and sat by the fire. 'Now resist the urge to complain about your lodgings while I read this.'

'A Chateau, servants, gardeners, a replete table, a stocked cellar, the Devil himself for occasional company. Who's complaining?' Kit drifted back to the board, collected the jug, and returned to the window where he slumped down in contemplation of the shirtless gardeners. The young men were laughing and chatting as they weeded the beds. 'I am learning French although for the exchanges I have in mind words are unnecessary.'

The Devil ignored him, sipped his wine as he read. Half an hour later he looked up. 'To be or not to be? Do you mean dead or alive?'

'Is there a difference?' Kit shrugged. 'I never believed in Heaven or Hell or the old man upstairs until I met you. Now I am left in a quandary, should I learn to pray?'

'My father never answers prayers. Only I do. They really should build Cathedrals to me.'

'You didn't answer me when I called you.'

'What do you call our arrangement?'

'Mutual convenience. I meant you are proof of your opposite.' He slugged back the wine, repoured. 'Everything has an opposite. Mine is Shakespeare.'

'He will keep your work alive.'

'He will be credited with my genius while I –'

'Live. Content yourself with the knowledge that your genius did not die with you. Cheer up, did you ever think you would live in a Chateau? Now please, silence while I read this.'

The fire crackled and hissed in the grate, more for atmosphere than warmth, the late spring sun beat down on the garden: a geometry of beds and borders bursting with marchpane-coloured flowers, the lawn truncated with established trees, fountains, statues, a maze and two follies, the grounds corralled within high walls of ancient stone. Beyond them the outside world teemed and plotted but within the precincts of the Chateau an altogether different world was being planned. After an hour of intense concentration, the Devil secreted the play in a silk budget.

'It's perfect. Your musings about death will topple those hypocritical institutions that enthrone my nemesis and the poisonous dripping into the King's ear will send ambitious courtiers scrambling to apothecaries for the means to dispose of the cadaver on the throne.'

Kit closed his eyes. 'You like it.'

'It's genius as well you know.'

'It's one thing for me to know.' Kit lurched upright, his eyes shining with tears. 'But the Devil recognises my genius and I didn't even sell my soul for it.'

'This is no Faustian deal, my friend. I've made that with Shakespeare.'

'Has he a soul to sell?' Kit ambled to the sideboard, unlocked a drawer and retrieved two scrolled manuscripts tied with ribbon. 'Give these to that charlatan as well. They're trifles, one a little sad, the other a fantasy. I dashed them off just after I died.'

The Devil read the titles. '*Romeo and Juliet* and *A Midsummer Night's Dream.*'

'The Dream is about Fairyland. In truth I started writing it in London, hoping it might restore my reputation with the Queen, but her ears had been so filled with poison, it made a ghost of me. The other I wrote here, disillusioned as I am with love.'

'You didn't sign them I hope.'

Kit clenched his fist, raised it then dropped it, defeated. 'No. I left a blank space as you instructed. He will sign it, assuming he can spell his name.'

The Devil laughed. 'He's not illiterate and he does have talent. The Queen adores him.'

'The Queen is a fool for flattery.' Kit poured himself another goblet of wine. 'How is the old virgin? Frustrated?'

'Feeble.' He placed the two plays in the budget along with the new work, *Hamlet*. 'I will have copies made in London. I will give the two *trifles* to the Bard first and in due course he will receive *Hamlet*, the masterpiece that will secure his fame.'

'In exchange for his soul?' Kit shook his head, the curls dancing.

'In the hopes of satisfying mine.'

Kit drained his glass, ambled across to the board for a refill. 'And what will you do with my originals?'

'Bury them in the graves of lepers here in France. By day rather than night. That's how I was killed last time.' He laughed. 'Don't look so horrified. No-one will exhume them but me. They're my insurance. I am investing heavily in your genius and Will's ambition. In five or six hundred years' time you and your nemesis may have become legends. If so, these plays will make me very rich. Of course, I will only resort to selling them if my own ambitions fail.'

'Your own ambitions? Remind me, what are they apart from burying my genius and living in abundance?'

'To rule the world.'

'Why do you want the world when you have Hell and all those fascinating inmates?'

'I enjoy the sun.'

'Then I'd start with Italy.'

'Too much God. Elizabeth will be dead soon. There will be a vacuum of power more easily filled than wrangling with a Papacy and systemic superstition. The old lady does not name a successor and she has no child that we know of. It would be perfect if the murdered Scottish Queen's son inherited the throne.'

Kit raised an eyebrow. 'Why? Is he in your thrall?'

'He will be. He is something of a poet and he adores theatre.'

The Abbey – 1600

Miriam had no idea how long she sat at the window hoping for a sign. A year? Two? Three? Time had a fluid quality like water. It split and flowed around her as if she was a rock in a restless sea, her position unaltering, her soul, if she still had one, frozen in a single moment of sterile hatred while life moved beyond her into a future potent with alteration.

She had tuned the lute, taught herself to play, another voice in her isolation. Stationed there on the uppermost level of the Abbey, her purchase was so high seabirds landed on the sill ignorant of her, resting before they took their seaborn passage. She studied their flight, the splayed wings that braced the air much as a ship floats on water. They were graceful on the wing; far more eloquent than they were on land with their knock-toed halting progress.

To fly over the ocean, twin the plane of blue as a hedgerow parallels a path would be to taste divinity, test death.

Freedom.

**

Seasons passed: winter rains lashed the Abbey, autumn winds swept the pockmarked cliff, summer suns burned holes in eternity and spring stars glittered like newly-minted coins, seemingly so close she could pocket one. Many flaming dawns rose over the indigo sea, many fiery suns set. Storms gathered, raged, and calmed; the seasons framed in the window's eyeless aperture. One magnificent winter she saw snow fall on the ocean; its brittle white chill captured a moment on the swell before melting into the unquiet grey-blue depths. At times thoughts of her mother fluttered around her like winged torments and she was gripped with the urge to weep but no tears flowed. There was no release of pain, no relief from her stagnant life, no routines to temper her days, no rituals to measure her years, no way to exact the vengeance she craved.

She wondered what had become of her rescuer. Had he abandoned her, left her to rot in a tower, there to suffer a lingering almost-death rather than the brief fiery one Master Rathe had condemned her to?

Then one day he arrived, blowing in like a leaf on the wind.

'Music,' he said, tossing a bundle of pages on the board. 'Learn it, give it voice that I may hear its beauty. What instruments did the nuns leave behind?'

'You found me.'

'I said I would. I always keep my promises.' He laughed softly as he strode around the room, examining her confines. 'That's untrue. This is the first promise I've ever kept. Ah, a lute.' He picked it up, plucked at the strings. 'Not the finest make. I'll bring you some well-made instruments next visit. Is there wine?'

She pointed at the board where a dozen leatherjacks remained unstoppered. 'How did you find me?'

154

'I sensed you, my dear. I have a talent, a nose if you will, for finding witches. You will never escape me.'

She moved from her place by the window to the centre of the room, watched as he opened a leatherjack and poured wine into the one silver goblet the murderers had missed.

'Why did you save me?' she asked.

He took a long draft of wine. 'Excellent vintage. I have been lonely. You are company.'

'You promised me vengeance.'

'And you will have it when the time is right.'

Noting his youth, around nine and twenty, she revised her initial impression of a man of middle years. 'I thought you were older.'

'Appearances can deceive. Was the coward who sent you to the flames young and handsome like me?'

'He was beautiful.'

'The Devil wears a beautiful face, they say.'

'He's not the Devil, just a man used to giving orders but he will rue the day he falsely accused me. Where have you been?'

'France.' He tossed back the wine, refilled. 'You won't drink?'

'I have no thirst.'

'Is there anything to eat? Or won't you eat either?'

'I have no hunger.'

'Then eat for pleasure. Is the larder stocked?'

'With what coin would I supply the larder? And with what foolishness would I show my face in the village Cheaps? There are eggs if you care to find them. A loan cockerel and his harem of hens roam the yard. There may be some eggs unhatched, or you could kill a chicken. What is the year?'

'1600.'

155

'Six years since my death. Take me to London so I can kill the man who destroyed me.'

'Soon. Will you cook the eggs and the chicken for me?'

'No. I will never serve again.'

'Very well.' He marched out of the room, his footsteps retreating down the stairs, a few minutes elapsed and he returned, tossed a coin purse and a bulging silk bundle on the table.

'Coins: angels, sovereigns, French livres. Clothes from Paris, the latest fashion. I guessed your size.'

'Should I dress for the ghosts or my own pleasure?'

'For me.' He nodded at the bundle. 'Choose a favourite and wear it tonight.'

'Who are you and by what magic did you cool the flames?'

He did not answer but prodded the bundle. 'Choose a gown.'

'I am lonely. I miss my mother. My child would have kept me company.' She looked out the window, at the sun's progress towards the horizon. 'Why did you kill my child?'

'I didn't kill your child. I killed you, stopped your heart. The child's soul flew.'

'Why didn't mine?'

'I compelled yours to stay.'

She swung around. 'Are you God that you have power over life and death?'

'I am neither God nor a Star Chamber judge.' He drank the wine in one long draft, refilled. 'Very well if you won't cook for me, I'll get drunk, equally satisfying.'

'Who are you?'

'The one who spared you an agonising death.'

'And cursed me with a living one.'

156

He upended the leatherjack and splashed wine into the goblet until it overflowed. 'Anyone would think you'd prefer the flames.'

'I sit alone day after day, week after week, year after year. I dare not go to the village for a little human company. They'd hang me for a witch.'

'You wouldn't die. They'd cage you as a freak! Stay away from humans.'

'I am condemned to an eternity of solitude.' She slapped her palms down on the table. 'You should have let me keep the child!'

'Children erase their parents.'

'What do you mean?'

'Mothers, fathers, the wretches whose lives are an endless struggle, place their hopes and dreams onto the frail shoulders of children who fail in their turn and blame their parents.'

'What kind of a life is it when I have no-one to share it with?'

'You have me.'

'A stranger. I miss my mother and my family: Master Trenery, Abigail, Rosamunde, Fyndern, Valentyne, Jonas, even Thomas.'

'They could never share your destiny. Their time will pass but you will live forever. The flames seared your soul into your flesh. Death will never release it. One day you will rule the world with me. I did not spare you from the flames for nothing.' He opened a second leatherjack. 'You really should drink.'

She returned to the window. 'I would see my mother. When will you take me to London?'

'It's still too dangerous. But I'm here.'

'Barely. You arrive without notice and will leave again when it pleases you while I remain here and rot.'

'You will never rot.'

'No, unfortunately. Well, if I'm to share eternity with you what should I call you?'

'Stanas Vedil. Satan Devil. A clever anagram, don't you think?'

'*You* are the Devil?' She turned slowly, faced him. 'When did I sell my soul?'

'You didn't. I took it. A beautiful woman about to burn for a crime she did not commit. I saved you.' He watched her, bas relief against the sea's restless struggle. 'Be kind, Miriam. I am lonely, too.'

'Surely there are wretches in Hell who would be grateful for your attention.'

'Grovellers and flatterers. You are honest.' He laughed. 'Brutally so. When I rule the world, none will dare cage you, your beauty will be recorded by every artist through the centuries, your magnificence celebrated in song and poem. You will be their goddess and I their god but whilst your face will remain unchanging, mine will alter as my host body sickens, ages, or dies.'

'You stole that body?'

'I steal all my bodies. I do like this one, so handsome, so healthy despite being hung, a pity I will have to discard it and find a new one in a few years' time. I cannot bear aging.'

'Why don't you still the heart as you have done with mine?'

'And lose my appetites? One needs hunger and juices to sate lust. The pleasures of the flesh glue me to earth. I would float away if desire did not anchor me.'

'What is my pleasure now that I am a living corpse?'

'Revenge.'

'For which I must wait.'

'Patience. Think how many men you can send to the flames when we rule the world.'

'I only want to send one man to the flames.'

'You'll get a taste for it believe me.'

'How did you get here? I heard no carriage entering the village last night. Did you walk from London?'

'I sailed from France.' He nodded down at the cove where a ship bobbed at anchor beyond the breakers. 'My crew are staying at a tavern in the village. I gave them coin for ale and whores, two ryals each and a bag of groats between them.'

'The village is too small for whores.'

'No village is too small for whores when women must feed their children.'

'Where does your crew think you are now?'

'Upstairs in my room at the tavern. With a woman.'

Miriam looked down at the vessel, its ellipsoidal frame lying prow to shore, three tall masts with lateen sails furled, the sterncastle locked watertight. 'A handsome vessel. Portuguese caravel. Who captains it?'

'I do. You know your boats.'

'Mam and I picnicked after church every Sunday on the banks of the Thames, weather permitting. We learned the types of vessels moored there, made up stories about their travels. How did you come by such a magnificent boat?'

'I bought it from a Portuguese nobleman who was tired of playing sea captain. It can only support a small crew, no more than five men but it's seaworthy. I could sail to the New World if I wished. Not yet though.'

She noted the workmanship, the immaculate condition of the hull, the neatly furled sails.

'If you are forever changing bodies, how do you acquire coin enough for such a fine vessel?'

'I also have a Chateau in Provence, an apartment in Paris and a vast fortune in antiquities.' He smiled. 'Over my many lives I have been a discerning collector of coins, jewellery, art and incriminating documents that might topple a kingdom. I bury my treasure in graves, dungeons, even more recently in my own backyard in France. Centuries later I dig it up and sell it for a fortune. This way I remain solvent and rich. As for my changing appearance I leave my estate to my next of kin, who is always male, always young and always me. It may take a month, or two, sometimes a year but when I find a new host I arrive with a Will confirming my claim on my own property.'

'Very risky.'

'It's worked for thousands of years.' He nudged the bundle. 'Won't you even look at what I bought you?'

'Later. When do you sail again?'

'Tomorrow. I have business in London two days' hence, then I return to France.'

'Take me with you.'

'The world is not ready for you yet.' He stared at the sea. 'I, too, long to sail beyond the horizon, conquer the world but while the Queen lingers on, my plans are stalled. There was a famine not long after you died, a drought that lasted three years until the heavens opened in 1597. But during those years the misfortune of the many unleashed the evil of the few. Engrossers bought up local supplies and sold them back to the poor at inflated prices. Greed worked like a slow poison in this land and the misery of the poor almost saw my plans come to fruition but tragically the Queen grew a conscience and did something about poverty.'

'She hung more paupers?'

'If only. That savagery would have served me. She passed a Poor Law in 1597, an act that levied a poor rate on each parish, relief for those too ill or too old to work, gave them *the parish loaf*, installed them in Alms houses. Perhaps at last she thought to secure a place in Heaven.'

'She belongs in Hell.'

'Fear not, my dear, I will welcome her in Hell ere long.'

'Can you be Master of two domains?'

'I prefer to be above ground.' He laughed. 'Neglect is a fitting punishment for my subjects below.' The laughter faded. 'I'm sorry she grew a conscience. The poor almost rose up until she made them comfortable. All the fight is gone from them now, but France may offer me a better opportunity. They have a new King, a baby born to a dead father and a mother jailed for his murder. There is a vacuum of power I could make use of.'

'Why wait for England? Or France? Why not conquer the New World?'

'Europe is my home. All my love affairs over the centuries were conducted in Paris and London, occasionally enroute. Call me sentimental but I can't leave all those delicious memories behind. And my treasures are buried there. I'd have to start all over again in the New World and the architecture would be so modern, so brutally Spanish.'

'Perhaps the locals built something more to your taste.'

'The Spanish murdered the locals and made ruins of their pyramids. No, there is no culture left there for me to inherit with my conquering. Maybe in a few hundred years we'll think about a visit. Speaking of visitors –' He collected the goblet, pulled a chair up next to hers, nodded down at the village. 'Has anyone been curious enough to climb up the goat track and call on you?'

161

'No-one. Sometimes when I sing I think they can hear me, especially on still nights when my voice carries. No doubt they think the Abbey is haunted.'

'I'd like to hear you sing.' He sipped his wine, gazed at the sea. 'Yes, the French Third Estate will rise. They have fire in their veins. This child, this new Henri is heir presumptive, Prince de Condé, his mother is a beauty wasting away in prison at Saint-Jean-d'Angély, accused of killing her husband. A very vulnerable family indeed.'

'Did she?'

'Did she what?'

'Kill her husband?'

'Not intentionally. He drank from a poisoned chalice. I may have had a hand in it. The woman is, as I said, a beauty and something of a devotee of mine. I have been a great friend to women. They have no power but spells and hexes, no friend but me. My father would have them hide their beauty behind a veil, serve men and bear children. I offer them power and appreciation. Yes, the beautiful Charlotte Catherine de La Trémoïlle turned to me when Catholicism failed to deliver comfort. I answered her prayers when no saint or angel did. My father was silent as usual.'

'And you poisoned her husband.'

'He was in the way, but dear Charlotte is no use to me in prison.' He leaned across, whispered in her ear. 'I did not save you from the flames to have you sit here like a corpse.'

'I have nothing else to do.'

'You sound just like Kit Marlowe! He was complaining last week –'

She swung around. 'I thought Marlowe died in a tavern brawl?'

'I paid the taverner to tell that story. The Queen was about to arrest him for heresy.'

'The Queen who believes in fairies? What a hypocrite.'

'A hypocrite who toadies to the Church.'

'She does not hide her love of Other.'

'The Church pays lip service to her fantasies even as they preach eternal damnation to her people. The English are too terrified to revolt against God's anointed vessel. A few Catholics have tried but they are buried in pieces. Yes, illustrious Gloriana uses torture as theatre to subjugate the masses. She signed off on your burning.'

'Where is Kit Marlowe?'

'In France, living like a king. I saved him from the pyre, too.'

'The Queen would have intervened for him. He's a national treasure.'

'He's dangerous: a genius and an atheist, a lethal combination. The lad was howling for me in the woods at Cambridge when he was an undergraduate, waking up the entire dorm.'

'Why didn't you answer him?'

'I had a perfectly good body and his genius hadn't yet flowered. I came for him when it was mutually beneficial. Kit Marlowe is alive and well and holed up in my Chateau in Provence where he writes plays with such scorching invectives against the elite, the common man will tear down the bastions of Church and State ere long and we may all leave our towers.'

'He cannot put his name to this work if he is dead.'

'I have another for that purpose. Marlowe's words will thresh the existing hierarchy and out of the chaos I will rise with promises of milk and honey.'

'People won't replace one tyrant with another.'

163

'They will for milk and honey.'

A smile broke across her face like sunlight for shadows. 'Marlowe lives.'

'Don't get too excited, my dear, he prefers men, preferably shirtless. Am I not handsome enough to please you?'

'You're not a creative genius.'

'I'm all you have. For eternity!' He marched across to the sideboard, retrieved the music and tossed it at her feet. 'Learn it. That's occupation enough for you until I rule the world.' Collecting four leatherjacks he slunk along the corridor and presently slammed a door.

Miriam picked up the wad of pages: First Booke of Songes or Ayres by John Dowland published in 1557, a book of single-voiced songs to be accompanied by the lute. She collected the lute and studied the first page, the music and words sirening off the staves. Plucking the strings, she began to sing, her voice drifting across the moonlit sea. A lone fisherman crossed himself against enchantment and in his room, suckling on his wine, the Devil curled his stolen body into a foetal ball and began to sob.

For the angel he once was.

For the family he had forsaken.

For all he might have been.

London 1600 – The Mermaid Tavern

The caravel was moored on the north bank of the Thames between London Bridge and the Tower, tethered in a forest of masts and furled sails, the vessels crawling with sunburnt brutes and lads scarce out of boyhood, all busy scalding and scrubbing decks while captains met with owners and investors to whom they gave reports of sales before receiving further orders. Stanas left his own crew to the same task, promising them coin for shore leave should he extend his visit beyond a single night. Otherwise they could wait for Marseille and La Rue Canebière, that colourful habitué of prostitutes, merchants and troubadours. In truth his business should only take two hours, the first hour in the arms of a lady whose rooms he paid for in Aldgate, the second with Will at the Mermaid Tavern. If all went as planned he should be back by midnight, asleep in his cabin, ready to sail at dawn.

**

His tryst in Aldgate took rather longer than planned, so intense was his need for reassurance after Miriam's slight and Kit's habitual lack of gratitude. He arrived at the Mermaid Tavern just as the Bowe Bells rang the eleventh hour. The crowd was young, loud, fevered with cheap ale and numbed by thwarted ambition. Standing in the doorway he scanned the room noting the shoulder-length hair and neatly cut beards and moustaches of the patrons. He would see a barber when he got back to France, catch up with the times, and advise Kit to do the same.

**

William Shakespeare had lied to his partners at the Globe, telling them he needed a week off to write a play so brilliant it would put their theatre at the forefront of English culture. A risky lie if his mentor failed to appear with the promised work.

'Meet me in the Mermaid Tavern in the last week of July,' Stanas had said in 1594 after handing William Shakespeare two superb scripts, *Romeo and Juliet* and *A Midsummer Night's*

165

Dream. 'I will have something even more extraordinary for you by then.'

Will had nudged the scrolled pages. 'These had best be good or the Burbages will suspect they're not my own work.'

'They surpass your work.'

The Bard winced. 'By whose measure?'

'Mine.' Stanas leaned closer, whispered, 'You want fame? These will secure it for you. Remember our bargain, Will.'

Will had swallowed his gorge and his pride. He needed to make his mark and quickly if he was to justify leaving his wife Anne and their three children in Stratford. He'd only been in London a year when Anne suggested he give up his foolish dream of theatrical fame, return to Stratford and take over his father's glove making business.

'I'll be here. Which night of the week and at what hour?'

'I'll be sailing from France; I can't guarantee the night or the hour. Tides and wind don't keep schedules. Just be here every night that week and I'll meet you when I can. With any luck the Queen will be dead by then and I can foment my plans.'

'Are you in line for the throne?' Will had asked.

'Every throne on earth. I am the Devil and you have just sold your soul.'

Will laughed but was silenced by a withering look.

'Put your name to those two plays and every subsequent play I give you and I guarantee you immortality.' Stanas collected his hat and stood up ready to leave. 'See that you keep our appointment in 1600.'

'1600!' Will sputtered. 'Six years' hence. How will I remember?'

Stanas narrowed his eyes. 'Write it down.'

166

Will muttered something under his breath and then said, 'How will *you* remember?'

'I never forget the deals I make. They're written in blood.'

Will swallowed. 'Deals?'

'Faustian. Immutable contracts. Your soul is mine whether you keep our appointment or not, so I'd advise you to be here, my temper is short and my reach is long.'

**

Will did not believe in the Devil, he wasn't fully convinced of God either, but he had great faith in providence. The plays his benefactor had given him had indeed secured his fame and if the gentleman imagined himself Beelzebub, Will was happy to play along, he was an actor after all. The truth was likely far more mundane, the author of *Romeo and Juliet* and *A Midsummer Night's Dream* wouldn't be the first peer of the realm to have his work staged under a pseudonym and Will Shakespeare, the emerging playwright from Stratford-upon-Avon, was happy to take his forgery to the grave.

**

As promised, William Shakespeare was at the Mermaid Tavern every night of the last week in July 1600. He sat at a window in view of the street, a bowl of oysters and a tankard of double beer in front of him. By Saturday night he worried his mentor had forgotten the meeting despite his claim that theirs was a deal forged in blood. He also worried he would be caught out in a lie by his partners, Richard and Cuthbert Burbage.

The Burbage brothers had built their own theatre in 1599 using timber from the theatre their father, James Burbage, had built in Shoreditch in 1576. They took out a twenty-one-year lease on a site in Southwark where they constructed a spectacular modern theatre they called The Globe. Will Shakespeare, the brightest star in the theatrical constellation since the death of Kit Marlowe, was offered a partnership. The brothers' confidence in Will's genius was affirmed by the two brilliant plays he wrote for the Curtain's 1596 season, *Romeo and Juliet* and *A Midsummer Night's Dream*.

The brothers offered to produce all Will's future work if he became a partner, illuminating his name for all time. He signed. It pained Will a little that his finest work was penned by someone else, but he squared his conscience with the thought that he was doing his anonymous benefactor a great service bringing his work to the stage. So when he had asked for a week off the Burbages happily granted it, laughing that if his new masterpiece overshadowed *Romeo and Juliet* and *A Midsummer Night's Dream*, the two outstandingly brilliant plays that had dwarfed his litany of Henrys, the lone Richard and his four comedies – Errors, Shrew, Gentlemen of Verona, and Love Labour's Lost – there would be no measuring his genius. They told him to take all the time he needed, a month if necessary.

'I might need a year,' he muttered, toying with the empty shells on his plate.

The beer was now tepid, the midsummer night's lingering warmth stultifying, his patience wearing thin and the expense of eating out every night on top of the rent he paid to the hairdresser for his room in Silver Street was eroding the savings earmarked for a three-storey house on the corner of Chapel Street and Chapel Lane in Stratford-upon-Avon, proof of his success when he retired and compensation for his long-suffering wife. He wished Ben Jonson had not lured him into a game of cards in the Mermaid's backroom at the beginning of the week. The debt meant he might have to give up *drinking in the smoke*, an expensive habit at 10 pence for a quarter of an ounce of tobacco but one that made bearable his grief and the subterfuge he cloaked, for the smoke had a strangely hypnotic effect, luring the mind into a place of absolute calm and benevolence where worry and grief evaporated like dew.

When the Bowe Bells rang the eleventh hour he gave up all pretence of hope, tossed back the warm beer, jammed on his hat, and resigned himself to dashing off a new play by Wednesday, probably another Henry if there were any left. Muttering to himself he marched straight into a gentleman dressed in a black velvet doublet and breeches, his fine cloak fringed with gold braiding and perched on his head, a hat with a waving tower of white ostrich feathers.

'Leaving so soon?'

Will looked up blearily. 'I've run out of patience and funds.'

'It's me, Will.'

Will blinked a few times, frowned. 'I've been here every night for the past week. I lied to my partners, lost at cards to Ben Jonson and have eroded my savings for my retirement and the house that will win back my wife assuming she hasn't been seduced by a local. Do you toy with all your accomplices, Beelzebub?'

'Keep your voice down. I may be a little late but I am here.' He ushered the disgruntled playwright to a corner table. 'I have what I promised and you mustn't be afraid of exposure for I assure you the writer can never be revealed. He is dead to this world.'

'Give me! Give me! Tell me not of fear.' He clawed the budget out of Stanas' hands, ripped at the knotted ribbon. 'So much depends on this. More than you know.'

'Oh? Has something happened?'

'I have lost someone since we last met.'

'Cheer up. This Masterpiece will make you immortal.'

169

Will peered at his mentor through a haze of smoke. 'More famous than Marlowe?'

'Marlowe is dead.'

'The Rose and the Curtain keep resurrecting him.'

The innkeeper materialised at the table, frowned at Will. 'Ben Johnson was looking for you earlier this evening, says you owe him money.' He turned to the well-dressed gentlemen opposite. 'What's your pleasure, my lord?'

Stanas handed the innkeeper a small bag of coins. 'A jug of your best wine, preferably French, and here is coin enough to cover my friend's debts.'

The innkeeper untied the bag, plucked a gold sovereign from within. 'This will see Master Shakespeare clear of debt and with credit.'

'Master Shakespeare is a genius. He deserves credit.'

'Every man is a genius when the wine persuades them.' He pocketed the coins and left.

Will teased open the budget and withdrew a script titled, *Hamlet, Prince of Denmark*. He dropped the pages, fell silent.

'Is something wrong?'

Will blinked several times. 'The loss I mentioned – it was my son, Hamnet. He drowned four years ago.'

Stanas cursed Marlowe under his breath. 'If I'd known –'

'But you didn't.' He returned the script to its silken womb. 'You did not need to buy my soul. I would have given it away for one more hour with my son.'

'I can only bestow what our bargain allows – immortality.'

The Abbey – 1604

170

Miriam ran her hands over the instruments – the virginals, the viol de gambier, an orpharion and a new lute. Beautiful pieces newly made and, apart from the lute, incomprehensible to her. She wished Master Trenery was there to instruct her, even Thomas could help but they were denizens of another world, another life, one side of a thousand conversations over supper or faces glimpsed in transit as they came and went from the kitchen. She wondered now if she ever really knew any of them apart from her mother.

Stanas had delivered the instruments piecemeal over visits between 1600 and 1604. Learning to play them would be occupation for her while his plans took shape he said. When she suggested he learn to play too he'd been churlish, claimed he had no time. She suspected he had no talent.

She had asked him if he'd ever heard the Music of the Spheres and after denying their existence he'd thrown a frightful tantrum and made a hasty exit. But on his next visit he attempted an explanation.

'I am mute in the expression of music.' He slapped his ears. 'These cloth ears muffle every melody I try to play but clarion the genius of others. If I am envious at all –'

'You are.'

'Thank you, Miriam, ever my conscience. I am envious of musicians and composers, those most radiant of souls, closest to –' he'd stopped speaking, tore away from the window, and retreated to the board where he poured himself a goblet of wine.

'God?' Miriam whispered.

'My father, yes. My father who lifts not a finger to relieve the suffering of –' again he stopped speaking, glowered into the middle distance.

'Humanity?' she offered.

'Me! In England right now there are composers of genius: John Farmer, Giles Farnaby, Michael Cavendish, John Dowland, Orlando Gibbons and William Byrd, all composing music of such elevation it echoes –'

'Heaven.'

'Heaven,' he muttered bitterly. 'What are they hearing, Miriam?'

'The Music of the Spheres.'

'The spheres do not exist.'

'But the music must or how can they hear it?'

'I don't know.' He gulped his wine, repoured. 'Have you heard it?'

'No. But I am only listening with my ears. I think it is heard with the soul and mine is forfeit now that it belongs to you.'

'I want to hear it!' He slapped the side of his head again. 'Why am I deaf to it when these musicians hear it so clearly? What is their gift? They are ordinary men. They have no special privilege. They sicken and die like other men. They love. They hate. They hunger and yet they are possessed of a genius I can only dream of. I am an angel, fallen yes, but an angel still with an angel's faculties and yet I lack the one talent that would have kept me home – the genius to hear music, not just any music but –'

'The Music of the Spheres.'

He rubbed his eyes. 'I couldn't hear it when I was bathed in light and witness to creation. I was cheated of the melodies my siblings absorbed like breath, the music that made my father weep.'

'Does God weep? The suffering here would argue against it.'

172

'He weeps for beauty.' He clenched his fists, trembled. 'I would make my father weep, if not for his lost son then for the music that issues from my soul. But there is none. My soul is mute.' He pierced Miriam with a look of such pain she took a step towards him, but he swung away savagely.

'Don't you dare pity me.' He swiped at tears, harnessed his emotions. 'Let us sit down together now. I will eat even if you won't.'

Miriam had cooked for him using the ingredients he had supplied: flour, eggs, butter, perch, garlic, onions, leeks, salt and sugar.

'The French cook everything in butter,' he said, hovering in the kitchen. 'Please cook the fish the French way.'

'Why don't you cook it?'

'I can't cook.'

'So you are mute in the culinary arts as well.'

He gave her a look that would extinguish anybody else. 'You're not afraid of me?'

She laughed. 'What can you do? Kill me?'

'Corrupt you.'

'Master Rathe did that. Take your seat at the table. I will serve you when it's ready.'

**

'This is delicious!' He skewered the last piece of fish. 'I am sorry you will not eat.'

'I have no appetite and what purpose would it serve? Forcing food into a corpse.'

'I wish you would try to see the benefits of your state. It's depressing the way you complain. You're no better than Kit.'

'I'd like to meet Kit.'

'Not if he lives a hundred years. You belong to me, and I am a jealous –' he shrugged. 'I'm not my father. He's a creative genius. I am mute.'

'You have plenty to say.' She picked up his soiled trencher.

'Please leave that. I have news from London.'

She stiffened. 'My mother?'

'No, the Queen. She died on the 24th of March last year.' Noting her puzzled expression he qualified. 'Last year was 1603, and James, the son of Mary Queen of Scots, was proclaimed King later that same day.'

'This serves your plan.'

He sighed. 'No, I thought the people would reject Mary's son but they love him.'

'Isn't that what you wanted?'

'I wanted them to hate him so much he feared for his life and then I'd –'

'Steal his inheritance.'

'Wheedle my way into Court and,' he shrugged, 'yes, take control but he was lavishly entertained by sycophantic English lords all the way from Edinburgh to London and when he arrived on the 7th of May, just nine days after the Queen's funeral, he was greeted by cheering crowds. He doesn't need me. But in better news Will Shakespeare is famous thanks to the genius of Marlowe –'

'The genius of Marlowe? What do you mean?'

'Shakespeare is the Bard who passes off Kit's plays as his own.' He refreshed his wine. 'I tell Kit what to write, propaganda against the Church and the Monarchy, and the Globe Theatre stages them.'

She frowned. 'Why would Shakespeare agree to such an obvious pretence? Anyone who loves theatre would recognise Kit's style.'

'They both write in iambic pentameter and even though his work has dramatically improved one might argue that every writer has peaks and troughs.'

'Marlowe doesn't.'

'I agree, which is why I saved him. Shakespeare is wildly ambitious. It was easy to buy his soul.'

'It's not fair to Kit.'

'Kit Marlowe died in a tavern brawl in 1593. How could I in all conscience let his genius die with him?' He took a long draft of wine. 'That's something my father would do.'

II

See how the moon lights up my smile
Ignites my hair like summer fire
And splashes silver in the corners of my eyes
My eyes are green
A summer field bewitched with dew
And emeralds too, and in my heart a woman's innocent desire.

The Abbey – 1633

She spoke the words out loud; aligned the rhythm to the melody she had notated. Now for the first time she played and sang her own song, the melody rising from the virginals she had taught herself to play in the timeless drift between visits from the Devil. Her first song began as a whisper and was now a full-voiced ayre, instrument and voice blending in perfect synthesis.

'I'm a composer.' She shook her head in disbelief, looked at the sky framed in the eyeless window. 'I'm a composer, Mam.'

The seasons had threaded into years; how many had passed she knew not for the outside world did not intrude or inform her stasis. She found comfort in the music and words that poured from her soul and now that she could give them voice they were company. The craving for vengeance had mellowed into pragmatism. With an eternity to fill she could bide her time. True enough, Master Rathe had escaped justice but England was full of Rathes and one would do as well as another to sate her hatred and wasn't it a service to rid the world of such carrion?

'How is Kit?'

They were seated at the table, the winter sun filling the room with tepid warmth and frail light. The terns had raised their young over summer and departed, migrating south to spend winter in the warmer southern climes. Their nests were empty, ragged and in need of repair.

The birds would return in spring, retracing their path over the featureless sea. They would find the Abbey, repair the nests, and start the cycle of life all over again.

'Forget Kit. He won't live forever like you.' He sipped his wine. 'My crew tells me that the villagers think the Abbey is haunted.'

Miriam froze. 'They must have heard me singing. On still nights my voice carries. I will try not to sit so close to the window next time I sing.'

'Let them think it's haunted. They'll leave you alone. Kit is well since you ask. He's writing even more brilliant plays and complaining that he's imprisoned.' Stanas laughed. 'He could leave any time he wished. Nobody would recognise him now. But he won't leave, he's too lazy and too comfortable. I must find a new playwright with galloping ambition and a soul he is keen to sell.'

'Has Shakespeare reneged on your deal?'

'Shakespeare died in 1616.'

'What year is it?'

'1633. Kit's plays have yet to plant the seeds of insurrection. If anything they have had the opposite effect, insulating the mob against servility. My plans are stalled, Miriam.'

'So I am trapped here?'

'Not forever.' He tossed a budget on the table. 'Kit's latest play.'

Over the years Stanas had brought Kit's plays to her to read before having them copied and delivered to

Shakespeare. The originals he secreted in France in lepers' graves ready to be disinterred in the distant future and sold for a fortune should his plans fail. Miriam was in love with Marlowe's words, half in love with the progenitor. Of all his plays the most chilling was MacBeth, the tragedy of a murdered King. Stanas had found it rather grim and wasn't sure if it sent the right message to the people but Miriam heard only the music in his words, the hint of Heaven that permeated even the darkest exchange.

'Kit's words could bring Heaven to earth.'

'I don't want Heaven. I want chaos. Witches, madness, evil, regicide. This is the way his mind turns after the long years of my hospitality. Do you still wish to meet him? He's scarce human now.'

'And what am I? A blushing maiden? I want to meet Kit and I'm sure he would love to slip his prison. I know I would.'

'Where would you go, Miriam? A woman alone. The world still treats women as second-class citizens, only useful for breeding and servicing men.'

'How many centuries must I wait before it is safe for me to walk abroad?'

'Your lot will change when I rule.'

She toyed with the pomegranates he had brought her as a treat. 'Did you only leave Heaven because you could not hear its music?'

He closed his eyes. 'The only deaf angel in Heaven, the only one lacking harmony. Everybody else knew the score.' He clenched his fists. 'Why am I different? Why am I so lacking in the gifts lavished on my siblings? Who made me?'

'Maybe you are base-born like me – father unknown.'

'I don't even know who my mother was.' He leapt up, paced. 'I want to be exceptional, admired, revered, worshipped, all the things that are an angel's due, but for that I must live amongst the similarly deaf, the inferior ranks of sentience, gross humanity who will worship me ignorant of my limited genius.'

Miriam split one of the pomegranates revealing a centre shiny and pink with glutinous clusters of seeds. 'There is no flesh. What do you eat?'

'The seeds.' He stared out the window. 'My father hates me.'

'He hates us all. What kind of father allows one son to be crucified, another lost and the rest of us suffering?' Miriam lifted a shiny cell of seeds to her mouth, tasted. 'The flavour bites my tongue. I'm sorry, it's too much for me to bear. My senses have heightened since my death.' She pushed the trencher away. 'Even among the deaf there are those here on earth who hear the music you cannot. Musicians, composers. It cannot be beyond you.'

He slammed his fist on the table. 'Must you always remind me of my shortcomings?'

'I'm sorry.' She ran her hands over the blue velvet stomacher and gown he had brought her. 'I did not thank you for this beautiful gown.'

He softened. 'That you wear it so beautifully is thanks enough.'

'I'm sorry, Stanas, I'm a bitter creature, full of grief, twisted with a vengeance I can never satisfy and I have no-one to talk to but the Devil.'

'At least I am here sharing the constraints of humanity.'

'And the pleasures now denied me.'

'We are both miserable creatures.' He sank back down. 'Shall we speak of other things, the world out there?'

179

'The world I have no place in?'

'That world.' He pointed out the window at the sky.

'Heaven? Why would you want to speak of your father's world?'

'I don't. I want to talk about infinity where new worlds are being born each moment. One day when science catches up with the birds and greedy men seek further conquests we will fly into that blue eternity in ships that defy gravity as surely as my caravel rides the tide. It will happen, it's in man's nature to seek,' he paused, 'bounty.'

She looked into the sun-bleached sky. 'The Church says earth is the only world, the centre of everything.'

'The Church and its self-aggrandising myths. Earth is a minor world in a vast empire of worlds and in our tiny corner of that empire the sun is the centre of –'

'The Spheres?'

'No. You must let go of this fantasy.' He squeezed his eyes shut for a long beat. 'The sun is the centre of our little family of planets of which the earth is a minor sibling and beyond our family there are countless other families stretching to infinity.' With his thumb and his index finger he circled the sun framed in the window. 'The sun is a ball of fire that will one day turn to ash. The earth is a lump of rock, a wanderer, as the Greeks call it and our little family of wanderers circles the sun held by the same force that plummets an apple to earth.'

She shifted her attention to the sentinel headland. 'Or a boy to his death when he missteps a ledge?'

He looked at her for a long moment. 'You saw this?'

She nodded. 'How do birds defy this force when they leap from the same headland?'

'They float on the currents of air much as a boat floats on water.'

'And do the stars float in the sky?'

'No, they are held fast by countering forces: gravity, momentum. Just as the planets defy the grip of gravity by flying forward, permanently trying to escape the sun's hold. If the planets were to slow even for a second they would fall into the sun and burn.'

'So everything is forever fleeing death.'

'Except us. We are immortal. We must keep faith with each other just as the stars must keep faith with their opposing forces. If they were to slow their transverse even for a moment they would plunge into the abyss that hovers like a spider at the centre of the universe, a spider with a hunger so voracious it will one day consume everything in its path.'

'But why does God allow the inevitable destruction of his creation?'

'So that he might have the pleasure of starting all over again. Father enjoys his games.'

'And what will become of us?'

'We'll be swallowed up along with the rest. My kingdom will be subsumed into my father's game. He must win, Miriam. He hates losing, even a sparrow's fall is marked. But we have time to explore before the end comes, time to make other plans, maybe even outplay him.'

She fell silent for a few beats. 'God is no better than the spider.'

'God *is* the spider.' Stanas poured a fresh goblet of wine.

'I saw a star fall straight through the spheres.'

'There are no spheres.' He waved his hand across the sky framed in the window. 'No walls dividing, not of glass or stone or rules. It goes on forever, eternally evading the spider.'

'What does the spider want?'

'Life. But nothing fills the empty space where a soul or a conscience might dwell.'

'Like the Queen.'

'You met the Queen?'

'Only in passing. Her eyes were empty and yet she gorged herself.'

'Like my father.' He yawned. 'I am tired. This body is getting old and needs more sleep. If a stranger finds his way to you in a year or two it's only me. I will bring you books next visit, Copernicus, Galileo, Gilbert. They will feed that hungry mind of yours.'

'1633.' She went to the window, leaned against the sill. 'My mother and everyone I have ever loved are dead. I caught my reflection in a pond yesterday. I have not aged at all.'

'You never will. Kit is an old man of nine and sixty but embalmed in my Chateau safe from plagues and worries he could pass for forty. He still wears his hair long; it dangles halfway down his back. I told him it was unfashionable, but enough of Kit Marlowe. Sing for me. I need music.'

She sang the song she had written about the boy who died, told in song how she had longed to kiss him and taste death in his final breath.

The Abbey – 1633

She had seen the boy die, watched from her eerie as he leapt from the cliff, his body falling like a leaf, curling and twisting before limply succumbing to death. He lay smashed on the rocks below, a smearing of pink and white flesh, the sea breeze quivering his green jerkin as if it were a broken wing. Her sights, so keen since her death, saw the dead face fixed in a silent scream, the tussled curls crusting with bright red blood that seeped from his shattered skull. To get a closer look at her fellow outlier she climbed down at dusk, crossed the beach in plain sight of the fishermen returning with their catches. Being swift and unexpected, they failed to notice the woman in a black nun's habit dashing barefoot across the sand.

She picked her way around the rocky platform at the base of the opposite cliff, mindful of the writhing return of scavenger crabs to their tidal pools, sanctuaries they shared with anemones and fry, oysters, cockles and tiny blue periwinkles. At the boot of the cliff she found the boy, the sea licking his feet, one bare, the other shod in a stained buskin. His vacant eyes were pale blue, glassily fixed on the sky, his freckled face was prematurely wearied with lines. The screaming mouth showed four blackened teeth and a coated yellow tongue. She examined the dead hand, the blistered palm, read there the years of labour. The potted belly, emaciated chest, corrugation of ribs spoke of hunger.

'I'm sorry the world drove you to this,' she said, resting the dead hand on the thin chest. 'They burned me.'

She kept vigil over the poor broken body until a single belching wave carried him out to sea where his body would feed her scaled masses. Under cover of dark she returned to her lonely roost, wondering if she might have tasted death had she been there, waiting beneath the waves when he plunged. If she had kissed him could she have shared his final breath and glimpsed Heaven in that bittersweet flight?

It was then that an idea was born. If she could risk the immersion in water she might be fortunate enough to be there next time someone leapt, might be able to taste death vicariously in a kiss, sense the spider, glimpse the light. With no need for air she could not drown. It was just a matter of facing her fear of water.

**

'Have you ever bathed?' she asked Stanas during his next visit.

He jerked his head up from his meal – fish again. 'Are you suggesting I smell bad?'

'No, I am asking you if you're afraid of water.' She refilled his goblet. 'Do you believe it opens the pores and allows the noxious fumes that carry disease to enter the body?'

'Water is safe if it runs, better yet if it passes through alluvial deposits or sedimentary rock –' he paused upon seeing her puzzled expression. 'Alluvial deposits are the effluence of rivers: silt, gravel, sand. Sedimentary rocks are porous rocks like sandstone. If water passes through these mediums it emerges free of putrefaction and can be safely bathed in or drunk. Likewise rain collected in a clean vessel is safe to drink and indeed *should* be drunk. Water flushes out the body's impurities. It is nature's cure for most ills.'

'Our wisest apothecaries and most skilled doctors believe that bathing is dangerous.'

'The Greeks have been bathing for centuries. They are far ahead of the rest of the world. In the fourth century BC a Greek explorer named Pytheas was mapping these isles while Britons were still hunting in packs. After exploring the frozen north, he returned to Greece with tales of a midnight sun, a sky burning with green fire, the earth wearing a cap of permanent blue ice, nights so short they passed in an hour and Britons so savage they still wore furs and lived in caves. This last revelation astonished his

184

countrymen more than anything else he reported and in the luxury of communal baths the nature of Britons was discussed. Were they animals or some long lost link in the chain of human evolution?' He laughed. 'The question remains.'

She looked at him for a long moment. 'Who's Pytheas?'

'A geographer, explorer and astronomer born in Massalia in 350BC.'

'And he bathed?'

'Yes, my dear Miriam, as well as exploring the known world he bathed.'

'Would seawater be safe to bathe in?'

'Too salty but you can swim in the sea if you can manage the tides and the undercurrents. Why? Do you think to swim?'

'I can't swim but nor can I drown so yes, I think to immerse myself in the sea.'

'Don't get washed out past the breakers. My boat may not be moored in the cove ready to rescue you.'

'I will manage.' She handed him a dish of marchpanes shaped into rosebuds. 'I made these to thank you for all the gowns and jewels you've given me.'

He took a bite, licked his lips. 'Perfection.'

'My mother taught me.'

'Why do you want to swim? Do you mean to drown a fisherman?'

'Perhaps.'

Stanas leaned back in his chair. 'He won't be the man who sent you to the flames.'

'I know.' She fretted the napkin into pleats. 'But somehow I must expiate my hatred.'

'The man who betrayed you is long in his crypt. You still live. Surely that's vengeance enough.'

'I barely exist let alone live. You promised me vengeance.'

'I am the Devil.' He reached for the leatherjack. 'I never keep my promises.'

Miriam's eyes glittered. 'Then you had best lock your door.'

'If you kill me you will never meet Kit Marlowe.'

'Another promise?'

'Miriam we only have each other for eternity. If you must have revenge drown some fishermen. It will make you feel better. Now some music please.'

The moon was a silver sickle, brilliant as a newly forged dagger. It cast a jagged light upon the crests, rimed the sill. Miriam plucked at the lute; sang the song she had written after seeing her reflection in the rock pool. Stanas closed his eyes and allowed himself to enter an altered world where ambition and plans reshaped into accomplishments.

III

Is that a wrinkle on my brow, a tiny frown, a marked disturbance?
Have I aged?
And in my hair, a thread of snow, a hint of silver or the moonlight
playing tricks
And does the sorrow in my eyes betray a feeling, an emotion?
Is it love?

The Abbey – 1ˢᵗ February 1649

The late winter's day was clear and warm. After being couped up throughout the long months of a sodden, grey, and seemingly endless winter, Miriam spread a blanket on the grassy knoll in front of the Abbey and sat in the sun to read one of the books Stanas had given her: *De Magnete* by William Gilberd, a physician, physicist and Natural Philosopher.

The sky was uninterrupted by cloud or breeze, the sea unruffled all the way to the horizon. She had started reading *De Magnete* earlier that winter but cast it aside confused by its complex concepts but sitting outside in the clear light of a mild winter's day Gilberd's ideas gained shape and traction. He wrote of a universe connected and held secure by an invisible force he called *electricus*, which meant *like amber*, the ancient resin formed from the blood of trees and possessed of a measurable power of both attraction and repulsion, as if it breathed.

'*There is a force, a general force that permeates everything*,' she read aloud. 'Everything,' she repeated slowly, looking out to where sea and sky met in a thin indigo band. 'Sea and sky. Heaven and earth. Me and this headland. The boy who died and the people who drove him to it. All connected by a force that both pushes and pulls us into action.'

The sea was so still it reflected the sky and a lone bird articulating slow circles in search of a meal. Gilberd went on to write that *between all solid objects there existed friction, a discernible "effluvium" and it was this friction that created the attraction that held the moon in its diurnal orbit around the earth and the earth in her annual traverse around the sun.*

Miriam glanced up at the sun, held her hand up to shield her eyes against its fiery glare. 'And what holds you in place?'

Perhaps the sun depended on an altogether different force.

She returned to the book and the ideas that were in such delicious conflict with Genesis.

'*The electric effluvia differ much from air, and as air is the earth's effluvium, so electric bodies have their own effluvia; and each peculiar effluvium has its own individual power of leading to union, its own movement to its origin, to its fount, and to the body emitting the effluvium.*' She looked up again. 'And by this measure I must still possess a soul. My effluvium?' She left the question dangling. 'My soul, if I still have one, would in turn attract other souls and yet I have been alone these many years, my only visitor, the Devil.' She shuddered. 'At least it's not the spider.'

She read on. '*The idea that there are spheres housing the fixed stars is nonsense due to the inordinate distance of the celestial spheres. If the spheres exist at all, it is an absurd idea that they would rotate every twenty-four hours, as opposed to the rotation of the relatively tiny sphere of the earth. How far away from the earth are those remotest of stars: they are beyond the reach of eye, or man's devices, or man's thought. Housed in thinnest aether, or in the most subtle fifth essence, or in vacuity*

– how shall the stars keep their places in the mighty swirl of these enormous spheres composed of a substance of which no one knows aught? What an absurdity is this motion of spheres.'

She stopped reading. 'But is there music?' She put the book aside, stared across the acres of blue to the horizon. 'I want to believe in the spheres if only for the music. I want to believe in God's Heaven for my mother. A spider weaves a beautiful luring web and the trapped may defy gravity for weeks, months, perhaps centuries before the spider feasts. I would risk God's web to see my mother again, to hear that music. But if cannot die I will never see my mother again and the music will play on without me.'

She sat a long time in silence, her body becoming her surroundings: the salt air, the vivid blue of sea and sky, the warmth of the sun, all felt as a faint ripple on her skin but failing to find traction within where her soul may yet be housed.

Into this void Stanas erupted.

'They executed the King!'

'You have a new body.'

'You like it? Kit's madly envious.' He tossed two bundles at her feet. 'New clothes from Paris, the latest fashions for you and food for me.'

She made no move to examine either bundle.

'I've bought you a red velvet gown and a purple cloak. You won't see their like at Court or in any fine house in the land.'

'Why not? The sumptuary laws allow the rich to wear whatever pleases them – silk, lawn, velvet – whilst their servants itch under buckram, bays and linsey-wolsey.'

He removed a scarlet velvet gown, held it up to the sun, the fabric glowing like flame. 'The scarlet dye is made from kermes, a parasitic larva from the Mediterranean. You won't see this colour on any lord or lady in England. Will you wear this gown tonight?'

'My old nun's habit will do. I have no callers apart from you and this old habit does not itch. It's been worn to smoothness. I would thank the previous owner for the comfort she provided but like me, she's dead.'

'I see there's no cheering you.' He folded the gown and returned it to the budget, flopped down beside her, stretched out his legs. 'The house of Stuart is dead. England has no monarch. The country is being run by a soldier!' He laughed. 'Charles managed to cause a civil war, incur debts of a million pounds, dissolve parliament and lose his head! I couldn't have planned it better myself. We're on our way, Miriam.'

'Who rules England?'

'Oliver Cromwell, not even a peer of the realm. Of course he couldn't have done it without an army behind him, but the man is a savage, famed for his brutality in Ireland. He won't last a year.' He lay down and closed his eyes. 'It's all going according to plan. We'll be a handsome couple on the coins.'

'There are no spheres.'

'I told you that.'

'William Gilberd declares it impossible, so there is no music.'

'We'll make our own. They beheaded Charles two days ago – the first time a King has been beheaded. It was marvellous.'

She collected the book and the bundles and stood. 'I will cook you supper.'

He sat up, grasped her wrist. 'Your skin is cold.'

'I am dead. What do you expect?'

190

'Warmth, I suppose. Never mind, very soon your life will be filled with celebration and music and joy. You will not mourn the life you had or long for a heavenly one. You won't even want revenge. You'll be happy, Miriam.'

Just then the circling seabird dived into the sea and rose with a fish flapping in its beak.

'That bird has been hunting all day.'

Stanas watched it a moment. 'Patience is always rewarded.'

The Cove – 1650

The sea rocked back and forth, testing the limits of its reach as a songbird might peck at the bars of its cage. Her hair floated around her like a veil lifted in the wind. She was naked, her skin silvered by moonlight, the water a nascent embrace, at once secure but also as tinglingly intimate as the coupling with Master Rathe had been all those years ago. The night amplified the slap of wavelets against the boot of the cliff, the sucking withdrawal of the tide, the soft groaning surge back again as the ocean rocked itself to unquiet sleep.

Midnight and the bells of the village church rang out the witching hour. She heard the stumbling footfall of a drunk expelled from the tavern, his complaints a blurred muttering. A momentary silence as he adjusted his passage and headed for the beach, his sudden change of direction doubtless the avoidance of an angry wife at home.

Miriam, treading water just beyond the breakers, watched him make his halting way to the water's edge where he swayed, looking up at the full moon. He had not seen her, could not expect her. Earlier that day she had made her way down the goat track, the first time since she had ventured out

191

to see the dead boy. She was ready to test the water and explore the submarine world at her doorstep.

Shedding and secreting her clothes in a cave above the waterline she dived off a rocky indent on the plateau where the sea was corralled in a deep green pool, its contours sheer and slippery. A sudden wave might smash her against those rocks, an impact that would shatter a living person like glass, but her body was *Other*, solid and fixed, even her hair could not be pulled from her head. She had tried. The result painful and pointless, not a single hair quit her skull, nor had it grown in the years since her death but retained its fiery fall to her knees.

The water had been bitingly cold and surprisingly dense, but having submitted to it she relaxed and began to explore a liquid world, strange and marvellous, sea grasses waving as if motioned by zephyrs, schools of fish, silver flashes turning in coordinated patterns like a dance. Deeper and the water shifted into meridian blue and turquoise tones, stray arrows of sunlight dappling the sand. She turned her body horizontally to the seabed and flapped her arms as she had seen the birds do. This created a forward movement like flight, adding a kick she began to fly over the corrugated floor. She quit the safety of the pool and ventured out into the open sea where the seabed dropped away as dramatically as the cliff's edge. Panicking, she reflexed a grip as if she was falling, but the water, seemingly infinite as the night sky, held her aloft with a reassuring pressure. Her heightened senses thrilled to a cornucopia of new sensations and she allowed the current to pull her away from the beach and further out to sea where the light faltered through water opaque and cloudy as a London fog.

Flashing past her, fish of all sizes, some with glittering scales, others with leathery grey skin. A sudden squall of snaggle-finned fish parted around her showing no curiosity in their silent, silver-eyed flight. Halting her own flight she assumed an upright position, gripping the stem of a giant seagrass in a gently waving forest, anchoring herself against the tide. At this depth, the water had a cloudiness that made phantoms of its occupants, but a sudden bright arrow of sunlight revealed a wrecked ship lying just below her on the seabed, masts streaming with ribbons of tattered sails. She let go of the kelp and dived down to inspect it. The wreck was a galleon, Spanish rather than French, the hull Carvel built, the prominent squared stern gashed with a cannon ball. It must have been a magnificent vessel, undoubtedly stolen by pirates who limped it all the way up the English coast hoping for safe harbour only to be wrecked within sight of land. She wondered what kind of cargo the ship had carried and was grimly informed when another shaft of sunlight flared on the white of bones of men chained together in the hold. Slaves. The ignoble trade in the New World was evidently so lucrative and so ungoverned that pirates could participate in the market until a cannon ball sent them to the bottom of the sea. There was no evidence of the crew or the captain, no doubt long consumed by the residents of a world beyond human governance. Why they had not unshackled these poor wretches only confirmed her opinion that mankind was inherently evil, a condition that should have made Stanas' ambitions to rule the world easily achievable had there not been so much competition for the stewardship.

Sickened by the sight of such inhumanity, she swam away from the wreck and headed back towards the beach, stopping a few metres below a surface brindled with elliptical shadows, the underbellies of fishermen's ketches. She picked her way through a tangle of lines and a trapping of nets and swam to the plateau on the far side of the beach, there to hide until sunset when she would make her way home but when day closed and a full moon silvered the crests, she lingered, enchanted by the beauty of a kingdom no man could trespass, where she was safe to observe the changing face of the unframed night. She was enjoying her autonomy until the drunk materialised like a ghost at midnight and ignited in her a longing that had been growing over the years of solitude. The longing for vengeance.

Time had fermented her loss into blame and blame into hate and as Stanas had observed drowning a fisherman might make her feel better. It might also gift her a taste of death and a glimpse of Heaven.

The drunk did not notice the water lapping over his boots, his eyes were upon the moon as if hypnotised. He was young, his face unlined, unlike the dead boy's whose weariness fissured him. Either the ale preserved his hope, or it erased his contempt, for nothing showed on his face beyond the foolish smile presently playing at the corners of his mouth.

Miriam watched him until the local church bells rang the solitary morning hour. The chime returned him to his surroundings for he shook his head and blinked as if released from a dream. That's when he saw her, his eyes widening in terror, his hand reflexing the sign of the cross over his chest. She had a split second to enchant him before he turned and fled.

She sang.

The sound of a human voice issuing from the lips of a mermaid gave him pause. The song was familiar, he had heard it in the tavern a hundred times or more but never sung so beautifully. Without losing a beat she began to walk through the sea towards him, revealing inch by inch, a woman of exceptional beauty, her body naked and silvered in moonlight. The young man watched her, bewitched and powerless to move beyond the edge of the sea. She was so unexpected and so beautiful he ignored the rising tide, the waters lapping around his ankles, his boots sinking into the wet sand. Miriam, her hair mantling a body perfectly proportioned and glistening wet as if she wore a second jewelled skin, held her arms out to him, beseeching, inviting. The familiar song ended and she began a new one of her own making with hypnotically suggestive words.

The water's soft against my skin
Sweet boy you're welcome to come in and drown with me
A single kiss, share your last breath
A taste of salt, a taste of death
Come in
Come in
The brilliant moon is beckoning
Forbidden love, delicious sin
Come in
Come in.

She did not mask her intentions and therein lay a brand of honesty. If he followed her into the writhing sea it was his choice. Holding first his eyes and then his hands she urged him into the waves. Entranced, he allowed himself to be led into the rising wash, the shock of cold, the loss of traction barely marked as he floated in her arms. Further and further out she drew him, past the breakers, past the horseshoe promontories and into the open sea where she stopped and there with only the moon to anchor them she ceased her song and in the ensuing silence her eyes, green and glittering, held him tranced.

'I cannot swim,' he said at last.

She smiled with a warmth that did not reach her eyes.

'Are you a seelie?' His teeth were beginning to chatter, the words hyphenated, disconnected. 'Where's your skin?'

She did not answer, but held him above the water, her legs moving in gentle circles that kept them both afloat.

'Can we go ashore now? My wife will be wondering where I am.'

'You had no thought of your wife when you followed me into the sea.'

'How could I help it? You are so beautiful.' His body stiffening into resistance.

'So her betrayal is my fault?' Her eyes grew suddenly wide, hate-filled, at odds with the kiss she pressed against his mouth. Resistance being futile he submitted to an embrace he never dared expect. The most beautiful woman he had ever seen was kissing him with lips icy and hard as stone. A flip of her legs as if they were a tail and she descended into the black depths with the young man in her arms.

Terrified, he thrashed and bucked but she held him in a vicelike grip, her mouth still covering his. The black water closed around them in an impenetrable suffocating fog. With all his remaining strength he attempted one last thrust against her hold. The unexpected force almost dislodged him, but she tightened her grip and inhaled, stealing the last gasp of air from his lungs which emptied and crumpled under the weight of the water. He died in her arms and she had not had the satisfaction of tasting death or feeling avenged. Her mouth filled with a pungent blend of stale breath fumed with ale.

Disgusted, she released the dead weight and swam to the promontory beneath the Abbey where an obliging wave deposited her on the plateau. She collected her clothes and hurried naked back up to her eerie where she sat on the edge of the cliff, watching the young man's body bob and rock on the tide and finally wash up on the beach, a deflated thing bearing little resemblance to the drunk she had despatched.

As the flaming sun rose a sense of justice warmed her.

'Stanas is right, after all. Patience is always rewarded. You betrayed your wife just like Rathe did,' she told the dead thing on the beach. 'I have rid the world of a cuckquean.'

Provence – 1655

The Chateau was quiet. Too quiet. Nobody greeted him when the carriage rumbled up the drive and came to rest outside the fan of stone steps that led to the double front doors. Those doors did not open. No servants emerged to collect his luggage. He alighted cautiously, checking the grounds, no sign of the gardeners.

'What has happened here?' he asked under his breath.

The driver was waiting for his fare. Stanas tossed a bag of silver livres, generous for a three-day trip from the port of Marseille to Provence, but the ingrate sniffed as he counted the coins.

'C'est généreux et vous le savez,' said Stanas, impatient for the fellow to leave but the surly wretch was taking his time counting the coins and it occurred to Stanas that his arrogance might be due to a shift in fortunes for his class. 'Y a-t-il eu une révolution à Paris?'

'Non.' The driver shrugged, then added, 'Il est grand temps qu'il le fasse.' He looked up at the banks of windows, sneered at the luxury and grandeur of the recently renovated façade. 'Vous devriez avoir plus de sécurité dans un Château que vous seul occupez.'

'I don't live alone,' Stanas snarled. 'Vous pouvez y aller maintenant. Vous avez le temps avant le coucher du soleil d'atteindre une auberge and you have more than enough coin for a whore to complain to as she warms your bed,' he added in English under his breath.

'Mes chevaux ont besoin d'eau et de foin,' growled the coach-driver, nodding at the two skinny nags that had miraculously completed the journey from Marseilles.

Clearly the wretch wanted a room for the night and clearly he believed Stanas lived alone. Who would be the wiser if a rich man's throat was cut in the night, his silver and plate loaded into an empty coach and if there had been a Revolution in his absence, who would care?

'You'd best find an Inn before sunset if your horses live that long,' Stanas muttered. 'I said, vous feriez mieux de trouver une auberge avant le coucher du soleil. Allez!'

The driver flipped the reigns with a curse, bullying his aged nags into a reluctant gallop. Stanas watched the carriage clear the grounds before he crept around the back. Trouble, if there was any, would find a salutary mark in the castle's châtelaine. He peered in through the kitchen window, saw only a scullery maid washing dishes.

'Où est tout le monde?' he asked as he pushed open the door.

The girl swung around startled, sudsy hand pressed to her chest. 'Mon Dieu!'

'Hardly.' He noticed that her eyes were red-rimmed, her face streaked with tears. 'Que s'est-il passé?'

'C'est M. Marlowe. Il est en train de mourir.' A fresh flooding of tears rendered her almost insensible. 'Il n'a pas quitté son lit depuis quinze jours! Quinze jours!'

'Fifteen days in bed? Hardly cause to send for a priest.' He clicked his tongue. 'Kit would never leave his bed if necessity did not drive him from it.'

The girl did not understand English but stared at him as if waiting for something: a word, an order, a miracle.

'Et c'est là que les restes du déjeuner de Marlowe?' Stanas asked the girl if Marlowe had stopped eating, suspecting he already knew the answer. Kit's appetites had scarcely diminished in all the years he had sheltered him and he doubted that even imminent death could dull that hunger.

This question about Kit's appetite elicited a hiccupping of tears. 'M. Marlowe n'a bu que le vin.' She sniffed. 'Beacoup de vin. Il ne pouvait pas toucher à son repas.'

So Kit could manage wine but not food. 'Quels vins?'

The girl dabbed her tears with the corner of her apron. 'Les vins appelés catépument, raspis, osy, Capri, Rumney.'

'All my best wines! If that ingrate wasn't dying before he will be now.'

'Monseigneur?'

'That damned knave. All right, arrêtez de travailler et allez pleurer quelque part. Aller!'

The girl scampered off into a hallway, one of the many tributaries he had never, nor *would* ever, bother exploring. He flung off his hat and coat, dropped them on the kitchen table and headed upstairs to Marlowe's bedroom to see if it was true that his dependent genius was in fact dying.

There were no signs of occupation along the hallways, no maids cleaning, polishing, or gossiping. It was as if the entire household had died or was in the process of dying along with Marlowe. Closer to the playwright's bedroom he heard the unmistakable sounds of whispered concern. The door stood open and he lingered a moment assessing the situation. Expecting to find Marlowe prostrate and beyond the reach of sympathy or prayer he saw his errant houseguest propped up in his bed on a plumping of red velvet cushions, the pages of a manuscript scattered over the brocade coverlet and within arm's reach a set of quills and pots of ink jostled for traction on a side table crowded with the remains of a sumptuous feast, two jugs and a Venetian glass half-full of red wine.

The entire household was attending him. The maids were applying hot compresses to his hands and the stockingless feet poking out from beneath the brocade, the two young male gardeners Stanas had hired last spring to replace the elderly originals were huddled in the corner with a brand-new staff member, a handsome young ostler, riding crop in hand.

Stanas judged Marlowe's imminent demise to be grossly exaggerated. He cleared his throat and everyone, including Marlowe, gaped at him as if a ghost had just appeared. A few crossed themselves.

'Hello Kit. I see you've learned sufficient French to puppet the entire household.'

'I am dying,' said Kit in a voice scarcely above a whisper.

'Not today I'd suggest.'

Kit sat bolt upright scattering the pages of the manuscript onto the floor, knocking the damp compresses out of the maids' hands. 'Aller! Aller!' he said with considerably more volume.

The startled maids scampered from the room.

'Et vous,' Kit added somewhat more gently to the three young men.

'I don't recognise the ostler,' said Stanas after the servants had left.

'He looks after the horses. I hired him last week when he came here begging for work.'

'How altruistic of you. Why did he bring his riding crop to your sickroom?'

Kit shrugged. 'Discipline never goes astray.'

'I'll have you horsewhipped if you don't recover instantly.'

'So now you presume to tell me when I may or may not die?'

'You are not dying Kit Marlowe judging by the amount of my best wine you've consumed and before you employ a boy to whip you –'

Kit opened his mouth to protest but shut it again.

'I am careful who I employ. You and I both share the distinction of being dead and the last thing we need is resurrection. Now get up.'

'Aren't you even curious about my new play?' Kit lifted a single page of the manuscript. 'Regarde ce que tu as fait à ma nouvelle pièce! Mon meilleur travail!'

'We can speak English. There's no-one to impress or seduce. We're just two corpses clinging on to life. You'll shake off this mortal coil soon enough and I may just get myself a new body. The young ostler's perhaps.'

'I'd like it first if you don't mind.'

'You've had my best wine. Leave the servants to me.'

'You only just upgraded. It would mean a new Will.'

'A minor inconvenience for such a handsome host.' Stanas collected the pages on the floor, sat on the edge of the bed and began to read. 'Writing about the Devil again?'

'They say you should always write about what you know.' Kit pushed back the brocade coverlet, swung his feet over the edge. 'I'm dying I tell you. I'm one and ninety this year and everything hurts. My back, my joints, when I make water.'

201

'And you add to your pain with a whipping?' Stanas put the manuscript aside, walked across to the window. 'If you drank more water and less wine you'd have no trouble making water.' He pulled the curtains back, threw open the windows. 'A little fresh air and some exercise would help too. Get dressed and we'll go for a walk around the grounds. I have news of London.'

Kit winced at the light but did as he was told.

**

The sun was warm, in contrast to the chill autumn air. As they walked along the borders Stanas slowed his pace to accommodate Kit's.

'I'm sorry you are aging but unlike my other charge you are merely mortal.'

'You can't mean Shakespeare?'

'The Bard is long gone. No someone altogether more interesting, an immortal.'

'I'd love to be immortal.'

'You will be. Your work will live forever.'

He groaned. 'Credited to a fraud.'

'Not all of it.'

'The best of it.' Kit moved slowly in Stanas' wake, scarcely regarding the regal stands of foxgloves and delphiniums that clung on despite the autumn chill and the carpet of bronze and scarlet leaves heralding winter's imminent return. 'I'd like to see London again before I die. I'd like to go to the theatre, see one of my plays.'

Stanas stopped walking. 'I said I had news of London.'

'They've named a theatre after me?'

'The theatres are closed.'

'The plague again?'

'Worse, far worse. Puritans. They've condemned theatres as nests of thieves. In 1644 they razed the Globe and built tenement houses.'

Kit crumpled down onto a stone bench. 'Did *he* know?'

'Shakespeare? No, he was long gone.'

'I may hate the fellow but I'm glad he was spared that sacrilege.'

'Sacrilege indeed. Destruction of Art is the one evil I cannot abide. Lechery, theft, betrayal, murder, all these are sharp arrows in my own quiver but a person who disregards Art is baser than the most grovelling of my houseguests in Hell.' He sat down next to his guest. 'It's not the London we knew, Kit. It's lost its soul.'

Kit gave a long sad sigh. 'Civilisation is dead.'

'It's unwell, but it will recover when I rule the world.'

'When you rule the world I'll be dead. If the theatres are closed I have no voice, no purpose. My life is wasted. Even Shakespeare's life was wasted.'

'Yours is the voice of the future. These Puritans will fail, Cromwell will die and his shrieking jackals with him.'

'It's all been in vain, all my good work, all my brilliant plays. Me.'

Stanas swung his arm around the garden in a gentle arc. 'See how the delphiniums and foxgloves hold on even as winter approaches with her white death. They trust spring will return and so they sink their roots deep in the ground and wait. Your plays, your ideas, my ambition are rooted in ground that has been well-prepared for revolution.'

'But I won't see it.'

'Sail with me next week.'

'Leave here at last? Where will we go?'

'To Lands' End.'

'What's in Lands' End apart from sheep?'

'Someone who's been longing to meet you. A woman who will restore your faith.'

'A woman?' Kit sneered. 'I'd prefer a whipping from the young ostler before you take up residence in his body.' He paused. 'Even after.'

The Tavern in Portloe – Midsummer 1655

'Another lad drowned.'

The little village of Portloe had concocted the myth of a selkie to explain the bloated bodies, all young men, that washed-up on their pristine little beach seemingly after every full moon. For centuries stretching back to the 1300s when a couple of fishermen and their families settled the productive cove of Portloe it had been untouched by an outside world pockmarked with plagues and scythed with wars. As if a Shangri-La enchantment hung over the little town visitors were rare and evil unknown until King Henry sent his butchers to the Abbey. But since then there had been no murders and the close-knit community depended on each other and the sea for survival. Now the sea was harvesting their sons.

'Smiling an' all, this one,' said a burly man of middle years, face red-veined from years of exposure to sun and wind.

Eight of the bell and the patrons of the Ship Inn Tavern were well on their way to forgetfulness but even the stupor of the ale could not stifle the terrifying truth – the fishermen of Portloe were being murdered, drowned in the very same sea that had fed them for centuries.

The taverner emerged from the back room where money changed hands on Friday nights in illicit card games that cost many a man his week's earnings, his wages lost to a land shark with luck on his side. 'He be laid out on table,' he said softly.

'Someone must tell 'is widow,' said the same red-faced fellow.

'I'll do it.' A lad of barely fifteen years but already taller than his father, pulled his woollen cap low over his ears. 'I'll go.'

'Good lad,' said the taverner.

The young man stood up and bowed his head to avoid cracking it on the beam. 'Do I mention the smile on 'is lips or nay?'

'Nay,' was the verdict in a unanimous chorus.

'Why trouble 'is young widow with details?' said a fisherman whose face was so lined his life's woes could be read upon it. 'Best get it over with so the poor lass can plan her grieving an' remarrying.'

The lad nodded, and keeping his head low to avoid the beams, went to the door. Opening it, a shivering wind cat-tailed around bent backs and blistered hands. When the lad was gone a low thrum of speculation erupted.

''Tis the fourth lad drowned this year.'

'An' all at night.'

'That makes twenty drowned this past five year.'

'An' all under five an' twenty.'

'What call do young lads have wandering down to the sea after dark? The day's fishing be done.'

'Some do pass by the sea on their way home. I do and I've never been tempted to swim,' said a middle-aged fellow with corn-coloured hair and ruddy cheeks.

'The mermaid only wants young men, Fyn.'

Fyn looked around blearily. 'Ye're safe then, Giles.'

The remark was followed by a sprocket of nervous laughter.

When the bell chimed midnight, the patrons of Ship Inn Tavern, fuelled with the courage of an evening's worth of ale, filed past the body of John Taylor and bid him farewell.

After the last man left, the taverner locked up, collected a leatherjack of wine, and crept into the back room to have a word with the deceased. In the flickering candlelight the dead man's mouth seemed to twitch into a broader smile as if he nursed some delicious secret.

'What were ye thinking lad? With your whole life ahead of ye, a fair wife and two little ones to feed.' He took a swig of wine from the jack. 'She must be a beauty, this mermaid. Twenty lads drowned in the cove in five short yers and only a single drowning death recorded in the previous hundred. What's bewitching the young men of Portloe?'

The bell chimed the lonely first hour of the new day and the candle waxed briefly before waning, shrouding the dead man and the taverner in darkness. The taverner sat a little longer, listening to the sea's slushed confession, her language strange and guilt-ridden.

'She knows who done this,' he whispered. 'And she harbours the fugitive.'

Faint as a seabird's homebound winging a voice purer than any he had ever heard wafted into the darkened room, the words indistinguishable, the tune unfamiliar but enchanting. Standing slowly he felt his way out into the night and followed the song as if it were a skein of thread down to the empty beach. Turning his head first left and then right he decided the song was coming from the Abbey.

'Haunted,' he said, crossing himself. ''Tis the murdered Abbess.'

His family had been Catholics and as a small child he felt their rage when his grandfather told him the story of King Henry VIII lusting after a witch called Anne Bullen. So great was his craving, some said bewitchment, he cut with Rome and made himself head of the Church of England. He sacked the Abbeys, Monasteries and Cloisters, murdering the nuns and priests who'd served their communities so faithfully, enriching himself on their plate and silver. His grandfather remembered the five men with hate-filled eyes who arrived at his tavern demanding food, ale and shelter in the name of the King. That night he had to serve those murderous rogues and endure their laughter over supper as they gloated about the innocent throats they would slice the next day, the virgin breasts they would pierce. The horror that awaited the nuns in the Abbey was echoed all over Britain as bloodthirsty men carried out the orders of the thralled King. After drinking themselves into a stupor the five men tumbled into bed. His grandfather said he wished he'd cut their throats that night rather than harbour the murderers of the nuns who had fed the poor and sheltered the homeless and never hurt a living soul.

The next day at dawn, the men climbed the path to the Abbey. His grandparents closed the tavern and drew the curtains before falling to their knees and imploring their Catholic God to save the Abbess and her sisters but when the men returned at midday, wiping the blood from their swords and hoisting budgets of silver plate onto their shoulders they knew their God was deaf.

No-one in Portloe heard a single scream that day but after the men had gone the townsfolk crept up to the Abbey and collected the hacked bodies of the nuns, placing arms, legs and heads together with torsos in hastily constructed coffins. They buried them deep in the forest where no man would find them and make further sport of them.

**

He listened to the song, his sympathy chiming with the ghost of the Abbess.

'But these young men you're sirening into the sea have not harmed you. Must you take your revenge on the innocent?' he said aloud. 'You were an innocent once yourself.'

Miriam stopped singing, listened, her heightened senses catching every word of the man's plea and something like a tremor moved her stone heart.

'I was until Rathe betrayed me,' she whispered. 'I waited for him in the room where love was made and forged in fire. He never came.'

She sang a new song echoing her lonely state.

A table set for two and a cold jug of wine
His place is here, and this place is mine
In the glow of a candle we'll talk o'er the day
And when the fire burns low we'll spirit away
It's a vision I've nursed and polished with tears
A dream I have clung to for so many years
My days have been watching
My nights spent the same
Looking out for my lover
But he never came
I was drawn to this dream like a moth to a flame
But my dream turned to ashes cause he never came
I linger, I linger, I linger on
Tis a dangerous moth who embodies the flame

208

The taverner listened until the last note drifted out to sea and settled like foam. He felt her pain, felt the antique rage of his ancestors, and wondered why God had not taken her to Heaven given her life of service. Nothing about the situation made sense and it left him wondering if an altogether different entity's hidden hand was at work. Had she changed allegiance in those last horrifying moments of her life as her sisters fell like threshed wheat?

He wouldn't blame her if she had turned to Satan for where do you put your faith when your King murders the clergy and then beheads the Queen he lapsed for? Who to pray to when his first daughter burned Protestants and his second burned Catholics? And all three God's representatives on earth, charged with caring for his flock.

Yes, Satan was at least honest about his evil and if she'd changed allegiance perhaps she was now harvesting souls for Hell rather than Heaven.

As the years fell away making chains of my days
Linking tighter the maypole circle of years
Spinning days into months, twining winters to springs
Spinning seasons to centuries over again
I linger, I linger, I linger on
My loneliness spinning a web of its own
One hundred summers, one million tears
Tis a dangerous moth who embodies the years.

The Abbey – 1655

'I give you Kit Marlowe.'

Miriam watched Stanas and his companion making their slow progress up the final twist of path. Last winter Stanas had cleared the tangles of gorse and heather covering the

209

hewn steps, making his coming and going swifter and easier. Beside the path and on the knoll there remained a scattering of trefoil, thrift and campion, those reliable little blooms she arranged in the nun's old wooden mazers to cheer the Abbey over the long months when Stanas was planning his conquest of the world in the comfort and luxury of Provence.

Stanas' companion was finding the climb difficult for he had to stop and rest frequently which gave her plenty of time to observe him: a man well past middle years with long white hair flowing out from beneath a brocade skullcap. His features were fine, his skin milky-white and remarkably unlined as if life sat lightly upon him. His mouth, open and gasping for air, was red-lipped and full. She judged him a libertine, a man who lusted excessively, for there clung about him an aura of both complaint and sated demand. Why Stanas thought to bring this old man to meet her was a puzzle until she heard him speak.

'What of my latest play? You may as well bury it in lepers' graves along with the others now the world has lost its soul.'

'Save your breath, Kit, you've barely enough to for the climb.'

'Kit Marlowe,' she whispered, her judgement of the man undergoing a swift reversal. 'Kit Marlowe is here.' She glanced back down at the old man presently clutching a tuft of campion for support. 'Well he'll be here *soon*.'

She swung away from the window, pressing her back against the wall for ballast as she ran her hands compulsively through her hair which had not seen a comb in sixty years and in truth had no need of one for she was frozen in the perfection of youth when no artifice or cosmetic device could have improved upon nature.

'Kit Marlowe,' she repeated, straightening her velvet gown.

She was glad of the instinct that had warned her to wear the red velvet gown Stanas had given her. It had been folded away in one of the nun's trunks along with the other fine clothes he had given her over the years. Only that morning she'd obeyed an impulse to open the trunk and see if her careful efforts had preserved the finery from moths and fleas. She'd wrapped the precious gowns, capes, stomachers and bodices in linen and secured them in a trunk to suffocate any living creatures that might have taken up residence in the seams. To her delight the clothes were as perfect as the day Stanas had delivered them.

She'd found the old trunk in the basement. It had contained a few linen gowns, a grey bodice and a pair of buskins, no doubt the clothes one of the novices arrived in when she joined the order and left the world behind. The murderers evidently judged the trunk and its contents worthless or too cumbersome to sell to an Irish toyle, so it served as a repository for Stanas' gifts. Only once had Miriam aired the expensive clothes to combat mildew, hanging them out in the sun for a whole day. Unlike the linsey-woolsey nuns' habits, velvet would not endure a washing board, soap and hot water. But after that initial care she'd forgotten all about them save the one blue velvet gown the Devil insisted she wear at supper when he visited.

When her idol finally staggered into the room she caught an unnecessary breath. He stopped in the doorway, leaned against the frame, and frankly stared at her.

'I give you Kit Marlowe,' said Stanas, making his way to the sideboard in search of wine. 'It may be a little late in the day, Miriam, but given that he would prefer a lashing from

211

an ostler rather than sharing his bed with a beautiful woman it matters not.'

Kit was out breath after his climb and unable to refute the charge. He slumped against the doorframe gasping for air and holding his chest as if his heart was about to burst.

'Please sit down Monsieur Marlowe and catch your breath. I will bring you wine and food.' Miriam glanced at Stanas. 'I assume you've brought me fish again?'

'Freshly caught today and a side of beef purchased in London yesterday. Needs cooking.'

Miriam shot him a withering look. 'Of course I do not expect Monsieur Marlowe to eat it raw.' And addressing Kit. 'Would you like the fish cooked in the French style with butter? The beef in pottage?'

'Pottage?' Kit, still leaning against the door frame, found his breath. 'English food. I have not tasted pottage since I,' he paused, '*died*. Madame, you are an angel.'

'I would like some pottage, too,' said Stanas. 'Can I help you, Miriam?'

'When did you find your way around a kitchen?'

Kit laughed, pushed his frail frame up to its full height. 'She has your measure, Stanas. If I may have some wine, Madame, I need it to dull a most insistent pain.'

'Your bones trouble you, Monsieur?'

'Worse, insanity grips the land. They have closed the theatres.'

Miriam reflexed an imaginary blow to the stomach. 'Who did this?'

'Puritans,' Kit spat the word.

'It won't last,' said Stanas, finding the one silver goblet and helping himself to wine. 'I'll bring more wine next visit. Zealots always end up on the pyre.'

'But not before they ruin an entire generation of genius,' moaned Kit.

'Have they no souls?' asked Miriam. 'Stanas, give Monsieur Marlowe some wine.'

Kit gazed at the vision presently framed within the gaping hollow of the solitary window. Behind her the sea was flung out like a tapestry of blue and gold, backdrop to the loveliest creature he had ever seen. The flaming red of her gown echoed the cascading fire-coloured fall of hair that cloaked her shoulders and breasts and hung to her knees. Her eyes were green and in them a fierce light shone.

'What kind of immortal are you?' he asked.

'Not your kind, not a genius, just a woman saved from Elizabeth's fire by the Devil.'

'He saved me too,' said Kit. 'Although now I see little point to my prolonged life.'

He laughed bitterly, his mirth causing such a spluttering and gasping for breath Miriam thought her idol was about to die. She rushed to the board and poured him a mazer of wine.

'Drink this.'

Kit grasped the wooden vessel she offered, drank deeply and met her eyes, triggering such a thundering in her breast it would have arrested a living heart. Under his intense scrutiny she felt a charge enlivening her like lightning striking. For the first time since her death she felt fully and thrillingly alive, even more so than her first submersion in the sea, even more exciting than her first kill or the many that followed: the fishermen, sailors, drunks, all the young men who answered her siren call and paid with their lives. But in all her kills she had never tasted Heaven and now standing a breath away from Kit Marlowe she imagined she heard its song.

213

'Will you stay?' she asked, without breaking the mesmeric hold of his gaze.

He finished the wine, nodded. 'I expect so. I'm an old man and unlikely to survive another sea voyage let alone the climb up here. I suspect our saviour has brought me here to die.' He handed back the mazer. 'May I have another drop, Madame?'

'Miriam. My name is Miriam.' She took the mazer. 'Where are your manners, Stanas?'

'I must have left them in Provence. If I leave Kit in your care you'll need to cook for him, clean for him, keep his mazer overflowing. He is incapable of doing anything for himself. He may even take to his bed and pretend he is dying but if you can keep him upright, or at least semi-prone, there are a few more brilliant plays in him.'

'I'll do anything for him. Except die.' She handed Kit the refreshed mazer. 'That I can't do for you. I can't even do it for myself. Monsieur Marlowe, crude as it is, the Abbey is your home if you choose.'

Kit's eyes filled with tears, heightening the amber colour of his irises. 'Thank you, Madame.' He pushed away from the wall, moved to the window. 'Such a glorious view and so far above the disease-ridden world. I feel remarkably well, Stanas. My appetite has returned.' He swivelled around. 'Where's that pottage?'

Miriam looked at Stanas who nodded in the direction of the kitchen. 'I've left two bundles on the kitchen table, enough to stock the larder and the buttery.'

'See that Monsieur Marlowe has all the wine he needs while I prepare midday dinner.' She paused in the doorway. 'I'm an excellent cook, Monsieur. My mother taught me.'

**

Over midday dinner of pottage, sauteed fish and sallat, Miriam studied her idol, looking for the traces of genius that separated him from mere mortals, but it was difficult to decipher that distinction in the man who wolfed down his food and reached compulsively for the wine to wash down barely-chewed mouthfuls of mackerel. She had baked some fresh manchets as well and these he ripped apart before dipping them in his wine, a combination of tastes he swore was ambrosia. Throughout the meal he complained volubly about Will Shakespeare and the Burbage brothers whom he accused of failing to recognise his superior genius. When he had said all there was to say about Shakespeare and the Burbages he started on the long-dead Queen.

'If I may interrupt this diatribe, Kit, I would like to compliment Miriam on a superb meal.' Stanas raised his goblet.

Kit raised his mazer. 'Your health dear lady.'

'And yours.' Miriam raised her mazer of rainwater, her preferred drink.

'You do not eat, Mistress Miriam?' asked Kit, torn manchet hovering above his mazer.

'I have no hunger.'

'How sad for you, my dear. All I have ever known is hunger.'

'And how well you have sated it, Kit,' said Stanas, reaching for the leatherjack and topping up his wine. 'I create Masterpieces for him and he begrudges me a drop of wine.' Kit shook his head and returned to his slandering of the Queen. 'She did nothing for women, you know, nothing to improve the lot of her own sex. It was a miracle that Isabella Whitney's poetry was published in 1566.' He stuffed a wine-soaked manchet into his mouth. 'Have you read her work?'

Miriam shook her head. 'Alas no.'

215

Kit leaned back. 'Then prepare to be wooed by her.' He began to recite.

The time is come, I must depart
from thee, ah famous city;
I never yet to rue my smart,
did find that thou had'st pity.
Wherefore small cause there is, that I
should grieve from thee to go;
But many women foolishly,
like me, and other moe,
Do such a fixèd fancy set,
on those which least deserve,
That long it is ere wit we get
away from them to swerve.
But time with pity oft will tell
to those that will her try,
Whether it best be more to mell,
or utterly defy.
And now hath time me put in mind
of thy great cruelness,
That never once a help would find,
to ease me in distress.
Thou never yet would'st credit give
to board me for a year;
Nor with apparel me relieve,
except thou payèd were.
No, no, thou never did'st me good,
nor ever wilt, I know.
Yet am I in no angry mood,
but will, or ere I go,
In perfect love and charity,
my testament here write,

216

And leave to thee such treasury,
as I in it recite.
Now stand aside and give me leave
to write my latest will;
And see that none you do deceive
of that I leave them till.

Miriam sighed. 'Lovely. Was it of London or a husband she wrote?'

'It was about the ungracious Queen and miserly old London,' said Kit. 'She was an artist with words and as you can hear hers was a rich palette.'

'She was marvellous,' said Miriam.

'She was dying,' said Kit. 'But what a prayer to leave to this uninspired world. Words are my religion, Mistress Miriam. I have knelt at their altar all my life.'

'When you weren't howling for me in the woods,' said Stanas.

'I long ago lost faith in you.'

'Disappointing people is my most lethal weapon.' Stanas laughed. 'It strips them of the will to live and then they are easily manipulated.'

'Closing the theatres has stripped me of my last shred of will,' said Kit. 'Speaking of death, will the lights go out with my last breath or may I expect a descent into your kingdom?'

Stanas pierced a chunk of fish with his knife. 'You think there are only two choices?'

'I doubt Heaven and I fear Hell.' Kit splayed the fingers of his upturned palms. 'Are there more destinations a lost soul can expect?'

'The destinations are as numerous as the stars in the sky. You, me, alas not Miriam but all of them,' he nodded down in the direction of Portloe, 'the simple souls who cast their nets and pray for mercy, even they have a tiny puddle of imagination and in that stagnant slick, dreams grow wings. These dreams fashion the life that greets us after mortal death.'

Kit narrowed his eyes.

'Why did you leave Heaven?'

A flash of pain momentarily darkened Stanas' eyes. 'It did not suit me.'

'He was deaf to its music,' said Miriam.

Stanas leapt to his feet, sending his chair clattering to the floor. He clenched his fists and froze in an attitude of imminent explosion. Then he swept away, snatched two leatherjacks off the board and marched out of the room. The sound of a door slamming indicated that they would see no more of him that night.

Kit reached across the table and collected Stanas' unfinished meal. 'No point wasting good food.'

'I saw *Tamburlaine* many years ago and I have read all your plays since my death. Stanas brings them to me.'

'What did you think of *Hamlet*?'

'I thought it a work of genius, expressing your agony over death, the horrifying prospect of surviving it. A worry I will never have.'

Kit looked up from the trencher.

'What deal did he offer you?'

'None. He saved me from the flames for his own purpose. There was no promise of fame or fortune in exchange for my soul like the deal in your *Dr. Faustus*. He made the decision without my consent.'

'He saved me from the flames, too. Elizabeth had me consigned to ashes after she learned Raleigh and I attended the same school.'

'She objected to your education?'

218

'Not University. We supposedly attended the School of Atheism.' Kit laughed. 'An empty appellation, for how can there be a study of nothingness? We were a group of poets, natural scientists and intellectuals who met and discussed everything forbidden by the Church.'

'Did Raliegh attend your meetings?'

'I never saw him there. Elizabeth thought she owned poor Raleigh and me. She was a deeply resentful woman, jealous of excellence. Some people resent excellence, Mistress Miriam, especially when it is unattainable to a merely serviceable intellect like Shakespeare.'

'What had Shakespeare to do with your imminent death?'

'Perhaps nothing. Perhaps everything. You see we did not invite him into our little coterie and his venomous envy took shape in that rather inferior play of his, *Love's Labours Lost*, in which the King of Navarre says "Black is the badge of hell / The hue of dungeons and the school of night" – a not-so-subtle reference to our imaginary School of Atheism. Of course Elizabeth, resenting her own exclusion, issued a warrant for my arrest. Enter Stanas Vedil, my saviour. Yes, dear Madame, my trafficking with the Devil was born out of human jealousy – Shakespeare's and Elizabeth's.'

'They were both fools.' Miriam's eyes shone with a fierce emerald light. 'I love you for your courage and your genius.'

'Then I am blessed. I am loved by an immortal and required by the Devil.' He laughed a short bark of mirth. 'What hope have I of Heaven?'

'You don't believe in Heaven.'

'I didn't until I met the Devil who is clearly proof of his opposite. We have been deceived, Mistress Miriam, first by our Queen and then by Satan and finally and most imperatively by God who did not stoop to warn or rescue or claim us.'

'We have each other.' Miriam reached across the table, took Kit's hand in a firm grip from which he reflexed.

'Your hand is as cold as ice.'

'I am dead.' She tightened her grip and this time he did not resist. 'When you leave will you find a way to –?' She fell silent, looked down. 'Forgive me, I ask too much.'

'Ask.'

'Help me die.'

'But you're already dead.'

'Promise me you will come back for me then.'

'Does he know you long for death?'

She nodded. 'He won't let me go. He's too lonely.'

Kit laid his warm living hand over her cold dead one. 'What does he want? Do you know?'

'His father's love.'

'And nothing else will do, I suppose.'

'He also wants to hear the music.' She placed her other hand on top of his. He reflexed from the icy contact but did not withdraw. 'Can you hear the music, Monsieur Marlowe?'

'Call me Kit.' He nodded. 'I've always heard it. You?'

'Sometimes I think I can but it's so fleeting I may have imagined it. I have made my own music to fill the empty spaces within and without.' Nodding at the sky.

Kit noticed the lute. 'You play?'

'And I sing for company. I'm alone most of the time.'

'Sing for me, please.'

Miriam fetched her lute and sat by the open window in view of the setting sun. She sang the haunting melody about the table for two and the lonely watching of the people in the village below, her voice carrying far out to sea, encincturing the drifts of enamelled cloud.

See there the fishermen casting out their nets and lines
And there the old men sit chattering over cheese and wines
And here the women come, flocks of pretty birds
Greeting men back from work bearing gifts of fish and words
These are the simple joys, signal marks of life
The happiness denied to me, not mother, friend nor wife
I linger, I linger, I linger on
My loneliness spinning a web of its own
I linger, I linger, I linger on
Tis a dangerous moth who embodies the flame.

'I should not sit by the window and sing. My voice carries like a haunting to the village below and,' she cast him a furtive glance, 'I have caused them enough pain.'

'How?'

She turned her face away, her profile bas relief against a sky preparing to bleed into night. 'I have drowned their sons to sate my hatred of a long-dead lover, stolen their final breath to taste death but I am no wiser about Heaven or its music or death nor have I felt vengeance.' She looked back at him, her face a mask of grief. 'When you are gone I will be alone eternally.'

Kit dragged himself to his feet, moved over to the window, placed a hand on her head as if in benediction. 'I will come back for you if it is within my power to live beyond the grave.'

She pressed her face against his chest and wept her tearless grief.

'Sing again now,' he said as the sun sank hissing into the sea. 'Sing here at the open window where every passing angel will hear you. Who knows, it may help free both of us.'

**

In the village below the midnight bell chimed. Miriam stopped singing and put the lute aside. 'I do not sleep. I have no need but there is a bed for you.'

'Thank you, these old bones have need of rest.'

Miriam collected a candle and offered her arm to the aged playwright but just as they were about to quit the room a ghost appeared in the doorway, an ancient woman in a black robe, her meagre frame trembling, her hands raised to her throat as if to ward off a spell.

The three occupants of the room stared at each other in silent apprehension until the ghost raised a living finger and pointed. 'Miriam?'

Miriam peered at the old woman and as if reading a map that held a known continent beneath an etching of lines, her entire body jerked with recognition and joy. 'Abigail!'

The woman caught her breath in a sob. 'I recognised your voice and followed it. But how are you so unchanged? How are you still alive? You were burned!'

Kit made a movement towards the door. 'I must rest these old bones. If you'll point the way, my dearest Miriam, I'll leave you to explain to your friend how you and I yet live.'

'Forgive me, Abigail this is Kit Marlowe.'

'The famous playwright?' Abigail leaned against the doorframe for support. 'Am I dead? For both of you most certainly are.'

'You live and so do we after a fashion. Abigail, please wait while I show Kit to his room.'

**

After settling Marlowe into a cell with a straw pallet, a warm blanket, and the promise of a hearty breakfast in the morning she returned to find Abigail peering out the window at the sea.

'Have you eaten?' Miriam asked her.

Abigail turned slowly. 'I've not. Miriam, what is this miracle? How do you yet live and why are you here?'

'Sit. I'll bring you supper and we'll talk.' She nodded at the leatherjack on the table. 'There are clean mazers on the board. Help yourself.' She collected the soiled trenchers and paused a moment before leaving the room. 'It's so good to see you. I've been alone these many years.'

The Tavern in Portloe – later that night

'Mum should have been home hours ago. Do you think she's drowned like the others?'

The taverner flushed the last drunk out the door before locking it. 'I didn't want to say this in front of the others but I heard singing last night. It were haunting, seductive. I think,' he adjusted his words, 'I *believe* that whatever lures the young men into the sea is female. She doesn't want women. So your mother's safe.'

'Then where is she?'

'Could she have forgotten her way home?'

'Her mind is sharp as ever and Ma knows these cliffs and coves so well she could walk them blindfolded.' He ran his hands through his corn-coloured hair. 'She's been so careful not to get caught all these years.'

'What do you mean?'

Fyn steepled his fingers, pressed them to his mouth. 'I've said too much. Still, I don't suppose it matters now since both my uncle and my Da have gone.' He flattened his palms on the table. 'My father did something in London. They had to leave in a hurry.'

The taverner pushed the leatherjack across the table. 'Were it theft or worse?'

'Worse, I think. I only ever heard snatches of conversations as a child. Whispers between my uncle and my Da when we lived with my grandparents. Da did something so bad it made them run as far from London as possible, all the way to my grandparents in Weymouth and after they died Mum and Da and Uncle Valentyne were on the run again. That's when we came here.' He gulped the wine. 'D'you suppose whatever mischief Da did has followed us here? D'you suppose it found Mum?'

The Abbey – later that night

'After your death,' Abigail paused her story, 'after your *imagined* death, Radclyffe House died too. Your mother drank poison the night you were burned.'

Miriam covered her face with her hands, her body jerking with dry sobs.

Abigail waited for the first flush of grief to pass before continuing. 'And then like flies they all fell, one after the other. Jonas and Master Trenery died of flux the first summer after you and your mother died. The Marchioness moved to Stanstead Hall after Master Rathe married again. She hated his new wife. We all did. She was a vain, silly woman, fond of giving orders. Rosamunde went home to her family in Stratford and when there was no hope of marriage with her Thomas signed on as crew for a ship bound for the New World, thinking to make his fortune. The ship was wrecked in the Channel. Thomas never saw another land beyond England.'

'Poor Thomas. He was kind to me when I was facing the flames. 'Tis a sad ending for him. And what of Fyndern and Valentyne?'

She smiled. 'I married Fyndern and the three of us left the house thinking to take our skills far from London. We left in rather a hurry.'

'You and Fyndern and Valentyne left together? But that's marvellous news. I wish I'd been at your wedding.' Miriam impulsively clutched Abigail's hand.

Abigail caught her breath. 'Your hand is like ice.'

'I'm dead. I'll explain later. Tell me more. So, the three of you travelled on foot all the way from London to Portloe? 'Tis a long journey. I know, I've made it.'

'We stopped for a time in Weymouth with my parents. I had my three children there.' Sorrow shadowed her face. 'Only one survived. My son, Fyn, named for his father. When my parents died we sold the house to escape the memories of all those losses and followed the coast until we found Portloe. Our son Fyn chose Portloe because he wanted to be a fisherman, so we bought a small cottage and a boat for him. He's a good fisherman, always manages to feed us.' She frowned. 'What is it? You look frightened.'

'He's still alive?' Miriam looked down. 'I've heard about the deaths in the sea.'

'My son is alive, thank the lord, but many others were lost.' Abigail shivered. 'It's been like a haunting, Miriam, the flower of our youth, so many healthy young men drowned. But how could strong swimmers familiar with the sea fall foul of her?'

'The sea has strange moods.' She looked back up. 'Did Valentyne marry?'

'No, he always loved you, no-one else ever held his heart as you did and he would not be parted from Fyn.'

'Do they yet live?'

Abigail shook her head. 'Death claimed them ten years ago. They died within a week of each other. Burning ague. I nursed them to the end. It was a mercy their souls flew together but I still have my son Fyn,' she paused, 'when his wife allows it.'

Miriam dared squeeze Abigail's hands. 'Stay with me if Fyn has no need of you.'

'I am a burden to Fyn's wife. She never lets me forget that I'm an extra mouth to feed.'

'I'll feed you. You'll be a joy for me.'

'I must tell Fyn where I am or he will grieve.'

'You can't. The villagers mustn't know about me. They would make a freak of me. Please stay with me and let Fyn believe you died this night.'

'Perhaps it may be best.' Abigail bowed her head. 'I died long ago when I lost his father, and the years do weigh heavily upon me.' She laughed softly. 'And I doubt I'd survive that climb a second time. But enough of me, tell me how you survived the flames and what you've become that you should look so young and feel so cold.'

'An angel saved me from the flames, rendered me immortal. I have no pulse, no need of breath or sustenance. My senses are heightened and as you can see, I do not age. I know not what I am, but I do believe I am the only one of my kind.'

'An angel saved you?'

'Of sorts. Stay with me, please.'

Abigail's face betrayed no emotion. 'Fyn has his wife, his friends, the life he wants.'

'No children?'

'Five, all dead.'

'I had a child. The angel sent his soul home.'

226

''Tis a rare and harsh pain losing a child.'

'I never knew my child and in any case it would have died long before me.'

'As will I.'

They were silent for a long beat, the only sound the moaning of the sea.

'I have not told you the real reason we left London.' Abigail's eyes widened as if remembering something fearful. 'Valentyne murdered Master Rathe to avenge you.'

'When? How?'

''Twas thirteen years after your death, 1606. He saw a play at The Globe Theatre and came home in a state of excitement, said he knew how to get away with murder because he had seen it done on stage and unlike the character he would never be troubled by a conscience because Master Rathe deserved to die. He told Fyn and I to be ready to flee London that night.

When the entire household slept he slipped into the Master's room and stabbed him in the heart. The three of us fled London that night.'

'*Macbeth*, that was the play. Kit wrote it even though Shakespeare claimed it. Abigail, I feel as if a shadow has been lifted from my soul. Dear Valentyne took the revenge I could not take and now I must confess something to you.'

'You've been drowning the young men in the cove.'

'You knew?'

'I worked it out tonight when I decided to follow your voice. Before every drowning I heard your voice or imagined I did. Will you strike again?'

Miriam's gaze fixed on her friend, her eyes green pools. 'Not if you stay.'

The milky blue of Abigail's eyes grew almost opaque in the waning candlelight. 'A hard bargain, never to see my son again in order to save his life.'

'He is safe from me.' Her eyes glittering. 'He's too old. I only drown the men who are Rathe's age when he betrayed me.'

'A small mercy.' Abigail looked around the cavernous space, the spare furnishings, table, chairs and sideboard, the cluster of instruments in the corner. ''Tis a cold house you keep after the warmth of my small cottage but I will share it with you. Would I have a bed of my own?'

'A whole cell and I would see to your comfort. My saviour comes and goes –'

'The angel.'

'Yes. He has no shortage of coin and he will furnish your needs.' She reached out her hand again, icy and firm. 'I will not strike again.'

'I must concoct a tale for my son. He will grieve if I just disappear this night.'

'If I let you leave tomorrow with a convincing tale do you promise to come back to me?'

'I swear. Of course I may not survive the climb again.' Abigail laughed.

'I will send Stanas with you. He will escort you to your son and bring you safely and discreetly back.'

'Stanas?'

'The angel who saved me. He lives in a Chateau in France but I keep a room for him here.' She laughed softly. 'He was ill-tempered earlier this evening but tomorrow he'll be pleasant and well-mannered. A night's sleep and a leatherjack of wine always restores his humour.'

'A strange sort of angel.'

'Fallen.'

'As was Val after he murdered Master Rathe. Some sins are necessary for justice and we are none of us so perfect we can judge another.'

Miriam squeezed her friend's hand. 'You were always fair-minded, Abby. I remember your concern for the chickens when Ma sent Val and Fyn out to despatch them for dinner.'

'I questioned God then. I expect I shall question him again when I meet him. This angel who saved you should have been welcomed home. His kindness to you should merit forgiveness and yet he is earthbound. What kind of father bars his own son from his house?'

Miriam laughed. 'You and Stanas will be great friends. Come now, I'll find a bed for you. Tomorrow you may choose any room you wish apart from Monsieur Marlowe's or Stanas'.'

Miriam led Abigail along the narrow corridor off which a dozen or more small doors opened into cells, each overlooking the sea and the cove. At the far end she stopped.

'This one will do for tonight.' She pulled her old friend into a tight embrace and whispered her thanks. 'I won't have you for long but you will bring me as close to my mother as any living soul can. I love you for that and for your own sake.'

Handing Abigail the candle she retreated into the impenetrable dark which no light – sun, star, or moon – would ever cheer and returned to her solitary post by the open window, there to wait for the rising sun which would hail a temporary change in her eternal life.

A cottage in Portloe – the next day

'Where have you been all night?' Fyn demanded, looking over his shoulder for support from his wife Alice who stood by the stove, arms folded, a frown furrowing her brow.

'I'm sorry if I worried you, sweetling –' Abigail began.

'He paced all night,' said Alice, 'worried himself sick about you and now you waltz in here bright as spring with a handsome young gentleman on your arm.'

Stanas bowed his head. 'You are too generous, Madame. I apologise for any inconvenience I may have caused but when I saw Mistress Abigail, my dear grandfather's servant from London, I had much to tell her and more to ask. Time just got away from us.'

Fyn's wife, a tiny woman as wide as she was high, squinted her black button eyes. 'You wouldn't have been born when she were in service. How d'you really know 'er?'

'True enough dear Madame, however I recognised her name at once when it was called out in welcome at the tavern. My grandfather spoke of her often enough and so fondly.'

Alice sniffed. 'That's as may be but where did you an' her spend the night? In your bed at the Inn?'

'At one and eighty I am no temptation,' said Abigail.

'But still you never came 'ome. Where'd you sleep?' persisted Alice.

'On my boat,' said Stanas, pointing out through the door towards the beach where a fine-looking caravel bobbed beyond the breakers.

'How'd you get out to it? Swim?' asked Alice.

'We ah –' Abigail looked helplessly at Stanas.

'We rowed the dinghy and your dear mother slept alone after we had reminisced.'

'That's right. Now enough of this nonsense. You would do well to remember this is still my cottage Alice. My son's when I die.' She smiled at Fyn. 'I'm sorry to be the cause of an anxious night, sweetling, but it is just as this gentleman has told you, your father and I worked for his grandfather in London.'

'Something doesn't sit right,' said Alice. 'Why would a gentleman want to spend time with a scullery maid, no matter how well she served his grandfather?'

'My grandfather said she was the best servant he ever employed,' said Stanas.

Fyn lurched backwards. 'You can't mean Master Rathe? I thought –' he adjusted his words. 'I had the impression he died young.'

'Master Rathe met his maker rather sooner than he expected,' said Abigail quickly. 'After he died, we were employed in a different household by this gentleman's grandfather.'

'What's 'is name then?' asked Alice. 'This fine gentleman who knew you by your married name when he hears it cried out fifty years after you left London.'

'Vedil,' said Stanas quickly. 'Forgive me I should have introduced myself. I am Master Stanas Vedil, Lord actually, but we can dispense with titles. My grandfather employed your mother –'

'And your father,' said Abigail quickly.

'– after Master Rathe met his untimely end. That's how it was, wouldn't you say, Mistress Abigail?'

Abigail nodded. 'That's precisely how it was. Your grandfather also employed my brother-in-law, Valentyne.'

'Ah yes, how is Master Valentyne?' asked Stanas.

'Dead,' said Alice curtly. 'Didn't she mention that when you was reminiscing?'

'I had news of my own, Madame.' Stanas glared at Alice.

'And plenty of it,' said Abigail. 'Lord Vedil's grandfather took your father, your uncle and me into his employ after Master Rathe so tragically died and –'

231

'And their service was impeccable. My grandfather said they were kind, honest, reliable and –'

'And that's why Lord Vedil has invited me to go to France with him.'

'France?' said Fyn and Alice in surprised unison.

'France,' declared Stanas and turning to Abigail murmured, 'Inspired.'

'To do what?' asked Alice slowly, dark eyes narrowed and suspicious.

'Keep house for me,' said Stanas airily. 'Maintain order with my servants.'

'How? She can't speak a word of French,' said Alice.

'I can learn,' said Abigail.

'At eighty?' Alice unfolded her arms, raised them in an exasperated huff. 'This is madness. Say something, Fyn.'

Fyn stepped up to his mother, hugged her. 'Go with God, Ma.'

'Or the next best thing.' Stanas cleared his throat. 'Mistress Abigail please collect anything you wish to bring with you to France.'

'You're not letting her go!' cried Alice. 'An old lady sailing to a foreign country where she don't speak the language and she 'as no lovin' family to protect 'er!'

'I'll help you pack, Ma,' said Fyn. 'Such a grand adventure. You and Da and Uncle Valentyne always did have adventurous spirits.'

'I love you sweetling,' said Abigail, drying his tears on the edge of her cloak. 'The house is yorn now. I won't see you again in this lifetime but I'll be there to greet you at the gates of Heaven.'

'Never mind the Pearly Gates who's going to cook for us if she goes to France?' demanded Alice.

'You might learn,' said Fyn. 'If Ma can learn French you can learn to light an oven. Come Ma, I'll help you pack.'

Abigail and Fyn disappeared into the gloomy interior of the cottage where a warren of tiny rooms served as bedrooms, reception and dining rooms for the family.

Stanas and Alice eyed one another warily.

'Why the rush?' asked Alice.

'The tide waits for no man, Madame. Don't worry Mistress Abigail will be well looked after where she is going.'

'And where exactly is that?' asked Alice, glaring at the handsome young man looming over her.

'To my Chateau in Provence.'

The Happy Years

A peel of laughter rang out like bells. Kit tied back a lock of hair that had escaped its ribbon, threw down his quill and heaved himself to his feet, his intention being to reach the open window before Miriam and Abigail passed out of hearing and scold them for interrupting his work. But at the window he was met with a picture of bucolic innocence: Miriam winding flowers into Abigail's wispy grey hair and Abigail smiling back at her with such love he felt chastened.

He returned to the table Miriam had set up for him in an airy ground-floor room, possibly the nun's dining room, now his study. Miriam had warmed the grey stone floors and walls with colourful tapestries and rugs Stanas had brought from his Chateau. With Stanas' reluctant help, Miriam had hauled the table up from the cellar, added four chairs from upstairs and arranged them in front of the window so Kit could enjoy the sea's changing moods as he created his Masterpieces.

Miriam had found a length of white linen in another old chest in the cellar. Once Abigail had washed it and bleached it in the sun for two days it made a nice tablecloth. The ladies dressed the table with jugs of wildflowers. Kit could be found in his study every day, head bent over a sheet of velum, a pot of ink at his elbow and a knife to sharpen the quills as they blunted on the stream of words that poured from his soul. Despite the theatres being closed and no Shakespeare to conduit his work, Kit declared himself inspired enough to create a new play, and over the weeks the pile of pages swelled into a manuscript.

The study, conveniently situated three doors down from the kitchen, meant the women could come and go with trays of food and jugs of wine without disturbing him. He said he was happier left to work alone rather than sit down for midday dinner and endure the conversations he deemed *gossip*: the reminiscing of Miriam and Abigail's shared history and the years in between when their lives diverged.

He did, however, join them for supper to discuss the progress of his play.

**

Miriam placed a crown of white flowers upon Abigail's head.

'You look as beautiful as you did when we were young, when you were forever washing our clothes.' She caught a flash of Kit's retreat from the window and grimaced. 'Oh dear, we've disturbed Kit.'

'Come, let's move away from the open window,' Abigail whispered. 'We, too, have important things to do.'

'Like collecting flowers and eggs!' Miriam laughed.

'Just so,' said Abigail. 'I've left a tray of food for him. Will he stop to eat, do you think? Too often I find his food untouched.'

'But all the wine drunk, I'll warrant.'

'Always!' She laughed. 'Look, I spy some purple flowers. Bees favour them, did you know?'

They wandered along the knoll keeping clear of the edge of the cliff that fell away to the rocks below where tidal pools kept their secret worlds safe from the surging waves that swept the careless into the sea. After picking a basketful of purple thrift they went around to the coop to collect eggs.

'What does Stanas do in Provence?' asked Abigail. 'Is he raising an army?'

'He would not waste his followers in a war. He means to reveal the fault in our stars through Kit's plays so that people demand change and then he will be that change.'

'He will feed the people?'

'I told him that, too, but he declares it too much hard work.'

'What will he offer them?'

'Lies and false promises like any ambitious man.'

'No change at all then.' Abigail thought for a moment. 'But how can he reach the people now the theatres are closed? I suppose he could pronounce Kit's plays in sermons from a pulpit.'

Miriam laughed. 'Stanas would never preach from a pulpit.'

Abigail stooped to collect a clutch of eggs, rose again slowly. 'My back takes time to unbend these days. I could not wash a tubful of cambric shirts and gowns now. This new world he plans, will people do their own washing and cooking and cleaning and fetching, or will there be slaves like us to do it?'

'I'm not sure he's thought that far ahead,' said Miriam, looking away quickly.

'He must have a vision for the world he wants to create or how could he remain inspired?'

'Inspired?' Miriam turned back to her friend. 'I don't think his mind turns to creating Heaven on earth, not since he fell.'

Abigail seemed not to hear as she counted the eggs. 'Only six. We need above a dozen if I'm to make a French cheesecake for Kit.'

'There are more eggs. The hens try to hide them but I know every nest. I've had years to find them.' Miriam knelt and pushed aside a loose rock propped against the old part of the coop. Reaching in she removed another six eggs, handing them one by one to Abigail who added them to her clutch.

'There is only one fallen angel,' said Abigail softly. 'Have you sold your soul, Miriam?'

'I've sold nothing.' She stood up, faced her friend. 'Master Rathe sent me to the flames. The Queen signed my death warrant. I prayed to God but he did not answer. The Devil saved me. I did not ask him to but I assure you I sold nothing for the eternal life he gave me.'

'But what does he want in return? Satan always wants something.'

'Stanas is impulsive. He takes what he wants when he wants it and worries about its purpose later, if ever. In this he acts just like Rathe.' Miriam hastened back to the Abbey, Abigail breathlessly trying to keep pace with her.

'Master Rathe was greedy like any other titled man,' said Abigail. 'Stanas is not of this world. There must be a reason why he keeps you in this state of permanent youth.'

'For company,' said Kit, appearing suddenly as they rounded the corner. 'Stanas is the loneliest person I've ever known, and I knew Shakespeare.'

Abigail took a moment to catch her breath. 'We're all lonely in our own way, Kit, but we do not cut people off from their own kind for company.'

'Oh, but we do,' he said. 'We stratify humanity into ranks, denying the lowest their due, rewarding the highest with stultifying worship, creating loneliness on every rung.' He looked out to sea as if the answer to humanity's madness lay just beyond the horizon. 'Do you realise how unnatural the class system is, how unfair? Even the Queen sat lonely on her throne. I promise you, dear lady, every person with talent or power feels the same isolation as the detested executioner.' He scanned the cove. 'I wonder what they are doing down there today?'

'They are preparing for a feast in the tavern,' said Miriam.

'How can you tell?' asked Kit. 'Your eyesight is exceptional, but I don't believe you can see through walls.'

'I can see what they are buying in the Cheaps: geese, blackberries and nuts. I bought these things often enough myself at this time of the year.'

'What feast is it?' Kit asked.

'Michaelmas,' said Abigail. 'The Feast of the angels Michael, Gabriel, and Raphael. Did you not keep the feasts when you lived an ordinary life?'

'As an atheist I kept only my cynicism.' He sighed. 'Which made me a very lonely man. I spent most of my free time in the tavern, drinking to forget my sorrow.'

'Fyn would be helping in the tavern today,' said Abigail sadly. 'All of Portloe gather in the tavern for the Feast of Michaelmas. Those that do not fish must complete their harvest for this day marks the turning of the seasons.'

'What day is it?' asked Kit.

'The 10th of October,' said Miriam. 'All England celebrates.'

'Except us,' said Kit. 'We three who have the Devil for company.'

The three outliers looked down at the cove, feeling the full force of their isolation.

'Now I understand the loneliness you spoke of Kit,' said Abigail.

**

The morning stretched and thinned into noon and still the three remained fixed on the knoll looking wistfully down at a human celebration they could never again be part of. A chill breeze, more zephyr than wind, teased the loose tendrils of their hair into a dance, troubled the hems of their cloaks, its cold fingers foretelling the imminence of autumn.

'It's as well Stanas is not here,' said Abigail. 'It was the archangel Michael who evicted Lucifer from Heaven. I doubt this day holds any joy for him.'

Miriam frowned. 'No-one asked him to leave Heaven, Abby. He wanted more.'

'And he came *here*?' asked Kit, a bemused upward inflection on the last word.

'Only because nowhere else in the firmament welcomed him,' said Miriam.

Abigail kept her eyes on the cove, her sights dim but her imagination keen enough to conjure her son Fyn moving through the Cheaps with a live goose tucked under his arm, its murder troubling his tender heart, so like her own. He had been known to lose a goose on the way home from the Cheaps in years past, enduring Alice's scolding with a secret smile at his mother.

'The poor cannot celebrate,' said Kit at last. 'They lack the means. Stanas may be a pariah in Heaven and a scoundrel on earth but at least he is honest about his selfishness unlike the rich who enclose their land and the Monarch who turns a blind eye.'

'Honest if a little vague about his intentions,' said Abigail.

'And yet here we are, safe from the unreliable world thanks to the Devil. Cheer up, ladies, we can have our own feast.' He glanced at the basket. 'Have you collected enough eggs for a French cheesecake?'

Abigail laughed. 'Is that why you have left off writing your Masterpiece and come outside? To make sure we had enough eggs for your cheesecake?'

'No, I thought to enjoy a little sunshine and give you the news.' He beamed. 'I have completed my play and I'd love to read it to you after supper.'

'Yes please,' they said as one.

'And Mistress Abigail, Stanas may be the Devil, but he is here on earth walking our paths, experiencing our pleasure and pain, being one of us, which is more than can be said of his father or that dragon-slayer, Michael.'

'But what kind of world does he plan?' asked Abigail.

Kit turned his palms heavenwards, shrugged. 'I have no idea, but can it be any worse than the one we have created ourselves?'

Marlowe's study – that night after supper

'The tyrant removes his lover's body from the tomb and makes her his queen. It's grotesque,' said Abigail. 'Can he not smell her as she putrefies?'

'He is so dazzled by her he doesn't notice,' said Kit. 'That's the whole point. He is mad with love.'

Miriam sipped her rainwater, her eyes fixed on her idol. 'I think it's brilliant.'

'Why?' asked Kit.

Miriam raised her eyebrows. 'Why?'

'Please tell me why my new play is brilliant.'

'It is love in all her twisted glory – dark, mad, divine, altering yet arrowed. And the king and the tyrant and the dead lady live in a thrall outside the world much as we do here but unlike us they are imprisoned in their passion.'

'While we are just left out of feasts,' said Abigail.

Kit touched his lips and then his heart. 'Thank you Miriam, I have never felt so completely understood in my life. I love you for it.'

Miriam's frozen heart fluttered. 'When eternity palls I will remember that Kit Marlowe loved me once.'

'But why did you set it in Spain?' asked Abigail, shattering the moment.

'Madame, you have no imagination. I was inspired by Cervantes and his story of Don Quixote.'

'Who's Don Quixote?'

'Stanas gave me the book,' said Miriam. 'I'll lend it to you.'

Abigail's wrinkled cheeks burned. 'I can't read. You offered to teach me but there was never time. Remember?'

'Reading should be mandatory,' said Kit. 'Books open worlds.'

'Tell me about this Don Quixote, please,' said Abigail. 'I want to understand what you've done.'

'Don Quixote was a man who wished to become a knight errant and return the world to chivalry and honour at a time when madness reigned, still does, in the form of the Inquisition.'

'The Inquisition is a group of self-righteous judges appointed to combat religious deviation.' Miriam explained to Abigail.

'Eliminate free thought and inquiry,' added Kit. 'Quixote is a dreamer tilting at windmills, a metaphor for all the injustices of the world.'

'A good man then,' said Abigail.

'A fool is often the best and bravest of men,' said Kit. 'Daring to speak truth to power.'

'But why have you set a play meant for an English audience in Spain? Is it because the theatres in London are closed?' Abigail persisted.

'Don't remind me. It's a literary jest. In this slew of adventures Don Quixote meets a man called Cardenio, a fellow whose madness has annexed him from society and whose plight, which should inspire pity, inspires instead emulation in Don Quixote who decides there is spiritual virtue in living as Cardenio does, as a hermit. But what drove Cardenio to this sorry state I asked myself? That, Mistress Abigail, is what I wished to explore in my play.'

Miriam shifted her gaze to the open window, to the moonless sky beyond, her sights tuned inward, remembering. 'Master Rathe swore eternal devotion to me. Vowed that no-one had ever captured him so completely. I owned him, body, mind, and soul, he said. How swiftly love can turn to hate.' She looked back at Kit. 'You have captured every foible of love with this Masterpiece.'

'When death intercepts a union, love remains eternally pure as it did for Romeo and Juliet. Miriam there will be no other love for me but you now because –'

'Because we have no visitors,' said Abigail.

241

'Because I will die soon.' Kit almost laughed. 'Mistress Abigail, you have no romance in your soul.'

'I am eighty,' said Abigail and softening added, 'But I love Fyndern yet.'

'The lights will go out for me the day you die, Kit,' said Miriam. 'The world will grow dark.'

'I will come back for you if I can. I promise.' Kit bowed his head. 'Now, shall I read Act Two? It is even darker.'

'Darker than sharing your throne with a corpse?' asked Abigail, shuddering.

'Much darker, my dear.'

'Oh, then please read on,' she said before sipping her wine.

'Mistress Abigail has a macabre soul after all.' Kit laughed. 'To continue: in his prison cell the king, Govianus, is visited by the ghost of his dead lady, who informs him of his usurper's morbid fascination with her dead body. Govianus plans his revenge.' He smiled at Miriam. 'And it is sweet. When eventually Govianus is released from prison he applies poison to the lips of his dead lady and paints her face so that she seems to have come back to life.'

'But the smell?' said Abigail.

'Top up her wine please Miriam. As I was saying, when the usurper sees his lady love looking so alive he cries out, "O, she lives again!" kisses her lips and dies.' He smiled at Miriam. 'I imagined kissing your lips when I wrote that, how cold, how perfect, how fatal your kiss.'

'I would never drown you.' She glanced at Abigail. 'I will never drown anyone again.'

'But how sweet that death as your kiss seals my fate, transferring death from your lips to mine. It's romantic,' said Kit.

242

'It's gruesome,' said Abigail. 'I love it!'

'Success at last!' Kit raised his mazer in a toast. 'Mistress Abigail loves my work!'

Just then the sound of voices raised in song floated up to them and by the slurring of the words and the lack of harmony they judged the progress of the feast. The people of Portloe were enjoying themselves, their bellies full of ale and goose. The three outliers fell quiet, lost in memories of other feasts, other songs, other loves, other lives. To cheer them Miriam picked up her lute and began to sing, her voice rising and falling over a melody that spoke of stars and moons and love's fleeting brightness and faith.

> *The colour of the night is in the moon*
> *A trail of silver drifts across the limpid ocean*
> *Heightening the hint of her perfume*
> *The salty taste of tears upon my tongue*
> *The colour of my passion is your touch*
> *Soft against my hand, a feather brush*
> *The whisper of my name, your breath upon my cheek*
> *My heart expands the feeling I call love.*

Kit sighed and scrolled his play. 'This will be consigned to the grave to be dug up centuries from now. Maybe I will be resurrected in more forgiving minds and hearts.'

'But you live at least for now,' said Miriam. 'And I will record every moment of your remaining years on my soul for when I am alone.'

'Stanas will be with you,' said Abigail.

'Stanas is a hollow bell,' said Miriam. 'No chime issues from his soul and even if it did, he would be deaf to it. No, once you two are gone, I will be utterly alone. Everyone I ever loved gone.'

Abigail wiped a tear on the corner of her sleeve. 'What have you called this play, Kit?'

'Cardenio.'

'Why? Cardenio was a minor player in Don Quixote. Does he even appear in your play?'

Kit did not answer but gazed at Miriam. 'If only the world could have been our oyster. Imagine how we could have informed it. But here we are, frozen in a tower, dead to the world, me creating Masterpieces destined for a leper's grave in France. You wasting away.' He glanced at Abigail. 'Thank God for your cheesecakes, my dear.'

'Who will bury your plays, Kit, and who will dig them up?' Abigail asked.

'Graves are where Stanas hides all his significant treasures. He plans to disinter them in a future world and sell them to the highest bidder. Art and death are as interlocked as love and death.'

'Love and death are symbiotic partners,' said Miriam. 'Twined, consuming, their sights turned to each other as if the universe did not exist.'

'The universe does not exist for lovers,' said Kit, tying a ribbon around the manuscript. 'Or for artists.' He cocked his head. 'The feast is over. They've stopped singing.'

Abigail eased herself to her feet, steadied herself against the back of the chair. 'My son now sleeps in his bed. Will he dream of me?' She released her breath in a sigh. 'No matter, I will dream of him and his father.' She smiled, collected a candle. 'God rest ye both.'

Miriam watched her friend leave the room, noting her frailty, the slow progress. 'She will leave us soon.'

Kit touched her frozen hand. 'We both will, my love.'

The Abbey – 1656

'He's here!' cried Abigail, half-leaning out the window. 'Kit! Miriam! He's here!'

Kit growled but did not stir from the table where he was working on a brand-new play. 'I'll never finish this with him prattling complaint.'

'He'll bring fresh supplies of wine,' said Abigail.

Kit laughed. 'In that case I'll welcome him with open arms!'

Miriam rushed to the window, eager to see the glorious caravel gliding into the cove. Her passion for boats and the adventures they conjured had never abated since she and her mother had woven stories around them on their Sunday picnics last century. The vessel was moving slowly through the sentinel Heads, harvesting sunlight on its gleaming Carvel hull, Medusa prow slicing the blue-green throw of sea. Presently it came to rocking rest in the cove, the anchor lowered into those alien depths, sails furled, and a dinghy with Stanas already seated in it lowered over the side. The instant it settled on the water the crew scrambled down rope ladders and began rowing ashore.

'Imagine the things they've seen,' said Miriam, 'while we've been holed up here.'

'I'd best light the oven for his dinner,' said Abigail.

'I'll help you,' said Miriam.

'Ladies, calm yourselves, he won't be here till nightfall,' said Kit, not rousing himself from his latest play, every page covered in notes as lines were torn apart and reshaped for poetic flavour. 'He'll go into the village first, pay for rooms in the tavern for his crew and himself before he sneaks up here.'

'The tavern.' Abigail caught her breath. 'Fyn will ask him about me.'

'I doubt Fyn will recognise him,' said Kit.

'Fyn never forgets a face.'

'I doubt it's the same face. He had his eye on the ostler in Provence.' Kit pushed the pages aside and joined them at the window. 'Miriam, your remarkable eyesight will tell me, is he altered?'

'He has a new body,' she said. 'I wonder who was hanged recently?'

'What do you mean *hanged*?' asked Abigail.

Kit caught Miriam's eye. 'She'll know soon enough. Stanas is the Devil and –'

'Oh, I know that. Miriam told me last year. It's the new body I don't understand. I thought he was immortal like you, Miriam.'

'You'd better sit down.' Miriam drew Abigail away from the window and led her to a chair. 'Stanas vacates his appropriated bodies when they sicken or age or otherwise inconvenience him and then he –' she looked at Kit helplessly.

'And then he steals another,' said Kit. 'He does not always wait until a body is conveniently hanged; neck unbroken of course. Sometimes his victims have an unfortunate accident, like drowning or heart failure through fright.'

'But he was young and healthy. Why would he vacate his body?' asked Abigail.

'For a handsomer one.' Kit smiled. 'There was a remarkable young ostler at the Chateau. I hired him when Stanas was away. He had his mark then, I'm sad to say. Mistress Abigail, casualties are what happens when you traffic with the Devil.'

**

Stanas arrived at dusk, thirsty as usual but with a fresh supply of wine, velum and ink for Kit, gowns and buskins for Abigail and Miriam and new stock for the larder.

'The ostler,' said Kit with a nod at Abigail.

'To your taste?' asked Stanas with a grin.

'I have found lasting love in your absence,' said Kit with a soft look at Miriam.

'Just when you're too old to do anything about it.' Stanas laughed as he helped himself to an over-brimming goblet of red wine. 'Miriam returns your feelings. She has made it clear enough. Ah, well, dear Kit enjoy your remaining months on earth.'

'A love like ours may endure beyond earth,' said Kit.

'Nothing endures beyond earth. My father's appetites are insatiable.' Stanas slurped back the wine and re-poured. 'You will be consumed like everyone else.'

'Into Heavenly grace and abiding love,' said Abigail, glaring at him as she placed the trenchers on the table in Kit's study where they ate their meals now that Kit and Abigail found the stairs challenging. The pair also slept in ground floor cells rather than the ones upstairs where Miriam had first accommodated them. Only Miriam still used the cavernous upstairs room with its far-reaching view of the sea.

'Believe that old myth if it makes you feel comfortable but I promise you no-one survives Heaven,' said Stanas.

'You did,' said Abigail.

'I left. Do you like the gifts I brought you, Mistress Abigail?'

'The gowns are more beautiful than anything I have ever laundered or worn and I am very grateful.'

'I've been to London if anyone's interested.'

'We're all interested,' said Miriam, delivering a platter of fish. 'Sit down Stanas and try not to drink all the wine you've just delivered.'

'He says Heaven is dangerous,' said Abigail.

'Ignore him,' said Miriam. 'Not everyone can hear its music.'

'You'll never see Heaven, Miriam, so the argument is moot.'

'Stanas please sit down and eat.' Miriam took her seat at the table with Kit and Abigail.

'Are the theatres open again?' asked Kit, loading his trencher with fish.

'Still closed.' Stanas plopped down at the table, skewered a chunk of mackerel dripping with melted butter. 'I'm famished.'

Kit's shoulders sagged. 'My new play will wilt then.'

'You have a new play?' asked Stanas, fish suspended mid-air. 'Let me see it.'

'After supper,' said Abigail.

Stanas gaped at Abigail then turned to Kit and Miriam.

'Does she know who I am? Does she realise I could strike her dead with a look?'

'I know who you are and you've no right to take a life, Stanas Vedil, no matter how tempting a handsome new body may be.'

'Another woman who insists on being my conscience. You think taking lives is my father's exclusive right?'

Abigail shuddered. 'I don't know what's right or wrong anymore. Did you see my son in the tavern?'

'He was drinking with his friends. He's as plump as a partridge. That wife of his must have learned to cook.'

Abigail lifted her mazer with both hands, took a long draft of wine. 'Does he miss me?'

'I could scarcely introduce myself with my brand-new body.'

'How did you despatch him?' Abigail asked. 'The ostler.'

'I daresay he was frightened to death,' said Kit. 'Or drowned in the fountain.'

'Both,' said Stanas.

'Poor soul.' Abigail crossed herself. 'So many young men die to satisfy the lust in this household.'

'I've never killed anyone!' Kit protested.

'And I won't kill again,' said Miriam.

'And neither will I,' said Stanas, pulling an old wooden drinking cup out of the silk budget attached to his belt and placing it on the table in front of him. 'It's over.'

'What's this?' asked Kit. 'Are you giving up the quest?'

Stanas stared at the cup for a long moment before answering. 'It's my turn to drink from this old cup and when I do I will die.'

Kit eyed the splintery-looking vessel on the table. 'It's just an old cup.'

'To you,' said Stanas. 'But it has the power to send me home.'

'To Heaven or Hell?' Abigail pushed a meagre serving of fish around on her trencher but did not eat.

'There's no difference,' Stanas muttered. 'I'm a stranger in both realms.'

'And what will become of me if you die?' Miriam asked quietly.

Stanas bowed his head. 'I'm sorry. I don't know how to release your soul.'

'You've cursed her with eternal life and now you're bored with yours?' Abigail pushed her plate away. 'You truly are evil.'

'Did I ever claim otherwise?' Stanas asked. 'This may be my last meal.'

There was a long pause and then Kit began to laugh.

'So dramatic,' said Kit, spluttering. 'He's playing the victim again, ladies. Ignore him. What's so lethal about that old cup? Is it poisonous?'

'He drank from it at his last meal before they crucified him. He gave it to me in the garden when I tried to help him, offer him sanctuary. He refused my help, said it was my turn to drink from the cup. Don't you see, he drank from it and died which means –'

'Nothing.' Kit skewered a piece of fish. 'Your brother upset the ruling classes and they got rid of him. You court them. Stop frightening Miriam.'

'I could have hidden him as I've hidden you all these years Kit but he was determined to be an example.' He slammed his fist on the table. 'He had to be remembered you see. That was his assignment.'

Nobody said anything for a while and then Abigail spoke gently. 'Our Lord could not write his ideas down cleverly like Kit. How else could he be remembered other than through martyrdom?'

Stanas' eyes shone with a fierce light. 'Father puppets us all, even me. No-one escapes the glare of his will.'

'Did the angels not receive free will like us?' Abigail asked.

Stanas sighed. 'No-one really has free will and I'm tired, so tired.'

'So you're giving up.' Kit shook his head. 'When it all gets too hard you give up. Coward.'

'Stay,' said Miriam. 'For me.'

**

By ten of the village bell Stanas was calmer, fortified by half a dozen goblets of wine. They still sat at the table; their trenchers cleared by Miriam who had been told to leave the lone cup where Stanas could see it, his glances returning to it from time to time as if the vessel held some special magnetism or the hypnotic power to ignite regret.

'You think bringing a new world to fruition is easy?' said Kit, with an edge of irritation.

Stanas glowered at him over the rim of his goblet. 'It should be easy for an angel.'

'Creation is a challenge for mortal and angel alike and you know why?'

'You'll tell me, I'm sure.'

'I will tell you.' Kit slurred his words after keeping pace with the Devil's drinking for most of the evening. 'Because no matter your skill, no matter your advantages, the page is as blank for an angel as it is for a mere mortal like me.'

'Mere mortal! Huh! Advantaged with rare genius,' said Stanas.

Now Kit slammed *his* fist on the table. 'I have worked hard for every ounce of inspiration I've ever had. Genius is discipline and hard work, Stanas Vedil. It's not about playing below your level like you do.'

Stanas raised his goblet, saluting Kit. 'Touché and merci. You have framed my chief inadequacy – laziness.'

'What value is an easy accomplishment?' asked Kit, refreshing his mazer. 'You will be left hungering for the fulfillment that follows effort. You think writing plays is easy for me?' He took a long draft of wine. 'Genius doesn't make the page any less blank.'

'I lack inspiration,' said Stanas flatly.

'Because you ease your path with wealth,' said Kit, holding the Devil's gaze in his own in a vicelike grip.

'I'm disappointed,' said Abigail, garnering everyone's attention. 'I thought you were inspired to change the world, Stanas. It's a crime not to use one's gifts and yours are many.'

'Madame, your belief almost shames me into revision.' Stanas raised his goblet to her. 'Thank you most humbly. Truly, I feel humble for the first time in living memory. Let's not argue any more tonight, Kit. We're both in our cups. Miriam, soothe us with a song?'

Miriam took up the lute and sang for them, her song conjuring remembrances of long-ago innocence and afterwards Kit read the first scene of his new play. When he lowered the page, silence enveloped the company as each soul retreated into their private worlds of loss and longings and unrealised gifts.

Stanas broke the silence, his glance returning to the old wooden vessel glowing dimly in the candlelight. 'They stopped looking for this, all those mad knights.'

Miriam and Abigail exchanged a puzzled look.

'He means the Knights Templar,' said Kit.

'Is this old cup the Holy Grail?' asked Abigail.

'It is,' said Stanas. 'A plain old cup, common as a million others, but he drank from it and made it exceptional.' Stanas' eyes had a haunted emptiness as if he had seen too much and understood too little. 'Why did he tell me it was my turn to drink from it? What did he think my death could possibly achieve?'

'Maybe it's the cup of life rather than death,' said Abigail. 'What did those knights think it could do for *them* if they drank from it?'

'They believed it would grant them eternal life,' said Stanas, dragging his gaze to Miriam. 'The cruellest cut of all.'

'Why have you brought it here?' Miriam asked. 'Are we all to drink from it? Even me?'

'Only me. I fear my time has come to risk the Grail. I will never rule the world.' His face a mask of sorrow. 'How can I compete with tyrants whose torture is more finely-honed than mine? How can I topple nations already on their knees?'

'By offering them milk and honey,' said Miriam. 'That's what you said you'd do.'

'I lied. I hate sharing and I'm far from generous.' Stanas shivered despite the warmth of the fire. 'Nightly my brother appears in my dreams, offering me this cup that I may drink.'

'Burn it,' said Kit. 'Be rid of it.'

'Drink from it,' said Abigail. 'Fulfill your destiny whatever it may be.'

'I'll be crucified.'

Miriam grabbed the cup, dashed her rainwater into it and emptied the contents in one long swallow.

Stanas caught his breath. Kit and Abigail clasped hands. All three stared at her, waiting for something, *anything* to happen. But when nothing changed Stanas sighed audibly.

'It has no power.' He turned the old cup over in his hands. 'It's an empty vessel.'

Kit smiled. 'Imagination is the only power it ever had. You and those mad knights imagined it had sacred properties.' He tapped his forehead. 'It's all in the mind, everything from religion to royalty. We fill vacuums with false power.'

'All these years I believed it was special but it's just an old cup.' Stanas looked at Miriam. 'I'll stay with you and –' He paused. 'Well, let's not plan too far ahead.'

The Abbey –1666

And then there were none.

Abigail died in her sleep in the winter of 1656, a merciful death, and a month later Kit followed her, albeit kicking and screaming that he was being plunged into eternal darkness. Miriam swabbed his fevered brow with cool presses of moistened linen and when his breath shortened and silenced his complaints she sang to him. It was on a magnificent high note, pure as a songbird's, that his soul finally flew.

She could not bring herself to bury her friends. Remembering the tyrant in Kit's play who kept his dead queen enthroned gave her the inspiration to arrange her friends' bodies at the table they had shared in happier times and secure them upright in their respective chairs. She placed Kit's unfinished play in front of him and arranged a bouquet of spring flowers before Abigail.

When the smell of their decay overwhelmed her, she sealed off the room and retreated upstairs to the window where she kept a lonely vigil over her borderless world.

**

A year passed and then another and when the sun had burned ten summers she dared unseal the room and visit her friends. Ten years had made skeletons of them, their clothes hung loose as shrouds upon their bones, but their empty eye sockets were turned to each other as if in conversation and between them the Holy Grail sat unyielding of salvation.

Stanas had not returned in all that time and she feared he had made good on his threat to abandon the quest and seek restoration in Heaven or sink back down into Hell. If he had gone to one ethereal home or the other she was truly alone.

254

Miriam made herself a small supper of boiled eggs, filled her mazer with wine for the first time since her "death" and joined her friends at the table. Over supper she spoke to them of the seasons she had witnessed from her perch, the generations of terns that had raised their young on the window ledge, the songs of migrating whales and her own songs, written since their passing, her musical voice rising and falling over a one-sided thread of observations.

If she listened closely she imagined she heard their whispered response.

London – 1666

In late 1664, a bright comet was seen in the sky over London and the people, ever superstitious, wondered what evil it portended. Stanas, holed up in his Chateau, saw the portent and decided the moment had arrived to revisit his quest, for nothing gave the Devil more traction than a perfectly normal astronomical event. The general run of humanity were nowhere near as inquisitive, irreverent or brilliant as Copernicus or Galileo. They would never countenance a heliocentric solar system with a cache of satellites looping the ringmaster sun. The comets and asteroids, flotsam and jetsam of a decaying galaxy, were not strong enough to escape the sun's grip but the valiant little scraps of dust and ice were willing to try and in that elliptical traverse the superstitious masses read doom.

A year after the comet, Stanas arrived in a London chaotic with plague. The gates at Ludgate, Newgate, Aldersgate, Cripplegate, Moorgate and Aldgate were locked but he was able to enter the city via the arterial Thames and take shelter on the lee side of London Bridge. From the safety of the river, he assessed the level of fear shredding the populace, gauging the right moment to present himself as their saviour and by whatever means possible persuade them of his benevolence. The city was in disarray. The age-old social stratification no longer applied for the rich had fled to their country estates and King Charles II had removed his family and his Court to Salisbury in September 1665. Later when the plague found its way to Salisbury he would move his entourage to Oxford, there to hide until it was safe to return to London.

The poor able to leave the city had to be armed with a certificate of health signed by the Lord Mayor of London but tragically they were often met with locked gates when villages, fearful of contagion, barred them entry. Rather than return to London and certain death they roamed the countryside, surviving on whatever they could scavenge in the open fields. But they were the lucky ones, the poor remaining in London had to subsist on goodwill.

Unlike the cowardly King, the Aldermen and the Lord Mayor of London, Sir John Lawrence, opted to stay at their posts providing much-needed ballast for London's sinking ship as businesses closed when merchants and professionals fled and the small number of clergymen, physicians and apothecaries coping with the huge number of victims began to die.

By the winter of '65 trade and business had dried up completely and the streets were empty except for the dead-carts and the dying and the last few remaining physicians hurrying through the streets hawklike in their long-nosed plague masks. With closed markets, sealed gates and no trade, it was a miracle the people did not starve but this was due to the foresight of Sir John Lawrence and the City of London Corporation who, working together, arranged for a commission of one Farthing to be paid above the normal price for every quarter of corn that landed in the Port of London.

Another food source they arranged was from the surrounding village farmers who sold their vegetables outside the gates, negotiating sales by shouting and collecting their payment in coins that had been submerged in a bucket of vinegar to disinfect them.

**

For a year the Devil watched, tacitly waiting for his moment to strike. With the King and his Court hiding out in Oxford the opportune time to overthrow the Monarchy would surely show itself in the form of a rebellion but as the months dragged on and illness crept from house to house like a thief in the night killing a quarter of London's population he began to wonder what kind of Kingdom he would inherit. Without the rich, all that remained was a broken rabble huddled in overcrowded tenements in a city stinking with open drains that made slippery sewers of the cobbled streets. Hardly the glamorous tenure he imagined.

When the stench of death and putrescence reached its tentacles across the river and into the hull of his boat, he considered retreating either to Provence or Cornwall, there to hide out until he had a plan guaranteed to supplant both the Monarchy and the irritatingly excellent Lord Mayor whose partnership with the equally excellent Corporation of London was saving lives. He was about to leave in the autumn of 1666, auspiciously his number, but paused, sensing something even more evil was brewing. London was eerily quiet and chillingly empty after the Black Death but something else was coming, he sensed it in the malevolent calm that presages a ship-wrecking storm at sea.

And then all the evil portended in the comet of '64 arrived in the form of – FIRE!!

**

Shortly after the Bowe bells tolled the midnight hour on Sunday 2nd September 1666, Thomas Farriner, a baker in Pudding Lane, removed the last batch of manchets from his oven and arranged them with the other twelve batches on high shelves where they would be safe from the hungry rats that swarmed the city. He had been lucky enough to buy a large quantity of unspoiled flour and sufficient butter and milk to continue his business when so many others were failing. Hopefully, he would sell all thirteen batches on the morrow and pay off the debts he'd accrued over the last couple of nightmarish years. As he brushed the ashes from the oven into a bucket he gave thanks his family had survived the worst of the contagion that had decimated London.

Before retiring, he took one last look at the loaves that would pay off his debts. For surety he mumbled a prayer of thanks to that amorphous presence that orchestrated the fates of men. No longer sure whether God was a Catholic or a Protestant he strung the words together in a hasty muddle hoping to excuse any misunderstanding on his part about God's preferred religion. Upstairs, after shifting into his nightrail and cap, he knelt beside his bed and rushed through a more formal prayer before slipping into bed and clinging to his plump, reassuring wife. The day had been long and hot and ruffled by an easterly wind that shortened tempers and stripped the last leaves of autumn off the threadbare trees.

Finding his wife's body too hot for comfort he released her and threw off his side of their shared woollen blanket. Tossing and turning he finally fell into a fitful sleep only to wake an hour later coughing and spluttering as ghostly tendrils of smoke crept under the door. His first thought was for his thirteen batches of manchets, his second was regret that he had chosen such an unlucky number, his third was that if he did not rouse his family immediately they would all die.

Moments later he and his family were scaling the wooden balconies between his house and his neighbour's, swinging perilously over a thirty-foot drop onto the cobbles below. But no sooner had they installed themselves in their neighbour's bedroom than the entire street emerged, gathering in front of his house, passing buckets of water to douse the flames that waved like sails from the lower storey windows.

Despairing, he watched as everything he owned crackled to ash: his manchets, his home, his debt-free future. It took the Parish constables an hour to arrive and judge that the adjoining houses, those of his kindly neighbours and several others, should be demolished to prevent the fire spreading further. But it was too late, the flames were marching in vermillion legions across rooftops, sparks leaping from one top-heavy upper storey to the next, devouring everything in their progress towards the warehouses and flammable stores on the riverfront.

**

Stanas was roused from a deep and comfortable sleep to the sound of supernatural crackling. Springing out of bed and tumbling onto the deck he saw an aureole of orange flames crowning the city. A strange discordant symphony of roaring and splintering accompanied the shrieking wind that had not ceased its bullying for three days. The banshee cacophony terrified everyone else but Stanas for whom it was music, the chords of triumph. He gave thanks to the forces that had conspired to visit one catastrophe upon the heels of another – two years of plague and now the fires of Hell.

For the remainder of that fateful Sunday night he watched the incendiary demolition of the city, his optimism rising with every falling building. By dawn, with the fire still raging, order broke down in the city as the rabble focused their hatred and blame on the French and Dutch immigrants whom they accused of starting the fires. Gratuitous acts of violence left many innocents dead or bleeding on the charred streets. All Monday the fires burned and on into the night there was still no relief as the banshee wind fanned the flames.

By Tuesday the fire had spread over the whole city. Flames destroyed St Paul's Cathedral and leapt the River Fleet threatening the King's Court at Whitehall. From the deck of his boat, Stanas watched the city being consumed, the people disordered and violent. He could not have planned it better: one plague upon another had reduced the populace to a lynching mob, fertile ground for a tyrant once guilt set in. The inferno drove Londoners to the high Roman wall enclosing the city, their meagre belongings bundled into carts or hand-held budgets. But when their escape was restricted to eight narrow gates, panic broke out with much screaming and wailing, their carts, horses and wagons creating an impassable bottleneck, trapping refugees in a blanket of intense heat and choking smoke.

In the small hours of Tuesday night while the fire still raged Stanas ordered his crew to row quietly out of London and seek refuge in the Chanel, there to ponder whether he would return to Provence or visit Miriam.

He decided to visit Miriam.

The Abbey – 1666

'Peace offering.'

Stanas heaved the solid gold chest he had lugged all the way up the goat-track onto the table in the upstairs room where Miriam sat watching the horizon. He took a moment to catch his breath and dab at the perspiration beading his brow.

'That track is overgrown.'

'No-one has been here to clear it,' she said without turning around.

'I've brought you a gift.'

'What use are gifts to me?'

'This one is rather special. The world thinks it's missing. It's the larnax of Alexander the Great, lost these many centuries. I stole it from his tomb in Alexandria.'

'You steal everything.'

'I'm hardly alone in that. Every fortune is built on theft.'

'The riches of genius are not built on theft.'

'I see you are not in the mood for company.' He sauntered over to the board, poured himself a goblet of wine. 'London has burned to the ground.'

She rose slowly and moved to the table. 'Cheapside?'

'Ash.'

'I'm glad.' She touched the lid of the solid gold chest. 'What am I to do with this?'

'Keep it safe until I need it.'

261

'And this is what you call a gift?'

'I've given you fine clothes and jewels that you never wear.'

'What use are jewels and fine clothes in an abandoned Abbey? The terns won't notice what I wear.'

Ignoring that he continued. 'Miriam it was spectacular! Flames consumed St Paul's Cathedral and the incinerating heat and choking smoke drove the populace to the gates where they were trapped! It was marvellous! When I return in triumph –'

'You will give them milk and honey. Yes?'

'No. I won't part with a sou or a ryal, but I will offer them false hope and this golden chest will convince them of my divinity.'

'It's just a pretty box, Stanas.'

'And the Holy Grail is just an old cup, and the Ark of the Covenant is just a wooden box and this larnax is just another faux symbol. Their value lies in the imagination as Kit said.' He drained his goblet, refilled. 'My brother's cup held the promise of eternity.'

'It holds flowers now.' Miriam nodded at the arrangement on the table.

'A far better use for it. The Ark holds two stone tablets, Aaron's fecund rod and a pot of manna. All symbols of life.'

'And what does the larnax hold?'

'My life. My future. My rule over the earth. People will follow whoever possesses it.'

Miriam shook her head. 'Always dressing up your inadequacy in gilt.'

'Why should I feel guilty? My father abandoned me not the other way round.'

'Gold, Stanas, gilt. You don't understand humanity. They won't be in the mood to be led. They will want practical help, new houses, food, work.'

He drank the wine in one swallow, refilled and sauntered back to the table. 'You think Alexander's army was comfortable when they followed him out of Pella? You think the people leaving homes and jobs behind in Egypt had full bellies when they followed Moses into the desert? I have lived long and –'

'Intermittently.'

'Regardless. I have observed humanity. They are deeply superstitious, always vulnerable to a well-made tale of supernatural proportions. Alexander conquered the world three hundred years before my brother was peddling his forgiveness-and-love philosophy. Alexander ruled with magic and the sword and he never let this chest out of his keeping.'

'Kit ruled with the pen.'

'Kit doesn't rule yet and speaking of the pen –' He ran his hands over the lid. 'Alexander kept his copy of the Iliad in this.'

'The Iliad?'

'A book by an ancient Greek writer called Homer. It was Alexander's bible, a tale of glorious conquest, the story of Troy and a beautiful woman.' He smiled. 'I have the larnax and I have you and with these two weapons I will conquer the world.'

'What will I do?'

'Sing. I will sail into a decimated London with the larnax of Alexander the Great and a songbird so gifted she once enthralled a queen. Yes, they will believe I possess supernatural power and they will turn to me for guidance. I will thrall the broken people with visions of a New World order. I will be their King and you their Queen.' He opened the lid of the chest, revealing an ancient, scrolled manuscript. 'The Iliad. I haven't read it. It's in Greek. But I know it glorifies conquest. Alexander imagined himself the new Dionysus, the vanquishing, liberating hero, a god no less.'

'You have no army; you can't fight, and you certainly won't feed the hungry masses. How exactly do you intend to conquer them?'

'By being far enough above their turmoil to be a beacon of hope.' He began to pace. 'Their scurrilous King fled to Oxford leaving his people to fry.'

'As did you.'

'They weren't my people but when I go back and claim them with a song and a talisman of victory they will be my slaves and I will inherit everything due a king.'

'You must feed them, Stanas. Even your brother did that.'

'And they crucified him.' He sloshed back his wine, refilled. 'I am burning with ambition for conquest. How do you suggest I do it?'

'You'll need a history and a plan.'

'My history doesn't read well, I'm afraid.'

'A dazzling plan then. Kit said a blank page is never easy to fill. But that is what you are Stanas: a blank page. It is time you wrote upon it. Perhaps that's what your brother meant when he said it was your turn to drink from the Grail.'

'My brother never wrote anything down. He never faced a blank page.' He slumped down onto a chair. 'How do I start, Miriam?'

She handed him a quill and a blank sheet of velum. 'With a single word. Write what you know, Stanas, that's what Kit said.'

He shivered. 'I know Heaven and I know Hell but I know very little of this world. I scarce know its language or its ways and now when I might conquer it I feel my falsehood most keenly. I am tired of failure, Miriam.'

'But you can't steal another's success,' she ran her hand over the larnax, 'no matter how brightly it shines.' She sat opposite him. 'What do you want for yourself alone?'

He turned his head from side to side, his lips moving over a cant. 'To be worshipped.'

'Hollow.'

'To be obeyed.'

'Empty.'

'To be –'

'Yes. Kit said it clearly. You have two choices, *to be or not to be*. Try being for the first time in your long and empty chain of lives.' Miriam touched his hand, her cold fingers conducing a shiver. 'Kit would tell you to face that blank page and write upon it.'

Stanas bowed his head and when he looked back up his eyes shone with tears. 'But what if I am not good enough? How can I bear more failure?'

A crack of lighting split the horizon and moments later a low grumble of thunder. Miriam removed the scroll from the larnax, teased it open. A craze of unfamiliar text flared off the page, the lettering geometric and sharp-edged but possessed of a compelling alien beauty. She did not understand the words but sensed the strength of their creator in the cribbed scrawl.

'You must make your mark Stanas, no matter how faint.'

He stood and looked over her shoulder. 'I envy Homer. To write so flawlessly of his times and ideals, his genius reaching across the labyrinth of two thousand years. I want to be remembered like that, Miriam. It would save me having to constantly reinvent myself. I don't want my mark to be faint, I want it to be a stain upon the earth that time cannot remove.'

He moved to the window to watch the brewing storm. 'I have no ear for music but I have seen more than any living being and if I could transmogrify my memories into verse —'

Miriam joined him at the window. 'Kit wrote of the Devil. You are the Devil. Write what you know.'

The sea rushed at the chiselled rocks below, gnashing and furious and impotent with rage against her confinement. Her rhythmic dashing against her boundaries congealed into an ominous rumbling and growling like some great chained beast. The sky matched her mood in a roil of green-tinged clouds that glowered broodingly overhead. Moored in the cove, Stanas' caravel looked small and frail and in imminent danger of uprooting its anchor and splintering against the rocks.

'Why do you keep them?' he asked without taking his eyes off his boat. 'Kit and Abigail.'

'For company.'

'The smell must have been unbearable for your heightened senses.'

'I locked myself in here while they rotted.'

'We must leave here. I need you with me in Provence now that Kit is gone. Ill-tempered and selfish he may have been but he was company. Of course you'll have to pretend to breathe and eat and drink in front of the servants and when I take you to Paris for new clothes.'

'Paris.' She whispered the name. 'Is it really as beautiful as the sailors in the Cheaps used to say it was?'

'Better and I speak French.' He smiled suddenly. 'Yes, I believe I will become a writer. The pen is after all mightier than the sword.'

'Kit did not come back for me,' she said softly.

Stanas paused on his way to murder a chicken for his dinner. 'Did he promise you that?'

'He said he would try.' She tracked the first sheets of rain blurring the horizon. 'Is he really lost in the dark or is my soul too shadowed to receive his light?'

'Kit would never escape the spider. No-one can. My father ravens for souls. I told you.'

She turned to him, held his eyes. 'Are you sure Stanas? Or is your own soul so lost you no longer recognise light?'

He shivered. 'I'll never know and neither will you. We are trapped in immortality.'

The Chateau – Provence 1715

'Miriam!'

She raised her head, listened. The cry came again. She thought about answering but knew it would be the same old scene. He would be sitting at his desk, a sea of discarded pages at his feet, his head in one hand, a quill dripping ink onto a blank page in the other.

Ignoring Stanas, she resumed her exploration of the garden, a series of outdoor *rooms* connected by a long colonnade covered in grape-laden vines. As she navigated the lacing of terracotta tiled walkways connecting the *rooms*, she hummed the tune she was hearing. Summer and the beds were aflame, the air fragrant with a mingling of perfume and flavours recognisable from her time in the kitchen: basil, rosemary, thyme and oregano. Bees drunk on nectar droned from one flower to the next like roués at a ball. Cascading down from the Chateau a series of lawns smooth as green velvet was aggregated with specimen trees that cast long, blue-green shadows. Spaced at intervals along the colonnaded walkway were stone benches where a tired soul might contemplate the scaped perfection.

The various garden *rooms* were walled in with a combination of stone and clipped evergreen shrubs. Each one featured a different colour palette but common to all were the life-size white marble statues of nude Greek men and partially-robed women permanently frozen in their various occupations: pouring water from an urn, playing an instrument or, in one instance, wrestling with an angel, but most were simply in contemplation of the landscape. And accompanying this visual and olfactory feast, the splash of fountains.

As she drifted from *room* to *room* the gardeners stopped their clipping to watch her pass. Too frightened to speak to her for fear of her brother's perplexing jealousy, they tracked her in silence, envious and awed that one so fair should live in their midst.

This was how Miriam and Stanas managed their arrangement.

He was her brother. When the body he wore was young and freshly-acquired, he was her younger brother returned from some foreign adventure. The turnover of staff was necessarily frequent and for the benefit of the newly-hired Miriam made a show of welcoming him home and as his body aged and hers remained youthful, the old staff were fired and new staff were told that Miriam's hermetic older brother was a writer holed up in his study creating great works too progressive for the world, hence the plays that were never staged, the books that were never published, the jeremiads never circulated amongst the discontented mobs of Paris. But in truth, despite fifty years of struggle Stanas had not produced one book, play or jeremiad.

And when he "died" Miriam would look after the Chateau until her "brother" arrived with a new Will leaving everything to him and the cycle would begin again with the welcome return of her profligate young and occasionally twin brother.

This pattern of deceit had been repeated without arousing suspicion for half a century.

**

'Miriam!' his cries were amplified by his removal to the balcony.

The gardeners looked up, Miriam stalled her exploration, arrested her melody, and retraced her footsteps, passing the gardeners whom she acknowledged with an amused nod, and to a chorus of increasingly irritated repetitions of her name she climbed the stairs of the glorious old pile she now called home and found her discombobulated "brother".

'You called?'

'And you ignored me and don't pretend you couldn't hear me; your hearing is supernaturally endowed.' He waved a copy of La Gazette in her face. 'Read this!"

'You know I can't read French.'

Stanas flung the magazine open to the first page and began to translate the main article: a peon of praise exaggerating the virtues of their King, Louis XIV. On and on it rambled about his tasteful renovations of Versailles, his talent for ballet, his wit and valour. The "Sun King" was God and State embodied in one glorious Monarch possessed of magnificent calves.

269

The King was a master fencer, an unparalleled vaulter, a consummate dancer who trained daily with his personal dancing master, Pierre Beauchamp. He had beautifully sculpted legs and a perfectly proportioned body, a match for his outstanding intellect and vision.

She held up her hand. 'Stop! It's just more of the same old litany listing the King's virtues. Why did you really call me, Stanas?'

Stanas flung his arms out wide sending a Chinese porcelain vase crashing onto the Turkish rug. His new body being taller than the last he had yet to adjust to his proportions. 'I didn't finish! He's dead. A month ago. September 1st. Gangrene.'

'Did he fall off his horse or was it a mistimed plié?'

He took a breath before continuing. 'I thought we might visit Versailles. Your remarkable beauty and musical virtuosity should be sufficient entrée into the narrowest of circles.' He ran his hands over his black velvet doublet. 'Ah, to be part of life again. Just the thought of it gets my juices flowing.'

She knelt, picked up the shards of broken porcelain. 'Some things can never be put back together as they were, but I would very much like a change of scenery.'

'And when you sing you will get me close enough to the Dauphin to eliminate him.'

She placed the broken pieces on the table. 'Why don't you just steal his body?'

'And be stifled by etiquette? No, my dear, I need freedom to rule my own way.'

'How do you intend to eliminate the Dauphin?'

'I'm very creative.'

**

The Sun King's extravagance had bankrupted France and the length of his life had kept many a noble in lifelong imprisonment at Versailles where the King carefully monitored their connections and hobbled their power, and all under the beam of his radiant eye. Freed at last by his death, the nobles who had managed to outlive him left Versailles in a chaotic scramble to reclaim their decades-long abandoned estates. It was upon an uncertain and largely empty Versailles that Stanas and Miriam descended in early 1716 and it was there that a series of tragic deaths occurred.

First the Dauphin, Louis, Duke of Burgundy, died of smallpox along with his wife and elder son. How the disease arrived at Court remained a mystery but rumours that the Bourbons were cursed began to circulate when the Duke's younger brother was killed in a riding accident one morning when out hunting with the newly-arrived Duc Stanas Vedil who, due to his youth and recent inheritance, had been fortunate enough to remain in his Chateau in Provence when all the rest of the French nobility were incarcerated in Versailles. The death of both the Dauphin and his brother left the Duke of Burgundy's two-year-old son Dauphin of France and all this was achieved before Miriam had sung a single note.

'Save your voice, my dear. Tomorrow we go to Paris where the Regent moved the Court almost before the Sun King's gangrenous body had cooled.'

**

Paris, the City of Lights, where on every street corner an oil lamp suspended on a post was lit at sunset, their warm halo providing some comfort for the homeless through the long, cold nights and offering sufficient illumination to help the cup-shotten Second Estaters find their way home, unlike in London where the cup-shotten depended on the moon and stars to light their stumbling way home.

Miriam and Stanas were installed in Stanas' Parisian apartment on la Rue de Sèvres, within walking distance of the Jardin de Luxemburg, the almost Italian home of the late Marie de Medici, the widow of King Henry IV. From the balcony Miriam could watch the city transforming into a replica of the night sky as the lamps were lit street by street.

'I want you to enchant the Regent.' Stanas called out from the candlelit interior of their top floor apartment.

'Come and look at the lights being lit.'

'I'm working.'

By working he meant he was drinking his way through a flagon of wine as he studied the gossip section of the Gazette: salacious accounts of sexual misadventures amongst the haute bourgeoisie and the Second Estate, all easily identifiable in crudely-drawn cartoons. 'He should be easy enough to seduce with a song. Are you listening?'

'You really should see these lights.'

'I've seen them before.' He yawned.

'You've seen everything before.'

'Ooh, here's a cartoon of the Regent and an article. It says that Philippe d'Orleans is a weak and sickly man whose wife frequents salons where she entertains her coterie of ambitious lovers. Yes, the Duc d'Orleans is a much-cuckolded, worn-out old man of one and forty. I deem him susceptible to a song.'

'One and forty is not so old.'

'It is ancient when your wife is a flirtatious beauty, daughter of the Sun King's mistress.'

She came back inside. 'His wife is base-born like me?' she whispered.

'No need to whisper. France has made it both fashionable and profitable to be born out of wedlock, especially to a king. Now we must get you fashionably dressed. I know a seamstress, a fine woman indebted to me for her rent and wine and upon whom I depend for certain other services. I pay her to keep free of the French disease. She'll be pleased to make my *sister* a robe battante. Don't look at me like that, it's the latest fashion.'

'Women look pregnant in those sacques.'

He laughed. 'That, my dear, is the whole idea. Hiding an illicit pregnancy was Madame de Montespan's plan when she designed them. Now these sacques are the fashion. I keep up with the trends unlike you and Kit.'

'Kit's gone.'

'I know but he never caught up with fashion. With your hair worn loose and adorned with a simple white lace mantilla in the Spanish style you'll be a magnificent contrast to the ladies of Versailles decked out in their gaud and glitter. Those remnants of the Ancien Regime were hopelessly out-of-date with fashion.'

'The Ancien Regime?' She poured herself a glass of water.

'The Monarchy. The Bourbon line will fray soon and when it does, I will pick up the threads and weave them so tightly they can never be broken. But first let me introduce you to Paris and Paris to you. We will dress you in pure white and while the ladies of Versailles teeter around on ten-inch heels studded with diamonds, you will wear four-inch heels with plain white leather uppers. We must never lose our balance, Miriam.'

Paris – 1716

273

For Miriam, the movement of Paris registered as pulse, the sounds as breath, the language as melody yet to be tuned into song. Parisians were more vibrant than Londoners, less gloomy despite the legions of poor dependent on the Vincentian Family, a group of people inspired by the saintly Catholic priest Vincent de Paul. The care of the poor should have been the concern of the late King but like Elizabeth he was careless of his flock and like his French predecessors he had been too busy expanding Versailles.

Still, the Parisians were a glamorous and spirited people, the women openly flirtatious, the men admiring and unafraid to kiss a hand or a cheek. At least that's how they seemed to Miriam, a foreigner for whom exchanges were music rather than gossip. From this linguistically removed distance she moved through the crowds like a bark upon water, revelling in the passage but never setting foot on shore.

**

They were sitting in Le Café Procope, a meeting place for savants, writers and actors from the theatre across the street, the Comédie-Française, and in addition to the artistic patrons, men from all walks of Parisian society gathered to chat over a cup of the newly-introduced brew called coffee that was delicious when mixed with a small quantity of cloves, cardamom seeds and sugar. The gentlemen sat at marble tables in groups of three, sometimes a crammed five, to discuss philosophy, science, politics, religion, art or merely to sharpen their wits. The cave-like interior was lit by crystal chandeliers, the narrow enclave cleverly expanded with wall mirrors. The absence of women was unremarked upon by the patrons who aired their views over a sorbet or a coffee served in a porcelain cup by waiters in exotic Armenian garb. Likewise the occasional presence of a woman was unremarked upon. Miriam and Stanas fell into the habit of frequenting Le Café Procope daily, Miriam to enjoy the proximity to other people after living so long alone and Stanas to discern the political and social currents.

While Miriam sipped her coffee, a delicious new sensation for her, Stanas listened closely to the conversations at the nearest tables, not always liking what he heard and often complaining of a headache.

'Stanas, can't you just enjoy being alive? You're always advising me to do so.' She took a sip of the exotic brew. 'The sun's shining, the air's fragrant and this coffee is delightful.'

'You don't know what they're saying,' he muttered. 'There's no traction for me in this divided rabble. No-one agrees about anything. How can I enchant them if I don't know their weaknesses?'

'How have you managed it in the past?'

'I haven't.' He glowered into the middle distance.

At a nearby table a young man was holding court, his audience a collection of earnest, poorly-dressed young men and one over-painted woman of middle years. Suddenly Stanas leaned forward listening intently and clinging to his cup, the dark brew cooling untouched. Miriam closed her eyes drinking in the musical rise and fall of the young man's voice, his calm reflective tone communicating a sense of hope. When he finished speaking the young men applauded and the woman nodded as if she had decided something. A waiter dressed in robes delivered a fresh cup of coffee to the speaker who said something that made his company laugh and applaud.

'What did he say?' Miriam asked Stanas.

'He said he finds inspiration in coffee and drinks fifty cups a day.'

'And what did he say in his speech?'

Stanas sighed. 'He argues for religious tolerance and freedom of thought. He wants to eradicate the hold of religion and weaken the priestly and aristo-monarchical authority. He sees a constitutional monarchy that protects people's rights as the only fair governance.' He rubbed his temples. 'I have missed my moment.'

Miriam looked across at the fellow, a young man scarce out of boyhood with a pleasant face and far-seeing eyes. A moment later those eyes met hers and widened as if he saw there something both marvellous and terrifying. Miriam smiled to reassure him that she at least was not the Devil. He returned a tentative nod before reengaging with his coterie.

The lone woman's voice now took over the conversation, the word theatre ringing the only familiar bell for Miriam. Presently Stanas groaned.

'What is it now?'

'She is the wife of the Director of the Comédie-Française and she has promised him a season with his new play. Yes, this fellow is a writer and he will spread his philosophy with his pen which is exactly what I saved Kit for and what I have been endeavouring to do.'

'M. Voltaire, vous avez ma promesse, votre pièce Œdipe sera présentée en première à la Comédie-Française l'année prochaine.' Her ringing voice making an announcement that drew further applause, this time from the entire café including the waitstaff.

Once again M. Voltaire's eyes met Miriam's and she read there uncertainty.

'Vous conduirez notre nation hors des ténèbres et dans la lumière. Vous apportez les lumières, M. Voltaire.'

A smile trembled on Voltaire's lips as the applause swelled to a crescendo. Miriam felt the ovation as a smash of glass upon rocks and she struggled against the impulse to dash from the candlelit interior out into the sunlit street. Voltaire once again caught Miriam's eye, his own widening and fearful as if the mantle of saviour sat heavily upon his shoulders. Stanas caught the look.

'Sing for him.'

She broke the hold, turned to Stanas, a protest half-formed on her lips. 'But –'

'I must disrupt this. To kill a snake you must strike off its head. He is the head of snake.'

'What about the Regent?'

'Forget the Regent. This young man is our mark.'

'*Your* mark. You cannot kill him with a song. He holds them in his thrall as the sun holds the earth. You could no more stop him than you could hold back the tide.'

'There is no room for both him and me in Paris.'

'Then you must leave Stanas. This is the change humanity has been craving for over a century. I have lived long enough to see the fault in our stars: the Monarchy, the Church, the wizened old beards that carry out our evil laws, like the men who sent me to the flames. He gives voice to the many who are tired of oppression.'

'Sing for him, enchant him, steer him from his course. I have lived longer than you and I know it only requires one voice, one command to drive a ship to wreck. Be that voice.' He reached out and squeezed her hand. 'For me.'

She withdrew her hand. 'I may sing but not for you. I sing for me, Stanas. For me.'

Voltaire still gazed at her and she looked back at him, recognising that same loneliness she had seen in the rheumy old eyes of the Queen. She wondered if perhaps that was what he likewise saw in her. The applause sustained, its rising tide crushing her with an intensity akin to suffocation. To stop it as much as to reassure the young man the crowd had elected as France's saviour, she rose and began to sing, her voice cutting through the crashing din as struck crystal silences a room of revellers. One by one the hands stilled and eyes turned to her, a vision in white, red-gold curls tumbling over her shoulders, her words an enchantment in a tongue only a few in the café understood.

Soft refrain, the song of the earth
As she binds the sun with the moon in train
Brother sun burns a holy symphony
Lights their way
Life is fantasy
Leavened mystery
Seasons changing winter to spring
Love is warp and weave
Binding all who breathe
Heart to soul as we sing
Sing of the wind-song harvesting seasons
Summer to autumn, winter to spring
Dying autumn leaves, greening symphonies
Life's sweet hymn another spring
Come hold me, please take my hand
Don't let me go, just hold my hand.

'He's yours. Now we leave.' Stanas rose, gripped Miriam's hand, and hurried her from the café. Looking back, she caught the look of terror on Voltaire's young face as if he saw a crown of thorns hidden in the laurel leaves of his imminent success.

Paris 1720-1723 – La Colombe Blanche

She was known as the White Dove, la Colombe Blanche, the exquisite young Englishwoman who wore white and sang songs that wove a hypnotic spell over her audience. Rumours of her beauty and angelic voice drew people to Le Café Procope where she sang daily.

She did not see M. Voltaire in the café again. His accusation in risky verse that the Regent was guilty of incest with his daughter resulted in his incarceration in the Bastille for a year during which time he penned an even more dangerous work, the epic poem, *La Henriade,* a satirical attack on politics and religion. Upon his release he left Paris and disappeared with his mistress, Marie-Marguerite de Rupelmonde, settling in the more tolerant Netherlands where he hoped to find a sympathetic publisher.

Miriam was sorry to have missed Voltaire but she did see the Regent.

Philippe, Duc d'Orléans, arrived one momentous day with the ten-year-old Dauphin in tow generating a flurry of genuflecting and craning of necks. After being shown to a table in the centre of the café, the Duc announced that they had only come to hear the famous White Dove sing. While the staff squirmed obeisance over these most illustrious guests the shy boy clung to his father figure avoiding eye contact with the mere mortals who would one day be his subjects.

At length Miriam arrived and took her usual place in the doorway so the passers-by could also hear the White Dove's song. Upon being informed that the Dauphin had come to hear her sing she smiled briefly at the young boy who would one day be king before she began.

I linger on
Memories chamber in my heart the echoes scream
I don't belong
Not in this world or the next or in between
My soul lives in the past, the distant London long ago
A century has come and gone and buried all I was
I should have died but somehow I lived on
I linger on
Is that a wrinkle on my brow, a thread of snow?
I haven't aged
My soul was seared into my flesh the day I burned
Bitter cold, half alive and feeling I was spurned
The hatred in my heart residual pain of being burned
They laughed at me and led me to the fire
The heartless mob
Gone, my almost lovers
Died in wars, lost at sea
Stabbed or rotted with disease
Or drowned by me
Give me death – the one thing I aspire to
Let me die
But I linger on
The sounds of life tease at my heart and taunt my soul
Humanity – a mob of tricksters, faithless preachers peddling lies
A curse for those condemned to stand alone and watch the moon
Tracing endless cycles without ever moving on
While brother sun ignites the day and burns his lover
I should have died.

'Charming sentiment,' murmured Stanas over the swell of applause.

'They don't know what I'm saying,' she said, bowing to the Regent and his charge.

'The future King of France is enchanted by you. Smile at him sister.'

Miriam smiled at the pale boy-child, an orphan, one of many in that airless stratosphere where few knew their parents but were farmed out to wet nurses and nannies and unscrupulous elderly uncles whilst still in their cribs. The Regent in contrast did seem to genuinely care for the boy and presently he beckoned to Miriam to join them.

'Go,' muttered Stanas.

'I don't speak French.'

'Nod and smile and wait for me to join you.'

Miriam joined the Dauphin and the Regent where they sat in a pool of light, seemingly better lit than everyone else in the café.

'You sang beautifully, Madame,' said the Regent in accented English.

'You speak English?'

'A little. But the Dauphin speaks fluently.'

The young boy looked at Miriam shyly. 'Your song was sad and violent. Is it a popular ballad in London?'

'It is my own creation.'

The hovering waiters rushed to replenish the cups of coffee for their famous guests, delivering at the same time, a fresh cup for Miriam.

'Drawn from your own experience, Madame?' asked the boy.

'I am hardly likely to admit as much, your Majesty. Let us just say I have lived fully and observed much.'

'Madame you are scarce one and twenty in my estimation,' said the Dauphin.

Miriam inclined her head. 'And you a boy of ten but we have both seen far more than is desirable or wished for.'

'I lost my parents to smallpox when I was two. My brother also.'

She lowered her voice. 'Be very careful of the company you keep. Perhaps after all Paris is not the healthiest place for you. Versailles is –'

'My parents died at Versailles.'

'I understand what it means to be haunted by loss but still you would be safer there.'

Stanas loomed over the table. 'Pardonnez mon intrusion. Ma sœur ne parle pas Francaise.'

'We speak English.' The Regent looked from Stanas to Miriam. 'Remarkable. There is no family resemblance at all. Please join us Monsieur –'

'Vedil, le Duc de –' he faltered.

'Le Duc d'Avignon,' said Miriam.

'Forgive me. I've never heard of you,' said the Regent. 'You were not at Versailles during the reign of our late King.'

'I was being educated in England along with my sister. The family Chateau is near Avignon, a tiny town in Provence. As for the family resemblance – our father was a passionate man who found much distraction in London. Alas, we do not share a mother, only a name and an inheritance.'

The Regent laughed. 'A common enough family tree. One that grows on both sides of the matrimonial covers.'

'Sadly I never met the late King but my sister and I were at Versailles when the tragedies struck.' He shook his head. 'To lose both your parents and your brother Your

Majesty, how lonely for you, and then to lose your uncle.' He feigned ignorance. 'A riding accident was it?'

'My uncle was out hunting with a friend,' said the Dauphin.

'Choose your friends wisely,' said Miriam, leaning towards the Dauphin.

'A king cannot choose his friends, dear sister.' Stanas laughed.

'Alas I had already moved the Court and the Dauphin to Paris when the tragedies occurred.' The Regent narrowed his eyes at Stanas. 'Or we might have met.'

'You must come and sing for us again, Madame,' said the Dauphin. 'Privately next time.'

'We'd be honoured,' said Stanas.

But by the time the official invitation arrived Stanas was dead.

Paris –1722-1723

Miriam was alone again. She pleaded illness when the invitation to sing at the Tuileries for the Dauphin arrived and in 1722 the Dauphin and the Regent left Paris and moved the Court back to Versailles where on October 25th that same year the twelve-year-old Louis XV was anointed King of France in the Cathedral of Notre-Dame de Reims. The Gazette reported that the boy-king threw himself into the arms of the Regent at the end of the ceremony where they both wept, either for joy or for sorrow. No-one knew which.

Meanwhile Le Comedie-Francaise, faithful to their agreement, had staged Voltaire's debut play, Œdipe in November 1718. The critical and financial success established Voltaire as France's greatest playwright and facilitated his safe return to Paris where in a tactical reversal the Regent presented him with a medal for service to the Arts. But this did not blunt his sharp pen and wit. His epic poem *La Henriade* was clandestinely published in Rouen, smuggled into Paris, and circulated in 1723 but by then Voltaire's star had risen high enough to afford him a degree of protection.

But the life of kings and courts scarcely touched Miriam who had seen many come and go. She occupied the spaces between the altering fortunes and faltering routines that measured the fates of men. Her essence was appended to the moon, the fixed stars and the music that coursed through her soul, assuming she still had one.

Simply to occupy her days and pretend to a human existence she kept up her routine of drinking coffee and singing at Le Café Procope daily, the loss of her brother occasioning her to wear black for a brief period. But when it was seemly she donned white again, imagining it gave her a lustre of innocence, a cover for the black heart that had murdered for a taste of death.

She added, upon its accidental discovery, a further divertissement: a daily visit to Catherine de Medici's gardens at Luxemburg where she sat by the Medici Fountain designed by Tommaso Francini, a Florentine fountain maker and hydraulic engineer gifted with great talent and the opportunity to use it for pleasure. Francini's grotto provided for Miriam a place of respite from a world corrupted by deceit and the brand of power-mongering that characterised men like Stanas, embroiled as he was in an insatiable quest for supremacy.

His last body had succumbed to the French disease, syphilis, the curse of the sexually promiscuous or plain unlucky who woke up one morning unable to make water without burning pain. Either the seamstress whose exclusive services he paid for had dabbled in forbidden fruit or the body Stanas had stolen was already infected for the rashes that covered him with pustulant weeping welts usually emerged after several years. Aware that his pleasure would be dramatically curtailed he opted to vacate the body by drowning it in the Seine in 1720, a few months after Miriam had sung for the Dauphin.

'It's incurable and the entire wretched Court of Versailles is riddled with it. Every courtesan in Paris has it and every attractive male body I might consider occupying is likely infected. I will have to hunt for a virgin in the countryside so I may be gone for some time.' He charged Miriam with the responsibility of maintaining the Chateau and the apartment in Paris until he materialised again as the male heir with the usual Will and Last Testament.

'Stay on in Paris and foster this relationship with the Dauphin. He may be a child, but he has an eye for older women of considerable beauty. You may yet become his mistress before I despatch him.'

'I will be no man's doll, Stanas. My body is cold. My heart too, I'm afraid.'

He nodded. 'Perhaps it is wise. You don't want this cursed disease.'

'My body could not catch it but no man would want to make love to a woman made of stone.'

'I would but I need your voice more.'

'Even you would find me cold, dry and disturbing.' She poured him a glass of wine. 'Drown yourself downstream please. I do not wish to be summoned to identify your body.'

'Ever the caring sister. Don't worry, my corpse will find its way to the sea before you next sing at the cafe. Don't wear black too soon or they'll get suspicious.' Stanas scratched his arm, lifting the crusted scabs off the rashes and wincing. 'Not that you need much given your lack of appetite but there's

285

plenty of coin in Alexander's old chest. It's under my bed.' He drained his glass in one swallow. 'Au revoir ma chère sœur, be ready to welcome your long-lost brother in due course.'

Paris – 1745

By 1745 she had lived for one hundred and seventy-two years, one hundred and fifty of them without appetite. She had her haunts, her minor joys, but felt no ecstasy and risked no emotional ties for she could not bear the loss of more love.

Everyone she had ever loved was gone and Kit who had promised to come back for her had not. If her mother had survived God's hunger for souls and was waiting for her somewhere in the ether she waited in vain because Miriam would never, *could* never die until that final reckoning when the spider consumed all life. But according to Stanas, even God's consumption of the earth and the spinning stars would not sate his monstrous appetite and by that measure Miriam reasoned God had no option but to create again. If only for a meal.

Yes, one day in a time so distant she could not imagine the changes, she would be consumed in that sacred hunger that surely cycled birth, death and breath. But before then she would remain stubbornly unaltering, immortal, lonely and lost.

If she had lost faith in God, she had come to despise humanity. Even the deaths she had caused, the young men drowned with a kiss, failed to stir pity in her for who were they other than adulterers betraying their wives just as Master Rathe had done? Which of them had not willingly followed her into the swell? She felt no remorse, certainly

286

no guilt. Kings and soldiers had done far worse than she. Her murders had been merciful compared with the hangings, burnings and quarterings performed in public for the entertainment of ghoulish hordes, not to mention the torture behind locked doors to extract the betrayal of friends. By comparison to these purveyors of human justice she was an angel and Stanas a saint.

She watched the water cascading from the Medici Fountain, sunlight catching and making beads of the droplets, the light refracting into rainbows. Beauty was a puzzle for which she had no ready explanation. If God could create such beauty why the appetite for its destruction? Why the hunger for more? He was no better than the earthly kings and nobles who were never satisfied with their lot, never awed by a rose or a fountain or a star. Even now in Versailles the sweet young Dauphin she had cautioned twenty-five years ago to choose his friends wisely had succumbed to greed and was betraying the Queen he once adored with yet another mistress. She knew this because she had learned sufficient French to read the headlines in The Gazette and the lampooning cartoons required no translation.

**

At a masked ball on 25th February 1745 King Louis XV met the twenty-three-year-old Jeanne-Antionette Poisson and even though she was married, he moved her into Versailles, there to occupy an apartment directly above his. The young woman of plebeian origins suffered much from the spiteful tongues and sharp claws of those whose blood was purer, bluer and less combined than hers. The King, to spare his beloved further insults, declared her the Marquise de Pompadour, a semi-official position reserved for the King's favourite mistress. Henceforth the cultured, beautiful and brilliant Jeanne-Antionette Poisson was known as Madame Pompadour and the vicious and spiteful nobility pretended respect for the woman the King depended upon for all his needs: emotional, physical and intellectual.

Madame Pompadour went everywhere with the King: on the hunt, to the gaming tables, to conferences and to bed where they discussed matters political, religious and personal. This most trusted and reliable confidante was also a wonderful singer who frequently performed for the King whilst accompanying herself on the clavichord and it was during one such private concert that King Louis XV, now a man of thirty-five, recalled meeting a woman who had amazed him with her virtuosity and voice twenty-five years earlier in Le Café Procope when his beloved Regent was still alive and buffering him against the storms of popular opinion.

Since her instalment in Versailles, Madame Pompadour had taken over management of the entertainment, organising operas and plays and private dinner parties for the King's pleasure and it was in this capacity that he asked her to find La Colombe Blanche and bring her to Versailles to sing for them for she simply must hear this songbird.

**

The invitation that arrived from Versailles was testament to the King's love of music and art. The summons, for that's what it was, was framed with etchings of cherubs swooning over musical instruments, the motifs festooned in vines and roses.

The invitation was direct and to the point:
Madame Miriam Vedil is requested to sing for King Louis XV and Madame Pompadour at Versailles Le Jeudi 24 Juin.

Miriam turned the invitation over, her first since the one she had declined twenty-five years ago. She ran her fingers over the card, feeling for nuances, a sticky trace of wine, a hint of perfume but whoever was tasked with scribing the invites to Versailles had been careful for there was no physical evidence of the author. How the King's messenger found her was perhaps less surprising than an invitation after all these years: she was well-known in Paris and anyone in Le Café Procope could have directed a stranger to La Rue Sevres where any neighbour could have pointed out her apartment.

A carriage was sent for her on the Monday of the second last week in June. It delivered her to Versailles where she was shown to an apartment and told to wait for the King's summons. In the meantime she was to enjoy the grounds and the banquets and acquaint herself with the guests but not the permanent residents unless they expressly requested her presence in their quarters.

She chose to do none of the above but sat alone in her room with a view of the splendidly articulate gardens, beds so perfectly coiffed they seemed to be apologising for their wild nature. While she waited she wondered when or if Stanas would return. She'd left the invitation on his bed where he could not fail to find it should he return with a new and, hopefully, healthy body while she was away. He may have been the Devil but he was also her only companion, the sole person remaining on earth who knew her secret.

All week she waited for the King's summons and when at last it arrived she felt unprepared, unsure what to sing for the woman rumoured to be an accomplished musician and brilliant stateswoman. Her escorts, a painted Chevalier with pockmarked cheeks and an eager young Marquise, hurried her along a corridor rendered seemingly infinite by a series of floor-to-ceiling mirrors battened in goldleaf. On either side of the corridor golden statues of cherubs and semi-nude maidens holding candelabras flanked her passage and dropping down from a fantastically painted ceiling depicting everyday life among the ruling classes, ornate chandeliers glowed with lit candles, even though daylight flooded the space. And reflected in the avenue of mirrors, the amputated trees, harnessed landscape and restrained blooms of the spectacular, manicured garden. The gold, the opulence, the hobbled landscape registered in her heightened senses as a scream, a rattling of bars.

'Is it much further?' she asked her escorts.

They shook their heads, uncomprehending. 'Tu parle Francaise?'

No, she had not learned sufficient French to have her solitary preambles disturbed by a comprehension of the daily struggles and petty strife of humanity. She did not want to know what was being said. But that much French she understood.

'Je suis Anglaise,' was all she said as she followed them, suppressing her repugnance of the overly-orchestrated surroundings.

At a set of gold-leafed doors the pockmarked Chevalier stopped and after knocking gently he stepped to one side. The young Marquise stood sentinel on the other side.

'Entrée.' The summoning voice from within was mellifluous, sweet and female.

The two escorts opened the doors, nodding for Miriam to enter. When the doors were closed behind her she stood quite still, her senses assaulted by a chamber carnal with blood-red embroidery: the coverlets, curtains, and wall dressings bleeding opulence. It took her a moment to notice the King of France and his mistress, a petite woman in an ivory and gold gown who presently stepped forward in greeting.

'Ma chérie, tu es exquise et nous avons tant désiré t'entendre chanter. Louis me dit que vous êtes tout à fait merveilleux.' Dark eyes perusing her face.

'Madame Miriam ne parle pas Francaise, ma chère,' said the King, whose body was almost lost in a swamping of purple velvet and ermine.

The dark brown eyes widened. 'Mais vous êtes rencontrés il y a vingt-cinq ans. Comment est-il possible que cette belle jeune fille ne parle pas Française et comment sa jeunesse est-elle possible?'

Now the King joined them, shaking off the robe and revealing an elegant blue velvet and ivory brocade jacket over simple blue pantaloons and white hose, his buckle shoes adding a few inches to his average height. 'My Jeanne-Antionette wishes to know why after twenty-five years in Paris you speak no French and how you have retained your youth. I too confess myself curious. You have not altered at all.'

But the King had. The shy thin boy had become a man of medium height with a comfortably padded girth, the fine, almost feminine, features an exaggerated version of the boy she had met a quarter of a century earlier. Only his eyes were unchanged, dark, and burdened with uncertainty, shadowed with loss and seemingly searching for something more than his considerable lot in life.

'I live quietly Your Majesty and I have learned no French because I have no need of conversation. My brother is the only company I keep.'

'You have no friends at all?'

Miriam shook her head, waited as the King translated this information to the woman at his side.

'Mais je serai votre amie,' she said, dark eyes fixed affectionately and somewhat sadly on her face. 'You will need a friend here at Versailles. I do.' This uttered in halting English.

'Will you sing for us now Madame? I have reported you an angel to Jeanne-Antionette and desire to be proven correct.'

At a slight touch on her elbow from the King Madame Pompadour moved backwards across the room without taking her eyes off Miriam and presently sank gracefully into a gilded chair, one in a row of four placed against the wall next to a massive four-poster bed. The King perched next to her on another of the delicate chairs, his hand presently resting in his lover's lap. After a moment Madame Pompadour placed her hand on his. Miriam noticed the hesitation and wondered if all was well in that gilded prison of a bed.

Quashing down the urge to flee the carnage-hued abundance, she closed her eyes and tuned into her internal world, the labyrinth where her secrets and her inspiration lay meshed and coiled. Recalling her loneliness after Kit and Abigail had died she began to sing.

I'm the girl who stands alone
Beneath the moon who hears her song
The fool who waits in vain
For a love that never came
But to love him from afar is fuel for fires, is dust for stars
All I have are memories, nothing to cling to or release
I am the one who's left alone
Bereft and weeping to the moon who watches with me

She whispers here she comes again
The lonely maid who lost at love and watches with me.

Jeanne-Antionette Poisson leapt to her feet applauding. 'Superbe. Exquis. Mais il faut qu'elle vienne à Versailles, ma chère. Elle doit chanter à chaque bal et pour chaque tête couronnée. Cette fille est le joyau de la France maintenant que l'Angleterre l'a abandonnée.'

'Oui ma chérie tu as raison.' The King stood also, bowed his head. 'Jeanne wants you to move to Versailles, Madame, sing for all the crowned heads and be France's National Treasure. Jeanne is a patron of the arts; it is for her a religion. But Madame, another sad song? Who hurt you or are your days often dark like mine?'

Miriam swayed a moment processing the onslaught of so much garish wealth. She knew she would feel even less alive surrounded by all this false allure corralled by a crippled garden but who could refuse the King and perhaps more prosaically, Madame Pompadour? But she had to refuse. It was a matter of finding the right words and delivering them in the right manner. She met the King's sad dark eyes and the searching, intelligent gaze of his mistress and asked, 'Have you ever seen a rose?'

'Qu'est-ce qu'elle nous a demandé?' Madame Pompadour asked the King.

'A-t-on déjà vu une rose?' King Louis smiled. 'We have seen and dismissed too many, Madame and yet we seek more.'

'One is miracle enough to lift the darkness.' Miriam bowed her head. 'There is a fountain I go to for comfort. Its beauty, so simple yet so pure reminds me –'

'That we are mere mortals,' said the King.

'If only,' thought Miriam. 'Just so,' she said and turning to the brilliant young woman beside him she answered in halting French. 'Je chanterai pour toi chaque fois que tu auras besoin de moi.' She smiled at the King. 'That is all the French I know. It is all the French I have needed these long years.'

The King inclined his head, remembering. 'How is your brother?'

Miriam looked down, affecting grief. 'He died not long after you met him, Your Majesty.'

'I am sorry to hear that but –' he looked confused, 'you said your brother was the only company you keep.'

'My younger brother. He should be back from London any day now.'

'You must bring him to Versailles next time you sing for us.' He laughed, a hollow, sad attempt at mirth that did not reach his eyes. 'Next time we have need of you.'

She curtseyed low and rising met a look of childlike longing in both sets of dark eyes, a look that came to haunt her over the coming weeks, months and years for she knew in time she would bring the Devil to Versailles.

Paris – 1755

Over the next ten years she sang for the King and Madame Pompadour many times and whilst the most powerful couple in France grew older and increasingly disconnected from reality, Miriam remained as youthful as a freshly-picked rose. Stanas had not returned and as the years peeled away she came to believe he had been recalled to that glacial region from which he had fallen, there to strike a deal with his father. Then one day she returned from singing at Le Café Procope to find a handsome stranger reclining on the chaise longue in her apartment.

'What's this then?' he asked, fanning himself with a gilt-edged invitation from Versailles.

'Stanas?'

'Who else? Were you expecting Kit?' He studied the invitation. 'How often do you get invited to Versailles?'

'Whenever they need me.'

'They?'

'The King and Jeanne-Antionette, his mistress, Madame Pompadour. He suffers from melancholy. My singing lifts his spirits and makes his management easier for her.'

He got up, went to the board, and refilled his glass. His new body was younger and even taller than the last and it looked healthy. 'It took me forever to find a virgin. Hung for being a Protestant.' He lowered the lace at his throat, revealing a yellowing welt. 'The neck did not break. Fortunately, the region of Cévennes is full of Catholic fanatics and sloppy hangmen.' A beat. 'How often do they need you?'

'They are good people, Stanas. I do not wish them any harm.'

'Sentiment, Miriam? You should know by now the folly of attachment. Mortals die, most in the fullness of time, others by accident. It hardly matters. They all die sooner or later. My difficulty is timing. These bodies do not last long enough to serve my purpose but you my beautiful immortal sister have secured for me the opportunity of a brief lifetime. You have gained entrée to Versailles' inner circle and from within it I will accomplish my task.' He drained his glass, refilled. 'I will spare Madame Pompadour. You deserve a friend. Next time you sing you will take me with you and introduce me as your brother, the new Duc d'Avignon now that our older brother is dead.'

'You may have trouble ruling the French, Stanas. Voltaire is famous now and his words ring loud.'

'Just as I predicted. He is the head of the snake.' He thought for a minute. 'Sometimes one must fight fire with fire. Time to translate Kit's unstaged plays into French. I will become a rival to Voltaire.'

'You will pretend authorship of Kit's work?'

'Don't get in my way, Miriam.'

'Kit worked hard and deserves credit for his genius.'

'Very well, I will follow my usual course. When you take me to Versailles the King will have an accident. His family are so prone to falling off their horses.' He thought for a minute. 'I didn't tell the Dauphin my full name at Le Café Procope all those years ago so I may keep mine of which I am fond and to which I will respond.' He poured himself a fresh goblet of wine. 'Did the King remark upon your youthful appearance?'

'He found it puzzling but not impossible.'

'Très bien, ma chère sœur, next time you visit Versailles you will introduce the King to your brother Stanas Vedil, Duc d'Avignon, recently returned from London having completed his education.'

Versailles – December 1756

The melancholy King was soon in need of a song and in December 1756 Miriam was summoned to Versailles to sing for him and his entire Court in a succession of Christmas celebrations to which all the Second Estate nobility of France were invited. Miriam brought a guest, her brother, the new Duc d'Avignon, recently returned from London. Just as she foresaw all those years ago,

296

Miriam brought the Devil to Versailles and how ironic that he should arrive in time for Christmas.

Stanas Vedil was warmly welcomed. His sister was a favourite of the Court, one of the few people who could coax a smile out of the King when sorrow gripped him. The young and handsome Duc d'Avignon charmed everyone with his fascinating tales of historical events that rang with uncanny realism, almost as if he had been there, so detailed were his accounts of the sacking of Thebes in 335BC by Alexander the Great, the construction of the Great Pyramid of Giza stone by stone, the flooding of mythical Atlantis.

'Oh yes, there was once a very great Kingdom called Atlantis.' Stanas assured his audience in French. 'Homer wrote about it but I met a fellow in India who had seen it, a sage so ancient his skin was like velum and his eyes like marbles, blind and quite blue, but when those eyes were sharp and dark as night and his skin smooth as polished ebony, he had seen Atlantis. I cannot say how old he was or how he yet lived but he spoke of glittering white cities clinging to cliffs verdant with strange and marvellous plants whose blooms were pale as snow and only opened under the full moon. But alas the Atlanteans had built too close to the sea and one day she rose up and swallowed the entire Kingdom.' On and on he spoke, weaving a web so lacunose Miriam was amazed his audience did not see through it. True, he had lived a thousand lifetimes but he was prone to exaggeration easily disproven by a glance at history's pages but the Second Estate rarely noted the lessons of history and moved in such narrow circles they were gullible enough to believe any fortune-telling pimp.

Yes, the idle elite swallowed Stanas' tales, wept and laughed where he compelled them to but most moving of all was his tale of the angel who tried to dissuade Christ from his course in the Garden of Gethsemane. Many a lace handkerchief was moistened during that story and when Stanas finished speaking he looked around the assembly, his gaze lingering on the King who was in a particularly melancholy mood.

'The destiny of the great is fraught with menace,' Stanas concluded in English.

'Mais oui,' murmured the King. 'Even if one has done no harm.'

Stanas held the King's gaze. 'The bourgeoisie and the peasantry do not understand a king who concerns himself with beauty or love as Christ did.'

'Christ was misunderstood,' agreed the King.

'The people wanted another David, a warrior king, un pugiliste non évolué, a man who would bankrupt his nation through war.' He affected a sigh. 'Violence is what the Third Estate admire most.'

'I detest violence,' said the King. 'I am a lover of art. Was Christ a lover of art do you think?'

'Christ was in love with love.' Stanas sighed. 'And look where it got him.'

'But we must try to love as he did. We must try.'

'Une chanson ma chère Miriam?' asked Madame Pompadour, with a concerned glance at Louis.

Miriam stood and was about to sing when Madame Pompadour began to cough violently. She pressed a lace hanky to her mouth and withdrew it stained with blood. The King placed a tender arm around her shoulders but Madame Pompadour shrank from his touch and presently excused herself. Without his confidante and protector King Louis sunk deeper into sorrow, his arms limp, his head drooping forlornly.

'Sortons demain matin de bonne heure,' said Stanas to the King. 'Just you and me hunting. We will see the dawn together, celebrate a new day, catch the stags unaware and bring venison to the table.' He leaned closer, lowered his voice. 'Nous parlerons des femmes et de la façon de leur plaire.'

Miriam caught only the English part of this exchange but it was enough to worry her. 'Stanas you detest rising early.'

'I will do it for my sovereign.'

The King smiled at Stanas. 'You and your sister are such a comfort to me. I did not like your older brother. I did not trust him, but you – you are as different from your brother as the night from the day. You are more like your sister. I would trust you both with my life.'

'Stanas, you hate riding,' said Miriam.

'I will do it for my King.' Stanas bestowed upon the King a smile that did not reach his eyes. 'Demain, nous chassons. Just you and me.'

Versailles – Christmas 1756

An hour after dawn the sun fully rose sending brilliantine arrows across the regimented gardens of Versailles. Miriam sat at the window watching the progress of two horses cantering past the curlicue lawns and along the gravelled avenue lined with potted trees. The riders were chatting amiably. They arced the circular pond, Stanas leading the way as they struck a direct course to the vast manmade lake beyond, there to detour into the forest and presently be absorbed into the immediate green and distant blue-violet foliage of linden and chestnut.

The King believed they were hunting stags. Miriam knew he was the quarry. All morning she watched and waited for the two horses to emerge and finally just before midday they did, the King laughing and victorious. Stanas looking glum.

'He has a very fine seat,' he told Miriam bitterly that evening after the silk and velvet-clad nobility had retired to their bedchambers. 'But everyone loses their balance eventually.'

Stanas persisted with the dawn hunts, never missing a single frosty winter morning that December. The King declared his optimism renewed after a week and looked forward to rising from his warm bed and bracing the brisk morning air to hunt with his dear young friend, the Duc d'Avignon. The combination of exercise and kill lifted his spirits enormously and restored his various appetites so completely he resumed his visits to Le Petit Trianon before and after midday dinner to meet with lovers whose names he never bothered to learn. They were simply relief. His heart belonged to Madame Pompadour and occasionally the Queen. That Madame Pompadour kept to her apartments alone was well-known. The Court assumed the King had tired of her but in truth she had ended their intimacy when the physical act of love became too painful for her. She did not end their friendship though for he relied upon her utterly.

The morning hunts continued into the New Year and Miriam grew increasingly anxious for her friends. No amount of pleading for an altered course would change Stanas' mind. He remained resolved to kill the King. That he had no plan beyond that did not bother him, unable as he was to write upon destiny's blank page. But like many an impulsive person driven by lust he believed the end justified the means. Still, the early mornings and the brisk rides were taking their toll.

'If he does not fall soon I will have to think of something else,' said Stanas one evening as he paced Miriam's chamber, a glass of wine in one hand, the other rubbing his aching buttocks.

**

The 5th of January 1757 dawned unusually cold, the sky green-tinged with a lacunose covering of clouds, but this did not dampen the enthusiasm of the King who was already waiting for Stanas with two saddled and snorting mounts. Presently Stanas emerged, Miriam watching from her window.

She had not changed her robe since she arrived. She had no need. Her body produced no odours or fluid so unless the gown itself became soiled or damaged she saw no need to shift. Let the other guests believe she had a dozen of the same gowns and indeed in the Paris apartment she shared with Stanas she did have a dozen white gowns but when she was summoned to Versailles she brought no change of clothes, no luggage, no jewellery: a strange penury few observed, self-absorption being the general run of the Second Estate.

But there was one who noticed.

**

A knock on her door, early, long before the guests had roused themselves for gossip, gorging and divertissement.

'Who is it?' Miriam called out.

'C'est moi.' A soft voice, mellifluous and familiar.

Miriam hurried to let Madame Pompadour in before a gossipy servant saw her and speculated about the substance of the visit.

'Were you seen?' Miriam asked, closing the door behind her friend.

'Let them talk.' She laughed and coughed, pressing the white linen handkerchief to her mouth and withdrawing it stained red. 'This cough will not heal.'

'Sit,' said Miriam. 'Asseyez-vous. I have learned a little French.'

'And I a little English. Louis has been teaching me.' She smiled sadly. 'So that I may talk to you, my only friend.'

Miriam sank down onto a chair beside her. 'You do not need friends like me.'

Madame Pompadour reached for Miriam's hand, withdrawing it suddenly with a startled cry. 'But your hand is like ice. Ah, the fire has gone out. I'll send for a servant.'

'I need no fire and we need no gossipy servants. Unless you are cold?'

'I am always cold but am content to shiver for your company.' She glanced at the bed that had not been slept in, the supper that had not been touched, the unstoppered decanter of wine. 'You do not sleep; you do not eat and you do not breathe. I have noticed. Nor do you bring luggage, jewels, or a change of gown.'

Miriam went to the board, poured herself a glass of water and drank it in one long draft. 'I drink.'

'Water.' She laughed and then whimpered, pressing her hands to her stomach, and wincing in pain.

Miriam was at her side in an instant. 'What is it? A child?'

When the spasm passed she opened her eyes. 'No child. Louis and I are no longer intimate. I cannot endure penetration; it hurts too much. My insides are rotting I fear.'

A bank of cloud passed over the sun laying upon the grounds a patina of pearly light. Frost scored off the trees, rising in wispy circles of breath.

'We've had no snow for two years now,' said Madame Pompadour, looking sadly at the clouds. 'I loved the white, so pure, so innocent and when it melted it was as if the world was reborn. I will not live to see another winter's snow.' Again she clasped her friend's hands and this time she did not flinch or withdraw. 'What kind are you, ma chère? I know you are not mortal.'

'I do not know. I was burned at the stake in London in 1593. I did not die but nor do I live.'

'I have read of immortals who drink blood. Estries. Succubi.' Madame Pompadour held her friend in a long steady gaze. 'But you drink only water.'

'And that rarely. I've lost everyone I ever loved. My mother. My friends. Mine is a lonely life.'

'Mine also. I have no friends, no remaining family. Both my children died.'

'My child died also.'

They held hands as the Palace stirred to life: footsteps in the hallway, whispered conversations punctuated with laughter, the gardeners emerging quarrelsome and reluctant to subdue the hobbled trees and curlicued lawns in the bitter cold.

'You have no love for your brother?'

'My brother –' Miriam halted. How to explain the Devil?

'Has hunger. I see it in his eyes. He lives as if he will never be satisfied. Who is he?'

'Immortal like me,' she said at last. 'If the King will listen please warn him against my brother. I tried once long ago. Jeanne, my brother is a friend to no-one, not even me.'

They left it at that, with Madame Pompadour promising to sour the friendship between the King and the Duc d'Avignon. But it was too late, Stanas had already found a man willing to sell his soul for fame and few sous. At 4pm on the 5th of January 1757 Robert-François Damiens broke through the bodyguards at Versailles and stabbed King Louis XV with a penknife.

Before being torn asunder by four horses at the Place de Grève Damiens told the slavering crowd that the Devil made him do it.

Paris – 17th of March 1757

Stanas rose early on the morning of the 17th of March 1757 hoping to beat the crowds and secure a front-row position at the Place de Grève where Robert-Francois Damien was to be executed for regicide. Miriam refused to go with him, citing that the grotesque spectacle would only trigger memories of her own execution. It was disturbing enough, she said, that human beings could find the torture of another human being entertaining but infinitely worse that there were individuals so lacking in humanity they could inflict it.

'You had no problem drowning young men in the Portloe Cove when you sought revenge.'

Miriam looked up from the page upon which she was committing a new set of lyrics. 'I was wronged.'

'You murdered for sport, my dear.'

'I was mad with hatred. What's your excuse? What's theirs?' She nodded in the direction of the Place de Greve where the sounds of a gathering crowd swelled.

Stanas adjusted his feathered tricorn hat. 'Damien's execution is a minor victory in my quest. It shows me how debased humanity has become. Their appetite for cruelty will be their undoing. The conscience plays a long game and when it pricks I will take control of the deflated masses. Do you like my hat? It's a little out of fashion but it suits me.'

'Who will notice you and your hat when so much blood is on offer?'

He studied his reflection in the mirror. 'I like this hat.'

'You'd best hurry if you want a good view of the torture you've set in train.'

'Don't wait up for me.'

'I won't lose any sleep worrying about you. I don't sleep anyway.'

Stanas walked across the room, leaned over her shoulder. 'A new song?'

She reflexed a protective palm over her words. 'You could have stopped this. You assured Damien he'd escape justice.'

'The King is dead, that's all I wanted and today I will bear witness to the ultimate weakness in humanity, its appetite for cruelty: a flaw my father refused to acknowledge in his penultimate creation, a tragic oversight on the part of my dear brother whose agonising despatch was testament to humanity's barbarism. Humanity is unfit for salvation.'

'Salvation? You mean fodder for the spider.' Miriam turned and looked up at him. 'Why do you want sway over them?'

'Don't you mean "why do *we* want sway over them"?'

'I am no longer human and as the years pass I identify with them less and less. Why do you want them?'

'For pleasure.'

**

The four hours of torture started mid-morning and Miriam could not shut out the shrieks of Damien or the cheers of the crowd who were mostly Third Estate bourgeoisie and peasants who hated the King but none-the-less turned out in force to witness the execution of his assassin. She closed the windows, sang her new song as loudly as she could but nothing could silence the ghoulish pleasure of the crowd or Damien's agonising despatch.

In her frustration her anger turned against Robert-Francois Damien, the fanatic Stanas had persuaded to assassinate the King. Why had he agreed? What possible outcome had he expected other than his prolonged torture and eventual death? The Palace guards said that Damien made no attempt to escape, seemed proud of his achievement, his mood elevated with excitement even as he was manacled and hauled off to Paris for a trial that would be no more than a formality.

Immediately after the stabbing Miriam had looked for her friend Madame Pompadour but was told she could not be disturbed as she and the Queen were keeping vigil at Louis' bedside, hoping for a word from him before his soul fled. The guards said that after making his final confession he had slipped into a coma and was expected to be dead by nightfall. It was unlikely that he would have a parting word for either his mistress or his wife.

Confident of victory, Stanas collected Miriam and took a fast coach to Paris to distance himself from the murder he had orchestrated. There was no further news from Versailles, no announcement of the King's passing and rumours began circulating that he had made a miraculous recovery. Stanas ignored them. He had instructed Damien to plunge the knife into Louis' left side where it would pierce his heart and Damien, an ex-soldier trained to kill, delivered the blade as instructed. Louis was dead. If Versailles was remaining silent on his passing it was to make sure the King's funeral did not overshadow the torture and execution of Damien and give the ambitious Courtiers time to shuffle the deck and decide who would be Regent while they waited for the two-year-old Dauphin to grow up.

At midday, a sealed message arrived from Versailles for Miriam.

It was a note from Jeanne-Antionette telling her only friend that the King had made a remarkable recovery but depression gripped him. Why, he asked repeatedly, was he so hated? Jeanne added that he had pleaded with the guards to go easy on Damien and was horrified to learn of the public torture intended for him. He had sent an urgent message to Parlement demanding that Damien be spared a grotesque ending, arguing that it would send an unwholesome message to the Third Estate, establishing in their minds that the First and Second Estates were beyond the reach of Christ and God, especially as the execution would be performed so soon after Christmas. But they refused him. They wanted their show, wrote Jeanne, to instil fear in the people in case they planned Revolution. They have not told the people that Louis still lives, she wrote, albeit under a cloud of despair, so the charge could not be commuted to attempted murder occasioning a lesser penalty. Finally she asked Miriam to return to Versailles and sing for the King whose soul had descended into such a dark place she feared he would never smile again.

Miriam folded the note and tucked it into her bodice.

Late that afternoon Stanas returned, elated and eager to celebrate.

'Two bottles of Vin Jaune from Burgundy,' he said, raising the bottles triumphantly. 'After the execution I walked along beside the river and thought about our next move.'

'Our next move?' Miriam patted the brocade bodice where the note nestled.

'Yes, now the King is dead there is a vacuum of power. I must move fast to fill it.'

'I thought you said the conscience plays a long game.'

'It does but hatred's game is swift and given the unhinged loathing I saw today I believe a Revolution is close. When I rule the world, women – apart from you – must never be given rights or a voice because they will use both to undo men. Men can be controlled by their appetites for sex, power and cruelty as long as women have no avenue to exact penalty. Men love torture, will cheer for it.'

'Women cheered too. I heard them.'

'Yes, but women did not swing the axe or spur the horses that tore him apart. Do you know what his last words were?' He grinned. 'The Devil made me do it.' Laughing as he prized the wax seal off the top of one of the bottles. 'Drink with me! Celebrate my victory.' He handed her a glass. 'Today I saw how my rule will be established. I will rule men through their appetites and women through their dependence. Salut.'

She took a sip of the wine, its heat coursing through her like fire, her hand resting on her bodice above the note from Madame Pompadour.

'This afternoon I paid a visit to my old seamstress, Anne Bécu. She did not recognise me in my new body. Time has been unkind to the once irresistible Anne, I would not pay a sou for her additional services now, but she was quick to offer me her fourteen-year-old daughter, Jeanne, a fetching little minx with blonde ringlets and huge almond-shaped blue eyes. I saw at once that Mademoiselle Jeanne Bécu is truly her mother's daughter, a greedy little flirt with an appetite for baubles. She will do well in Versailles after I have trained her in Madame Quisnoy's establishment.'

'Madams Quisnoy?'

He refilled his glass. 'A brothel-casino catering to the debauched tastes of the Second Estate. I am a loyal client. That's where I purchased this wine. Yes, my old seamstress was very happy for her little Jeanne to start earning her keep in the family business.'

'Sewing?' Miriam asked, feigning innocence.

'Prostitution.'

'You are so confident men are without conscience and women without voice.'

'No-one spoke up for Damien today.'

'Someone did.' She withdrew the letter, handed it to him. 'The King pleaded for clemency for his would-be assassin.'

'Would be?' Stanas swayed.

'The King lives, dear brother, and I have been summoned to Versailles.'

Versailles – 1764

By 1764 Voltaire was a French icon, a national treasure unmatched in literary genius, an intellectual celebrity, champion of the unjustly persecuted, a cynic who hated religion yet advocated for its tolerance, but most disturbingly for the King he was a great friend of Madame Pompadour and it was in this capacity that he was summoned to Versailles in March 1764 to say goodbye to his dear friend and most powerful ally as she lay dying of tuberculosis.

**

'How fares the King?' Her voice a whisper, her face whiter than the pillow upon which her head rested.

'Save your charity for yourself, ma chérie. The King will manage his grief assisted by a coterie of servants and a bevy of false friends.' Voltaire poured a tumbler-full of wine, slipped an arm behind her head and held the glass to her cracked, blue-tinged lips. 'Drink a little. It will numb the pain.'

'Ma chère amie, pas si près, cette contagion est cruelle et facile à attraper.' This concern accompanied by a fit of guttural coughing that suffused the wad of linen pressed to her mouth with fresh blood.

Voltaire withdrew the wine, waited for the fit to pass before he spoke.

'I am too stubborn to die my dear friend, although this creaking old body reminds me every day that I have seen seventy summers.' He spoke in English for the benefit of their mutual friend, Miriam, sitting by the bedside where she had kept a constant vigil, day and night, ever since the King had summoned her to Versailles to say goodbye to her friend. The only time she left the sickroom was when the King desired to be alone with his beloved.

'The world will benefit from your long life and inestimable genius,' Jeanne whispered. 'Me, the woman hated by the Court and despised by the Third Estate, they won't miss.' Followed by a hollow hacking cough that convulsed her frail frame.

'I will miss you,' said Voltaire, his eyes glittering with tears.

'And I.' Miriam's eyes were dry and fixed on the friend who would soon pass from the world leaving her lonelier for having dared love again.

'It seems to me absurd that an ancient pen-pusher, hardly able to walk, should still be alive, while a beautiful woman in the midst of a splendid career should die at the age of forty-two,' said Voltaire. 'If ever there was an argument against God it is you my dear Jeanne.' He looked

310

at Miriam. 'And if ever there was an argument *for* God it is you with your miraculous eternal youth.'

'My dearest friends I must sleep a little while I can.'

'Bien sûr, ma chérie,' said Voltaire, rising slowly.

Miriam kissed her forehead. 'Fear not, sweetling, I cannot catch this disease or indeed, any. I will be back later to sit with you as usual.'

Madame Pompadour gripped Miriam's icy hand. 'Ma chère amie do good in this world. You have time.'

'I will try.'

Madame Pompadour released her friend's hand and closed her eyes, her breath wheezing, shallow and soon to be silenced forever.

'I am slow but walk with me, Madame?' said Voltaire.'I was in London after my last little stay in the Bastille. I have learned your tongue and I now have an English publisher who is far less hostile to my inflammatory philosophy. No manmade idea is spared my pen, Madame, so I count myself multipartite in my condemnation of religion and politics.'

Miriam walked slowly to accommodate Voltaire's immobility: the pain in his joints evidenced by the occasional pause for which he apologised before resuming their progress and their conversation.

'How are you so unchanged, Madame, and why are you immune to disease and why does our beloved Jeanne-Antionette urge you to do good in this world?'

'Shall we sit awhile, Monsieur? I have a favourite fountain.'

'I would like to see where you find respite in this flamboyant cage.'

They took the path arcing to the right of the main parterre and moving deeper into the wooded area reached a clearing where a bronze statue of a lion bringing down a wolf gushed twin jets of water.

Voltaire eased himself down onto a bench. 'A violent theme. You draw calm from this.'

'Life is violent Monsieur. Even now our friend dies in agony, her body rotting from within.'

'You do not believe in a merciful God or a life-affirming Nature?'

'Neither. Nature is cruel. She predates upon herself and God allows so much suffering it argues against his mercy.'

'A puzzle I have agonised over these many years. I have done my best to soften the hearts of men but have had no avenue of appeal to God whose indifference to suffering I find barbaric. I will ask him to explain himself when I see him.' He laughed. 'But what of you? How is this youthful permanence possible? Our dear friend Jeanne seemingly declares you immortal with time to do good in this world.' He looked directly ahead through the falling rainbows. 'What I must know, desire most fervently to know, ma chère Madame, is are you proof of God?'

'I am proof of his opposite.'

'Ah, so we have been looking in the wrong direction for benediction and to the wrong source for angels.'

'I am no angel, Monsieur. I have killed for vengeance and I hate the God who allows my permanence.'

They said nothing more for a while but sat in communion listening to the sibilant hissing of the twin streams issuing from the victor and the victim's gaping mouths.

'I acquainted myself with the work of Monsieur Shakespeare when I was in London,' said Voltaire at last. 'Once my grasp of your language was firm enough I went to one of his plays: Hamlet. You smile. You have seen this play?'

'I read this play when the ink had scarce dried.'

'You met Shakespeare?'

'I knew Marlowe.'

Voltaire turned to her. 'Marlowe penned Hamlet?'

'Marlowe penned all of Shakespeare's plays after *Taming of the Shrew*.' She smiled. 'It was the bargain he made with the Devil for his life.'

'And The Bard? What bargain did he strike with the Devil?'

'The usual. Fame and fortune.'

'And you, Madame, did you sell your soul for the immortality you now regret?'

'I sold nothing. Permanence is the curse the Devil placed upon me when he spared me from the flames.' She noted the look of horror. 'Yes, Monsieur, I was burned at the stake in London in 1593. My condemner was the father of my child. The Devil saved me without my consent but Kit gave his.'

He swung around, mouth dropped open in surprise. 'Kit Marlowe is still alive?'

'No. My dear friend passed from this world in 1666. Kit was to be arrested and burned for heresy. The Devil saved him from the flames that he might use his genius. Kit lived for 102 years and drew his last breath in my arms whilst protesting the shadows. I miss him every day. It is dangerous for me to love, Monsieur, for I am in a permanent state of loss and yet I loved Jeanne-Antionette dearly.'

'We both have.' Voltaire lifted his face to the sky. 'To look upon this beauty eternally. I can't imagine a greater gift or curse.' And without turning. 'Tell me about your brother, Madame.'

'My brother is the Devil.'

He took a sibilant breath. 'What does he mean to do with us?'

'Rule over you.' She touched his hand and he flinched at the chill. 'But do not fear, Monsieur, my dear brother has no plan and no desire to earn his distinction as you and Kit have done through hard work. Like many a lazy despot he expects supremacy to fall into his lap.'

Voltaire laughed. 'Out of the sky? Like manna?'

'His father would never be so merciful.' She rose. 'I must return to our friend.'

'And after her passing what will you do?'

'What little good I can. I will sing for those who need respite from their trials.' A pause. 'I will never kill again.'

'Are you sure, my dear? Perhaps it is your nature.'

'I will never kill again. It brought me no relief. None of them was Rathe.' She smiled at his puzzled look. 'The man who sent me to the flames.'

'Ah, bien sur. But you will sing and bring joy to all who hear your song.' He kissed her frozen hand. 'Few of us make such a difference.'

Versailles – 1764

Jeanne-Antionette Poisson died on the 15th of April 1764. It was a Sunday. She was forty-two.

The King was inconsolable and the permanent residents crept around Versailles like mice. They wore black and even the ones who had hated La Pompadour were impressed with her courage and dignity in her final weeks.

**

Stanas found her sitting in front of the fountain. Unlike the rest of Versailles she wore white.

'I've been looking everywhere for you, sister. The King is beyond the reach of mere mortals. Sing for him. I need an audience with him.'

'I am in no mood for singing right now.'

Stanas released an exasperated sigh. 'Your heart will be constantly broken if you insist on caring about people.'

'There is still a vestige of humanity left in me, Stanas.'

'That may yet be useful. My father may want you back. You will be my bargain for my own salvation.' He followed the passage of a hunting hawk. 'I will tell my father that no-one gets to you except through me. I rather like the irony.'

Miriam rose. 'If you don't need me I will walk now. I'd like to be alone.'

'I just came to tell you we'll be returning to Paris at the end of the week but I must speak to the King first.' He loomed over her, blocking her retreat. 'I have a plan and I am keen to put it in action. One song is all I ask. Remember who spared you from the flames.'

Miriam sighed. 'Very well, one song.'

'Thank you, dear sister.'

Paris – 1767

While Miriam kept to herself, avoiding company, and sitting for hours in contemplation of the Medici Fountain, Stanas oversaw the education of his former seamstress' daughter. Jeanne Bécu had blossomed into a delectable young woman with keen appetites. A woman with appetites usually has a history and by 1767 Jeanne and her mother, Anne, were well-leafed, overwritten pages. How they managed the number of scandals that trailed them like strays

315

at a fair was due entirely to the omission of any shred of moral fibre. Jeanne had managed to escape the convent at age fifteen cutting short the education one of her mother's lovers was paying for and within a year she and mother were thrown out of the household where Anne served as cook and occasional lover, forcing them to return to the cramped abode of Anne's long-suffering husband, Nicolas Rançon.

Having shucked off the shell of respectability, Jeanne was eager to cross her itchy palms with silver, if not gold, so she began selling trinkets on the streets of Paris until her beauty caught the eye of an elderly widow who had spied her through parted curtains. The job of companion to the partially deaf and constantly dyspeptic old lady paid three sous a week in addition to a warm bed and generous meals. For a few extra sous she provided the widow's two married sons with the delights lacking in their spousal beds: an arrangement bound to shatter and soon Jeanne returned to the cramped benevolence of her mother's husband.

**

And that is how Stanas found them, soiled, bored and ready to be inspired.

His proposal was both grand and forward-thinking: they would move into the brothel-casino run by Madame Quisnoy where Anne would once again work as a cook and Jeanne would learn the art of paid pleasure, and when she was ready Stanas would take her to Versailles where she would replace Madame Pompadour as la maîtresse-en-titre.

'But first we must find Jeanne a husband,' he said, in English, summing up his plans.

'Why do you speak in English?' asked Anne.

'For privacy.' He nodded at young Jeanne. 'Tu comprends?'

Anne scratched her palms. 'I understand enough to know this is folly. Men don't marry courtesans and why should Jeanne soit retenue,' she rephrased in English, 'be tied if she is amusement pour le Roi?'

'Because ma chère Madame, the King likes his mistresses married and above reproach.'

Anne laughed out loud. 'Nous sommes employés dans un bordel! Courtesans!'

'A minor detail and leave the husband to me, laisse-moi le mari.' He added under his breath. 'I have many acquaintances in debt to me.'

**

Within a year Jeanne Bécu had married the Comte Guillaume du Barry who owned the brothel. Once Stanas explained his plans, the Comte recognised the enormous money-making potential of being married to the mistress of the King. The ceremony included a false birth certificate created by the Comte's younger brother, Jean-Baptiste, who added a little extra icing by subtracting three years from Jeanne's age and concocting some noble ancestors.

On the eve of his marriage, Guillaume told his brother that the Duc d'Avignon had great plans for his wife.

'Versailles,' he said, tapping the side of his nose.

'But I thought once she was married her career would end,' said Jean-Baptiste.

'Au contraire dear brother, it will just be beginning.'

Stanas' patronage of Jeanne du Barry nee Bécu saw her moving in the highest echelons of Parisian society where bored Second Estate gentlemen paid generously for the services of the highly creative Madame du Barry. No recalcitrant member was beyond her grasp or rigidifying.

**

Meanwhile in the little town of Ferney, Voltaire had found sanctuary.

In 1758 he bought an elegant Chateau on the French side of the Franco-Swiss border, far from the toxic atmosphere and fickle benevolence of Versailles and the Parisian Parlement that awarded him medals one week, incarceration the next. Harboured and safe he wrote some of his most scorching diatribes against the Church and the Monarchy. To shore up acceptance with the locals he invested in cottage industries that produced some of the finest potters and watchmakers in France and to demonstrate tolerance for the religion he castigated he built them a new church along with a theatre where he produced his own plays.

Here he wrote his remarkable novella *Candide*, a vehicle for airing his contempt of religion, nationalism, war, government, philosophy and philosophers, and above all, the false optimism that kept humanity enslaved and impotent. It was a copy of this book, translated into English, that Voltaire sent Miriam along with other "scribbles" written on randomly sourced parchment of quite startling irregularity: the backs of old jeremiads, a loosely stitched assortment of invitations and letters, the remaining pages of an incomplete diary.

The bundle was delivered to her with a note that read: Pour la Colombe Blanche immortelle so she remembers the boy, François-Marie Arouet, who became Voltaire.

**

While Stanas schemed world domination and groomed Madame Jeanne du Barry, Miriam went to the Medici Fountain and read Voltaire's letters.

My dearest Miriam, I have come to despise priests of every religious sect, these leachers of light who rise from an incestuous bed, manufacture a hundred versions of God, then eat and drink God, then piss and shit God. But I reserve my most stinging contempt for our national religion, Christianity, assuredly the most ridiculous, the most absurd and the most bloody religion which has ever infected this world. You and His Majesty will do the human race an eternal service by extirpating this infamous superstition, I do not say among the rabble, who are not worthy of being enlightened and who are apt for every yoke; I say among honest people, among men who think, among those who wish to think. My one regret in dying, my dear Miriam, and I fear it must be soon because I can scarce rise from my bed these days, is that I cannot aid you in this noble enterprise, the finest and most respectable which the human mind can point out. Yes, I admit to the most insufferably selfish hope that you my dear with all eternity to fill and the Devil at your command will be the architect of the ultimate fall. Do I assume too much?

Miriam stopped reading, sinking into an empty place no light pierced, for hers was as cynical a view as Voltaire's but rather than bother with humanity she was tempted to abandon it, never risk love and loss again. She closed her eyes listening to the song of life: the bell-like tinkling of the fountain, the chittering of birds whose simple lives merited a full reiteration each evening to their fellows, the crunch of carriage wheels along the distant boulevard, the rhythmic press of footfall on the cobbled lanes and the sounds of laughter as Parisians pursued whatever pleasures they could afford.

After a few minutes thus distracted she returned to the pages and read on.

As Christianity advances, disasters befall the Roman empire – arts, science, literature decay – barbarism and all its revolting concomitants are made to seem the consequences of its decisive triumph – and the unwary reader is conducted, with matchless dexterity, to the desired conclusion – the abominable Manicheism of Candide. I have concluded, my dearest Miriam that instead of being a merciful, ameliorating and benignant visitation, the religion of Christians would rather seem to be a scourge sent on man by the author of all evil. On that wholesome note how fares your brother?

Planning a Revolution, she thought, and using a greedy little whore to do it. If the uncultured du Barry replaced the brilliant Pompadour and if her excessive greed for glitter was met by the grieving King, the Third Estate would finally have cause to forge dissent. But she did not write any of this in her return letter to Voltaire later that evening. He would anticipate and no doubt welcome a Revolution anyway. She wrote instead that she had composed another song. Stanas had bought her a new lute and while he oversaw Jeanne du Barry's education each evening she played her music, the occupation providing satisfaction and a degree of contentment. A tame enough letter in response to her friend's turmoil of mind and soul.

In a perplexing mixed vision he had also written the following:

Having decried Christianity I must acknowledge the self-sacrifice of Christians. Perhaps there is nothing greater on earth than the sacrifice of youth and beauty, often of high birth, made by the gentle sex in order to work in hospitals for the relief of human misery, the sight of which is so revolting to our delicacy. Peoples separated from the Roman religion have imitated but imperfectly so generous a charity. But their charity does not sanction the ramblings of a text that defies science, a fairytale no less, bizarre and dangerous, and those who can make you believe absurdities can make you commit atrocities. Give my regards to your brother and tell him I applaud his desire to crumble the pillars. I won't be alive to see what rises from the rubble but it must surely be better than what currently stands.

She made a neat pile of the letters and placed them in the larnax of Alexander the Great, one of the few things Stanas had brought with him from the Chateau. She ran her fingers over the elevations of a battle sculpted on the lid, more vanity and casual loss of life and for what? Alexander died at thirty-two, felled by a mosquito apparently. The chest itself was almost certainly not a larnax as Stanas believed but a receptacle for plans rather than ashes. Homer's Iliad now had to share the hollow with Voltaire's letters and her lyrics. Stanas had come to understand it was just a box possessed of no more power than the Holy Grail. It would never win a kingdom.

He needed a Courtesan for that.

**

Miriam returned to her place by the window and her lonely vigil over a world that increasingly convinced her that humanity was destined to be snuffed out by a piece of universal flotsam defying gravity, the same ending the dinosaurs had suffered.

Incinerated.

In an instant.

It was fitting somehow for a species that had outgrown its Creator.

Versailles – 1768

He moved her lute closer to the door. 'You'll need your lute.'

'There are lutes in Versailles.'

'You prefer your own. Bring a change of gowns. You must appear human in front of those vultures. Hurry and pack, the carriage will be here at 10am.'

One additional gown would scarcely take hours to pack. While Stanas scurried from room to room on the point of panic she calmly finished her letter to Voltaire.

It seems we return to Versailles, she wrote, and this time Stanas descends upon the Court armed with a Courtesan who comes with the very highest of citations, although none of her referees would put a name to their praise.

'Jeanne is traveling with us in the carriage,' said Stanas, enroute to his bedroom.

'No!' Miriam abandoned her letter and followed him. 'I will not share a carriage with that creature. Jeanne-Antionette was my friend. I will not befriend her replacement.'

Stanas ignored that. 'This body is getting old. I see the beginnings of wrinkles.'

'I won't travel with that whore.'

'She speaks no English and you refuse to learn French –
'

'I understand plenty of French. I just won't engage in mindless gossip. My nationality protects me from the insipid and the vacuous like Madame du Barry. I can't believe any decent man agreed to marry the woman and give her the veneer of respectability.'

'Guillaume du Barry is hardly decent. He and his brother own the brothel she works in and a more delightful pair of pimps I have yet to meet. They were easily bought.'

'In exchange for fame and fortune? The usual fee.'

'Yes, my dear, I am now in full possession of their shabby souls and once I establish Madame du Barry as la maîtresse-en-titre that pair of rogues will have all the fame and fortune their tawdry hearts' desire.' He studied himself in the mirror. 'I can't abide wrinkles but this is the body the King will recognise. Louis and I may even resume our hunting.'

'He's a sad old man of eight and fifty, prone to depression. He cannot live much longer. Why don't you wait Stanas?'

'Because the Third Estate is restless. Your friend Voltaire has cloaked their bloodlust in intellectual sanctity. He almost provides the banner under which they will march. All they need is a nudge and the Monarchy will come tumbling down and with it the unholy alliance of Rome and any semblance of civilisation. I must be ready to take the reins.'

'Voltaire sends his regards by the way.'

'Does he indeed?'

'He supports the fall of the First and Second Estates but has not quite realised they cannot be replaced by an illiterate Third. How do you intend to rise above this carnage?'

He smiled slowly. 'I intend to translate and produce Kit's last play and pass it off as my own. Yes, my dear sister, I will become the new Voltaire.'

Miriam quashed the urge to laugh. Stanas could no more discipline himself for fame through literature than he could maintain it through rule. This plan of his was doomed to fail before it even found traction.

'I'll bring my lute and one change of clothes and I will share a carriage with Madame du Barry but I will not speak to her.'

Versailles – 1768

The accidental meeting of the King and Jeanne du Barry née Bécu occurred when Stanas and the King were out hunting one morning, the King's first cheerful company since the loss of Madame Pompadour he told his friend the Duc d'Avignon when they were far enough away from the Palace where every wall had an ear and every doorway an eye.

'I live to serve you,' said Stanas. 'I am so glad you were stirred from your bed to hunt again, just you and me, no baying hounds, no gaggle of nobles.'

'I will not hunt with hounds,' said the King. 'It gives the hunter an unfair advantage, and those dogs are so noisy, not to mention the chattering nobles. I treasure this quiet time with you my dear friend. You've been too long away from Court.'

They rode on, plunging deeper into the forest. Stanas hoped du Barry had remembered to rouse herself so they could accomplish their own hunt.

'I miss Jeanne-Antionette,' said the King. 'She made me laugh.'

'Could you love again my friend?'

The King sagged in the saddle. 'Love? Was it love I felt for Jeanne-Antionette?'

'You doubt it?'

'I'm not sure I believe in love anymore. I was almost murdered by one of my own people. They do not love me and yet I love them.'

'Don't let one madman destroy your faith.' Stanas reined in his horse, waited for the King to draw level with him. 'You are a passionate man. I believe that what you felt for your beloved Pompadour was grand and selfless but could now be eclipsed with a passion such as you have never known.'

'There is no woman at Court who inspires me apart from your sister but I know she is not quite of this world and must remain unsullied.'

'If I could find you a woman who would set your loins on fire and restore your faith in love –?'

'You would deliver Heaven, my friend.' Suddenly he sat up straight, a finger to his lips, his eyes fixed on a point a little ahead in a copse of linden and oak.

Stanas followed the King's gaze and saw there a magnificent stag frozen in an attitude of wariness, its body almost camouflaged but not quite. The King took aim with his favourite Lorenzoni rifle and before Stanas could block his ears Louis had discharged the weapon with a deafening report. The stag fell. The King let out an ear-bleeding cry of triumph and spurred his mount on to inspect his kill. Stanas, ears ringing, followed and pretended glee when they reached the writhing animal who looked up at them terrified, the whites of his dying eyes showing.

'One shot and no hounds!' cried the King. 'Come, my friend, we'll alert the servants so they can deliver the coup de grâce and butcher him. I have worked up an appetite. Breakfast?'

'Indeed. Let's ride back via the Evening Fountain.'

'That will delay breakfast. We'll take the more direct route.'

'We may find my sister there. She loves to sit by the Evening Fountain and practice her songs.'

'Ah well, then we shall make a slight detour. My Jeanne-Antionette declared your sister immortal and I must concur. She retains an unnatural youth and beauty.'

'My sister lives only for her music. The trials of mortal life do not touch her, hence her ageless beauty.'

As they approached the fountain where Stanas had laid his honeyed trap they heard a trill of laughter and a splash. Clearing the grove they were met by the spectacle of a naked woman frolicking in the pond, her discarded gown and hose draped over a statue of Cupid with bow drawn and arrow aimed.

'Oh,' she shrieked fetchingly, almost covering her breasts with her plump pale arms. 'Vous m'avez surpris en train de me déshabiller. Je ferais la révérence, mais …'

'A naked water nymph,' said the King. 'How delightful. How surprising. Who is she?'

'She is our guest, a friend of my sister's,' he lied. 'Permettez-moi de vous présenter Madame du Barry. Jeanne, c'est le Roi.'

'But how delightful. The three of you must come to a private supper in my chamber this evening.' He lowered his voice. 'Do you mind sharing her, my friend?'

Stanas smiled. 'She is my gift to you, Your Majesty.' And addressing Madame du Barry whose lips and fingers were turning blue with the cold. 'Retrouvez-nous dans nos chambres pour le souper ce soir. Nous allons maintenant prendre congé. Profitez de votre baignade.'

The King inclined his head. 'You have brought me back to life, my dear friend. A kill this morning, love this evening and now breakfast. Truly all my appetites have returned.'

Paris – 1772

She had not found the courage to sit by the Siene since their move to Paris. The fear of memories of Sundays when she and her mother had picnicked by the Thames kept her to her familiar haunts. But with Stanas ricochetting between Versailles where he directed the King's love life and Paris where he frequented Madame Quisnoy's brothel, her days and nights were long and she felt the need for fresh occupation, even if it occasioned a flux of grief.

So one Sunday morning she walked to the river and found a tract of ground where picnickers had spread blankets and launched pleasure boats. Settling a brief distance from them she opened her picnic basket and ate a little bread and cheese just to appear human. The river, daubed with pleasure boats, murmured its ancient song and blooming on the opposite bank clusters of spires and pitched roofs punctured a sky stippled with undecided cloud.

Almost two hundred years since she and mother had sat beside the Thames sharing the leftovers from Saturday night's feast while they fed the swans. Two centuries since they had unravelled the sermon they'd just heard or speculated about the play they might see. Life had been uncomplicated then and beyond their intervention: two base-born servants lacking the power to change the course of history, unlike in France where the Thirst Estate felt entitled to opportunities, if not equal to the privilege of the First and Second Estates, at least within reach.

In London she had been victim to the whims of her betters now she had within her grasp the means to fire alteration and sow the seeds of equality and all because she had access to Versailles, a route oft taken via the boudoir. And her dear friend Voltaire had given her the greatest gift anyone can proffer: hope.

**

Voltaire had a clear vision for mankind, a philosophy based on the one religion he admired, Buddhism, that Eastern practice that sanctified life. He wrote of it often in his letters and hinted at it in his books and plays and the more he forged a path for peace the more convinced Miriam became that a nirvana-like state was possible on earth and she would live to see it. Even her beloved Kit was merely tilting at windmills compared to the root-severing incisors of Voltaire. While Stanas grew ever more desirous of rotting the social paradigm Miriam grew more certain that elements of it could be preserved under a more egalitarian banner. Stanas kept his plans from her these days, aware that she had the means to unravel them should she befriend the young Dauphin and his teenage wife, the Dauphine Marie-Antionette.

When he was home he drank and schemed in his room while she buried herself in her letters and books. Their paths only crossed at mealtimes when he insisted she sit down with him, their companionship forced, and when the King summoned her to Versailles for a song the carriage rides were endured in silence as each retreated into their private worlds. Miriam knew Stanas would never find traction in the world Voltaire envisioned, a world that drummed equality and toppled despots. He could install a dozen du Barrys in Versailles but people fuelled by greed tire quickly whilst those who march for justice stay the course. It was just a matter of time before fortune flipped. Du Barry was a temporary hiatus not a re-coursing and Louis was old and ill.

Versailles – 1772

By 1772, Louis had enjoyed four years of unparalleled sexual gratification at the hands and various regions of Jeanne du Barry, but after a lifetime of reliably pointing north his compass was beginning to drift south. He was sixty-two and du Barry a year shy of thirty. They were both showing their ages, he in un-saluted nights and she in the accumulation of flesh under her chin. Whilst the King mourned the southward drift of his penis, Jeanne mourned the loss of her beauty and came to dread her reflection in a Palace merciless with mirrors. Her despair made her impatient in the bedroom where Louis needed time and skilful attention.

To reassure his Mistress, Louis commissioned the Parisian jewellers Boehmer & Bassenge to create a necklace so spectacular no-one would notice her chins. The quoted fee was two million livres. He did not balk, the gowns and baubles he had bought her over the past four years had cost the taxpayers well in excess of this new investment in his pleasure.

**

Madame Quisnoy's establishment had lately acquired a young woman whose aptitude for sex, theft and deception interested the du Barry brothers who saw in her a possible replacement for Jeanne whose years were starting to lengthen and whose temper was starting to shorten.

A comely twenty-four-year-old, Jeanne de Valois-Saint-Rémy had a lineage that required no forgery. Indeed it could be traced back to Henry II, albeit on the wrong side of the covers, but none-the-less the blood running through her veins was royal Valois blood, perhaps more lilac than blue but sufficiently tinted to gain her entrée to Versailles when Madame du Barry exhausted the King's coffers and patience. Stanas was introduced to her one Saturday evening after

329

taking his usual pleasure with his usual provider, a woman whose exclusive services three times a week he paid well for as he was not about to lose another body to the French disease.

A subtle knock on the door signalled that his two-hour appointment was up. He dropped an extra dozen livres, coin by coin, between her breasts, kissed her hand, retied his breeches and slipped out of her bed.

'Jusqu'a mardi. Gardez-vous propre ma chère.' He reminded her.

She blew him a kiss and waited until he left her room before counting the coins.

Stanas sauntered along the hall, past the closed doorways of rooms that were in service, past the semi-open ones through which scantily-clad ladies could be seen reclining on beds sipping wine as they waited for their next client. Sighs, moans, and the clink of coins accompanied his passage to a room at the farthest end of the hallway from which no sound issued. Two short knocks followed by one loud report and the door swung open releasing a billow of smoke and the fumes of brandy.

The tables were full, the game of Belle, Flux et Trente-et-Un was in full swing, dishes of coins filling and emptying in equal measure. Velvet and gold-frogged coats hung over the backs of chairs, lace at throats was loosened and judging by the fog of smoke and the heavy silence but for the shuffling of cards, the first game was drawing to an end. The losers, purses lighter, would go home to irate wives, the winners might stay on and try to increase their winnings. Either way a chair and a new game would soon be available to the Duc d'Avignon whose pockets were so deep many a poor Comte dared their borrowed livres in a game with him. If they managed to win, their reward was

330

a purse full of Gold Louis for he and the Du Barry Bros only paid their debts with the highest coin in the land. But Stanas rarely paid. His luck was uncanny, almost divine.

While he waited for a game, Stanas poured himself a brandy and sat in the corner.

'Bonsoir Monsieur.' The voice soft, purring.

He had not noticed her: a young woman sitting alone in the shadowy corner of the room, an unstoppered bottle of Vin Jaune and a half-full glass on the table next to her.

He cast a glance her way, nodded. An ordinary young woman, too pale and lacking the curves that might tempt him but dressed in an immaculate ivory and gold gown replete with panniers and a frothing of lace at the bodice, a gown one might expect to see at Versailles.

'Vous êtes inattendue Madame,' he said. 'Êtes-vous un invité du les frères du Barry?'

The girl pulled her chair closer, lowered her voice so she did not disturb the game. 'Je dois apprendre ce jeu et trouver des clients pour la chambre à coucher.'

Guillaume du Barry tossed down his last card, an ace, eliciting groans at his table. Collecting his winnings, a dish of Gold Louis, and thanking the gentlemen for the game, he looked around for Stanas. Finding him, he crossed the room and sat next to him.

'Wait for the next game. This is the young woman I told you about,' he said, speaking English so she could not understand. 'She will help us commit a crime unequalled in the history of theft.'

'I have a long history of crime, my dear Comte.'

'What I have in mind will topple all your former accomplishments and mine.' He inclined his head to the young woman. 'Jeanne de Valois-Saint-Rémy rencontre le

Duc d'Avignon. Stanas let us retreat to another room where we can speak privately.'

'Un plaisir de vous rencontrer Madame,' he said rising and following Guillaume.

***

'Another Brandy?'

Stanas accepted the crystal tumbler and leaned against the marble hearth. 'Who is she?'

'She claims nobility, Valois blood. It's dubious but enough to get her into Versailles with you next time your sister sings.'

'My sister has become unreliable and I am missing the game,' he said, glancing at the door.

'There is a far bigger game afoot, with a stake of two million livres.'

Stanas drained his glass. 'I'm listening.'

Guillaume refilled their glasses, indicated the chair opposite him. 'The King has ordered a necklace for Jeanne, the most elaborate ever seen, one row of seventeen diamonds as large as filberts from which three-wreathes of smaller diamonds drop and, framing it, four pendants of pear-shaped and star-shaped diamonds. The fee is two million livres but work on it goes slowly.'

He shrugged. 'Why?'

'The jewellers are struggling to source the filbert-sized diamonds.'

'So, Jeanne must wait for her bauble. What of it?'

'The King is unwell. If work goes too slowly he will die before it is completed and then the jewellers intend to sell it to the Dauphin. This is already in their minds.'

'How do you know?'

'They are clients of mine. And the young woman you just met has a new client, Cardinal de Rohan, a former French ambassador to the Court of Vienna, a wealthy man who seeks to regain favour with the Dauphine Marie-Antionette. Too much wine, a loose tongue and the wrong circle of friends cost him the friendship.'

'What do you expect me to do?'

'You must persuade your sister to sing for the Dauphine.'

He shook his head. 'My sister has developed a great sympathy for the Third Estate.'

'I see, then we must rely on my new employee to get us into the good graces of Marie-Antionette.'

'Why are we bothering with the Dauphine? She is hugely unpopular with the people.'

'But not with Cardinal Rohan.' He smiled. 'He imagines himself in love with her, and my excellent new Courtesan is using his weakness to her advantage. She has told the Cardinal she is a confidante of the Dauphine's and she has offered to remit a letter to her, a letter Cardinal de Rohan has written in the belief that it will restore favour with her.'

'A mere flurry of a jaded heart. What has this to do with me and where is the swindle?'

'I'd like you to take Jeanne de Valois-Saint-Rémy to Versailles as your guest. You've seen her gown. She would pass as minor royalty at Court. She and the Dauphine are of an age. The friendship is up to her and from there she can orchestrate the romance that will make us rich.' He paused. 'Richer.'

'One can never be too rich. And if the Dauphine will not forgive de Rohan?'

He smiled. 'Jeanne de Valois-Saint-Remy is an excellent forger. She will write a letter of forgiveness for the lovesick Cardinal if the Dauphine will not.'

'A delicious deception but how does that get me closer to two million livres?'

'If the King dies before the necklace is completed, the smitten and very rich Cardinal de Rohan will buy it for the new Queen of France, Marie-Antionette.'

'Too much riding on too little, dear Comte.'

Guillaume leaned forward as if to play his ace. 'I never play with a straight deck. If Jeanne cannot befriend the Dauphine we have a new girl here, Nicole Le Guay d'Oliva who bears an uncanny resemblance to Marie-Antionette. Seen in the right light, the gardens of Versailles at night for instance, a man might believe he had just made love to the Queen of France.'

Stanas smiled. 'And he would buy her this necklace if she asked for it prettily enough.'

'Exactement.' He raised his glass. 'And who better to deliver the necklace than the Queen's close friend, Jeanne de Valois-Saint-Rémy.'

'A delicious plan but the lady must be married if she is to gain entrée into Versailles, royal blood or no.'

'I have just the man, a gendarme named Marc-Antoine-Nicolas de la Motte, young and handsome and poor. He plays cards here when his regiment is in Paris. He always loses and is forever in my debt. He will be easily persuaded to marry anyone of my choosing if I offer to clear his debts.'

Stanas finished his brandy. 'When will the necklace be ready?'

'When Charles Auguste Boehmer and Paul Bassenge find the diamonds. Last week they were complaining they only had ten.'

Versailles – May 1774

In late April 1774 Charles Auguste Boehmer and Paul Bassenge sent a message to the King requesting a part payment of the fee so they could purchase more diamonds. Their own funds were running low and with an order of this magnitude they could not cover the ballooning costs themselves.

Their request arrived the same morning Louis complained of a headache and nausea. That evening, still feeling ill, he sent for the Court physician, Le Mariniére, who diagnosed *petite variole*, a cause for optimism as he'd already survived smallpox and was therefore unlikely to die. Madame du Barry had immunity and was allowed to remain with him but the young Dauphin and Dauphine had never had smallpox and were asked to leave his room.

A few days rest should see an improvement his physician promised. However, when angry red eruptions broke out all over his body he began to fear for his life. On the 3rd of May, after studying the eruptions on his hands, the King sent du Barry away and on the 7th of May, Louis was given the final rites. Two days later the eruptions had darkened to an ominous shade of bronze and at 3:15 a.m. on the 10th of May 1774 Louis died without having read the letter from the jewellers begging remittance for the purchase of more diamonds.

Stanas was in Paris when he heard the news and after his usual Saturday night visit he sort out Guillaume du Barry.

'Marie-Antionette is now Queen of France. Have the Cardinal's affections altered or can we set our game in train?'

Guillaume handed him a glass of Brandy. 'He remains true and will do whatever it takes to win her heart.'

'In that case, arrange the girl's marriage and I'll present her at Court.' Stanas raised his glass. 'Let the games begin.'

'Here's to a fat stake of two million livres.'

'You usually only deal in Gold Louis.'

'I'll make an exception.'

'And we steal a diamond necklace.'

Guillaume frowned. 'Forget the bauble. You could never sell it, not even on the blackest of markets.'

'Leave the necklace and its despatch to me.'

Versailles – 1784-1785

The Duc d'Avignon had not been back to Versailles since King Louis XV's death and when he did return in January 1784 it was not with his magnificent sister, La Colombe Blanche, but with a fetching young woman named Madame de la Motte whose gowns and demeanour argued for the drop of royal Valois blood she claimed and whilst the gendarme husband might suggest Third Estate impoverishment, her friendship with the Duc d'Avignon gave her entrée to Court.

That year Madame de la Motte and the Duc d'Avignon visited Versailles thirty times and the trips were relayed in detail and in bed for Cardinal Rohen who relished every detail pertaining to the Queen. A tiny inflation of the truth, she and the Queen were close friends, earned her a Gold Louis. A small lie and one she believed would soon become truth.

One evening after the usual service had been provided the Cardinal asked Jeanne if she would take yet another letter from him to her friend the Queen. He was happy to pay five Gold Louis for the favour. He dropped the coins onto her bed.

'Mais bien sûr,' she said, fingers itching to clutch and pocket the coins.

'Et si elle devait répondre –' he jiggled a purse of coins in front of her nose.

For such a lucrative reward what was a little harmless forgery? A week later the Cardinal received his first letter from Queen Marie Antionette and Madame de la Motte received ten Gold Louis from the Cardinal.

The letters from the Queen kept coming until:

'Je veux rencontrer la Reine.'

**

'Il veut rencontrer la Reine!' Jeanne's heels beat a staccato rhythm as she paced, her fingers twisting her lace hanky into anxious knots. The evening's card games were over and Stanas and Guillaume were counting their winnings when Jeanne had burst in declaring they would all end up in the Bastille if her forgery was discovered.

'He wants to meet the Queen.' Guillaume smiled at Stanas. 'Nicole Le Guay d'Oliva. Might the Cardinal be convinced if they met in the garden at night?'

'A man in love is easily convinced,' said Stanas. 'I'm going back to Versailles in August. Too soon?'

'Qu'est-ce qu'il dit?' Jeanne asked, looking from one to the other.

'Timely I think. The hook has been well-baited,' said Guillaume. 'Take Nicole as your maid and Jeanne as your guest and let our little herring beg the Cardinal for a token, a two million livre necklace. Are you in?'

'I am,' said Stanas.

'I told you it was a crime unequalled in the history of theft. Now to snare the prey.' Again they exchanged a glance. 'Another letter for the Cardinal suggesting an assignation in the garden at midnight?'

Stanas smiled. 'I'll dictate.' He handed Madame de la Motte a gold pen and a perfumed page with the Versailles insignia etched on its parameter and issued a single direction. 'Écrire.'

**

On a balmy night in August 1784 Cardinal Rohan met Queen Marie-Antionette in the gardens of the Palace of Versailles. Bolstered by months of correspondence inflaming his hopes, he gave her a rose and dared kiss her hand and when she asked him to purchase the necklace commissioned for du Barry for her as a token of his devotion he swallowed hard but agreed.

'N'importe quoi pour toi ma Reine.'

**

Charles Auguste Boehmer and Paul Bassenge had spent their own fortunes and a small borrowed one on the completion of a necklace for the maîtresse-en-titre who no longer lived at Versailles having been chased away by the new Queen who detested her. Having lost the initial purchaser they tried without success to persuade King Louis XVI to buy the necklace for Queen Marie-Antionette and indeed the King had offered it to her but she could not be persuaded to wear the diamonds intended for the vain breast of Madame du Barry.

Having received an official refusal from King Louis XVI it was therefore surprising when they received another official letter claiming that a young woman called Jeanne de la Motte would act as an intermediary for Cardinal Rohan who would purchase the necklace as a gift for the Queen. The letter went on to explain that due to her lack of popularity with the Third Estate and rumours of over-spending in Versailles she could not buy it herself.

Madame de la Motte arrived in person with a sachet full of letters between Cardinal Rohen and the Queen attesting to this arrangement. She said the Cardinal would pay in instalments after receipt of the necklace. The jewellers were convinced.

**

On the 21st of January 1785, Cardinal Rohen collected the necklace from Charles Auguste Boehmer and Paul Bassenge and negotiated the instalments he would repay. He then hastened to the establishment he had frequented for the past decade and laid the extravagant lure on his mistress's bed where it glittered and seduced like a lamia.

Following strict instructions from the Duc d'Avignon and Comte Guillaume du Barry, Madame de la Motte suggested she deliver the instalments as well as the necklace to protect the Cardinal from scandal and to ensure his position at Court and ultimately in the Queen's bed. And it all would have gone smoothly had Charles Auguste Boehmer not asked the Queen what she thought of her gift. Marie-Antionette informed the jeweller that she had neither ordered nor received the necklace. A scandal broke and by August 1785 arrests were made, starting with the lovesick Cardinal Rohen.

**

Stanas arrived at Madame Quisnoy's at midnight on the 22nd of August 1785 to find a house in disarray: empty beds, a hastily tidied gaming room, his friend Guillaume du Barry gone and Madame de la Motte in a state of high anxiety. When he entered her room she almost fainted.

339

'Seulement moi,' he said, eyeing the half-packed valises on the bed, the gowns in chaotic piles. 'Are you leaving? Partez-vous?'

She did not answer but kept packing, throwing gowns and shoes into bags.

'Où est le collier?' he asked.

She tossed a silk bundle embroidered with the three fleur-de-lys and double rooster heads of Versailles at him. 'Take it! I cannot have it on me or –' she made a slicing motion across her neck.

'You do speak English.'

'Enough. Take it. C'est du poison.'

And so with the diamond necklace tucked into his waistcoat the Devil left Paris.

Paris – an hour past midnight on the same night

'We're going back to Provence.'

Miriam looked up from the last letter she'd received from Voltaire, written only a few months before he died on the 30th of May 1778. She had read it so often it was known by heart but still she kept returning to it, her anchor and weight in a world sullied by intrigue and poisoned with greed. She said nothing and Stanas stood unmoving, his mouth set in a grim determined line.

'If you do not come with me you will be arrested and locked up in the Bastille and likely executed.'

She turned slowly at this. 'I would die?'

'Probably not. You'd linger in your half-life clinging to your head.' He unclenched his fists and relaxed his stance. 'Anyone associated with Madame de la Motte and Guillaume du Barry will be hunted down on suspicion of theft.'

340

'Of what?'

He upended the bag, poured its glittering contents onto the table. 'This.'

'Isn't that the necklace Louis ordered for Madame du Barry?'

'Yes and I must bury it.'

'Why do you want it, Stanas, if you can't sell it?'

'I'll sell it next century.' He glanced out the window. 'Pack please. I've ordered a carriage and paid the driver in Gold Louis to drive all the night. We can't even risk an Inn.'

Provence – 1793

'Empty bellies seed revolutions,' said Miriam. 'If you want to rule you must acknowledge the people. You must be one of them.'

'How can I be one of them? I'm an angel, set above them by God and it is simply a matter of time before I occupy an earthly throne. Greedy men have done most of the work for me and nature will do the rest. Observe how power is concentrated in a few hands: the Bourbons, the Habsburgs, the Savoys, the Guises. They inter-marry, co-mingling their blue bloodlines. But nature has a sweet vengeance for the incestuous nobility – the purer their blood, the weaker their flesh until their inbred bodies can no longer sustain a strong heart or clever mind. They can scarce hold a sceptre, let alone wield one and that is when I will take over.'

'When there's no resistance.'

'Précisément.' He drained his glass, grimaced, and pressed his hand to his gut. 'Ulcers.'

'What of translating Kit's last play and passing it off as your own?'

'Who goes to the theatre these days?'

'Do you want love Stanas?'

'Why would I want love?'

'It brings much meaning to this weary existence.'

'Power brings more.' He grimaced. 'I must rest.'

**

The following morning he re-emerged, greeting the new day with further complaint. 'My bones ache. Food is intolerable and no part of me wants to rise. I must acquire a new body. I only kept this one to complete my little intrigue at Versailles. We'll need new servants and you must look after my assets. Are you listening Miriam?'

'I will look after your bounty, don't worry.' Miriam smiled without looking up from her drawing, a redesign of the garden, taking the best elements of Versailles: the secret fountains, the copses gated with faux ruins, the addition of deer to "wild" the woodlands. 'You must hire some fresh young gardeners, one to accommodate your tarnished soul, the rest to create my vision.'

He glanced over her shoulder. 'What's wrong with the garden the way it is?'

'Everything can be improved with a little imagination.'

He growled. 'Where do you find your inspiration? I am too impatient for the cultivation of excellence.' He ran a fingertip over the diamond necklace festooning the neck of a life-size statue of Venus rendered in bronze. 'I am taking a little trip into the countryside today. Would you care to accompany me? We might take lunch at an Inn. I'd like to hear the gossip from Paris, what they're saying about this necklace for instance.'

'I am happy with my current occupation, Stanas. You go and bury your latest theft.'

'Very well.' He lifted the diamond necklace off Venus and slung it into a coarse linen budget. 'It may be best if I travel alone. I can be more discreet.' He also collected his brother's old wooden cup, the Holy Grail, dropped it into the bag with the necklace. 'I can take a shovel and do my own digging.'

'Who dug for you before?'

He laughed. 'Dead men.'

'We both have far too much blood on our hands, Stanas.'

**

He was gone all day.

When dusk purpled the green and gold land he galloped up the gravel drive, horse hooves beating a frantic rhythm. Moments later he erupted into the room, threw down a copy of the Gazette.

'Look at the front page.'

Miriam left her sketching, picked up the paper which carried a full-page illustration of an implement of death upon which the King's prone body lay headless.

The headline read: LE ROI EST MORT.

'It's a guillotine,' said Stanas. 'A swift death that does not discriminate between the Estates. Today the King died and the crowing sans culottes have announced a Reign of Terror that will end the Ancien Regime. The rule of Kings is over, Miriam. My dream of occupying Versailles and from there making my seal upon the earth is dead.' He sank into the nearest chair. 'They'll be coming for us next; the sans culottes have tasted blood and if you know anything about hounds –'

'I don't.'

'Once a hound has tasted blood it cannot be trusted. The appetite is wetted and must be satisfied. These leeches will storm every Chateau, murder the chatelaines, and take what is not theirs.'

'You cannot hear the irony can you?'

He wasn't listening. 'I will take you back to England where you must hide in the Abbey until this madness is over. What is happening in France will inspire the English to do the same.'

'Do we leave before or after you get your new body?'

'There will be no new body.' He gave her a long look. 'I may have to go away for a while.'

'How long this time?'

'Just until the treasure I buried today can be safely exhumed.'

'That may take a hundred years.'

'It may take a thousand.' He smiled. 'Will you miss me?'

The Song

And all that remained was her song and the sea's, at times in harmony, at other times dissonant and in conflict depending on their respective moods.

**

They took only the larnax, the lute and a few clothes with them in the carriage to Marseilles where Stanas hired a crew. Without risking another day in France they sailed to Cornwall and there Stanas directed his crew to carry the larnax and the lute up the old goat track to the Abbey. If they had questions a bagful of Gold Louis silenced them.

After directing Miriam to wait for his return, Stanas and his crew rowed back to his caravel and set sail. She watched until his boat was a blink on the horizon over which it presently sank.

When she had asked him where he intended to go if not back to France he had given her a forlorn, defeated look and declared humanity a lost cause, riven with a malevolence far exceeding his own. He said he would visit those regions beyond the imagined spheres, there to hear the music that was second nature to her. When he heard the music he would return to her and make fresh plans. She had begged him to take her with him but he said it was a journey that could only be taken in spirit and whilst his was soiled, hers was trapped.

Perhaps it was his intention to join the legions of the sunken, free his soul and sacrifice his crew. Or he might change his fickle mind and sail to the New World, test its tolerance of fortune hunters. Whatever he decided she envied his choice. She had none in her living death.

**

Other than a deeper layer of dust and bird droppings the Abbey was unchanged. Kit and Abigail were still fixed in their eternal conversation, their flesh clinging in leathery strips to their skeletons. That summer she buried them and sang over their bones. All night she sat by their graves, the full moon echoed on every crest and rise, her tethered orb shivering a silvern path to the boot of the cliff. Having laid her friends in the cold earth she dared an adventure, climbing down the goat-track under cover of night.

Keeping to the clifftops and shingled coast she ventured east towards London, retracing the route of that long-ago departure. She toyed with the idea of visiting the city where she had lived and died but grief overwhelmed her and she changed course. Sometimes she wandered inland via the tributary rivers that ran homeward to the sea, curious to mark the changes, the rise of steepled villages buzzing with human exchange.

She had abandoned her white battante robes, replaced them with a simple white linen shift, an undergarment freed from the restraints of a basquine and hopefully bland enough to bridge the march of fashion. If she met a fellow traveller on the backroads she would enquire about the state of the world, the date and current atmosphere religious and political. In exchange for news she would sing for them, giving rise to a rumour that a beautiful young woman wearing the white shift of a corpse roamed the countryside gifting wanderers with a song. Some called her a ghost, others a djinn, still others believed her a sidhe or fairy.

One night she slipped into the sea and headed for France. With no need of either boat or breath she crossed the Chanel, exploring the world of fin and scale and wrecks.

**

For almost two centuries she was seen all over Europe becoming first myth then legend, an exquisite immortal who sang with the voice of an angel. She enchanted with her song, cementing the illusion she had dazzled the Queen with, a fairy who left no trace of her visit other than a melody that lodged in the soul. She was careful never to give her name, leaving no fixed identity. One day she visited the Chateau where she had lived with Stanas. Scaling a wall she perched in the bough of one of the ancient oaks in the wild woodland area she had intended to fill with deer. From there she had a clear view of her old home: Kit's and Stanas's sanctuary. Crawling over the lawn like ants and stomping up and down the front steps were men in black breeches and coats. They seemed angry, these mostly young men who barked in a foreign tongue.

346

She dared not approach them to enquire who now owned her old home. After a day and night of observation she concluded that they lacked the ears and soul for a song. Where were the women and children that might soften them?

Dispirited, she travelled north towards Paris through meadows and forests. After a week, her passage was halted by an unearthly booming that set the sky on fire. Moving cautiously towards the aural dissonance she saw a meadow gouged with dry riverbeds corrupted with dead men. The stench of their decay was so unbearable she withdrew into the woodlands, found a river, and sank into it, continuing her journey under its watery blanket.

Closer to Paris, she emerged, intending to continue on foot but the usually quiet backroads were crowded with metal carriages that moved horseless between lines of young men in ugly brown breeches and jackets, their eyes empty, their youth fledged, their souls semi-flown. She would have thought them ghosts but for the rhythmic thump of their marching feet.

If Hell had found its way to earth it had done so without the Devil.

Miriam watched these horrors from woodland lairs or the safety of rivers and it seemed that humanity had sunk to depths of depravity no light could penetrate. These men who wore brown and black as if all the colours had been stripped from the world, showed no glimmer of light, no semblance of joy, no hint of a soul.

Eventually her heightened senses – assaulted with the stench of death, the screaming fissures in a sky infested with roaring metallic birds that dropped exploding eggs, the loss of colour and song – could take no more. She returned to the sea and hid in its twilight depths suckling silence.

Silence but for the hiss, caw, sigh and whisper of the sea at night when the horror was suspended and she was safe to rise up and float on the sea-skin, mapping the infinite region where dreams are born and music sings them to life, where the Devil was listening for the music that might save his soul. At dawn when the sun fired up another day of metallic birds searing the sky and dropping their evil eggs on the desecrated land she sank back down into the indigo, there to drift on the sucking/shucking tide until the weary sun drowned itself beyond the green isle and once again she floated up to pattern eternity.

Once she had asked the Devil why he saved her. He said she was bait for God, a light that would lure his father to her rescue surely as a moth to a flame.

'And when my father comes I'll be waiting with my net,' he had said.

'Am I the net?' she had asked.

'You are lure, net and bargain. He cannot have you without me.' He raised a warning finger. 'But you must stay clean and bright and pure. He must want you.'

She had killed since then.

**

When the world grew silent again, broken and sad and bent on repair, she returned to the Abbey and watched the fishermen casting their nets just as they had done in 1600. Time had stood still in Portloe and therein lay a small comfort, a familiar pattern she could measure her days by. As summer cooled into autumn a new generation of terns took their fledged brood south and she was alone with her lute and the music that poured from her soul. She had no concept of time other than as a conduit for the creation of the songs she sang to comfort herself and fill lonely fishermen with a belief in mermaids.

Four hundred years since she had been burned, sent to the flames by the man she loved.

Her life informed by senses heightened enough to find closure in a fragrance, comfort in a sunburst, joy in a sound, was richer than Versailles, more useful than a sunken treasure, further reaching than a melancholy King's domain, more joyful than the sodden bliss of wine but still she wished for company, someone to share her abundance with.

'I will sing for you,' she told the night.

Thru my eyes
I see the world in colours made of sound
A storm is purple tears upon my weary face – falling through
space – seeking ground
When day breaks
I hear the sound of birdsong and I wake
To a world alive with laughter
Crowds of mercury, silvery streams ocean-bound
Daylight ends when a seabird cries
Night descends in whispers shivering sighs
The stars unroll crackling silver runes
Green the weeping tide implores the moon
Thru my eyes
The colour of the night is sweet perfume
And I'll sing a song to show you how it looks to me
A world made of sound – colour-bound

Colour-bound
The world may clock, measure passing time
Tick away the years in metered rhyme

Life is potions of memories, laughter hinted ruby-tinted wine
Thru my eyes
I can read a person's story in their song
I can tell if they're happy or have lived too long
It's all in the sound – colour-bound.

The Abbey – 2024

The sea was restless, all night she had been sighing, resisting the shackles of shorelines altered by storms and the powdery corrosion of white cliffs but when the sun rose brilliant and clear as an angelus bell she settled to her bed where wrecks beyond salvage kept their secrets.

Miriam stood with her back to the door, keeping her usual vigil at the window where she watched the sea and dreamed of flight. The first notes fell between the spaces of the sea's capitulation and she failed to sense the presence that had entered the room. Perhaps his soul-deep alteration made him too unfamiliar for registration until the music swelled into an aria, syncopating with the melody of her soul.

'Stanas?' whispering his name, half-turning.

'I said I'd come back.'

She turned and saw a stranger spotlit by the rising sun, a violin resting on his shoulder, a bow caressing the strings. He was handsome and young, his eyes full of fury and wisdom and joy, hallowed and home at last.

'You heard the music?' She took a breath, the first she had needed in four centuries.

Without breaking the thread of melody he nodded and played a series of notes bold and original.

'My music, Miriam. I'm hearing it in my soul and playing it as she taught me.'

350

'She? God?'

'Mary Granger, a composer as brilliant as you who taught me to listen.'

'Where is she?'

'In Italy surrounded by her family but longing for death and wings just as you are.'

She shuddered another breath, her eyes stinging with the first tears in four hundred years.

He began to play an exquisite piece of music, haunting and haunted. 'This song is hers. She wrote it for an angel who was her lover.'

'You?'

'Gabriel.'

The stream of bewitching notes homogenised in her frozen body as winter's thaw. A crack, a creak, and an ancient cog ground to life, articulating a single rotation that shocked her heart to spluttering life. She took another breath and another, her body unfreezing in a tingling of vivification, nerve-endings shivering and aching with life, and just as the music reached a soaring crescendo her body dropped from her like a discarded winter coat.

Stanas rushed to the window, stepping over the shell that was Miriam and shouted a single word: 'Fly!'

Raising the violin to his shoulder again he held the bow suspended, listening for the music that would wing her flight. Hovering there over the tumble of cliff into grinding tide she heard a trickling, tripping of notes that echoed the song of the sea and the sun and an explosion of life coursed through her ancient soul and thrust her twinning the indigo plane of sea.

Beyond the horizon her path altered, coursed upwards to the stars and brushing luminescent, counter melodies, harmonies, souls in escort, her mother and Kit and Abigail,

Jeane-Antionette and Voltaire, all the people she had known, even Rathe, rushed her winged passage beyond the manmade spheres and into that place where dreams are born and the music of Heaven plays eternally for a spider who is not so much hungry as enchanted.

Printed in Great Britain
by Amazon

58383290R00201

WHAT SHE DID NEXT

EVE SIMMONS

WHAT SHE DID NEXT

What to Do When the Life You Planned is F**ked Up

dialogue
books

DIALOGUE BOOKS

First published in Great Britain in 2026 by Dialogue Books
An imprint of John Murray Press

1

Copyright © Eve Simmons 2026

A CIP catalogue record for this book
is available from the British Library.

Hardback ISBN 978-0-349-70509-5
ebook ISBN 978-0-349-70511-8

Typeset in Berling by M Rules
Printed and bound in Great Britain by
Clays Ltd, Elcograf S.p.A

John Murray policy is to use papers that are natural, renewable and
recyclable products and made from wood grown in sustainable forests.
The logging and manufacturing processes are expected to conform to the
environmental regulations of the country of origin.

Carmelite House
50 Victoria Embankment
London EC4Y 0DZ

The authorised representative
in the EEA is
Hachette Ireland
8 Castlecourt Centre
Dublin 15, D15 XTP3, Ireland
(email: info@hbgi.ie)

www.dialoguebooks.co.uk

John Murray Press, part of Hodder & Stoughton Limited
An Hachette UK company

For Alex Pepe

Contents